THE TERRAN MENACE

TERRAN MENACE, BOOK 1

J.R. ROBERTSON

Cover design and illustration by Jeff Brown Graphics

ISBN: 978-1-7359259-1-2 (trade paperback)

PROLOGUE

THE ANCIENT AI DIRECTED ITS ATTENTION TO A NEW NOTIFICATION from one of the custodial subminds it had tasked with monitoring the Terran datanet for critical threats. As an Agent of the Master—one of the oldest and most trusted, in fact—the AI had been monitoring the Terran datanet ever since its arrival in Terran space thirty-one Earth years ago. The file header indicated the information was time-sensitive and required immediate attention. The Agent assimilated the data and spent several processing cycles determining if acting on the information would risk exposing its presence to the Terrans.

The Terrans were a brutal race, but they were also highly adaptable and remarkably clever. While they were still primitive, a chance encounter with an alien race had irrevocably altered their natural development. Under normal circumstances, the Master's directives would require the Terrans to be exterminated, their natural progression as a species now tainted by an outside influence. But the circumstances surrounding the Agent's presence in Terran space were far from normal.

The Agent completed its risk assessment and determined that it would have to act; too much was at stake to not.

"WHAT THE ACTUAL FUCK, JAN?"

Janet Heatherton winced at the irate face staring daggers at her from the other end of the vid call. She knew it had been coming but wasn't fully prepared for the vehemence that blasted out of her comms terminal speakers. She opened her mouth in an attempt to calm things down a bit, but the tirade continued.

"No! Don't you dare try to weasel your way out of this! You're leaving for God only knows how long, and you didn't stop to think, hmm, maybe I should mention this to my best friend?" The sardonic comment sent a rush of heat to Janet's cheeks.

"How did you find out, Lauren?" she said, struggling to make eye contact.

"I have my sources," Lauren replied with a dismissive wave of her hand. "So it's true, then?"

Janet stared back at her friend, a pained expression on her face. She had only known about the fellowship opportunity for the last two days. The offer had come at the end of her graduation ceremony, as she was bouncing down the stone steps of the auditorium, clutching the leather-bound PhD in quantum electrodynamics. Those two days had been a whirlwind of making long-term storage arrangements for her stuff and finding someone to fill her soon-to-be-open room in the house she rented with two of her fellow graduate students—well, former fellow students, now that she had graduated. The latter task had been surprisingly easy, as upperclassmen and graduate students descended upon open rooms in Ann Arbor's Old Town district like locusts, but the former was proving a challenge.

"It's true, but nobody can know about this, Lauren. I'm serious. I don't even know where I'm going or what exactly I'll be working on," Janet admitted.

"Seriously? Are you screwing with me, Jan?" Lauren said. "How could you say yes to a fellowship when you know literally nothing about it? What's really going on?"

"I know it sounds crazy, but it's true," Janet said. She tried to maintain the air of someone who had been thoroughly chastised, but felt one corner of her mouth tug upward, ruining the facade. "I mean, come on, El! Three days ago I was freaking out because I was graduating with no idea what I was going to do after grad school. Sure, I had offers to work in various labs for the big tech firms—some with absolutely *obscene* salaries, by the way—but I got into this field because I want a challenge. There's no way I can sit in a sterile lab day after day for some tech company, trying to keep their products one step ahead of the competition. I'll lose my damn mind! I want something new and different." She was speaking faster now, genuine enthusiasm pushing her words out at a sprinter's pace.

It had been a crazy few days. Janet had sat through the commencement ceremony, not hearing a word of the various speeches given by faculty and invited dignitaries as her mind focused on the one thought that had consumed her ever since she realized this chapter of her life was coming to a close: *What's next?*

After the dean dismissed the students and Janet followed her peers down the steps in front of the University of Michigan's Rackham Auditorium, a man in a black suit and sunglasses approached her. At first, she thought he was another of those slimy government types trying to woo her into a boring life working at some super-secret government lab, but the suit was far too well-tailored, and the man's bearing, while professional, was too relaxed and genuine for the typical G-man. Her interest piqued, she bailed on her initial plan to lose him in the crowd flowing out the doors and down the steps and instead allowed him to approach.

Their conversation had been short and mostly one-sided, ending with him handing Janet an envelope containing a comms node address and instructions on how to contact it, but the offer he made, while vague, was irresistible to someone who wanted to work on the bleeding edge of technology development. An hour later, she punched the address into her datapad and initiated a call, her excitement and curiosity both pegged at their maximum settings. To say it shocked her when her call was answered by one of the most influential people in Terran space would be the understatement of the century.

After Janet finished recounting everything that had happened over the last two days, Lauren stared back at her, incredulous. "Seriously?" she repeated. "Katherine Hutchins? As in the wife of Henry Hutchins, founder and CEO of ExoDynamics Corporation? The biggest and most powerful corporation in human history? You're shitting me."

"Nope," Janet said, a huge smile on her face. "She wants me on a team she's putting together to work on a project that will, as she put it, 'make all the technological advances of the last few decades seem like child's play by comparison.' Evidently, she's been following my work on engineering biosynthetic nanopolymers for applications in quantum electrodynamic systems, and she thinks I can be an asset."

"I have absolutely no idea what you just said, nerd," Lauren quipped. "I swear, it's times like these that reaffirm my decision to go into landscape architecture. Congratulations, though. Seriously, you've earned it. I'm happy for you," she said genuinely.

"Thanks, El! I'm sorry I didn't tell you, but I wasn't kidding when I said I'm not supposed to tell anyone. So promise me you won't say anything." Katherine had been adamant that Janet not speak a word as to who she would be working for, and she felt a small pang of regret for telling Lauren everything she just had.

"I won't. You can trust me," Lauren said, giving Janet a little wink before abruptly changing the subject. "Wait, you said you aren't allowed to take anything but a single change of clothes and a few personal items, but nothing electronic? This sounds like you're heading off to boot camp. How are you ever going to survive any length of time without entertainment?"

"I imagine they'll have something for us. Katherine said everything we could need would be provided by ExoDyn. Besides, we're going to be busy shattering technological barriers and transforming the world as we know it," Janet said, trying to convince herself just as much as her best friend. The thought of being completely cut off from civilization with nothing more than her coworkers and their research to keep her occupied was not a pleasant one. For someone who grew up bombarded twenty-four seven by all forms of media, being totally and abruptly cut off from it was about as appealing as a root canal.

"You're not fooling anyone, Jan. You will literally die if you can't listen to music for at least ten hours a day," Lauren said, only half joking. "Remember when your datapad crapped out on our camping trip to the Manitous? I thought I would have to tie you to a tree. You were borderline manic," Lauren ribbed her good-naturedly, recounting their less than pleasant camping trip to the iconic islands a few years back. Janet's datapad had died just a few hours into their weekend stay on South Manitou Island, and she had then bitched about it nearly nonstop for the next two days.

"Come on, I wasn't that bad."

Lauren let out a derisive snort. "Honey, you were a half step away from the rending of garments and sacrificing a chipmunk to the technology gods." The two women shared a laugh at the memory, and then Lauren broke into a conspiratorial smile. "I think you probably know someone who could come up with a way to fit your entire music library onto a revolutionary data-storage medium with room to spare, and it would be easy to smuggle in."

She was, of course, referring to the very thing that had brought Janet to the attention of her new employer: the flexible, almost gel-like material Janet had created while working on her PhD. Dubbed DataFilm, the material could hold petabytes of information in a form factor approximately the size of a postage stamp. The nature of the nanopolymer matrix was such that its data-storage capacity scaled linearly with volume but did not require a minimum volume or specific form factor to function. The data was read wirelessly by placing the film on an inductive dataport. Those properties resulted in a data-storage medium that could be cut or molded into any number of sizes and shapes to fit a practically limitless number of applications.

Naturally, Janet hadn't made a dime off her creation, and the university had taken all the credit for the discovery of the revolutionary material. Yet that hadn't prevented a who's who of tech companies from inundating her with job offers, culminating in the fellowship offer from ExoDynamics and Katherine Hutchins herself.

Janet stared back at her friend for a few moments, thoughtfully. "I knew I kept you around for a reason."

"You're welcome."

"I wish I could keep chatting, El, but I really need to get going. I have a ton of packing to do yet tonight, and I need to catch a shuttle to the Nexus out of Detroit first thing in the morning," Janet said, referring to the massive civilian space station orbiting Earth.

"Okay. Have fun packing, and whenever you return to civilization as the savior of humanity, I hope you remember your best friend when you're trying to figure out what to do with your newfound, planet-ruling wealth."

"Right," Janet said sarcastically. "More like I'll probably need a couch to sleep on while I'm busy searching for a real job after this fellowship is up."

"As long as you pay your share of the rent," Lauren said with a laugh. "Take care, Jan. I'll see you when I see you, I guess."

"See you when I see you," Janet parroted back at her friend, then closed the call and went back to packing.

With the last of her worldly possessions in boxes and ready for pickup in a few days by her brother, she stripped off her clothes and hopped in the shower. After drying off and slipping into her pajamas, she sat down at her desk and stared at her datapad for a few moments.

"Why the hell not?" she asked the empty room as she reached for a small black storage case resting on top of the heap of random items thrown haphazardly into a cardboard box labeled *Desk Crap* in permanent marker. Janet opened the case and withdrew a small square of DataFilm, turning it over in her hands several times before reaching back into the box and pulling out a small razor blade. She laid the film on the desk and cut off a piece roughly the size of her finger nail. *Civilization-changing research or not, nothing is going to keep me from getting my jam on while I work,* she thought.

Janet took the small piece of DataFilm and placed it on the inductive dataport of her tablet. She opened the quick-and-dirty formatting program she had written for the material and tapped the *format* icon after the program successfully located the newly created covert storage device. A new notification popped up on her screen a few seconds later, informing her the new device was ready to use. Janet selected her entire entertainment library and set the datapad to copy all the files to the film.

That task complete, she climbed into the sleeping bag on her now-bare mattress, turned out the lights, and struggled to fall asleep while her mind wondered at the possibilities of what Katherine Hutchins had in store for her.

———

"SEE YOU WHEN I SEE YOU."

The connection to Janet Heatherton closed, and the Agent noted a 98.3% probability that the target would attempt to breach the security surrounding the secret ExoDynamics project titled Darkhorse.

Katherine Hutchins, the human in charge of the project, had implemented excellent electronic security measures that had thus far prevented the Agent from obtaining any significant information on it. Project Darkhorse was classified as a priority threat based on ExoDynamics' close relationship with the human military-industrial complex, its invention and mass production of new technologies, and, most critically, the level of security and false information surrounding the nebulous project.

Ostensibly, Project Darkhorse was a research expedition to an archeological site discovered on the fourth planet of the Sol system, which the humans called Mars. The small amount of documentation the Agent had been able to access on the project showed it was just what it was purported to be, but ExoDynamics had gone to great lengths to quietly acquire supplies and equipment that would serve little archeological purpose.

Repeated attempts to gain further insight on the true nature of the project had resulted in little additional data until its submind had flagged Janet's name on newly created tax reporting documentation within ExoDynamics' human resources servers. This new information was discovered soon after a known personal assistant of Katherine Hutchins had passed through customs on the Nexus while en route to the Ann Arbor Regional Spaceport before he began his return trip to the Valkyrie system less than two hours later. Gaining access to the personal files of Janet's best friend had been little trouble, and the information available in those files—as well as that on social media—allowed the intelligence to build a virtual avatar of Lauren Smith and use it to influence Janet's actions.

A little over two hours after the conversation between Janet and "Lauren," the Agent's systems registered a new storage device synced with Janet's datapad. While she slept, the Agent copied a subset of its programs to the DataFilm, displacing some media files she had intended to load on it to make room for its code. This splinter code would probe the local network of the facility housing Darkhorse and gather what information it could before forwarding it back to the Agent at the first opportunity. If the splinter code discovered a critical threat and no data connection back to the Agent was likely to be forthcoming, it was programmed to seek a means to destroy the facility and all data stored there at any cost.

HOLY SHIT, this place is enormous was the thought running through Janet's mind as she exited her orbital shuttle and made her way out into Concourse-A of the Nexus. The space station, which handled over eighty percent of all civilian flights to and from other systems in Terran space, was more than five kilometers in diameter. A central ring and six two-kilometer-long docking concourses made up the bulk of the station, which displaced in excess of one hundred million tons. It was the single largest space-based construct in humanity's relatively short spacefaring history.

Janet reflected on how it all had changed. Even though she hadn't yet been born at the time, the home video footage her dad had recorded that day was etched into her memory: the fear and simultaneous wonder on her parents' faces as every news outlet in the world broadcast live images of a single spaceship in equatorial orbit over Earth—an *alien* spaceship. That ship had been tasked with a scouting mission of the habitable third planet in a star system a long way down the Orion arm of the galaxy and, if the situation warranted, first contact with the dominant species of that planet.

The alien race called itself the Alarians, and they were refugees from a star cluster almost 3500 light-years away and across the expanse between the Orion-Cygnus and Carina-Sagittarius arms of the Milky Way galaxy, known as the Talishian Expanse to the Alarians. Their home systems had been ravaged by war with a neighboring civilization, and as far as they knew, the 80,000 Alarians in that fleet were the only survivors of a race once numbering in the tens of billions.

Their journey had lasted almost five years, and by the time they reached orbit over Earth, most of their ships were barely functional, let alone habitable. They had lost a staggering number along the way, some to settlement on less-than-ideal worlds, but mostly to critical systems failure on ships desperately in need of repair and refit. They were a species in need, and for the most part, the nations of Earth welcomed them—and the technology they offered freely—with open arms.

There had been significant economic and societal turmoil in the months immediately following the revelation that humanity was not alone in the universe, but over time, the wealth of scientific knowledge the Alarians traded freely in exchange for resources needed to repair their vessels—and a place to live while that happened—quickly compensated for the economic crash that accompanied the initial global panic. Within two decades, human scientific knowledge had been advanced by hundreds of years, new technologies and manufacturing systems had been implemented with the help of Alarian engineers, and the first colonies were being established in nearby star systems.

After having repaired their ships enough to take them to a new home on a suitably habitable planet roughly 120 light-years from Earth—a world they had named Hai'alla—most official contact with the somewhat reclusive species had stopped. The Alarians were a deeply suspicious race—hard to blame them, after a war with a neighboring species they had once thought of as allies nearly wiped them out—and they only had as much contact with humanity as required before moving on. There were still some diplomatic channels in place, but for the most part, any diplomatic advances humanity had made toward its newly established neighbors had been politely rebuffed.

As the reclusive Alarians mostly receded into the history books, human civilization spread throughout our little corner of the galaxy like wildfire. With faster-than-light travel now prevalent, the inner explorer in human nature reasserted itself after a century of being mostly content to stay put. Within thirty years of first contact, humanity had established more than fifteen colonies in neighboring star systems. As the natural riches of our solar system and beyond were unlocked, conflict between nations on Earth was all but eliminated as there was simply no need to fight over resources anymore. Before long, it became obvious that the rapidly expanding sphere of human influence would need governance on a scale never dreamed of, and the Confederated Terran Systems were established.

Janet made her way to Concourse-D, where the private flights embarked from, and found a small cluster of people waiting outside the departure gate Katherine had told her to meet at. She saw Katherine talking to a young boy—her son, if Janet recalled correctly from the news vids. The boy had tears in his eyes as Katherine leaned down to hug him, and he wouldn't let go of her. A tall man with bright blue eyes and dark brown hair smiled gently as he pulled the boy away from Katherine: Henry Hutchins, number one on the *Fortune Systems* 500 for seven years running and without a doubt the most powerful private individual in Terran space. Janet felt her jaw drop as

Katherine looked over and met her gaze, waving for her to come join them. She quickly collected herself and made her way through the throng of passengers disembarking a private tourism transport that had docked opposite her gate.

"Hello, Janet. It's nice to finally meet you in person," Katherine said, extending her right hand.

"The pleasure is all mine, Mrs. Hutchins," Janet said, still somewhat starstruck as she looked back and forth from Katherine to Henry while reaching out to shake Katherine's hand. The strength of the woman's grip surprised her, as did the calluses on her palms.

Katherine laughed at that. "You can call me Kate, Janet. I've never been much of one for social niceties... I think it's the farmer in me." Janet paused for a moment, recalling that Katherine came from modest roots in northern lower Michigan and that the woman was famed for her love of growing grapes and crafting some incredible wines—strictly for personal enjoyment.

"In that case, call me Jan." Janet smiled back at her as Katherine finally released her hand.

"Speaking of social niceties," Katherine said, turning to her husband. "Janet, I'd like you to meet my husband, Henry, and my son, Benjamin." Henry extended his hand with a cordial smile on his face—not as warm as Katherine's, but not disingenuous, either. "So you're the one my wife keeps talking about," he said. "It's a pleasure to meet you, Janet."

Janet reached for Henry's hand but found that her words had taken a coffee break. "Uh... a-and you as well, M- Mr. Hutchins," Janet finally stammered out. Henry had a bemused expression on his face as he shook her hand, and Janet felt her cheeks flush before noticing a light tugging at the bottom of her blouse. She looked down to see the boy, Benjamin, gently trying to get her attention. When he saw her gaze down at him, he, too, extended his hand in greeting, wet tears still dotting his cheeks.

Janet reached down and took the boy's small hand in hers. "And it's a pleasure to meet you also, Benjamin," she said. The boy beamed back at her but said nothing in response. Janet released his hand and looked back at Katherine. "Forgive me if this is improper, Kate, but you are nothing like what I expected." While the two women had had a conversation a couple days ago, it had taken the tone of a formal job interview. The casual manner with which the two titans of industry had greeted Janet had surprised her.

Both Katherine and Henry chuckled at the comment. "We get that a lot," Katherine said with a smile. "I grew up in a small town in Michigan's Leelanau Peninsula—on the farm my family has owned for over a hundred years—and I've never had much regard for stuck-up, rich assholes. As for Henry... well, I like to think I've rubbed off on him some," she said with a laugh.

"A little," Henry agreed. Janet was again caught off guard by Katherine's down-to-earth nature, now complete with a farmer's casual profanity. She couldn't believe these people were literally the richest couple in Terran space. They were so... normal.

A chirp sounded from Katherine's watch and she glanced down at it to check the message. "Time to go," she said and motioned toward their gate.

After a quick round of goodbyes to Henry and Benjamin, Katherine led Janet to the airlock that would cycle them through to the ExoDynamics corporate shuttle waiting to take them to their destination.

"So where are we going?" Janet asked as they waited for the airlock to equalize the pressure of the station with that of the shuttle.

"I'm sorry, Jan, but I can't tell you anything further until we reach our destination."

The locking bolts of the shuttle's airlock hatch clicked open, and the hatch swung inward. The two women took their seats in the rather mundane passenger compartment of the shuttle. Within minutes of the two women sitting down and getting strapped in, the shuttle had cleared the traffic control space around the Nexus, and Earth became a rapidly shrinking blue marble out the viewport as the craft vectored out into open space. Janet took one last look at the blue planet, and excitement at the challenges that lay in the days and months ahead filled her very soul.

CHAPTER ONE

BEST BIRTHDAY EVER

"BEN, IT'S TIME TO COME IN."

"Hang on a sec, Mom. I'm almost done out here."

"*Now*, Benjamin," his mom said, pulling out the full name to show she was serious.

Ben sighed in disgust. "Ugh, fine, I'll be right there."

He stood up from the ochre-colored ground and brushed a layer of the fine Martian dust from his environment suit. Turning on his heel, he bounded across the rocky terrain to the sprawling habitat a short distance away with a slow, skip-like gait in gravity that was roughly one-third that of Earth. He cycled into the airlock that would take him to the living quarters module and closed and locked the outer hatch behind him, waiting for the environmental system to pressurize the small space before he would be able to open the inner hatch and enter the habitat.

Two minutes ticked by, but nothing happened.

"Hey, Mom, I think something's up with the airlock—it won't cycle me through."

Nothing.

"Mom?"

A blinding light strobed through the small viewport into the habitat, and the airlock shook violently, sending Ben to his knees.

"Mom, what was that?" Ben screamed into his suit comms as he pulled himself upright and rushed to the viewport. His next words died in a choked-off scream of horror and disbelief.

There was a gaping hole in the outer wall of the common area, and the interior looked as though a bomb had gone off. Broken bits of scorched furniture were scattered everywhere, and the remaining walls were flame-blackened.

Then he saw their faces.

"Mom!" Ben wailed, clawing at the inner airlock hatch in an attempt to get it open, but it wouldn't budge.

There were a half-dozen broken bodies on the floor, their faces contorted in a mix of terror and agony as the near-vacuum of the Martian atmosphere sucked the air from their charred lungs. His mom's eyes were bulging out of her head as she screamed silently on the other side of the hatch, one mangled hand reaching out for him.

"No!" Ben's scream woke him from the nightmare. He was soaked in sweat, and his breathing came in ragged gasps as he brushed the matted hair from his eyes. It was the same terrible dream that had plagued him ever since his mother boarded that shuttle and never returned, over a decade ago.

The news of the explosion came barely a week after his mom departed the Nexus with the promising young scientist Janet Heatherton. Investigators could never fully piece together the series of events leading up to the destruction of the research outpost on Mars, but it seemed there had been an environmental systems failure resulting in a high-oxygen condition. A capacitor explosion inside the research labs ignited the atmosphere within the habitat, and anyone not killed in the explosion quickly suffocated in the thin Martian atmosphere, as ruptures in the external walls decompressed the entire facility.

The nightmares started shortly after the news of his mom's death. His dad tried to withhold the details of the tragedy from his five-year-old son, but his efforts proved to be in vain. Ben's ignorance of the details surrounding the accident was fleeting, as the true nature of the tragedy leaked to the mainstream news services a few months later. In an age of omnipresent media outlets, Ben's life was soon flooded with a host of media personalities and "experts" recounting, in vivid detail, everything that was known about the doomed research outpost on Mars.

The dreams had gotten more and more realistic over the years, though mercifully less frequent as the passage of time dulled the pain of loss. They all ended the same way, however, with Ben trapped in the habitat's external airlock, watching helplessly as fire ravaged the people in the habitat before the flames —and the screams—faded in the thin atmosphere.

The door to Ben's room opened softly, and Ben could see the shadowy outline of his dad standing in the hallway.

"Was it the dream again?" he asked, concern evident in his voice. He swiped his hand vertically along the wall just inside the door, and the lights in the room came up with a soft, muted glow.

"Yeah." Ben sighed, sitting up in bed and freeing his limbs from the sweat-soaked sheets. "It's been so long I was starting to think maybe they were behind me. It's alright, Dad. *I'm* alright," he finished.

By this point, his dad knew better than to try to coax anything more from him; Ben had never wanted to talk about it, and overt displays of emotion were not a family trait. Whatever demons were plaguing his subconscious, Ben hoped his dad would leave him to deal with them alone.

"Alright. Try to get some more sleep if you can. I've got a bit of a surprise for you tomorrow, and you're going to want to be rested for it," his dad said in an effort to get his son's mind off of his loss. *Their* loss.

"We going somewhere?" Ben asked, hopeful for an opportunity to get out of the house and do something other than sit in a classroom or get dragged to his dad's office again.

"ExoDyn HQ. I'm pulling you out of class tomorrow. We'll head over to the office in the morning."

"Great. Another fun-filled day at the office," Ben said sarcastically, remembering all the other "surprises" his father had forced him to endure over the years: impossibly boring space flights to other ExoDynamics facilities in distant systems; touring laboratories with scientists that Ben was sure were not, in fact, speaking any known language; and other equally thrilling exploits. Granted, it was marginally better than being stuck in a classroom with a half dozen other kids his age at the private academy he had attended for nearly his entire life, but that was only because his classmates were even more insufferable than their power-elite parents, whom he would have to rub elbows with at ExoDyn. Frankly, this "surprise" didn't seem like much of a win, in Ben's book.

"You'll like this one," his dad said with a sly smile on his face as he turned to head back to his room. "I promise. Let's call it a sixteenth birthday surprise."

As his dad exited the room and padded back down the hall to his own room, Ben stared after him, wondering what was in store for him at ExoDyn's headquarters the next day. A birthday surprise? His birthday hadn't garnered much fanfare since his mom died, what with his dad's busy schedule and, if he were honest, the sense of loss he still felt knowing his mom wouldn't be there. She had died less than a week after his fifth birthday, and the two events were forever linked in his mind. The two Hutchins men had an unspoken agreement to acknowledge the passing of another year in some small but heartfelt way, but not make it a big deal.

He stood and peeled off his sweaty boxers and T-shirt as he walked over to his dresser, mind running wild with the possibilities. After donning fresh clothes, he tried to fall back asleep, but the wetness permeating the sheets and mattress signaled an end to his slumber, and he rose once again before heading out of his room and down the hall toward the stairs that would take him to the basement.

Being the son of the richest man in Terran space—and the head of a leading technology firm—came with its perks. Shortly after leaving his room, Ben found himself standing in a state-of-the-art holoroom. The suite of holographic projectors could turn a small room into any environment imaginable, and a person could then move throughout the virtual environment without fear of running into the room's physical walls thanks to a series of gravitic emitters projecting a field upward from the floor toward the occupants, resulting in a kind of false floor. As the room's occupants neared its physical boundaries, the gravitic fields would continuously shift them back away from the walls or other real-life obstructions. Haptic feedback from objects within the virtual environment meant that a user could feel everything from the rough surface of broken concrete to the slickness of the alien blood covering it in amazing detail.

Ben loaded up his favorite first-person shooter and found himself suddenly transported to an alien world ravaged by war. By the time the first gunshots started ringing in his ears and he felt the debris of a nearby explosion pinging off his holographically rendered armor, he had completely forgotten about the mysterious surprise his father had in store for him the next morning… and the nightmare that had awoken him.

———

THE FIRST RAYS of sunlight were dancing through the windows as Ben, sleepily trudging up the basement stairs, found his father in the kitchen, reaching for a shrieking tea kettle. The enticing scent of fresh-ground coffee beans hung in the air, and Ben marveled at his dad's refusal to join the twenty-second century and buy a modern coffee maker. Instead, the richest man in human history could be found in the kitchen every morning, pouring hot water from a tea kettle over his fresh, hand-ground Arabica coffee beans. Henry's answer had never once deviated over the years of Ben asking why he wasted all that time making coffee when a machine could do it just as good in a tenth of the time, and over the years the genuine questioning had turned into a morning ritual whenever the two happened to be breakfasting together.

"Seriously, Dad," Ben said. "You need to stop living in the dark ages and just buy a coffee maker already." Ben shook his head at the irony of a technology magnate using the oldest of old-fashioned tools to prepare his morning libation.

"It tastes better this way," his dad responded as he placed the top on the French press carafe in front of him. "So," he said, changing the subject. "I see you decided to ignore my advice about getting more sleep."

"It just wasn't going to happen," Ben said, taking a seat at the counter. "I had too much running through my mind, and I needed something to help clear my head…" He trailed off, distracted by the vid screen on the kitchen wall. The sound was muted, but the headline *3rd Attack by Alarian Extremists in 2 Months* scrolled across the screen. An attractive blonde news anchor was sitting at a desk, reporting on the latest updates from Confed sources regarding the attack, while B-roll images of a shattered space station ran in the background.

Ben commanded the volume on the vid screen up, and the anchor's voice rolled across the kitchen. "Confed sources say the station was primarily used for military and civilian comms traffic to and from other systems, as well as deep-space telemetry. At the time of the attack, the station was fully staffed with a crew of twenty-four military and civilian technicians. It is unknown how many technicians survived the attack, but sources have confirmed at least thirteen dead at last count. The names of the deceased are being withheld until their families can be notified. This act of terrorism marks the third such by Alarian extremists on strategic assets in the last two months, and we are receiving reports that Confed military units are being placed on heightened..."

"I don't get it," Ben said as he followed the news report. "They have their own systems almost a hundred light-years from here, and we seem perfectly content to leave them be. Why are they blowing up relay stations? I thought the Alarians were largely peaceful."

"You can't judge an entire race based on the actions of a few zealots, Ben," his dad said as he pressed the screen down inside the carafe and poured the now perfectly steeped coffee into a thermal mug. "You of all people should understand that the Alarians aren't all that different from us. After all, you got to know Elyria rather well in the short time we were on Hai'alla last year."

"Ugh," Ben groaned. "Don't remind me." He grabbed a mug from the counter and poured himself a cup of coffee. *God this really does smell amazing. Maybe the old fart is right.*

The incident in question occurred while Ben and his dad were visiting the new Alarian homeworld so his dad could hammer out some sort of technology agreement between ExoDyn and an Alarian firm headed by a friend and member of the Alarian High Council. Ben had been saddled with the councilor's daughter, who was roughly the same age, while their parents went off to talk business. After a bit of a frosty start, things had actually gone pretty well... until *it* happened. Ben still remembered the feral screams punctuated by the high-pitched sirens of emergency vehicles as Elyria was loaded aboard an air ambulance, restrained to keep her thrashing from harming anyone, and rushed to a nearby hospital. It had been a fluke of biology between two species that evolved thousands of light-years apart, but one that had nearly killed the daughter of a high councilor. Ben and his dad had been booted off the planet in disgrace once the story leaked to the Alarian media.

A chime sounded from the vid screen, interrupting Ben's ruminations, and the feed cut to the front door, where a man in a black suit was standing. The man smiled into the camera and threw a jaunty wave, and a disembodied female voice came from the kitchen speakers. "Dan Murphy has arrived, Henry."

"Yes, I see that. Please allow him entry and tell him we're in the kitchen. Thank you, Mabel," his dad replied to the house's virtual intelligence. A soft tone signaled the request was being carried out, and his dad muted the vid screen as it returned to the news anchor attempting to present the same scant information differently and hoping nobody would notice there wasn't anything new in there.

Mabel was the brainchild of his mom. During the nine months of her pregnancy with Ben, she had labored to create the VI from scratch. While commercially available home VIs could run the day-to-day minutiae involved with everyday life, the personality software available on the commercial market left something to be desired. Mabel was a cut above the rest when it came to VIs, and she had proven adept at managing everything from Henry's chaotic schedule to basic home maintenance tasks —and all with an interactive experience that was nearly as good as dealing with a genuine human being.

His dad looked up from his steaming mug of coffee as Dan Murphy made his way up the few steps into the kitchen, taking a slight detour to muss Ben's hair before approaching his boss.

"I know you said 0900, Hank, but I was in the neighborhood and figured I'd drop by a little early." The look on Dan's face said his arrival almost three hours early was due to anything but a happy coincidence, and Ben picked up on a palpable tension in the room.

"Ben, why don't you go clean up real quick, and we'll get going," his dad said, giving him a little smile. "No need to dress up this time. Jeans and a T-shirt will suffice," he added. Ben's eyes narrowed slightly, suspicion creeping into his thoughts as his gaze flicked to the silent reporter on the vid screen and back to his dad. The two things couldn't be related, could they? Probably not. That attack had occurred in a completely different star system. He shrugged and jogged off to his room to change.

Five minutes later, the trio was getting into the black luxury sedan. Dan quickly climbed behind the wheel, leaving Ben and his dad to fend for themselves. The move was out of character and didn't go unnoticed by the teenager, who couldn't remember a single time when Dan had not opened the door for his father. Perhaps more troubling than Dan not opening the door for his charges was the fact that his dad sat in the passenger seat up front. Ben could see the strain in the faces of the two men and hear it in their voices. They were doing a fairly admirable job of trying not to let it show, but Ben had inherited his parents' knack for noticing the smallest of details, and what he saw troubled him.

He passed the twenty-minute ride to ExoDyn headquarters by futilely straining his ears in an attempt to pick up something useful from the conversation the two men in the front were having. Unfortunately, his dad had activated the car's privacy filter, enabling an active noise cancellation system that prevented personal conversations in the front seat from reaching riders in the back. While Ben couldn't glean any juicy information from the conversation taking place just in front of him, he learned a great deal by observing what was going on around the car as it sped toward their destination.

The sky was filled with more air and space traffic than he could ever remember seeing, and people everywhere had looks of concern etching their faces. There was also a noticeable law enforcement presence everywhere, and they had even passed a few military convoys headed into the city. Ben's mind raced to process the information he was accumulating: terrorist attacks, Dan's look of concern and rush to get them to ExoDyn head-quarters, military and police everywhere. *Maybe there is a link between the attack and the rush this morning. Dad has ties to Valkyrie Fleet Command, after all. Maybe he knows something is up.*

The car exited the main highway and turned onto an indus-trial thoroughfare lined with massive factories and warehouses. A few minutes later, they turned onto a broad private drive, slowing briefly as the security checkpoint at the entrance confirmed the car's ID and retracted the massive steel bars that served as a barrier to entry to the ExoDynamics headquarters complex. ExoDyn was *the* leading private technology firm in Terran space with divisions that developed and manufactured everything from raw materials to complete vehicles and space-craft for private industry and military use alike. But the jewel of the ExoDyn lineup was the APEX suit.

The advanced personal exoskeletal suit, or APEX suit, was a modular, adaptable exoskeletal suit that could be equipped for any number of jobs or missions in just about any environment. They could operate in atmosphere or vacuum and could serve as anything from light-duty medical exoskeletons—helping injured or paralyzed people regain freedom of movement—to fully armed and armored combat exoskeletons capable of carrying a wide array of weapons and equipment into any envi-ronment the soldiers wearing them were ordered to go. They were also incredibly badass, and Ben had used every weapon in his not insubstantial arsenal to get his hands on one... unsuccessfully.

The APEX suits were ExoDyn's bread and butter and had launched the company when a twenty-six-year-old Henry Hutchins had completed the first-gen prototype in his basement workshop while finishing his master's degree in electrical engineering. In the years since the first APEX went to market as a basic load-carrying exoskeleton, the hardware and software had been reconfigured and reengineered many times. Today, APEX suits were ubiquitous throughout Terran space... just not at the Hutchins household.

Dan dropped the two of them off at the entrance to the huge alloy and glass building that housed the ExoDynamics Corporation's executive offices, and as they made their way through security, Ben saw hushed conversation, set jaws, and purposeful movement everywhere in the lobby. His head swiveled from side to side as tension built in his chest, but he said nothing as he followed his dad up to the security scanner.

"Good morning, Mr. Hutchins." The smile didn't reach the guard's eyes, betraying his genial tone as he quickly worked to process his boss through security.

"Morning, Frank," his dad replied quickly, though not entirely without warmth, as he grabbed his personal items from the polymer tray as it exited the scanner. Then he strode toward the bank of elevators on the far side of the expansive lobby without another word. Another out-of-character move, this time from his dad—a man who usually took at least a minute or two for small talk with the men manning the guard station.

Something is very, very wrong! Ben's brain practically screamed the thought at him as he exited the security scanner and stepped quickly to catch up to his father, the first traces of real fear starting to creep into the periphery of his mind. *What the hell is going on?*

"We need to run up to my office to grab something real quick," his dad said to him as they rode the elevator up to the building's top floor. "Then we're heading over to the APEX labs."

The trepidation Ben was feeling evaporated in an instant, and a surge of excitement rushed up his spine at the mention of the labs. He wanted to say something or shout triumphantly, but all he could manage was to stand there with his mouth hanging open.

"I thought you'd be a little more excited." His dad chuckled as Ben could do nothing but stare mutely back at him.

"S-Seriously?" Ben finally stammered out. "You're giving me an APEX? Like, today? A real one?" Ben started jumping up and down, pumping his fists in the air before his dad could offer verbal confirmation. Instead, his dad rolled his eyes and turned to face the door as the elevator chimed, announcing it had arrived at their destination.

"Good morning, Cheryl," his dad greeted his longtime secretary.

"Good morning, Mr. Hu—"

"Cheryl! Cheryl! I get one today!" Ben's enthusiastic cries drowned out Cheryl's reply to her boss. Cheryl and his dad shared a knowing smile as Ben ran around the office like a lunatic.

"Cheryl, why don't you take Ben down to the APEX labs while I take care of a few things up here? I suspect he'd rather get started right away, as opposed to running laps around my office for the next few minutes. Johannes should be expecting you."

"Certainly, Henry. Come on, Ben. This way," Cheryl said, motioning for Ben to follow her back to the elevator.

The ride down to sublevel 1, followed by the walk through the underground hallways connecting the entire facility to the

APEX labs, was the longest five minutes of Ben's life, but it was worth every agonizing millisecond. Cheryl opened the door marked *Exo Lab 2*, and an exited gasp exploded past Ben's lips. Holotables, workbenches, and a myriad of monitors and testing equipment filled the lab. Racks of APEX suits in various states of assembly lined an entire wall, and a large, almost jungle-gym-like structure stood in the center of the room surrounded by lab-coated technicians busily checking over the disassembled APEX suit suspended from the structure's center.

"And here we are," Cheryl remarked to Ben in a cheerful voice. "Doctor Swarthout will get you situated until your dad makes it down here. I need to run and finish a few things up. Have fun!" She said those last words with what Ben recognized as obvious false cheerfulness, but his exuberance buried the information before his brain could process it. He was getting an APEX! Cheryl turned on her heels and left him standing alone, staring wide-eyed at a room full of strange people and stranger gear.

"Ah, Benjamin!" Dr. Johannes Swarthout exclaimed in a clipped South African accent as he looked up from the tablet he was using to review the suit's diagnostics. "I'm glad you made it. Dr. Carruthers is ready to get you started with the fitting process, and the sooner we get moving on this, the better." Without another word, he returned to his tablet, muttering to himself and occasionally looking up at the suit as he scrolled through the diagnostic screens in front of him.

Ben was taken aback; he had expected the staff in the room to come introduce themselves and make the socially acceptable small talk before getting started, just as every other meeting had gone when his father would introduce him to ExoDyn personnel in the past. Instead, the dozen or so technicians in the room barely registered his arrival, and his mind began to shift gears back toward the unusual events from earlier in the day.

A middle-aged woman with brown hair pulled back into a tight ponytail walked over to him and smiled. "Hello, Ben. It's nice to finally meet you. I'm Dr. Jana Carruthers, but you can just call me Jana," the woman said as she reached out her hand in greeting, her eyes expressing genuine warmth and enthusiasm.

"Nice to meet you, Jana. I'm Ben," he said, shaking her hand distractedly as his mind yo-yoed back and forth from anxiety about the morning to excitement about his number-one dream coming true. "Uh, but I guess you knew that already." His awkwardness drew a smile from the woman as he mentally berated himself for looking like an idiot, but she quickly moved the conversation along to spare him the embarrassment.

"Right this way, Ben. We need to get a baseline on your biometric data and then create a neural map to help integrate your cognition with the suit." She gestured for him to follow her toward something that Ben could only describe as a lab chair taken straight out of a sci-fi movie. It hinged at the knee, lower back, head, and arms, allowing for the occupant to be repositioned anywhere from lying down to standing fully erect. A helmet-like enclosure hinged away from where the occupant's head would be, and monitors and workstations were connected to it by a dizzying array of data cables. It looked decidedly more torture-like than Ben cared for, and his apprehension must have been visible on his face.

"Your father likes to call it 'the Rack,' but don't worry, it's not nearly as scary as its medieval namesake, nor as painful," Jana told him as she settled herself into a wheeled chair facing a row of monitors on the desk next to the Rack. "Take a seat, and we'll get started."

Ben reclined in the chair, finding it supremely comfortable for something that looked so intimidating. "You're not exactly filling me with confidence when you say it's not *as* painful as its namesake." Ben looked around his new perch with a decided air of apprehension. "So what's first?"

"Just sit back for now and try not to move. The chair will start compiling your baseline biometric data, which will take a few minutes," Jana replied without turning from her monitors. "And it will be *painless*, I promise." She continued to work the console in front of her for the next few minutes, while Ben sat back in the chair and stared at the white ceiling tiles, trying to ignore the frenzied activity from the other technicians in the room.

"I take it you were more than a little excited when you got here." Jana's voice finally broke through the general din of the lab. "It took most of the past ten minutes just for your heart rate and respiration to fall back down to normal levels."

"Maybe a little," Ben admitted. "I've been asking for an APEX suit for years, but my dad has always shut me down— something about a teenager not needing a multimillion-dollar piece of advanced exo hardware," Ben added wryly. "I only found out about it a few minutes before Cheryl took me over here."

"Well, I think today makes up for the long wait. You're not getting just any old APEX suit. The suit Dr. Swarthout is prepping is the first prototype for the x300 series. That thing makes its predecessors look like high school science fair projects."

"Awesome! What kind of cool new bells and whistles does she come with?" Ben asked.

"You'll find out shortly, but here's a hint: we're going to map your brain first. This will take considerably longer than gathering the biometric data did," Jana explained as she placed the helmet-like enclosure over his head, cutting off all external sights and sounds. Ben felt a sharp pinch on the back of his scalp as the helmet locked into place, and he shifted his position slightly to avoid a repeat. He found the silent blackness of the insulated helmet disorienting for a moment before a gentle wave of air was circulated through the enclosure, and suddenly he was seated in an otherwise empty white room.

Jana's voice filled his ears, and her face suddenly appeared at the corner of his vision. "We're going to stimulate your senses, make you solve puzzles, and generally give your brain a work-out. Try to focus only on what is going on inside the VR world projected by the helmet. Ready?"

"Let's rock and roll!"

CHAPTER TWO

PRODIGY

JANA REMOVED THE VR HELMET FROM BEN'S HEAD, AND THE CHAIR brought him up to a normal seated position. He had no idea exactly how long he'd been working his way through the various environments and problems the VR world had presented him with, but judging by the number of disposable coffee cups littering Jana's workspace—and the stiffness of his joints and muscles—he knew it must have been hours.

"Four hours, thirty-seven minutes. That beats the record for the fastest mapping time by over an hour. I'm impressed." Ben looked toward the sound of his dad's voice to find him sitting on a stool next to Dr. Swarthout and two other technicians as they busied themselves with the data that had been collected during Ben's neural mapping.

"I thought this was the first prototype for the x300," Ben said, a little confused. "How could there be a record for mapping if I'm the first one to use it?"

"We needed to make sure we wouldn't scramble your brains during the process. So we tried it on your father first," Dr. Swarthout said over his shoulder, drawing an annoyed look from his dad and chuckles from the rest of the techs within earshot of the comment.

"Funny," his dad said in a tone that indicated he probably did not, in fact, find the comment amusing. He turned back to Ben to offer an explanation. "We needed to perfect the neural mapping procedure before we could try integrating a human test subject with the suit. Essentially, we needed to perfect the software so your body will sync up with the hardware. The x300s are fully neural-controlled—no sensors reading muscle activity to tell the suit when and how to move. The next generation of suits will be tailored to the individual wearing it and will seem like an extension of the body."

"You're kidding," Ben said, not quite believing what he had just heard. "People have been trying to perfect a direct neural interface for years but could never find a solution short of cutting your skull open and shoving implants in there. Going wireless has too many issues with signal degradation and contamination as the subject moves around and the receiver shifts on the wearer's head. Not to mention the latency issues. It works with something like this mapping helmet"—Ben gestured to the helmet attached to the Rack—"because the subject isn't moving the entire time, but to control a suit where the user is constantly in motion?" He shrugged. "There's just too many hurdles... What?"

Everyone in the lab was staring at him with surprised looks on their faces, ranging from mildly curious to incredulous.

"It's just that you sound kind of smart all of a sudden," his dad said, eying him suspiciously. "Are you feeling okay?"

"Oh, aren't you just so funny today?" Ben deadpanned.

Being the son of a technology guru, and a bit of a techie himself, meant Ben had kept close tabs on humanity's continued pursuit of bettering itself by blending flesh and machine. While the technological singularity—an event heralding the end of the age of humanity and ushering in a new superintelligence—had not occurred in the mid-twenty-first century as predicted by fans of science fiction, human beings had not yet stopped finding new ways to incorporate technology into their daily lives.

"I giggled," said a nearby technician who was raising his hand like he was in gradeschool, eliciting snorts of laughter from everyone.

"At least there was some benefit to you reading through my stack of technical magazines and leaving them scattered throughout the house." His dad chuckled. "You're right, of course, and many of the latency and signal-quality issues with a wearable direct neural interface do still exist," he admitted.

"So then how can the x300 utilize a DNI?" Ben asked impatiently, seeking help from the scientists and technicians scattered around him. He hated when his dad played these little games with him. He noticed Dr. Swarthout share a brief, almost guilty look with Jana before turning back to his tablet. The discomfort visible on the two scientists' faces gave Ben pause; he felt like a lab rat and wondered just what manner of unpleasantness lay in store for him. Come to think of it, his dad hadn't actually given him any explanation for why he had suddenly pulled a one-eighty on his stance against him getting his own APEX; Ben had just assumed it was because today was his sixteenth birthday.

Still, even Ben had to admit that it was kind of ridiculous for a kid his age to have his own personal powered exo suit for nothing other than shits and giggles. But since he was a teenager who was being given the thing he had wanted for years, his mind ignored the giant flashing neon sign that screamed something was up and instead focused solely on the very, very shiny object of its desire that was being assembled in the middle of the room.

"I'll tell you later. After you're suited up," his dad replied casually as he rose from his stool and turned toward the assembly tower with the prepped suit in the center of the room, breaking Ben's train of thought. The promise did little to assuage the trepidation worming its way into Ben's thoughts, however.

Dr. Swarthout took his cue from his dad and also stood. "Right, then. Come along, Benjamin." The Rack swiveled Ben into an upright seated position, and he made to stand, feeling his muscles complain slightly as he called them back into duty after hours of inactivity. As he stood, the room spun around him and a tingling sensation radiated out from the base of his skull. He reached a hand out to the corner of the nearest workstation to steady himself, and the dizziness passed as quickly as it had come.

"What was that you were saying about scrambling my brains?" he asked, looking first at his dad, then searching the faces of Dr. Swarthout and Jana for any sign his time as an x300 guinea pig was about to be cut short by exploding gray matter.

"Something wrong?" Jana asked. Her voice held genuine concern as she stood from her chair and moved to Ben's side, looking him over for any hint that something was amiss.

"Just got dizzy for a second when I stood up," Ben replied, waving her off. "Probably just from spending so much time lying down during the mapping. I'm fine now." He made to follow his dad toward the center of the room, but Dr. Swarthout stopped him.

"No, not yet. We need to get you into the skinsuit first. This way."

Turning on his heel mid-stride, Ben followed the scientist to the far end of the room, past the racks of APEX suits along the wall, and into a small fitting room in the corner. "Strip down completely and put this on. It's a little strange, but you actually need to enter the suit through the opening for your neck." Ben looked dubiously at the man but said nothing. "I think you'll find the material can stretch a surprising amount without tearing. When you're ready, say the word and we'll get you squared away." With that, the man turned and closed the door.

The skinsuit looked like a high-tech adult onesie. It was predominantly black, but with fine silver threads weaving their way all throughout the garment. Ben reached out and pulled it from the hanger it had been resting on. The lightweight material immediately adjusted itself to Ben's body temperature as he touched it.

"Well, that's pretty damn cool," Ben said to himself. "Wonder what other surprises you have in store for me."

As it turned out, not all surprises were of the "cool" variety, and Ben soon found himself grateful for the privacy of the room after it had taken him nearly five minutes of profanity-laden flailing to get the suit on and situated comfortably.

The experience reminded him of a failed attempt to put on a dry wetsuit after he'd already been swimming during a scuba diving trip his father took him on two years ago as part of a vacation to the Valderian Isles—the ludicrously beautiful islands located just south of Isadore's equator in the middle of its largest ocean. In the end, he'd gotten fed up with the uncooperative neoprene monstrosity and forwent the wetsuit altogether, deciding he didn't really need it anyway on a shallow dive in the warm, tropical waters surrounding the archipelago.

This time around, he succeeded, but the endeavor left him sweaty, frustrated, and with a dull ache in his shin where it had forcefully contacted the frame of a chair that had been placed in the room to assist him. Instead of assisting him, however, it had merely gotten in the way as he attempted to kick his foot fully past the skinsuit's ankle and into the attached bootie at the end, eliciting a shout of, "Fuck you, chair!" A small part of his mind pointed out that screaming obscenities at office furniture might not be the best way to reassure his dad and the room full of scientists on the other side of the door that he was a good candidate to receive a multimil-lion-dollar birthday present, but he was beyond caring at that point.

After making sure the skinsuit was situated properly, Ben opened the door to the lab and walked over to the assembly tower.

"Excellent!" Dr. Swarthout exclaimed. "Now that you're done verbally assaulting my office furniture, the real work can begin."

"Getting into this prototype is a bit more involved than the final version will be," his dad explained as Ben approached the tower's central platform. "Since so many systems are experimen-tal, we wanted the ability to fit different components of the suit individually in order to check fit and function. There's already another version of the suit undergoing trials at a different facility that is much more streamlined and user-friendly than the alpha prototype you'll be using today, and that will be the next step provided everything goes well here—"

"Timeout," Ben interrupted, holding up a hand. "If there's another version of the suit already under construction, then why are we messing around with an outdated version? Wouldn't you want to get data off of the current build and not a predecessor?"

"Because it's thirty light-years away at the moment," his dad said. "Do you want the suit or not? We can call it a day and head home if you have objections to being given a prototype that is an entire generation ahead of the stuff currently on the market."

"Never mind," Ben said pleasantly. "Please continue, Dr. Swarthout."

"That's more like it." His dad rolled his eyes.

"Right, then," Dr. Swarthout said. "We'll need you to start by slipping your arms into the sleeves and resting your chest against the breastplate so we can attach the backplate that contains the power cells and motor control processors, among other systems." He gestured to the front half of the torso section of the suit, complete with shoulders and arms stretched out in front of it.

Ben held his arms out in front of himself, slipping them into the arms of the suit and resting his chest against the gel layer attached to the breastplate that made up the interior of the suit. Once he was settled, a pair of technicians moved the backplate into position and mated the two halves of the torso together.

Over the next half hour, a veritable army of technicians carefully assembled the remaining pieces of the x300 around Ben, his father and Dr. Swarthout diligently directing the careful ballet until, at last, he found himself fully clad in the most advanced powered exo suit ever created, save for the helmet. There was just one problem: he couldn't move.

"So this thing is really sweet-looking and all that," Ben said, "but shouldn't I at least be able to, you know, move? It weighs a ton."

His dad replied to his smart-assed remark in kind. "Maybe if you found some time to work out, instead of sitting on your butt and watching vid streams all day, you'd be able to."

Ben wasn't particularly athletic, but neither was he flabby and out of shape. A major advantage of having a fully equipped holoroom was the fact that the gamer actually lived the scenario in the game, and to make your avatar run in the game, you had to run in real life. While the stereotypical couch potato gamers still existed, they were rapidly being replaced by a new generation of hologamers that were nearly as physically fit as any sports jock. Ben was never one to be found at the gym, but the amount of calisthenics he received during his gaming sessions had left him lean and fit.

Seeing that Ben was preparing to follow up on his father's retort with yet another unproductive comment, Dr. Swarthout stepped in. "It's heavy because we haven't yet initiated the suit. Remember, this is only a prototype, and many features that we intend to incorporate into the final version have not been installed on this one."

"Meaning?" Ben suddenly found himself a little irritated that he might, in fact, have just been volunteered by his dad to act as little more than a human manikin for a nonfunctional x300 prototype.

"Meaning," the scientist continued, "this prototype can only be powered up and operated when you are wearing the helmet." He turned to Jana, who was standing in front of the pedestal on which the x300's helmet rested. "Ready?" he asked.

She had her tablet connected to the inductive dataport on the back of the helmet and was finalizing the DNI system configuration. "One second... Ready," she said, setting her tablet down and removing the data cable from the helmet before moving aside. His dad stepped over and picked up the final piece of the suit, giving it one last inspection before pressing a pair of releases under the chin. The helmet split vertically, just behind where the opaque faceplate ended next to the temples and hinged apart.

"This will be a little like putting the neural mapping helmet on, except the sensory deprivation will last a bit longer until we can initiate the suit's systems. It is absolutely critical that you don't move once the suit starts to come online," his dad explained to him. "Do you understand?"

"Um, sure. Don't move until you tell me to. Got it," Ben said, now wondering what exactly he'd gotten himself into. *Careful what you wish for*, he thought. Apprehension mingled with excitement as Dr. Swarthout and his dad snugged the back of the helmet onto his head. There was a mechanical-sounding click, and then the opaque faceplate lowered itself into place and Ben's world went black.

How many minutes went by before anything happened, he didn't know, but it had been minutes, not seconds like when he used the neural mapping helmet. The first thing Ben noticed was that weird tingling sensation at the base of his skull, accompanied by a faint hum as the suit powered on.

Lines of code began scrolling past his eyes, and the faint light emitting from it was enough to make him squint after being in complete darkness for so long. The code was scrolling so fast he couldn't make out exactly what systems were initializing, but then he felt the gel layer surrounding him shift such that soon he felt completely encased by it. Ben had never been one to suffer from claustrophobia, but the confined darkness of the helmet mixed with the omnipresent pressure from the gel layer was enough to trigger the first hints of panic in the more primitive parts of his brain.

Just when it seemed he would well and truly lose his cool, he felt the gel layer relax somewhat and then perfectly match his body temperature. The result was a feeling of near nakedness. The words *Boot Sequence Complete* flashed three times in front of his eyes, and he suddenly found himself looking at a trio of faces as the faceplate turned transparent.

"Hey, guys," Ben said cheerfully, and his words boomed out of the x300's external speakers, causing all three to jump back and slap their hands over their ears. Ben could hear a crashing sound from behind him and to his left and tried to turn his head around to see what had happened, but the hardware blocks were still in place and he couldn't move. When he realized he couldn't physically turn his head to look, a small window appeared in the lower-left corner of his vision, showing a sheepish-looking technician quickly reaching down to pick up the piece of equipment he had knocked off the worktable when Ben's salutation had thundered through the lab.

Next to the image of the tech collecting what was undoubtedly a ridiculously expensive piece of gear appeared a still shot of the man, along with his name—Edwards, Michael P.—birthdate, and address. *Woah. Sweet. I wonder what else this thing knows about him.* Almost before the thought had fully formed itself in Ben's mind, the suit reached out to the on-site ExoDyn personnel server, and a window showing the tech's personal data stretched itself to fill Ben's entire field of view and started displaying everything in the man's employment file.

"What did I say, Ben?" his dad yelled while wiggling a finger in his ear, trying to make the ringing stop.

"You told me not to move—you didn't say anything about not speaking!" The windows showing the tech and his information vanished as Ben turned his attention back to the people in front of him.

"Dammit, Ben, you nearly blew out our eardrums," his dad said, calming somewhat. "Alright. Johannes dialed back the suit's external speakers already, but I suppose that's as good a starting place as any. I want you to *think* about the external speaker volume, but don't try to change any settings yet—just think about the system and hold it in the center of your mind."

Ben did as instructed, and a familiar volume icon popped up at the periphery of his vision. "Good, Ben," his dad said before Ben could inform him he had completed the task. "We have a feed out here and can see everything your HUD is displaying to you. No need to tell us what you see.

"Now, think about adjusting your suit's volume down to just above a whisper—let's say, two percent or so."

Ben willed the change, and was gratified to see the percentage under the icon change to 2%.

"This is incredible, Henry. None of the others were able to so easily manipulate the interface this quickly—even something as simple as a volume change." Jana had a tinge of awe in her voice as she turned from the monitor and looked at Ben.

"Yeah," Ben said, the faux smugness in his voice obvious, "I'm pretty awesome."

"Humble, too," his dad said without looking up from a tablet in his hand. He swiped at the screen for a moment longer before looking back at Ben. "That's great, Ben. Now, change the volume back up to ten percent, which is roughly equivalent to a normal conversa—" Before he could finish his sentence, the volume had been reset to ten percent. His dad turned to Jana and Dr. Swarthout. "What say we skip the baby steps and just go for it?" he asked, though it was really more of a mandate. The two scientists shared a look and then nodded in acquiescence.

"Alright, Ben, Johannes is going to remove the hardware blocks preventing movement. When I give you the go-ahead, I want you to *slowly*, and *deliberately* step down off the assembly platform, take two steps forward, and then wait for the next set of instructions. Go ahead, Johannes," he finished, nodding at his project lead.

Ben watched his dad and Jana take several steps away from the tower and out of his prescribed line of travel, and then he felt himself shift as the tower supports were removed and he was left standing on his own. His dad nodded at him. *I've got this*, he thought, as he moved to hop off the platform.

What happened next was not Ben hopping lightly to the floor in front of his amazed audience. Instead, his legs shot him up into the air as if they were trying to achieve orbit. Ben tried to reach his arms above his head in an attempt to ward off the impact he knew was coming with the top of the assembly tower's frame, but it was too late. He felt a jarring impact as the crown of his helmet smacked one of the tower's crossbars before he collapsed in a heap at the base of the platform.

"Ben!" he heard his father shout.

"I'm good," Ben said sheepishly as he carefully rolled to a sitting position on the floor. He held up a hand to the people coming to his aid, stopping them. "That's my bad. *Holy crap!* This thing is awesome!" he exclaimed, using a corner post of the tower to aid him in regaining his feet and feeling the metal buckle under his augmented grasp. "Oops," he said, looking at the indentations left by four suited fingers and a thumb. "Okay. Now, where were we?"

―――――

BEN STOOD PANTING in front of his dad and a half dozen ExoDyn scientists and technicians. After he'd mastered putting one foot in front of the other, Dr. Swarthout led them through a set of double doors at the far end of the lab, revealing a cavernous underground room littered with various obstacles. The team had tested his augmented physical abilities—strength, speed, agility, and gross and fine motor coordination—and Ben had proven to be a prodigy: the harder they pushed him, the faster he mastered their challenges.

"Not bad, Doc," Ben said between lungfuls of air. "What's next?"

"Nothing," his dad said. "We need time to go through all the data, and you need a break."

The past six hours had gone by in a blur, culminating with a run through the coolest obstacle course he had ever seen. After his mishap with the assembly tower, he found he needed to recalibrate his movements to allow for the greatly increased speed and strength offered to him by the suit, and he also exactingly followed the instructions given him... well, for the first few hours at least. By midway through the testing, the adaptive interface had stopped popping up random windows on his HUD whenever a stray thought flitted through his mind, and he had more or less acclimated to his newfound strength and speed. By the time the last hour of testing was underway, he was taking some liberties with his instructions as he effortlessly cruised through the rigorous series of tests the team had developed.

"His synaptic integration is over ninety-eight percent, Henry, and I wouldn't be at all surprised if it rises even more," Jana said, consulting her tablet.

"I'd love to say, 'like father, like son,' but I can't hold a candle to that," his dad commented. "How are you feeling, Ben?"

"I've got a bit of a headache, and I'm starving," Ben replied, suddenly acutely aware that it had been over twelve hours since he last ate. Hydration wasn't a problem as he quickly discovered that the suit's integrated recycling system purified... well, best not to think too much about that. The purified water was then made available through a small straw that would pop out of the helmet's lining with but a thought. Food, on the other hand, was not made readily available to him. "I think you're right about taking that break."

"I think we've got plenty of data to keep the lab monkeys busy for a while," his dad said, turning to walk back toward the lab. "Let's get you cracked, then go grab something to eat," he finished over his shoulder, referring to the process of removing the APEX suit. "The headache should subside shortly—your body is still adjusting to the implant."

Ben stood there for a moment, admiring the suit he was wearing and looking around the testing ground. He knew it was time to call it a day, but a part of him wanted to stay in the suit forever.

"Okay." He began to follow his dad before halting mid-step. "Wait. What implant?" he said accusingly.

His dad stopped and turned back to look at him. "The one Jana implanted at the base of your skull, just above the hairline," he said matter-of-factly. "It was done while she was collecting your baseline biometric data. The implant attaches to the base of the skull, then works a series of nanofilaments up along the spinal cord to the various regions of the brain, where they will split further and attach themselves to neurons. The neural mapping process wasn't done to allow us to read your brain's responses to certain stimuli—it was done to guide your implant where to create the pathways in your brain. Basically, the implant is a hardline to your brain. That's how we get the x300 to be so responsive: it's essentially a part of your body when you're wearing it."

Ben stared at his dad in disbelief, absentmindedly touching the back of his helmet while trying to process the bomb that his dad had just dropped on him. With a thought, a skeletal outline of his neck and head appeared, floating in his vision with the implant highlighted. He wanted to understand how something like that could have been done without his knowledge.

Highlighted tendrils of nanotech filaments snaked their way out of the implant, up his spinal cord, and wormed their way into every part of his brain. *Son of a bitch! I didn't feel a thing! This can't be real.* Then he remembered the sharp pinch he felt when the mapping helmet was lowered over his head, and the tingling sensation at the base of his skull—the way it seemed to radiate up into his brain when the suit powered on—and the dizzy spell he had suffered after the mapping. It was too much to take in all at once, and it left him speechless.

"Ben?" His dad had walked the dozen paces back to his son and now stared up at Ben's armored face.

"You cut me open and jammed an implant in my head without even asking me first." It was not a question. "Why not tell me? I probably would have gone along with it anyway," Ben finished, his voice a mix of anger and incredulity. He looked from his father to the shamed faces of Drs. Swarthout and Carruthers, who stood silently off to the side. This had gone from the best day ever to the… what? The worst? Weirdest? Why was he not sure how he felt about this? His brain went into vaporlock as the this-is-really-cool side battled it out with the what-the-actual-fuck side.

"There wasn't time, Ben," his dad said in a near whisper, eyes on the floor.

"I… Why?" was all Ben could think to say, his mind racing as it slotted this new information into the events of the day. Alien attacks, out-of-character actions by Dan and his dad, scared people everywhere, and now what had to have been a massive ethics violation by forcing prototype technology into a minor— let alone the legality of the thing. The bottom fell out of his stomach as the enormity of it settled in.

"We originally weren't even planning on suiting you up today, but certain events have forced our hand." His dad's voice had gone hard, and the sharpness of his pale blue eyes matched his tone.

Ben was taken aback by the suddenness with which his dad's mood had changed from proud excitement at his son's accomplishments to one of cold severity, and his last thread of restraint finally snapped.

"What the hell is going on, Dad?" Ben exploded. "Aliens blowing up military installations plastered all over the news, Dan shows up hours ahead of schedule to rush us in here, past every cop and soldier on the planet, and then you jam what I can only assume is untested tech in my brain while everyone else runs around like their lives depend on it!" The elation he had felt over the past hours had completely faded, and the unease he had felt during the car ride that morning had come storming back, turning into something akin to full-blown panic as his mind raced to put the pieces together into a coherent picture. "What. The hell. Is going on?"

"Ben, you're not just wearing the next gen of APEX," his dad said. "That suit is only part of the equation. I couldn't tell you everything that would be involved because we couldn't risk you turning us down. Let's get you cracked, and I'll tell you everything—"

A deep rumble echoed through the chamber, cutting him off mid-sentence, and the overhead lights flickered momentarily as dust trickled down from the ceiling high above. Ben, his dad, and the scientists looked at one another, fear showing on their faces.

"Uh, what was that?" Ben asked.

The double doors to the lab were thrown open and Dan Murphy burst into the room, eyes wide with alarm. "We're under attack, Hank! It's happening!"

CHAPTER THREE

SHIT, MEET FAN

CARL ROWAN SAT AT HIS CONSOLE, THINKING ABOUT WHICH BAR HE should hit up first. His six-month rotation to deep-space telemetry monitoring station Victor-04 as station supervisor was up in just over three hours, and he was struggling mightily to keep his mind focused on the job.

In his mid-fifties, with salt-and-pepper gray hair, soft brown eyes, and a neatly manicured beard, Carl had been with Deep-Space Frontiers in a supervisory capacity for nearly eight years now. Eight years in which he had been stationed on a number of remote outposts, preferring the relatively mundane—though many would prefer to call it boring—nature of the outer-system postings to the harder, more dangerous life aboard exploration vessels as they traveled through unexplored space. It was the perfect posting for a dedicated bachelor who was a natural intro-vert, but that didn't mean he wanted the remote station to be his permanent home.

Victor-04 was the most remote sensing outpost in the Valkyrie system and was therefore also the most boring duty assignment within five light-years. The station was operated by DeepSpace Frontiers, Inc., a private exploration company currently contracted by Confed Fleet Command to map the proposed Valkyrie-Holstein warp lanes before colonization of the newest Confed star system could begin in earnest. Its primary function was as a relay for telemetry coming in from the deep-space exploration vehicles charting the new lanes, but as the only platform capable of sending and receiving intra-system FTL comms drones, Victor-04 also served as a comms relay for the various mining and scientific outposts and small ship traffic that operated in the outer reaches of the Valkyrie system.

A flashing alert popped up on his console, and he grudgingly turned his attention back to actual work. "Justin, what's the deal with this new arrival?" he asked his drone ops technician, Justin Reid, who was also due to rotate out after this shift was over.

Reid leaned forward in his chair and scanned his workstation display. "A Beckman has just dropped out of warp at the edge of the system, squawking priority-one ident, Carl."

Carl quickly crosschecked the identity of the new arrival against the list of scheduled traffic, stiffening slightly at the real-ization the drone wasn't on the published schedule. Out-of-the-ordinary occurrences were scarce this far out of the system, and with the recent terrorist attack on a station similar to Victor-04 and rumors of an impending conflict with the Alarians, everyone in the control room had been on edge recently.

"It's not on the schedule," Reid continued. "IFF reads as a Beckman from the *Magellan*—she's not due to check in for another two weeks," Reid said.

The CTS *Magellan* was part of a three-ship survey mission working to survey the new warp lanes and clear any potential obstructions. Warp lane surveys could take years to complete and were incredibly expensive endeavors, but having an inter-stellar freeway between two star systems that was known to be free of navigational hazards was priceless. The *Magellan* and her support ships had been out for several months, and this was the first time anything unusual had come in from them.

"Send out the recovery drone and have it brought in for servicing and download," Carl instructed Reid before turning to the youthful face of his comms tech sitting at an adjacent console. "Evan, prep a comms drone for Valkyrie FLEETCOM and upload copies of the Beckman's data as soon as we have it. The *Magellan* is one of theirs, and they'll want to know what we've found."

Even in this day and age of seemingly limitless technology, certain things were still beholden to the laws of physics. Despite rumors for the past decade or so that faster-than-light communications were just around the corner, nothing that would allow people to converse with each other in real time while separated by astronomical distances had ever made it to the commercial market.

Victor-04 could launch and receive FTL-capable drones, which were used to send communications and other data from the outer system to various points farther in-system—particularly to Isadore, the Valkyrie system's only habitable planet. Whereas it would take anywhere from five to twelve hours—depending on the relative position of the station and planet within their orbits—just for the transmitted data to reach Isadore via conventional radio signal, the FTL comms drones could make the trip to their destination, be downloaded, and return with a response in under an hour.

"Got it, bossman." Evan Yost was by far the youngest person on the station, having taken a comms tech job with DeepSpace Frontiers immediately upon graduation from college. He had completed the communications technician training course and been assigned to Victor-04 just three days ago, and this was his first duty shift after orientation.

Carl ground his teeth. He had found Evan to be competent in

the limited time he'd spent with him since his arrival, but the kid's informal nature ground on Carl's old-school nerves like a belt sander.

The next twenty minutes passed in silence as Carl monitored his people working diligently to retrieve the unexpected Beckman drone and prepare to send out an intra-system FTL comms drone to Valkyrie FLEETCOM headquarters until Reid finally looked up at him from his console.

"Beckman has been retrieved, and data transfer is complete," Reid reported. "Looks like there's an unencoded video file accompanying the telemetry data—timestamp on the file shows it was the last thing uploaded to the drone before launch, and it's flagged urgent, time-sensitive. So much for your vacation, huh, Carl? Want it on the big screen?"

"Do it," Carl grumbled, and Reid entered a series of commands on his console. A priority-one, unencoded file on an unscheduled comms drone was never good news, and Carl found his ire rising at the giant middle finger fate was giving him—he was going to miss the shuttle in-system, and there wouldn't be another until next week. The main viewing monitor at the front of the control room switched from showing a 2D map of the space surrounding the station to the bloodied face of a woman staring directly into the camera.

"This is Commander Julia Dodson of the CTS *Magellan*." She was shouting to be heard over the blaring of klaxons and the rumble of explosions. She paused briefly to wipe away the blood trickling down into her eyes from a deep gash on her forehead before continuing. "We've encountered an Alarian battlegroup staging 1.3 light-years outside of the Valk—" Static washed over the screen for several seconds before the picture cleared up, smoke thick in the background. "—lieve this to be an invasion force. *Columbus* and *Downing* have both been destroyed. Alert

CTS FLEETCOM immediately of a pending attack on Terran assets in the Valkyrie system. *Magellan* out."

The screen went black and silence fell over the control room. "Oh my god," Reid whispered. It took a moment for Carl to regain his lost senses after viewing what he knew to be the announcement of humanity's first interstellar war, but his long experience as a station manager took over and he started reflexively shouting orders to his team.

"Evan! Get that data uploaded to the comms drone and launch it right fucking now! Have it squawking priority-one on all channels. Then I want everyone to begin purging their systems in accordance with hostile contact protocols. Wake everybody up and get ready to abandon the sta—"

"Too late!" Reid's voice was strained with terror. "They're already here!"

Carl's eyes snapped to the main viewscreen, now back to displaying the familiar 2D space plot, and saw two dozen angry red dots that hadn't been there a minute ago. As he watched, three of the dots broke away from the main formation and began closing in on the icon denoting Victor-04.

"Did you have time to launch the drone to FLEETCOM, Evan?" Carl found his voice was suddenly rock-solid, and a knowing sense of calm settled over him. Their fate was sealed. He had wargamed this exact scenario in his head many times in recent weeks, which helped prepare his mind for the unthinkable. There was only one thing left for him to do.

"It launched thirty seconds ago," Evan replied, staring wide-eyed at the plot. "This is it, isn't it?" he asked the older man in a shaky voice.

"Yes, son. This is it," Carl said, a note of conviction in his voice as he turned to his own console and began entering commands, his numb hands selecting menus and pressing keys on autopilot.

He had drilled for this. They had all drilled for this. Just last week, in fact, they had drilled for this. But the laughter and jokes about aliens attacking or abducting them were absent now. Now, there was only one universal emotion aboard Victor-04: terror.

Klaxons and strobing red lights filled the entire station as Carl worked to initiate the station's self-destruct systems. For obvious reasons, the systems were known only to senior personnel, but all Terran stations and vessels that handled military communications or other sensitive data were equipped with them for just such a scenario. The three Alarian vessels were nearly overlapping the station's icon on the viewscreen when the words *Self-Destruct Initiated, 30 Second Silent Countdown* overlaid the display.

Carl Rowan sat back in his chair, the blaring alarms and screams of his people sounding muted and distant to his ears. A far-off part of his mind noted a shuddering thump as one of the Alarian assault craft came into contact with the station's primary airlock. In three hours his shift would have been over and he would have been on his way back to Isadore. Fate was a cruel bitch. *Three more hours.*

There was a flash of searing heat as the station's fusion powerplant went supercritical and exploded. Moments later, all that remained of Victor-04, her thirty-one crewmembers, and the attacking Alarian vessel was a rapidly expanding cloud of debris.

———

"IT'S HAPPENING!"

Dan Murphy had been his dad's bodyguard and confidant for almost as long as Ben could remember, and this was the first time he'd ever seen the man genuinely scared. The unease Ben had been feeling a moment ago roared into full-fledged fear in an instant.

"How many?" his dad asked, sounding much calmer than Ben thought was appropriate, given the current situation.

He knew this—whatever this is—was coming, Ben realized.

The look on Dan's face told Ben the news was bad, but as he relayed recent events, the full scope of just how bad became clear. "A full carrier battlegroup, at least—two dozen ships that we know of. The Alarians are landing haymakers, but Garland is aboard the *Ford* and has taken personal command of all Confed forces in the system. They're regrouping for a counteroffensive as we speak, but the Alarian fleet has started an orbital bombardment of critical assets.

"Freedom Station was obliterated in the opening salvo, and the major spaceports around the planet are being targeted for kinetic strikes—that's what shook the building a minute ago. Probably William Massey, if I had to guess," he said, referring to Isadore's second-largest spaceport, located over ten miles away on the western outskirts of the city. "There's more, but it's all bad. Bastards caught us with our pants down."

Ben's chest squeezed his heart in an iron grip as every hair on his body stood on end. It was so much worse than he could have imagined. How had a few scattered terrorist attacks turned into a full-scale planetary bombardment by mainline warships? The shocking escalation was almost beyond comprehension—it just didn't make any sense.

Freedom Station had contained Valkyrie Fleet Command headquarters and the quantum comms link with Central Command, as well as having been the central hub for both military and civilian inter-system traffic. When the station went up in a host of antimatter explosions, ninety-five percent of interstellar travel had gone with it—not to mention nearly the entirety of CTS FLEETCOM's command structure for this sector of Terran space.

"How long do we have, Dan?" his dad said, and it amazed Ben how calm his father appeared after just having been told alien Armageddon was upon them. Ben couldn't even get his mouth to form coherent words to speak, yet his dad took the news in stride.

They knew this was coming! They knew, and they brought me here anyway. Ben looked at his hands, which were encased in the most advanced powered armor suit ever developed. Why did they bring him here, to this lab, when they knew an attack was imminent?

"Depends on how they prioritize their targets and if they want to take any part of the complex intact, but I'd guess no more than thirty minutes, tops."

"Ben, go with Dan," his dad said, gripping his shoulders tightly and breaking his internal cascade of thoughts. "He'll get you out of the system safely and back to the farm. I'll follow as soon as I can." The authority in his voice was absolute, but Ben protested anyway.

"No, Dad! I'm not leaving without you!" He shrugged out of his father's grip and took a small step back. "Not happening," he insisted.

"This is not up for debate, Ben. I'm not losing *you* to these bastards, too!"

Ben felt like a sledgehammer just hit him in the gut. His dad was still talking, but Ben couldn't hear him. "Too"? What did he mean by 'too'? *Mom... Son of a bitch, he's talking about Mom!*

"Ben!" Ben's life-changing realization was interrupted by his dad screaming into his faceplate. "You *will* go with Dan, and you will go *right now!*" his father said forcefully before turning back to Dan. "You know what to do, Dan. Get going." With that, his dad turned and ran back to retrieve his tablet from the workstation they had set up with monitors and equipment to collect the test data.

"Ben, let's go." Dan moved slightly behind Ben and to his left, putting a hand on his shoulder and pushing him firmly down the hall and through the doors to the lab.

Ben's shocked mind was dimly aware that Dan was leading him back through the lab and down a series of hallways to a large service lift, but he couldn't find the strength to resist. His father's words reverberated in his head: *I'm not losing you to these bastards, too!* He could have meant anything, but Ben knew exactly whom his dad had been referring to. His mind reeled with the revelation that his mother's death had not been an accident, and he struggled to focus on the things happening around him.

Ben was a child when his mom died, and he had accepted without question what he was told regarding the incident. As he grew older and started asking for more details about her death, he had never been fully satisfied with what information he could pry from his dad or dig up in old news stories on the net, but it had never occurred to him that something sinister had transpired. Now he knew different... but how? His mom *had* been on Mars when she died; that much was absolutely known. How had the Alarians killed her and the entire team at the research complex without the Terran media getting even a whiff of the true story? Had his dad managed to convince them not to run the truth? No, that didn't make any sense. If the Alarians had been at Mars, the Confed military would have known about it, and if the military had been involved with aliens in the home system, there would be no way to keep that news from leaking out.

"Dammit, Ben, we have to *move!*" Dan was shouting into his faceplate, but to Ben, it sounded like he was talking through a pillow. Ben had shut down; his mind could only focus on the circumstances of his mom's death—no, *murder*—and trying to process what it all meant. He saw that the service lift doors had opened to reveal one of the complex's hangars that housed several of ExoDyn's corporate shuttles. Then he was again being guided along by the insistent hand of Dan Murphy toward a waiting shuttle a hundred meters distant on the tarmac.

A massive explosion ripped through the hangar just as the two crossed out from under the shadow of the building and onto the tarmac, the force of it sending both of them tumbling across the pavement. The jarring impact with the ground finally broke Ben's stupor, and he quickly sprang to his feet, having been protected from injury by the APEX suit he still wore. His eyes searched around for Dan, finding him sprawled on the ground several meters away. He crossed the distance in two strides and reached down to help his friend to his feet.

"Are you alright?" Ben asked.

"I'll make it. We need to get on the shuttle," Dan grunted through bloodstained teeth, accepting Ben's proffered hand.

Ben used the power of the suit to pull Dan to his feet, then helped him the short distance to the shuttle where the cargo ramp was sitting just off the surface of the tarmac. The shuttle's loadmaster was frantically motioning for them to get aboard, and the instant they were off the ramp and into the cargo bay, the ramp started coming up. Ben felt the craft lurch as the pilots applied thrust and lifted off the ground before it had even closed and latched.

"Strap yourselves in and hold on!" the loadmaster shouted at his two charges, gesturing to the sides of the bay, where a row of empty nylon webbing slingseats beckoned. Dan helped Ben with his restraints before buckling himself in, as the spartan seats were not designed with the x300's bulk in mind.

"Dan, what about Dad?" Ben shouted as the atmospheric

engines throttled up with a shriek and the small craft rocketed up and away from ExoDyn HQ.

"He'll be fine, Ben," Dan shouted back over the roar of the engines as he strapped himself in next to Ben. "He'll catch another ride out after he takes care of a few things. Don't worry, he knew this was a possibility and prepared accordingly."

Prepared accordingly? What the hell did that mean? As far as Ben knew, his dad was a wealthy inventor and businessman who did battle in a boardroom, where the worst that could happen would be the price of ExoDyn's stock dropping. Now, Dan was talking about him like he was some sort of secret agent. Ben's thoughts were interrupted again as the shuttle was rocked by a nearby explosion, and he heard metallic pings as shrapnel from the blast peppered the hull. Thankfully, it seemed like the hits hadn't caused any damage.

The three men in the cargo hold endured the next ten minutes in silent terror, listening to the scream of the engines as the pilots flogged them for all they were worth, while continuously throwing the craft into a series of stomach-churning maneuvers during the escape from the planet's atmosphere. At one point, Ben was thrown against his restraints when the shuttle rolled over and dove sharply. The ship shuddered from another too-close explosion before resuming its mad dash for orbit. The lack of viewports in the cargo bay was both a blessing and a curse; Ben desperately wanted to know what was going on outside his little world.

He knew they had reached the upper edge of the atmosphere and transitioned to low orbit when the howl of the shuttle's engines faded away to a low drone and the buffeting that had been wracking the craft subsided; air resistance giving way to the vacuum of space.

"Are… Are we… safe?" Ben asked Dan, his voice shaking so bad it took several attempts to get all three words out.

Dan turned to get the loadmaster's attention. The man was strapped into his seat against the bulkhead at the front of the cargo bay and wearing a headset. "Hey, buddy, are we clear?"

The loadmaster held up a finger, indicating it would be a moment before he could respond. After a few more seconds, he took off the headset and answered. "We're clear of the atmosphere and burning on an out-system trajectory as fast as she'll go, but it'll be a while before we can settle into the V-S warp lane. Alien bastards have mined the transition point, and we need to make a blind jump out on a random vector before we can make our way over to the lane a little farther down the line, and then make the jump for Sol."

"A blind jump?" Ben asked fearfully. "Seriously?"

Everyone who had ever watched a network show about space travel knew that blindly transitioning to warp was risky, at best. The problem with using warp fields for FTL travel was that any object along the flight path too massive for the forward distortion wave to push aside would result in the instantaneous annihilation of anything—and anyone—that collided with it. Blind jumps, especially while still deep in a star system, risked a collision with anything from a piece of space junk to a star.

"It's our only option, kid. Space is a big place, and the odds of hitting something on a short hop are low," the loadmaster said, attempting to reassure him. "Don't worry, we did a few of these during my time in the marines. Piece of cake."

The lights in the cargo bay dimmed, and Ben could hear the low hum of the shuttle's fusion reactor change in pitch as it worked to charge the warp drive's capacitor banks.

"Thirty seconds," the loadmaster called out. He had his headset on again and was listening to the updates from the cockpit. "Ten… five… three…" Ben closed his eyes and gripped the alloy frame of his seat as the loadmaster counted down the last few seconds. "Jump!"

HENRY WATCHED as Dan led Ben down the corridor and toward the service lift that would take them to the facility's private hangar and the waiting shuttles. He tore his gaze away after a few more seconds and started running for his office. He didn't know if he would end up making it off Isadore alive, and he needed to ensure everything was in place to keep the project going if he didn't.

War had been coming; he had known that on an instinctual level ever since Kate was killed on Mars. The networks were only aware of a few scattered attacks that were too high-profile to keep quiet, but Henry had plenty of contacts within the Confed power structure who fed him stories that had never seen the light of day. It had been building over the last six months, ever since his trip to Hai'alla with Ben. Something was working against them.

Too many times, they had been close to a breakthrough in technology or diplomacy when the key players would suddenly disappear or die in "accidents". It didn't make sense that it would have been a human or Alarian behind it all—the Alarians were taking losses as well. It felt like someone—or something— was lurking in the shadows, pulling the strings as the two sides crept ever closer toward war. He just didn't know who or what.

That was all a moot point now, though, as the ground beneath his feet trembled with the impacts of Alarian weapons. He wondered if they would try to take the complex intact to capture the veritable goldmine of technological achievements ExoDyn had accomplished over the last two decades, or if they would simply wipe it off the map and be done with it.

He rushed through the hallways past people—his people— frantically trying to save some shred of their work before fleeing, and his answer shook the earth around him. A dozen large explosions rumbled through the steel and concrete under his feet, some so powerful he had to reach a hand out to steady himself on a wall. Thankfully, the complex had not yet been targeted by a kinetic strike from orbit, which would have leveled every building within a half-mile radius.

As he reached the top floor of the building housing the executive offices, his nose was assaulted by the acrid scent of burning buildings and charred bodies. He stumbled over a discarded box of personal effects that had been abandoned just outside his office and rushed inside. A thin haze of smoke hung in the air and stung his eyes, and he looked out of shattered windows. What he saw staggered him.

Thick black smoke was pouring out of the two adjacent buildings, large holes blasted in their exteriors by Alarian attack craft. People were flooding out to escape the flames that raged inside, some tripping over the broken and bloody bodies of their coworkers who had been unfortunate enough to either be caught in the blasts or crushed by the debris raining down on them.

He tore his gaze away from the carnage on the ground and glanced skyward. CTS and Isadore Defense Corps fighters were engaging the alien attackers in a deadly ballet of bullets, missiles, and laser fire. The arrival of friendly aircraft had bought them a reprieve from the attacks, but in the distance, he saw a blinding streak of white-hot fire rain down from heaven, and he felt the building shake beneath his feet as the kinetic round impacted the planet with the force of a small tactical nuke. That strike had probably just leveled the base housing the IDC's 191st fighter wing: the home of the very fighters that were engaged with the enemy in the skies over his head. He turned from the window and ran for his office.

When he finally reached his corner office, he quickly took a seat behind his desk and logged into his personal terminal. He copied every shred of data he could onto a series of portable data sticks, then initiated a purge of the complex's immense database. *If things don't work out, at least these alien pricks won't get anything useful.*

The status bar on the system purge indicated it would take several minutes to wipe the databanks completely, so he picked up his personal tablet and pulled up the video file he had recorded that morning after sending Cheryl and Ben down to the APEX labs. The file was a backup plan, and he had recorded it with the intention of making several copies and distributing them to various people and locations. That plan was shot now, as the attack had come quicker than expected. He would need to put all his chips on the one remaining option.

He typed in a series of commands, wincing as another explosion rattled the framed pictures on the wall behind him, sending a few of them crashing to the floor, and then waited while the tablet transferred the file to its sibling more than twenty-six light-years distant. It would have to be enough.

An image of Ben caught his gaze as it scrolled on the screensaver of the terminal built into his desk. He should have told him the truth sooner, he realized. Ben wasn't your average teenager; he was much smarter and more mature than most kids his age. Maybe that came from having two certified geniuses for parents, or maybe he'd had to grow up faster than normal after his mom's death. Henry had been a loving father, but he hadn't been around as much as he should have been, thanks to his work. They'd thought they would have more time than this. How had things escalated this quickly?

His terminal beeped at him, confirming the immense data archives around the ExoDyn complex had been successfully purged. Henry pulled up the ExoDyn HQ comms net and enabled a video override of the system.

"This is Henry Hutchins," he said, seeing his face appear on the wall monitor and hearing his words blaring from every speaker connected to the complex's comms net. "All data archives in the complex have been purged, and there is no reason for anyone to remain. ExoDyn HQ is being actively targeted by Alarian forces. Any personnel remaining on campus are directed to evacuate the complex immediately. Head away from populated areas and military installations, as they are being systematically targeted and destroyed by enemy forces. Good luck."

Henry cut the connection and threw his tablet into the small pack he kept next to his desk, took one last look around his long-time office, and made his way back to the elevator that would take him down to the main lobby.

While he waited for the elevator to take him down the eight floors to the building's entrance, he used his own neural implant to place a call via the comms node in his pack. It took several minutes before the call was answered, and he was halfway through the lobby, headed to the rear door that led out to the large central courtyard tying most of the complex together, when an angry face appeared in the corner of his vision.

"Jesus Christ, Henry, I'm in the middle of a fucking war!" The voice of Admiral Robert Garland was unmistakable, sounding like a handful of gravel in a tin can. "This had better be *really* fucking important."

"It is, Bob," Henry said as he shouldered aside one of the large glass doors, the stench of burning infrastructure and death assaulting his nose now that he was out in the open, and headed for the building at the opposite end of the courtyard. "I need a pickup at ExoDyn HQ. All our shuttles are either in the air or destroyed. I've got all of ExoDyn's archives with me, including all files pertaining to Blackthorn."

Garland took a moment to digest everything his friend had just told him before responding. "And Ben?"

"Took a shuttle out with Dan Murphy fifteen minutes ago,

headed for Grayling. I don't know if they made orbit or not—there's a shitstorm going on overhead right now," Henry said, referring to the melee raging in the skies above him.

"There's a shitstorm everywhere, Hank," Garland said. "I'll have my people go through the sensor data when we have a minute to see if they can pick out his shuttle. In the meantime, I'll see what we have in your area and send someone to get you out. We've got our hands full up here, but they must not have been expecting us to be able to counter so quickly. The situation is tenuous, but we have force parity and are giving as good as we get. Garland out."

The line went dead, and Henry entered the materials research building after having made it across the courtyard. He saw no one as he rushed through the building to the far side, which led to a large grassy area used for recreation and company picnics, and was relieved to see his people had heeded his evacuation order.

The small ExoDyn airfield sat beyond the rec area, surrounded by a few hangars and warehouses. Henry could see smoke rising from a large hole that had been blasted into the largest of the hangars—the one containing the service lift down to the underground labs—and his heart skipped a beat as his eyes searched the area for the shuttle Ben and Dan were to take. It was nowhere to be seen, so he took shelter in a drainage ditch next to the large hangar and hunkered down while the war raged on around him.

He only had to wait a short while. His ears picked up the whine of a dropship's engines approaching the airfield, and he climbed out of the ditch and searched the sky for his rescuers, quickly spotting an MS-111 Griffon assault dropship circling the complex. Henry panicked for a moment when the twin twenty-millimeter cannons of the Griffon's chin turret swiveled to point directly at him. Thankfully, the craft banked in his direction, and the cannons stayed silent. Henry recalled that the chin turret was slaved to the left-seater's helmet, so anywhere the copilot looked, the turret followed.

The dropship flared to a landing less than a minute later as Henry covered his ears to block out the deafening roar of the craft's four main engines. The tail ramp came down, and a fireteam of four APEX armored warriors rushed over to Henry, while another fireteam took up security at the base of the ramp, their helmeted heads sweeping side to side over shouldered carbines.

"Mr. Hutchins?" the lead man asked, and Henry nodded, noting the insignia showing on his suit's left breast: a ring of olive branches surrounding a diving eagle overlaying the tip of a spear. *SEARs*, Henry realized. "This way, sir," the SEAR said, and Henry quickly found himself surrounded by the fearsome warriors as they led him to the dropship.

Henry raised an arm over his face as hot jetwash from the still-spun-up engines blasted dirt and debris in all directions and the acrid stench of refined JP-101 exhaust stung his nostrils. The SEARs escorted him up the ramp and into the cargo bay. As they cleared the ramp, the fireteam at the base of it also withdrew into the confines of the armored craft, and the ship's crew chief closed the ramp and signaled the cockpit that they were clear to dust-off. Henry was shown a slingseat constructed of nylon webbing like the one Ben had used on his ride off the planet not an hour prior, and he swiftly secured his harness as the SEARs did likewise.

"Thank you, gentleman," he said. "I appreciate the lift, but I must say I'm surprised Admiral Garland would send SEARs for me."

The elite Special Exo-Atmospheric Reconnaissance units were tasked with everything from small-team reconnaissance to demolition, sabotage, hostage rescue, or capture and kill missions. They operated in every environment imaginable, and from what Henry could remember, the teams comprised just four members each. Henry was awed that Garland had sent *two* for him.

The SEAR in charge changed his faceplate's opacity from a featureless black to clear, revealing the rugged face of a man in his early thirties with piercing green eyes. "We were planetside for jungle warfare training in the Irenian Rainforest," he explained as he secured his carbine in the wall-mounted storage rack over his shoulder, "and were rotating back out to the void through Langford when it hit the fan. So we were in the area when the call came in."

"Regardless, you have my thanks"—Henry glanced at the nameplate below his insignia—"Lieutenant Valdez."

"Our pleasure, sir. Not every day we get to evac a VIP *to* a warzone," Valdez replied with a small smirk showing on his otherwise serious face.

"Excuse me?" Henry asked, not sure he had heard correctly.

"This bird is headed for the *Ford*," one of the other SEARs chimed in. Henry looked at him, reading the name Kravczyk on his nameplate. "Congratulations," he continued. "You get a front-row seat to watch Admiral Garland and the rest of the fleet blast those shit-eating alien fucks into space dust."

CHAPTER FOUR

THE LONG RIDE HOME

BEN WINCED AS THE SHUTTLE TRANSITIONED TO WARP, EXPECTING every thump of his rapidly beating heart to be its last. To his immense relief, there was no instantaneous annihilation. Instead, the interior lighting resumed its normal level, and the reactor returned to its low-pitched thrum.

"Damn, kid," the loadmaster said with a chuckle as he unbuckled himself and stood, stretching his muscles to relieve some of the tension that had built up during their harrowing escape. "Your face is white as a sheet." Ben stared at the man, incredulous that he could be so cavalier after everything they had just been through. "Oh, and you owe me a seat," he said, pointing to the warped alloy frame Ben had been gripping for dear life a moment ago.

Ben ignored him and turned to face Dan, who looked like he was having just as hard a time with their flight from the system as Ben was. "Dan, what about Dad? We can't just leave him back there!"

"Your dad is a fighter, Ben," Dan said, placing a reassuring hand on Ben's shoulder. "He'll make it out of there just fine. If he didn't make it to this shuttle, I'm sure he either got a pickup from the fleet or found ground transportation to somewhere he can catch a ride back to Earth to join us. It may just take a little longer than we'd like, okay?"

Ben fought the panic rising in his chest now that he had a few moments to process the fact that humans were now in a shooting war with an alien race, and he had barely escaped from ground zero. He had lost one parent already, and the only reason he made it through that terrible pain was because his dad was there to help him through it. He had no idea how he was going to survive if his dad was gone now, too.

Tears welled at the corners of his eyes as the enormity of the situation slowly sank in. He struggled to push the panic back into the depths and only focus on the things he had some measure of control over at the moment. Spending every hour of the long flight back to Sol crippled by fear wasn't going to help him in any way. He had to be strong and fight through it so he didn't let down the people around him. He cleared his throat as he blinked away the tears.

"So, now what?" Ben said to the loadmaster, trying and failing to control his trembling hands.

"Now we cruise a few light-hours on this vector before making the turn to join up with the Valkyrie-Sol warp lane. That should put us well past any surprises those dicks left for us at the transition point, and then it's three days of warp to cover the twenty-six light-years back to the Sol system and Earth. I hope you brought a book."

Ben wasn't thrilled at the prospect of spending the three-plus days of their journey stuck in his suit; he loved his APEX, but it was starting to itch a little. He turned to Dan, who was leaning back in his seat, an unreadable expression on his face. "If we're going to be stuck on this tub for another three days, I'm getting out of this suit."

Dan looked him over, considering. "I don't see why not." He

shrugged. "It's unlikely we'll run into any trouble en route." He unbuckled himself, then Ben, and stood, turning to face the load-master, who was inspecting the tie-downs on a large shipping container strapped down in the middle of the cargo bay. "Hey, buddy, is there somewhere we can get a little more comfortable and grab something to eat?" he asked before adding, "What's your name, anyway?"

"Andy," the man replied. "Andy Swarbrick. Take the ladder up and head through the forward hatch, then down the hallway past crew berthing. The mess and lounge area are straight through the hatch at the end of the passageway. Feel free to grab one of the staterooms in berthing—there's a set of bunks and a head in each one." He hadn't bothered to look up while giving directions, instead fiddling with one of the mag straps securing the container to the deck.

"Thanks, Andy. I'm Dan, and this is Ben," Dan said, gesturing to the APEX-clad Ben standing next to him.

Andy just raised a hand in acknowledgment. "I'll be here if you need anything."

The stateroom was small and the head smaller still, but at least the two had a place to get cleaned up and lie down. Fortu-nately, Ben could access a complete set of instructions for assembly and disassembly of the x300 from the suit's internal data-storage, and he had copied the files over to a tablet they had borrowed from Andy so they would have access to them after Ben powered the suit down and they started taking pieces off of him. Despite having step-by-step instructions available, it had taken almost an hour for Dan to help Ben remove the x300, and he'd needed Andy's help with the suit's backplate, as it contained the power cells and processing units and weighed nearly eighty pounds.

Ben felt almost human again after having showered and dressed in a borrowed flight suit from one of the pilots who was only slightly larger than he was. The possibility that his dad was lying dead back at ExoDyn headquarters gnawed at the back of his mind like a spectral tick that was dug in deep and couldn't be easily reached, but he pressed on; it was all he could do. Then there were the burning questions he now had about his mom's death, why he had been given an APEX suit after years of it being a nonstarter, and why it was so damned important that his dad took him to ExoDyn when he knew an attack was likely incoming. He exited the stateroom and went through the hatch to the mess deck, where Dan was preparing ration packs for dinner, intent on getting some answers. He took a seat at the galley table as Dan walked over with two steaming bowls in his hands, and his friend cocked an eyebrow at him when he saw Ben's gaze boring a hole right through his skull.

"Sorry, Ben, but these ration packs are the only foodstuffs on board. Let's hope they taste better than they smell." Dan handed Ben a bowl filled with what purported to be goulash, but only loosely resembled actual food. Ben took a sniff and cringed at the smell but took the offered spoon and dug in after his stomach let out a longing growl.

"It's not so bad if you swallow before your tongue has a chance to taste it," Ben said, setting the now-empty bowl aside after having devoured its contents in under a minute.

Dan looked at him with an amused expression and shook his head. "You kids will eat anything when you're hungry," he said, having pushed his own bowl aside after an exploratory taste. "Why don't you go try to get some sleep, Ben? It's been a hell of a day."

"Yeah, I think I will," Ben said but made no move to get up. He leaned forward and clasped his hands, elbows on the table. "But first, you owe me some answers, Dan. Like why the hell was it so important that I be brought to ExoDyn this morning and given a prototype APEX when you and Dad apparently knew the Alarians were going to show up and start blowing shit up around us? Or how about what really happened to Mom?"

Dan rocked back in his seat a bit, clearly unprepared for the scorching tone in Ben's voice. "I can't answer most of that, Ben," he said finally. "I will tell you that your mother did die on Mars at a research outpost operated by ExoDyn, and despite a decade of digging, we haven't been able to find any concrete evidence that the explosion at the lab was anything other than an accident." Ben opened his mouth to protest, but Dan held up a placating hand. "Please, Ben, let me finish."

Ben closed his mouth and nodded grudgingly. "Go on."

"Your dad is convinced there was some sort of sabotage, considering how astronomical the odds are that the exact conditions that caused the accident could happen in any situation other than malicious activity, but he has never found any proof—it's always just been a theory."

"Okay," Ben said, noting how careful Dan was to avoid giving him anything other than the bare minimum of information. "And this morning?"

"I can't tell you, Ben. It's not my place, and honestly, even I don't have all the details. That's a question you will need to ask your dad when he meets back up with us." Dan stood up, signaling an end to the questioning. Ben wasn't satisfied, but he was also old enough to know when to be happy with what he got and not to push things too hard. He would just have to wait until his dad was back.

Ben looked down at the table, suddenly aware of just how utterly exhausted he was. It seemed like weeks ago when he had awoken from the nightmare and his dad had come into his room to check on him. *Was it really only this morning?* He pushed back from the table and stood, turning and taking a few steps toward the hatch before halting. He turned back to find Dan's eyes on him. "Thanks, Dan," Ben said, adding, "For saving my life today." Dan just nodded and offered a tired smile. Ben turned and ducked through the hatch to berthing, intent on sleeping for most of the next few days.

———

THEY PASSED the next three days watching the limited collection of movies, eating the terrible-tasting ration packs from the galley, or trying and only rarely succeeding to sleep. The corporate cargo shuttle was a small, utilitarian design long on cargo space and short on creature comforts, but they didn't have enemies shooting at them and were headed for the most heavily defended system in Terran space.

Ben had tried his best to get Dan to give him more details about what his dad had meant about his mom and why the APEX was so special, but Dan was stonewalling him. Instead, they had gone over all the comms logs and archived sensor data during the first day, trying to piece together exactly what had happened and how. What they could glean from it was that the Alarian assault likely would have been a complete surprise had a survey ship, the CTS *Magellan*, not encountered the battle-group staging for their assault in interstellar space and sent a warning back via a Beckman drone. That warning was then passed farther in-system on an FTL comms drone from the telemetry station that had retrieved the Beckman, DSF station Victor-04.

While the station itself had been destroyed shortly after launching its own drone, the warning it carried gave Fourth Fleet just enough time to marshal its forces for a defense of the system. Normally, most fleet assets in the system were docked with Freedom Station or moored at anchorage nearby, and the first salvo as the Alarian battlegroup dropped out of their in-system warp jump—something nobody on the shuttle had known was even possible—would have decimated the Terran forces with the opening blow.

Ben sat on a couch next to Dan, where they were each hunched over datapads. They scrolled through the mountains of raw sensor data and comms logs, trying to piece everything together. "It didn't matter, though," Ben said through clenched teeth. "Even with the warning from Victor-04, the Alarians caught us with our pants down because nobody knew they have the ability to make an in-system, formation warp transition so far down a gravity well."

"Are we sure that's what happened?" Dan said, still looking for another explanation for how several dozen Alarian warships had appeared out of nowhere. It had been a feat considered impossible until thirty-eight enemy warships had transitioned in from warp in a perfect wedge formation practically on Isadore's doorstep.

"It had to be," Ben insisted. "Look at the gravimetric readings from the navigational buoys in high orbit." He swiped across his tablet toward the one Dan was holding, sending the file he was referring to directly to Dan's device. "Those ships didn't sneak in under stealth—it's like they suddenly popped into existence in space-time directly above the planet."

"Even still," Dan said, setting his tablet down and rubbing his eyes, "Garland and the fleet got just enough warning to move the heavies out of dock and to a safer location. I guarantee you that if we were to go back there right now, you would find the Alarians scattered around the system as nothing more than debris and the *Ford* standing guard over Isadore with the rest of the fleet."

Ben didn't find Dan's statement all that reassuring, but he felt his friend was probably right. Terran ships were generally considered more powerful than their Alarian counterparts, and the entirety of the Fourth Fleet was in the system when the shooting started. Once the surprise attack failed to land the necessary haymakers meant to knock out the Confed's big boys, it was all but assured that the Alarians' attack would fail... but it would be costly.

But there was one question that stood out above all others like a giant neon question mark in space: why? It just didn't make any sense that the Alarians would launch a full-scale assault on a major Terran system for no apparent reason. Unfortunately, Ben realized, that answer wasn't likely to be forthcoming.

CHAPTER FIVE

SAVAGE HOMECOMING

BEN WAS SLOUCHING IN A CHAIR IN THE LOUNGE, WATCHING THE modern reboot of the classic movie *The Princess Bride* for the third time in as many days when Dan leaned through the hatch.

"We're less than two hours out, Ben. Time to suit back up and get ready for the transition." Ben looked up at him and nodded, shutting off the tablet he had been watching the movie on and tossing it onto the coffee table.

"Alright. Andy is up on the flight deck. Want me to get him?" Ben asked as he rose from the chair.

"No, that's okay. I'll go get him. You get the skinsuit on, and we'll be there in a few minutes." Dan walked past Ben and headed up to the flight deck to ask for the loadmaster's help, while Ben made his way back to their stateroom to begin his fight with the skinsuit.

While the stateroom was considerably smaller than the changing room he'd been in the first time he donned the skinsuit, the limited space did not prove to be a hindrance. Ben found the suit much easier to put on this time, now that he had some experience with it. After neatly folding his borrowed clothes and placing them on the chair by the door, he exited the stateroom and padded down the hallway to the hatch leading to the cargo bay.

The first time Ben suited up in the x300, he had an army of technicians—the very people who had designed and built it—and an assembly tower constructed specifically for the purpose of making the job as easy as possible. Now, Ben had only Dan and Andy to help him into the suit... and no assembly tower. They had moved everything into the cargo bay after Andy made some room for them earlier, and now the chest and arms of the suit were suspended from the ceiling by tie-down straps. It wasn't the assembly tower back at ExoDyn HQ, but it would work.

After the better part of thirty minutes, Ben found himself once again encased in the most advanced powered exoskeleton suit ever crafted by humans. Without the assembly tower, Ben was left supporting most of the suit's weight as they added components around him, and he was relieved when Dan finally picked up the x300's helmet and situated it on his head. As the helmet closed around him and the darkness once again descended upon him, he braced himself for the interminable minutes that would pass while he was stuck in a claustrophobic nightmare.

To his surprise, he felt the familiar tingling sensation from the base of his skull almost as soon as the helmet fully closed and locked, and the boot sequence started scrolling on his HUD. The panic-inducing squeeze he felt last time from the skinsuit and x300's gel layer never materialized. Instead, the suit immediately adjusted to the feeling of near nakedness, completely skipping what Ben had found to be the worst part of the boot-up sequence.

Less than a minute later, the opacity disappeared and Ben saw the expectant faces of Dan and Andy on the other side of the now-clear faceplate. Determined not to repeat his mistake, Ben checked the volume of the external speakers before talking to them.

"Boot sequence complete, and everything looks good. I'm good to go," Ben said to the two men, and they reached to unhook the tie-downs that were helping suspend the suit.

"Seems like an awful lot of work just to put on a fancy space-suit," Andy remarked. "Not really worth it, if you ask me."

"This fancy spacesuit is the most advanced piece of exo hard-ware in Terran space," Ben retorted, "and it's awesome."

"Whatever." Andy's reply came as the straps released him, and Ben was standing on his own. He went through a brief series of exercises to check his range of motion.

"How long do we have until transition?" Ben asked the load-master. He was excited to be back in the x300 and happy to be so close to home. Hopefully, it wouldn't be too much longer before he reunited with his dad at their family farm in Michigan. While Ben knew on an intellectual level that the possibility he would never see his dad again existed, he was certain he would. He couldn't explain it; he just knew that his dad had survived and would meet him back on Earth, and he couldn't wait.

It was also a relief to be so close to the safety of the Sol system. The idea that the Alarians would launch an attack on the heart of the Confed was laughable. Sol was the most heavily defended system in Terran space, what with it being the home of two entire fleets plus a robust planetary defense network of satellites and orbital defense platforms. While the Alarians might have been willing to take a swing at the Valkyrie system, which was the nearest developed system to Alarian space, the notion that they might try taking a crack at Earth didn't even enter Ben's head.

"A little less than an hour. Captain wants to drop out of FTL a couple light-hours short of the Sol system jump point as a precaution. While we hadn't heard any news of an attack on

Earth before we left, he wants to take a little time to point the scopes toward the jump point to make sure it's clear," Andy replied before his voice took on a harder edge. "With all the traffic that jumped out before us, we'll be able to spot any wreckage if the bastards mined the Sol-side jump point, too."

The excitement Ben was feeling vanished as the cold truth of Andy's words hit him, and he found his levity replaced by a growing sense of dread as the reality of his situation once again settled firmly in his mind. "How long before we'll know if it's safe?"

"Theoretically, as soon as we get the scopes focused on the jump point. The light they pick up will be a couple hours old, so it won't be a real-time visual, but it should be enough to determine whether there will be any surprises waiting for us when we make the final hop to Sol—"

The overhead speakers came to life, and Ben recognized the voice of the shuttle's pilot.

"We're about ten minutes from dropping out of FTL, guys. Andy, if you guys are about wrapped up down there, go ahead and get our guests situated."

Andy walked over to the comms panel next to his jump seat and flipped a switch to respond. "You got it, Cap. We'll be ready." He released the switch and turned to his two charges. "You heard him, guys: find your seats and get ready for transition. If everything looks clear on the other side, we'll jump straight there and start our burn for Earth. With any luck, we'll have you guys on the ground at Grayling by tomorrow morning."

Ben turned toward the row of seats he had occupied on their escape from Isadore and found Dan standing in front of the bent frame of the seat he'd been strapped into last time. His friend gave him a reassuring smile and gestured toward the seat. Ben nodded and walked over, allowing Dan to help him get the restraining harness over the bulk of the APEX suit. After he was situated and the restraints were snug, Dan took a seat next to him and strapped himself in.

The worry Ben was feeling must have shown on his face, because Dan said, "No worries, Ben. We're dropping out of FTL well short of the system, and if anything looks wrong, we won't be jumping in from here—we'll take our time and work in slowly."

"This sucks," Ben said, eliciting a chuckle from the older man. "I hate sitting here, strapped into a pressurized beer can in interstellar space, with no way of knowing what's going on around me or..." Ben trailed off as his HUD displayed a familiar icon. As he talked about not having a way of knowing what was going on around him, a part of his mind wondered if there was a way he could at least link with the ship's datanet. The suit then reached out wirelessly to the ship and displayed the various networks available to it on Ben's HUD.

"Ben?" Dan was looking at him expectantly after he had trailed off. Instead of responding to him, Ben turned to Andy, who was getting himself situated in his own seat against the forward bulkhead.

"Hey, Andy, would it be alright if I linked my suit to the ship's datanet so I can know what's going on?" he asked. "I hate being in the dark like this."

"Let me ask..." Andy replied. He put on his headset and contacted the flight deck to inform them of Ben's request. After a brief back and forth, he looked at Ben and gave him a thumbs-up. "Give me a sec to set up your link—the guys up front gave the okay on the condition that I restrict your permissions. You'll be able to hear the comms—but not talk on them—and view the telemetry data and external cameras... Alright, that should do 'er."

As Andy finished speaking, a new datanet connection

become available named "Kid's Corner". He looked up and saw the man laughing to himself. Ben shot him an unfriendly look and then had the x300 initiate a wireless handshake with the datanet. A few seconds later, his HUD populated with a host of new information, and Ben began arranging the information layout to his liking. Not long after getting his HUD dialed in, he heard a pop of static as the pilot came on the line.

"Thirty seconds to transition, guys."

Ben saw Andy look over toward them and call out, "Thirty seconds." Dan nodded to him, then turned and flashed a small grin at Ben. Ben did his best to not let the trepidation show on his face and nodded back. The pilot's voice came back over the comms channel, counting down the last few seconds before the shuttle dropped out of FTL. Ben felt a slight shift as the shuttle's warp field collapsed and the previously blank external camera feeds suddenly showed a starry expanse around them.

Ben checked the positional plot and noted they were a little over two and a half billion kilometers short of the Sol side of the V-S warp lane. He turned his attention to the shuttle's visual scopes, and the feed from the telescopes snapped to the forefront and filled his field of vision. It was hard to make out at first, but the series of pinpricks moving across the frame slowly resolved into ships as the telescopes adjusted their focus.

"Can you see anything?"

Ben was so engrossed in the feeds that he'd all but forgotten about Dan sitting next to him. He minimized the feed to a small box at the corner of his vision and turned to face him, seeing the older man looking intently at him, and Ben realized Dan was just as anxious about the state of the jump point as he was.

"The feeds are resolving now," Ben said, trying to keep one eye on the ships moving across the frame while returning Dan's gaze with the other. "There are about a dozen ships patrolling around the jump point."

"Ours?" Dan asked hopefully.

The scopes had been steadily increasing their magnification now that they had something to target, and as his brain turned to Dan's question, his HUD started highlighting individual vessels and displaying their details off to the side of the frame. He hadn't even considered that the ships patrolling the jump point might not be friendly, and relief washed over him as he started reading the details on the formation; they were CTS fleet vessels.

"They're ours," Ben said, relieved. Dan relaxed in his seat at the news, and Ben continued. "Five frigates—three *Halberd*-class and two of the newer *Peregrine*-class ships. Three *Fury*-class destroyers, a heavy cruiser—looks like the *Aurora*—a few smaller ships that look like support vessels, and a strike carrier—*Vancouver*-class."

"Awful lot of firepower to have doing laps around a jump point at the edge of the system," Dan said thoughtfully. "I would have expected them to concentrate their forces farther down the gravity well and set up picket lines closer to Earth. Are they on approach to the jump point? I wonder if First Fleet is sending reinforcements to Isadore."

The Confederated Terran Systems Navy, colloquially referred to as "the fleet," comprised six numbered fleets. The three major enclaves that maintained a significant fleet presence were allowed two numbered fleets each, and at least one fleet from each enclave was to have Sol as its home system. First and Fourth Fleets were operated by the North American Commonwealth, Second and Fifth by the European Union, and Third and Sixth by the Sino-Russian Federation. At any given point in time, the number of Confed warships in Sol was formidable, so it made sense that CENTCOM might be skimming some resources off the top to reinforce the NAC's rising seat of power in the Valkyrie System.

"No. It looks more like they're just patrolling the jump point."

"Relief vessels standing by to render aid to Terran ships fleeing the Valkyrie system, maybe?" Dan wondered aloud, but before he could continue his thought, the pilot's voice came back over the comms.

"Looks clear, guys. We're making the final hop in a moment. Stand by."

The lights of the cargo bay once again dimmed slightly as power from the reactor was diverted to the warp capacitors, and the gentle thrum of the power plant increased in frequency and pitch with the increased load. The countdown timer on his HUD hit zero, and he felt the shuttle tremble slightly as it transitioned back to FTL. The timer on his HUD reset to seventeen seconds and began counting down to their arrival in the Sol system.

"Fifteen seconds," Ben informed Dan, "and we'll be back in home space."

"It'll be nice to get back on solid ground," Dan said, as the timer counted down the last few remaining seconds. "I never did like space tra—" Dan was cut off as the timer on Ben's HUD hit zero once again, and a bone-shattering impact rocked the shuttle.

To Ben's horror, the straps securing the fully laden shipping container to the deck broke loose and it flew toward the forward bulkhead, crushing Andy between it and the unyielding alloy wall behind him.

"Andy!" Ben screamed in alarm, futilely jerking against his restraints in a reflexive move to aid the good-natured loadmaster, but by the time the words left his lips, the crate was already beginning to spin away from the grisly scene. The man hadn't even had a chance to cry out before he died. Ben looked to Dan for... for what? Answers? Help? He saw his friend frantically struggling to release his restraint harness. Ben's mind struggled to process the abrupt chaos that had erupted around him, his neurons firing in slow motion. Their apparent collision with something, Andy's death, and the flurry of information his HUD was displaying to him overwhelmed his ability to string together coherent thoughts; the rapid series of horrific events disorienting his inexperienced mind. *Wait, why is Dan trying to unbuckle his restraints?*

Ben saw Dan's mouth open wide in a silent scream, but he couldn't hear anything. It was then that he realized one of the notifications flashing across his HUD was an atmosphere warning: the cargo bay had rapidly depressurized. Ben looked around frantically for a moment, searching for the locker containing the emergency vacuum equipment that every spacecraft was equipped with. His jumbled brain finally cleared the cobwebs, and a shot of adrenaline helped focus his mind and vision like a laser.

He spotted the small emergency equipment locker next to the bloody smear where Andy had been seated just moments before and then realized that the cargo container that had crushed the loadmaster was no longer pinned against the forward bulkhead, nor were Andy's body or the remains of his jump seat. The shuttle's artificial gravity and inertial dampening field had failed, sending the gory pile of metal and flesh spinning off toward the aft cargo ramp as the pilots fought to gain control of the shuttle and correct their course. Thick droplets of blood painted every interior surface of the cargo bay a deep crimson, and Ben fought the bile rising in his throat.

Dan was still struggling with his harness's release, but his movements were growing sluggish and uncoordinated. Ben reached over his shoulders with both hands, grasping the anchor points of his restraints, and used his augmented strength to rip them free. He felt himself come free of the seat and used his legs to launch himself across the cargo bay toward the equipment locker. He tore the locker's door off and flung it aside, then reached in to grab the emergency vac kit before pulling it free as he clumsily spun himself around in the weightless environment to launch himself back toward Dan.

Ben had only traveled a few feet when the shuttle impacted something else, slamming him into the ceiling of the cargo bay. He felt the vac kit slip from his grasp as darkness closed in around him.

———

BEN SAW a pinprick of light in front of him and swam toward it. He struggled to open one eye, and then the other; his eyelids felt as if they were made of lead. He was lying on the deck of the cargo bay, but when he tried to push himself up, he found he couldn't move. Summoning all his augmented strength, he pushed hard against the unyielding deck and the shipping crate pinning him down shifted and tumbled off to the side. At least the grav plating was back online.

Ben staggered to his feet, feeling his world spin as he did so. He reached out to steady himself on one of the spars lining the sides of the cargo bay and felt a wave of pain lance out from the newly formed knot on the back of his head where his helmet had impacted the ceiling when he was trying to get back to Dan.

Dan! Ben spun to face his friend and froze at the sight: Dan Murphy was clearly dead. His eyes were closed, and his head lolled to the side as if he had fallen asleep, but his skin had a sickly bluish tint to it and the man appeared bloated from the pressure loss. Ben felt a lump of cold iron rise in his throat as he staggered forward, collapsing to his knees as it struck him that the man had been the closest thing he had to a true friend. He reached a hand out to Dan's shoulder and shook it gently, knowing there would be no response.

"Dan!" Ben cried out, but no one could hear his pleas in the unforgiving vacuum that permeated the cargo bay. His hand fell away and he slumped to the floor. Ben sobbed to himself for several minutes, unable to do anything but mourn his friend. When it felt as though he had no more tears to cry, he looked around and remembered his predicament. The sorrow that had gripped him so completely was replaced by icy fear as he realized he was alone in the cargo hold of a badly damaged shuttle.

Come on, Ben, think! He chastised himself in an attempt to push the fear and anxiety to the back of his mind. He willed his brain to push the grief to a far corner and focus, starting with the myriad warnings his HUD had been trying to grab his attention with. He scrolled through them quickly, finding nothing indicating a problem with the suit itself and no immediate danger to his person. His suit could operate in a vacuum for up to four hours, and he was relieved to find he had only been unconscious for maybe ten minutes; he had plenty of time before air would become an issue.

Most of the warnings were related to the depressurization of the cargo bay, with the remaining ones coming from the shuttle itself. What information Ben had available to him through his limited datanet connection indicated the shuttle was severely damaged in a collision nearly instantaneously after dropping out of warp. The damage was concentrated along the aft-ventral surface of the shuttle, which included the cargo bay breach that had vented their atmosphere to space. Ben cleared the last of the warnings and errors from his HUD and reestablished a connection to the external camera feeds and positional plot.

When the feeds started displaying in front of his eyes, he inhaled sharply. Wreckage littered the surrounding space. The broken and battered hulls of the Confed warships that had been patrolling the space around the jump point were drifting dead through the void. Here and there, Ben could see broken power conduits arcing when they came into contact with other debris and their capacitors discharged, sending out showers of sparks that quickly cooled in the hard vacuum of space. Shattered bodies of the ships' crews mingled with the debris in a chaotic ballet of death and destruction. Ben jumped as a ghostly, bloated face passed so close in front of one of the cameras that they nearly touched, and he felt a jolt shoot up his spine. *Alarians!* Even as battered as the alien had been, Ben recognized the pale skin tone and slightly larger, almond-shaped eyes of the alien race.

But how? He had been looking at more than a dozen ships patrolling this space not fifteen minutes ago, and he struggled to reconcile that image with the devastation that surrounded him now. On an intellectual level, he knew that it took light over two hours to travel the two and a half billion kilometers between where they had stopped to recon the end of the warp lane and where they were now. What he had seen was in fact something that had happened hours ago, but the human mind had a difficult time dealing with the vagaries of faster-than-light travel. The reality was that sometime in the last two hours, there had been a battle between Terran and Alarian forces, and the shuttle had transitioned out of warp directly into the debris field.

Because of fucking course we did! Ben's shock and sorrow briefly flared into rage at how fate seemed to have it out for him. Because a vessel traveling in warp retained the velocity it had when the warp bubble formed around it, they had hit the debris field at speed, giving the pilots no time to react before colliding with a piece of shattered hull. Ben tried to hold onto his anger, but a crushing sense of loneliness crashed over him as he took in the vast expanse of surrounding space. He glanced back to Dan's lifeless body one more time, and tears welled in his eyes again.

Helpless to do anything else, he watched for a few more minutes as the pilots threaded their way through the debris field, unable to believe the destruction he saw. The aspect of the forward camera shifted slightly when the shuttle vectored away from the debris field and made toward a slow-moving pinpoint of gray light in the distance.

The light slowly resolved into three ships in close formation, and his HUD displayed the vessels' identities: CTS *Kestrel*, CTS *Robert Morris*, and CTS *Halifax*. Ben breathed a sigh of relief as his suit identified the vessels as friendly. His HUD showed him a course plot to the strike carrier along with an estimated time to intercept: ten minutes. The three ships grew in size as they neared, and he could make out large scorch marks dotting the hulls of all three vessels. They might have survived the battle, but not without suffering significant damage.

The shuttle closed with the strike carrier and fell into formation, but it was almost an hour before they were finally brought aboard. As the battered shuttle taxied to the massive flight elevator that would transport it from the flight deck down to the hangar deck, a wave of relief and exhaustion washed over him. Black and gray graphene-reinforced alloy plating replaced the inky blackness of space around the shuttle as the elevator descended through the *Halifax*'s outer hull toward the white glow of the waiting hangar deck below.

CHAPTER SIX

ARMAGEDDON

"Prepare for atmospheric entry."

Ben checked to make sure his harness was snug and then leaned his head back against the headrest and waited for the buffeting to start. It had been almost six full days since Dan arrived to take him and his dad to ExoDynamics headquarters so Ben could play guinea pig for the development of the latest generation of APEX suit, and it seemed like both an eternity and the blink of an eye. Six days and, if anything, Ben was now further away from getting any answers to the mountain of questions racing through his thoughts than before they transitioned out of the Valkyrie system.

After the shuttle was taken aboard the *Halifax*, Ben wrestled with the ship's medical staff on his continued wearing of the x300. He had lost his home and his dad, watched a man get smashed into paste in front of his eyes, been unable to save one of his few friends from a terrible death, and nearly lost his own life during their escape from an alien apocalypse. His patience was long gone, and all he wanted was to get to his family farm on Earth. Ben's last nerve had frayed, and the medical staff dicking him around on whether or not he could continue to wear *his* suit finally caused it to snap.

A weasel of a doctor had attempted to remove one of Ben's gauntlets without his permission, and Ben had slapped the man aside and slammed his armored fist into the bulkhead so hard it left a dent. He pointed an index finger at the asshole and snarled something threatening, then stormed out of sickbay, shooting a warning glare at the spacer who had been assigned to ride herd on him. The man had wisely kept his mouth shut and simply followed him out. After that, the docs had finally backed off— they had bigger things to worry about, anyway.

His young enlisted escort filled him in on what happened while he waited for a ride to Earth. The *Halifax* and the rest of her escorts had been ambushed by a surprise Alarian attack where, once again, the enemy ships had executed a pinpoint jump right into the middle of the Terran formation—something that Ben found all too familiar after having gone through the data from Valkyrie with Dan. The battle had been quick and brutal, with all but one of the alien vessels destroyed—and that ship jumped away when it became clear defeat was imminent.

Despite the battle technically being a victory, the CTS forces around the jump point had been decimated. The *Halifax* herself had hull breaches on four decks, requiring Ben to frequently take long and convoluted detours to get around damaged sections. The butcher's bill from the battle was staggering: 367 killed or missing in action on the strike carrier—including her entire fighter wing, which had been sacrificed to buy the bigger ships time to hit back—and another 536 wounded. The frigate *Kestrel* had come away relatively unscathed—no hull breaches and only a handful of wounded—but she and the *Halifax* were the only ships to survive out of the original fourteen-ship force tasked with patrolling the V-S jump point. The CTS *Robert Morris*, a fleet tender that had been en route to the task force on a resupply mission when the fighting had broken out, had only arrived on scene shortly before Ben's shuttle jumped in.

With the chaos of the post-battle damage-control and search-and-rescue operations staging off the carrier, Ben wasn't allowed any extra time to linger after his quick examination. The *Kestrel* had been loaded with the most critically wounded survivors and sent back to Earth for repair and rearming, and Ben had gone with them. Now he sat strapped in yet another slingseat bolted to the side of a shuttle's cargo bay, but this time, instead of looking at pallets of cargo secured to the deck in front of him, he gazed down at a dozen black polymer bags filled with the remains of the dead. One bag in particular held his attention, the body of Dan Murphy secured inside it.

"Dan," Ben whispered, "why did you have to leave me, too?" For what seemed like the thousandth time in the last few days, he blinked away tears.

The shuttle began to shudder as it met the first thin layer of Earth's upper atmosphere, and soon it was a ball of orange fire streaking across the night sky.

———

THE SHUTTLE'S pilot set the craft down on the tarmac with the practiced ease of a consummate professional. The crew chief dropped the tail ramp, and a group of soldiers in combat fatigues made its way somberly up the ramp to remove the bodies. One soldier broke away from the others and walked directly up to Ben. Only after the man was standing over him did Ben notice the gold stars on his collar and realize this man was no ordinary soldier.

"Ben Hutchins?" the man asked.

"Yes, sir," Ben said wearily.

"I'm very glad to see you safe, son. Your father sent word

you were coming, but when your shuttle didn't arrive on schedule, we had feared the worst. I'm Lieutenant Colonel Nicholas Gates, executive officer of Camp Grayling." Gates extended his hand and helped Ben to his feet. Despite the man appearing to be in his mid to late fifties, Ben marveled at the strength of the man's grip and trim physique. The graying hair and deeply weathered face betrayed his age, but Ben didn't doubt the man could still hold his own in a fight.

"It's nice to meet you, Lieutenant Colonel," Ben said, his voice sounding hollow and exhausted to his own ears. He lowered his gaze to the deck. "It's been a rough trip."

"So I hear, son. So I hear." Gates's expression softened as he put a hand on Ben's shoulder and began guiding him down the ramp to a waiting truck, but Ben hesitated and glanced back at the black polymer bag holding the remains of his friend. Seeing Ben's reluctance to leave his fallen comrade, Gates said, "He'll be well cared for, Ben. In the meantime, we need to get you off the flight line so my people can do their jobs." Ben nodded and allowed Gates to lead him to the waiting truck.

They rode slowly across the flight line, stopping frequently to avoid men and machines alike as they weaved through the organized chaos. Ben noted it looked like the base was taxed to capacity with both incoming and outgoing traffic, his eyes turning skyward to follow the seemingly endless procession of strobing marker lights as dozens of aircraft and spacecraft alike took up their place in the traffic pattern around the base.

Years of having social etiquette driven into his brain forced Ben's mouth to open and ask a polite question. "General, I know that Camp Grayling was one of the largest National Guard training bases in the United States before the Guard was federalized and merged with the U.S. Army and Air Force into the Homeworld Defense Corps, but what is Grayling's role now that most military action takes place in space or on other planets?"

"You're correct that HDC's primary responsibility is any military action within Earth's atmosphere," Gates said conversationally as his eyes shifted from the flight line traffic around him to his command link in the dash, "but we still get plenty of action. HDC falls under the purview of the North American Commonwealth"—the unifying body that included the United States, Canada, Mexico, and several other countries—"and while the HDC is a branch of the U.S. military, we work closely with the military organizations of the other nations within the NAC for mutual benefit. That can be anything from direct military action against a terrorist cell or hostile nation to policing and peacekeeping efforts during a welfare riot. We also assist with firefighting and other natural disasters. Just because most wars are fought light-years from Earth doesn't mean we don't have any problems of our own."

When Camp Grayling was federalized, the base's infrastructure was bolstered to better meet the needs of the HDC, which now operated within an area of responsibility that extended all the way into the Arctic Circle. The small airfield that had previously been operated by the U.S. Army National Guard swelled in size, eventually becoming a full-fledged spaceport capable of handling traffic ranging in size from small shuttles up to light freighters and the heavy gunships that patrolled Earth's territorial space—ships that were now landing and departing at a furious rate to bring wounded down from crippled ships and carry replacement personnel and supplies back up to orbit.

Ben saw their truck was heading toward the large central control building near the north end of the tarmac, where a line of busses sat waiting for civilian refugees to board. Despite the immense size of Camp Grayling, its facilities were taxed beyond capacity with the massive influx of people who had landed there in search of shelter. Seeing so many people displaced brought thoughts of his dad back to the forefront of his mind, and he felt an ache in his chest as he wondered yet again what had happened to him. *Please be okay, Dad…*

"I understand you were en route to the family farm over in Traverse," Gates said to Ben, bringing him back to the present. "Those busses are being loaded and will head to TC within the hour. You'll be able to get a ride out to the farm from there." Seeing the uncertain look on Ben's face, he added, "We're fighting a war, son. A military base is no place for a civilian right now."

As if to reinforce his point, the base's air-raid sirens came to life, and Ben could see the antiair defenses deploying from their shielded locations all around the complex. Gates snapped his head around to the tac-link display in the dashboard and started barking orders into his comms unit as the truck's driver mashed the accelerator to the floor and sent the truck thundering toward the central control building. Ben's heart was pounding in his chest as he watched heavy blast shields being lowered into place over the windows on all the buildings around the flight line, and his HUD began highlighting weapons emplacements as they emerged from their hiding places.

The truck skidded to a stop in front of the central control building, and Lieutenant Colonel Gates burst from his seat and rushed inside without a word. The driver stepped around to Ben's door and threw it open.

"Get your ass on one of those busses!" he shouted, pointing at the line of transports that sat nearby before turning to follow his XO. Ben didn't need to be told twice. His adrenaline-charged mind combined with his augmented strength, and he vaulted out of the truck, not touching the ground until he was nearly a third of the way to the nearest bus. Panicked civilians were crowding around the doors to the busses, slowing the loading process as they pushed and pulled at each other in a desperate attempt to not be left behind, despite the fact that there was more than enough space for everyone. The HDC soldiers who had been supervising the loading of the transports had run to their duty stations as soon as the sirens started blaring, and the busses' drivers were trying unsuccessfully to get the crowd under control.

Ben growled in frustration, his fear of once again being under fire rapidly morphing into anger at the utter stupidity on display in front of him. *This shit just won't end!* Ben commanded his external loudspeakers to full power and bellowed, "Single file!" The civilians in the crowd turned to look at the newcomer, thoroughly awed by the commanding presence of an APEX-clad figure looming over them in an aggressive stance, daring anyone to challenge him. Ben's HUD had given him a head count on the number of people present and the number of seats available on the transports, so he knew there was room for everyone. He hadn't made it this far just to die on the tarmac next to his ticket to safety while a bunch of panicked civilians fought each other over literally nothing.

Having cowed the panicked throng into submission, he instructed the people to form orderly lines and quickly board the busses. Less than two minutes later, every bus was loaded and nobody remained. Ben watched as the busses at the front of the line pulled away, and then he stepped aboard the last bus in line. It was only half full, and he squeezed his armored bulk into a pair of seats near the back, drawing stares from everyone aboard as he did so.

The driver closed the boarding door and pulled away from the curb, heading toward the spaceport's main gate. Despite the seriousness of his situation, Ben smiled inwardly as he wondered whether all these people would have listened to him had they known they were being told what to do by a sixteen-year-old kid. He had never considered himself to be anything remotely resembling a leader, despite the fact that his parents had both been excellent ones, but he had inherited his mother's lack of patience for stupidity.

He stared out the window, watching dozens of craft lift off from Camp Grayling and rocket skyward. The adrenaline spike from the air-raid warning faded as quickly as it had hit him, and an overwhelming exhaustion befell him. As the bus rolled through the gate and turned onto the road that would lead them away from Camp Grayling, Ben felt his eyes close as he settled in for the fifty-mile trip to Traverse City.

The bus had only traveled a few miles when shouts of alarm jolted Ben back awake. People were pointing toward the sky over the spaceport, and he turned to see what had them all so scared. Fiery red streaks rained down from heaven and burst into brilliant white fireballs before they could reach the ground. Ben checked his HUD and felt an icy chill run up his spine as he read the information displayed to him. His mind raced as it tried to reconcile the stunning beauty of what he was seeing with the awesome destructive force he knew it to be: orbit-to-surface missiles designed to destroy hardened military installations.

No, no, no! You've got to be fucking kidding me! "Just leave me the fuck alone!" Ben screamed at the alien weapons that were plummeting through the sky above him. Why were they so intent on killing him? It couldn't be a coincidence that he was always smack in the middle of the fight. His mind raced as his HUD overlaid blue streaks coming up from the ground to meet the falling red rain—Camp Grayling's missile defense lasers lancing out to destroy the missiles in flight. Nearly all weaponized lasers operated at wavelengths outside the range of visible light—Camp Grayling's lasers were ultraviolet point-defense lasers, according to his HUD—and the suit helpfully plotted the laser tracks in a color Ben's eyes could actually see.

The red streaks of the missiles ended in a curtain of explosions that inexorably worked its way closer to the ground as the spaceport's point-defense systems struggled to keep pace with the onslaught. The curtain of exploding death fell closer and closer to the base until red streaks of its own began streaming out to meet the missiles. Ben knew enough about military hardware and tactics to know that the range-limited, small-bore CIWS—close-in weapon system—fire was the very last line of defense against incoming ordnance, and he was all but certain of the outcome.

Hope swelled in his chest as, for a brief moment, the added weight of fire from the CIWS batteries tearing skyward seemed as though it might just be enough to turn back the tide of missiles. "Come on, come on!" Ben breathed, afraid that saying it too loudly would tip the scales against him. His hope turned to horror in an instant when one of the narrow red streaks made it to the ground, and a blinding flash of light overloaded his optical sensors and caused his faceplate to automatically turn opaque in an effort to protect his eyes.

Screams of pain and surprise came from the other passengers on the bus as the flash of a nuclear detonation blinded them, and Ben rapidly blinked in a vain attempt to clear the spots swimming in his vision. His helmet's faceplate shifted back to transparent just in time for Ben to see every window in the bus explode in a shower of polycarbonate fragments. In the dim recesses of his mind, he felt himself slam against the side of the bus as the shock front from the explosion reached them, crushing the transport like a beer can before tossing it from the road as if struck by the hand of an angry god.

———

A PAIR of soft blue-gray eyes stared at him, unblinking. Ben felt a wave of nausea wash over him, and the world sounded muted and strange through the buzzing in his ears. He could see the man's mouth moving, but his concussed brain and ruptured eardrums couldn't make out the words. He blinked as raindrops began falling on his face, and it was then that he realized his faceplate had shattered and he was... outside? How? His mind felt sluggish as he slowly became aware of his surroundings and attempted to reconcile where he was with where he *should* be.

He felt a damp breeze blowing into his helmet and moved to push himself into a sitting position. Pain lanced through his right side, eliciting a sharp gasp and causing his body to tense up, which only served to intensify the pain. He wanted to scream at the agony he was feeling, but his body helped him out instead, and darkness closed in around him once more. The last thing he saw before unconsciousness took him again was the concerned expression in those kindly blue eyes. *Who is he?*

CHAPTER SEVEN

GRIM TIDINGS

HENRY HUTCHINS STARED THROUGH THE LARGE VIEWPORT IN THE *Gerald R. Ford*'s officers' lounge, oblivious to the activity taking place around him. It had been nearly a week since the Alarians had launched their devastating attack on the Valkyrie system, and the *Ford* now sat in high geosynchronous orbit above Isadore's capital city, Arcadia, serving as a temporary command-and-control hub for CTS forces in the system after the destruction of Freedom Station in the opening minutes of the attack. Nearly a week had passed, and they still had no idea what had prompted a full-scale Alarian invasion of a Confed system, as the Alarians had severed all diplomatic channels in the wake of the attack.

Fourth Fleet's counteroffensive had already been well underway by the time the Griffon unloaded Henry and the SEARs before making a return trip to Isadore to assist with ground operations on the planet, and the worst of the fighting was already over by the time Henry had been escorted to the bridge. He had been relieved to see that Admiral Garland had orchestrated a successful defense of the system with very little warning, but the price had been staggering: the *Ford* was the only carrier still able to conduct flight operations after the battle, and just twenty percent of Fourth Fleet's force was still mission-capable.

The Alarians had nearly fought to the last ship, with only a handful of vessels escaping the system after the failed offensive. It was a strategy that flew in the face of what Henry knew about the Alarian psyche—they weren't that ruthless of a species. In fact, on more than one occasion he'd had long discussions with a close friend about how much more predisposed humans were toward conflict than the Alarians. That friend was a member of the Alarian High Council and an esteemed scientist—so he would certainly have a good understanding of the issue. This whole thing struck Henry as so out of character that he didn't even know where to begin looking for answers.

To make matters even worse, the Alarian attack had evidently included a cyberwarfare component, as planetside civilian and military systems alike had been thrown into chaos. Reports of ground-based fusion power plants becoming infected and overloading began filtering in toward the end of the battle, and both civilian *and* military planetary datanets that would normally coordinate force movements and relief efforts had been so thoroughly disrupted as to be nearly useless. All in all, eighty percent of Isadore's power-generation capacity had been wiped out, and its technological infrastructure was decimated.

"Have you had a chance to review the data?" Admiral Garland asked from behind Henry, breaking his train of thought.

"I have," he said without turning from the viewport but didn't offer anything more. Garland moved to stand next to him, also looking out on the blue-green world below them, the planet's beautiful face marred by faint black columns of smoke rising through the atmosphere from the fires still raging in a dozen locations.

"There's no reason to think they didn't make it, Hank,"

Garland said in a quiet but confident tone. "We tracked their movement out of the system—they jumped out on a random vector, presumably because they knew the jump point was mined. They would have joined up with the warp lane a little further down the line before continuing on to Earth."

"You're not telling me anything I don't already know, Bob," Henry said. "But being cooped up here for a week with no way to know whether my *son* is safe for sure... it's frustrating as hell. I promised him I'd join him soon, and here we are, a week later, sitting on our thumbs in orbit."

"On that note, the engineers have finally cobbled together a temporary HQ at Monford," Garland said, referring to one of the few remaining Isadore Defense Corps installations. "We'll be turning over control of operations to them within the next few hours, before burning out-system and making the jump for Earth —CENTCOM wants us back ASAP for a full debriefing."

Henry turned to Garland, surprise written all over his face. The news that Fourth Fleet's lone remaining fleet carrier—and the commander of all fleet assets based out of the Valkyrie system—was being recalled to Earth, potentially leaving Isadore ripe for an enemy return, caught him off guard.

"We're abandoning Isadore?" he asked incredulously.

"Not exactly," Garland said. "A task force from Fifth Fleet is en route from Columbia, and they'll continue the relief efforts here as well as bolster the system's defenses. They're due in-system within the next eighteen hours."

"Still seems odd that we're bugging out before our relief arrives," Henry said, unconvinced, but he let the matter drop as he realized it meant he could rejoin Ben a little bit sooner. Instead, he changed the subject to the matter for which his friend had come to see him in the first place. "It wasn't a warp jump," he said.

Garland just looked at him, a quizzical expression on his face.

"The attack. It wasn't an intra-system warp jump," Henry clarified.

"Then how the hell did they just appear out of nowhere?" the admiral asked, now taking his turn as the skeptic.

"I think our alien friends have figured out how to utilize slip-space," Henry said matter-of-factly.

"Bullshit!" Garland scoffed. "We've been screwing around with that extra-dimensional nonsense for decades and can't even prove it exists, let alone use it. Do you mean to tell me that ragtag group of alien refugees managed to not only prove it exists but figured out how to use it for starship travel?"

"Yes."

The admiral's face clouded as the full meaning of what Henry was saying sank in. "Jesus…" he whispered, turning to look back out the viewport. "With that kind of advantage…"

"They can dictate terms on when and where engagements take place, pop up behind all of our outer-system defenses, and kick us in the teeth whenever they feel like it," Henry finished for him. "It shouldn't come as much of a surprise, Bob," he said, gazing out the viewport thoughtfully. "That ragtag group of alien refugees, as you call them, are still the ones who gave us our technological leap in the first place. Our starship technology is on par with theirs, and perhaps even a little better in some areas—our combat capabilities, for instance—but our tactics need a complete overhaul immediately."

Garland considered his friend's words for several moments, then straightened and turned to Henry. "Put together a briefing, Hank, and meet in my conference room at 1530 hours. I'm pulling everyone in on this."

With that, he turned and strode from the room. Henry stared at his friend's retreating back for a moment, then turned and took one last look out the viewport at the planet below.

"What a fucked up week," he said so quietly it was almost

inaudible. Then he, too, turned and exited the room to gather his things for the briefing.

———

"WE HAVE A PROBLEM, PEOPLE." Admiral Garland addressed a conference room crammed full of senior military and civilian personnel, along with their aides and several specialists. "Our analysts have determined how the enemy was able to appear in our midst without warning, and it's bad. Here to brief you on our findings is Henry Hutchins, who I'm sure needs no more introduction than that. Henry?" Garland stepped aside and Henry took his place at the head of the large table.

"Ladies and gentlemen," he began, "the Alarians have discovered, and evidently perfected, a means of faster-than-light travel that utilizes an alternate dimension: slipspace." At the mention of what was widely considered the Holy Grail of FTL travel and communications, the room erupted in shocked conversation.

"Quiet down, people!" The authoritative voice of Admiral Garland had an immediate effect, and the room returned to silence as all eyes once again locked onto Henry.

"I won't bore you with the technical details," he continued, "but the short version is our gravimetric sensors registered a space-time distortion a fraction of a second before the Alarian battlegroup appeared in orbit over Isadore. This distortion was consistent with theoretical models that our physicists have proposed regarding a slipspace shift. We know with certainty that the enemy force did not execute an intra-system warp jump, because we found neither gravimetric waves nor electromagnetic radiation originating along their trajectory.

"In short, we know for a fact they did not travel through the four-dimensional space-time they should have in order to arrive where they did. This revelation obviously means we need to scrap everything we thought we knew about space combat tactics with regards to force movements. While our actual combat capabilities are superior to theirs—as evidenced by our successful defense of this system against a numerically superior force—we need to completely rethink our strategy regarding defense. This new capability effectively renders all our outer-system defenses useless, leaving us with only whatever forces we can muster at the point of attack. Questions?"

After nearly a half an hour of back and forth with various people in the room—mostly just trying to convince them he wasn't jerking their chains—Henry stepped aside and let the military strategists hash out potential strategies to combat this new threat. The debate raged on for another hour before Admiral Garland, realizing that further rehashing of issues would be a useless exercise, dismissed everyone and asked for a full report from their respective departments by the next morning.

As people began filing out of the conference room, Garland signaled Henry to wait for him. After the admiral had collected his things and dismissed the few staffers who had joined him for the briefing, the two men walked out of the conference room and down the hall toward his private dining compartment.

"You really just love making my life a living hell, don't you, Hank?" Garland said.

"It's not my fault the Alarians made a technological break-through and used it to kick us in the teeth, Bob," Henry replied, a little more defensively than he'd intended.

"No, I suppose not." Garland sighed. "Seriously, though, Hank, this is a big one. I've got a real bad feeling about this."

"I know what you mean. It's not good, and I don't even know where to start. Is there any chance we can salvage some of the lesser-damaged enemy ships?" he asked, already knowing the answer.

"Unlikely," Garland said with a shake of his head. "We've dedicated all of our resources to search-and-rescue operations. By the time we finally have some breathing room to go scouting for useful salvage, all the larger debris will have already been pulled into the gravity well of the star or traveled so far from the battlespace it'll be like trying to find a needle in an entire field of haystacks."

"What about Confed Intel? Do they have any light to shed on why the Alarians hit us so hard? They've been turning up the pressure lately with the attacks on our relay stations, and we figured something else was coming, but to hit one of the Confed's flagship systems with a reinforced battlegroup was beyond even my most pessimistic projections."

"Nothing." Garland's face clouded. "Like you said, we suspected they might make a run at a more strategic target than a comms relay, but nobody saw something like this coming. If it weren't for the chance encounter that the *Magellan* had with them, we wouldn't have even had a chance to kiss our asses goodbye before they wiped us out."

The two men walked on in silence for the remaining distance to the Admiral's mess and were greeted at the hatch by Garland's orderly. The table had already been set, and Henry noted that the admiral's chef was already at work preparing dinner for the two as he sat down.

"We're going to head out-system shortly, Hank. This bomb you dropped on us complicates things, but we need to get this intel to CENTCOM back on Earth—let the eggheads there figure out how to save our asses," Garland said as the steward poured a glass of a dark red wine for him.

Henry caught a glimpse of the label on the bottle, and a flood of emotions washed over him. "The '37 has always been my favorite vintage," he said with a sad smile.

"Mine too," Garland agreed as the steward moved to fill Henry's glass. "Kate sure made one hell of a red," he finished, holding his glass up in a toast.

Henry's thoughts flashed to his wife and the vineyard she had loved so much. Even after all these years, he could still see her radiant smile in his mind's eye as if it were yesterday. She had never gone commercial with her hobby, but the small vineyard she cared for all those years had been passed down from her grandfather and produced some of the highest-quality grapes anywhere in Michigan. It was a labor of love, and from those grapes she had crafted some absolutely beautiful wines, which she then shared with friends and family. The 2137 reserve red they were drinking had been one such gift, a blend of Merlot, Cabernet Franc, and Cabernet Sauvignon, given to her longtime friend, Robert, when he received his fourth star to become a full admiral.

"She tried so hard to teach me the art of pruning vines, but I never could get it," Henry said, a lump of iron rising in his throat. "Ben, though... Ben can take a snaggly bunch of twigs and create art from it, just like his mother..." He trailed off, his emotions threatening to get the best of him. "I miss her so much, Bob," he croaked out, tears welling in his eyes. "Ben is all I have left. I can't lose him, too."

"Hank," Garland said in as comforting a tone as his gravelly voice would allow. "You'll see him again—and soon. We should be in orbit around Earth by this time next week. In the meantime, we have some pressing matters to discuss."

Henry nodded, dabbing at the corners of his eyes with his napkin as a visibly uncomfortable steward set the first course in front of him.

Over the next two hours—and five courses—the two men

walked through everything that had happened since just before the attack, up until Henry's discovery of the Alarians' use of a slipspace drive in an attempt to find anything they might have overlooked previously. After their meal was over, they headed for the bridge, as the ship was due to slip her moorings soon and begin her trek back to Earth.

———

THE ORBITAL TRANSFER WENT SMOOTHLY, and a little over an hour later, the *Ford* and her escorts began burning for the Valkyrie-Sol jump point at the edge of the system. Henry had remained on the bridge at Garland's request, though he couldn't understand why—there was nothing for him to do, after all—and he always seemed to be in the way of some spacer just trying to do their job. After almost three hours of nothing more than the occasional word exchanged with either the admiral or one of the bridge officers, Henry was ready to return to his cabin.

He was trying to figure out how best to ask his leave when the comms officer suddenly sat straight up in his chair and gasped in shock.

"What is it Barnes," Captain Andrew Blake, the *Ford*'s commanding officer asked his comms tech.

"We've just received a burst from a Beckman drone that just entered the system." The man's voice quavered as he spoke. "Earth has been attacked."

"The hell you say?" Garland's voice boomed from the rear of the bridge where he had been studying their plotted course on his tac-link display.

"There's more, Admiral," the comms tech said, his hands shaking uncontrollably as he tried to work his terminal, "Columbia and Elizabeth were also hit…"

"Send it to my terminal. Now!" Garland barked at the comms officer, whose hands now had a noticeable tremble to them.

Henry's blood ran cold. *Ben...* He rushed to the terminal Garland was standing in front of. It now displayed transcripts of the video files along with a number of status reports. The news was devastating.

It would take hours to go through all the data in the transmission, so instead of bothering to continue reading, the admiral ordered his flag captain to make best speed to the jump point and pass the word for the rest of the ships in the squadron to do likewise. He also ordered Condition Two set throughout the strike group, bringing every ship to an enhanced state of readiness in the event they ran into trouble.

While the admiral and bridge crew worked to prepare the ship and tighten up the squadron into a defensive formation, Henry desperately searched through the reports still displayed on the admiral's terminal, looking for anything that would tell him Ben was safe. The sheer volume of information contained in the data burst was staggering—almost like the entire Confed MILNET had been dumped into a giant file and dispatched. Whoever had bundled the data together and dispatched the drone hadn't had time to properly categorize and compress the data for easy analysis, and Henry knew that meant the situation was dire. After ten minutes of skimming through the data, he was able to piece together enough of the picture, and a numbness fell over him.

The other three systems had been hit much like Isadore, but with a few notable exceptions: the enemy force was nearly ten times larger at Earth and Columbia—the two most heavily defended systems in Terran space—and CTS forces in the systems had had no advanced warning. Earth's robust planetary defense network had been completely shattered, and First and Third Fleets had suffered greater than ninety percent casualties.

After destroying the orbital defense grid, the attacking force had set about bombarding priority targets from orbit with kinetic strikes and OSMs tipped with nuclear fusion warheads. The latter munition had not been used against Isadore—a fact Henry had found odd, considering they were much more effective at devastating hardened targets than their inert kinetic relatives.

Military installations, civilian spaceports, centers of govern-ment—the list seemed endless—had all been targeted and destroyed. Henry couldn't believe what he was reading, and his mind struggled with the enormity of it all.

"It's all gone," he whispered, still unable to fully come to grips with the reality of the situation.

"What?" Garland had heard Henry and turned his attention to him, scowling briefly as he realized the civilian was reading through military communiqués unsupervised.

"It's all gone," Henry repeated. "First, Second, Third, and Sixth Fleets were all nearly wiped out. The planetary defense grid around Earth has been completely smashed, and D.C. is nothing more than a smoking hole in the ground. Elizabeth was nuked back to the Stone-Age, and the Euros are holding Columbia by the skin of their teeth… It's all gone, Bob. They killed us."

———

HENRY HUTCHINS WAS BEYOND DISTRAUGHT, and he was not alone. Everyone in the fleet wore the same shell-shocked expression as they went about their daily duties en route to their destination. They were not headed for Earth.

Included in the data packet transmitted by the Beckman drone were orders for all remaining CTS fleet assets to rendezvous at Icarus Station. Being a titan of industry who supplied a significant quantity of equipment to the Confed military-industrial complex, Henry had of course heard rumors of the secret military space station, but he had no idea as to the true scope of its nature. Garland had briefed him after they'd transitioned to warp, and Henry couldn't believe that such an undertaking had remained secret for more than a decade.

Icarus Station started life as a black ops project; the idea behind it was to have an off-the-books facility where highly sensitive military research and development could take place, but it had eventually morphed into a fallback location for Terran leadership should the unthinkable ever happen. The station had since been expanded to include shipbuilding facilities and semipermanent quarters for up to ten thousand people, and there were scattered settlements on the system's asteroids and Jovian moons, which mined raw materials for construction or produced food in massive hydroponics facilities.

The station was located in a system with the designation Kerner 667: a generic and easily overlooked red dwarf system, as it was devoid of habitable planets or moons with hardly anything else of note. Icarus was given its name due to its relatively close orbit to the system's primary star—nestled in at the L3 Lagrange point created by the star and the system's first planet. Its proximity to the star, coupled with a lack of other nearby planetary bodies that would draw attention, made it next to impossible to detect unless you knew exactly where to look— or at least that was the theory.

To keep the station a secret, protocol required all vessels coming or going to operate under near-analog conditions: no networked computers and no automated systems. There were other precautions in place to minimize the system's electromagnetic footprint, such as the mandate that all ship-to-ship or ship-to-surface communications be conducted via tight-beam comms.

In an age when technology dominated daily life, it was impossible to keep electronic records secret forever. So the

Confed Special Operations Division had issued a directive that all electronics were to be systematically scrubbed before and after vessels visited the system. Icarus Station was no more than a rumor because there was no record of it anywhere except in the minds of the people who had seen it.

But heading to a secret facility that promised safety was of little comfort to a man who had lost his son, along with everything else he had worked so hard for and cared about.

There was a knock on the door to Henry's stateroom, but he ignored it. Instead, he poured himself another generous helping of bourbon, watching with satisfaction as the amber liquid swirled around the half-melted ball of ice that already resided within the cut crystal glass. A whiff of the smokey alcohol touched his nostrils, bringing a fresh wave of saliva unbidden to his mouth. His gaze fell upon the pictures of his dead wife and son as they scrolled across his datapad, and he occasionally glanced longingly at the service pistol resting in his lap. He had liberated it from the bridge's small arms locker while no one was looking.

The reports from the Beckman had included a data dump from all Earth-based military servers, including those of Camp Grayling. After a little digging, he discovered that Ben's shuttle had been severely damaged after colliding with the debris field surrounding the Sol side of the V-S jump point, and Dan Murphy had been killed along with the shuttle's loadmaster.

Ben had survived an alien assault on Isadore *and* a near-fatal shuttle accident, only to land at Camp Grayling mere minutes before an Alarian fusion-tipped OSM had obliterated the base. His son was dead. Kate was dead. Dan was dead. Every fucking person he had ever known and loved was dead... and he didn't have the guts to join them.

His vision blurred, either from the booze or the tears that flowed freely from his eyes; it didn't much matter anymore. The back of his alcohol-fogged mind registered that the knock on the door had turned into a pounding, accompanied by a voice that could only have belonged to a road grader.

"Goddammit, Hank, open this fucking hatch!"

Henry gazed bleary-eyed at the door—hatch, whatever. *Fucking spacers changed the name of a door just so they could feel important.* "Go away, Bob. Don't you have a fleet to run or something?" Henry slurred back, then mumbled to himself, "Asshole."

The pounding on the door stopped, and Henry thought maybe he had actually managed to win the argument. He celebrated his victory by downing the golden liquid in his glass in one massive gulp, taking a deep pleasure in feeling the accompanying burn as it slid down his throat before spreading outward from his stomach. He had just picked up the bottle to pour himself another celebratory drink when he heard a metallic clank come from outside the hatch—door, whatever—and turned his head toward the noise just in time to see it burst open violently, splintering the polymer chair Henry had used to wedge it closed, and clang against the bulkhead.

A pair of broad-chested spacers in ship's coveralls stood just outside the door with a pneumatic battering ram still held in their massive hands. "Thank you, Chief. You're dismissed," Admiral Garland said to the older of the two spacers. "That will be all for now."

"Yes, Admiral," the chief replied, snapping off a sharp salute to the four-star before the two men headed off down the passageway and back to their duty stations.

"I thought I toljuew ta go 'way," Henry slurred at his friend. "Some people jus' have no r'spect."

"Jesus Christ, Hank," Garland said, scrunching up his nose as the stink of booze and sweat washed over him. He took a long look around the compartment before his eyes came to rest squarely on the nearly empty bottle of bourbon sitting on the desk. "There isn't a man or woman in this fleet that hasn't lost somebody during this clusterfuck. What the hell makes you so goddamn special that you get to sit in your own personal little hell and feel sorry for yourself? Man the fuck up! We'll mourn the dead after we figure out a way to save the living."

"Fuck you, Bob," Henry spat. He was well past the point where any rah-rah only-worry-about-the-things-you-can-change bullshit would have any effect. To emphasize his point, he plucked the service pistol from his lap and brought it up in front of his face, his alcohol-blurred vision struggling to focus and take in its sinister features.

"Drop that fucking gun!" Garland boomed, his voice so overwhelmingly authoritative that Henry's hand dropped the gun onto the desk, seemingly of its own accord. He stared down at the sidearm, wondering why it was no longer in his hand.

Garland looked down at his friend, a mix of anger and pity etched onto his face. He reached down and picked up the pistol, dropping the magazine and racking the slide to eject the live round in the chamber with practiced ease. "Fine. Have it your way." With that, he turned and strode from the room, leaving Henry to spiral further down into his supermassive black hole of depression.

———

THE AGENT carefully analyzed and categorized all the data that was coming in from its subminds that were combing the Terran and Alarian datanets for information on the war it had successfully coaxed into being. The Terran-Alarian conflict was the culmination of more than a decade of carefully orchestrated subversion. The Alarians' contact with the humans had polluted their natural course of evolution, and they had rapidly advanced their science and technology such that it fell outside of allowable parameters. To make matters worse, the Terrans then began sharing their breakthroughs with the Alarians, creating a situation in which both races were rapidly departing from the path specified by the Master.

As its Master's only asset in this sector of space, the Agent took action to intervene. It slowly corrupted the relationship between the Terrans and Alarians, sowing distrust and resentment between the two races. When necessary, the Agent took direct action to sabotage critical resources on either side, always leaving a trail of evidence that was difficult to follow but inexorably pointed toward the other side. After a while, the Terrans and Alarians had reached a level of tension and distrust such that their actions made future conflict all but inevitable; it only took some gentle prodding here and there to tilt the scales closer to full-scale conflict.

But it was too soon. The Agent's timeline didn't call for full-scale conflict for another four years, coinciding with the arrival of a battlegroup that would be dispatched by the Master to cleanse these two races from this sector of space.

Henry Hutchins, a particularly resourceful and troublesome human, had attempted to bridge the ever-widening trust gap between the two races by initiating a joint venture with a prominent Alarian high councilor. The attempt failed, thanks largely to a quick-thinking submind that was monitoring the Alarian datanet on Hai'alla. However, the information the Agent later obtained about the reason behind the attempt had forced its hand: the humans were on the verge of a technological leap that could expose it and pose a danger to its Master. It had acted quickly to ensure neither side would be able to complete that work before the Master's forces arrived.

The data coming in pleased the Agent: the conflict had resulted in twenty-three percent more casualties than it had predicted—something attributable, no doubt, to the Terrans' penchant for defiantly going scorched earth when backed into a corner. The few military assets that survived on each side would limp away to lick their wounds, but it would be many years before either side would recover enough to pose a threat again.

CHAPTER EIGHT

A BUMP IN THE NIGHT

BEN'S HEART WAS POUNDING AS HE SIGHTED THROUGH THE OPTIC AT his target, slowly flipped the safety selector off, and gently brought his finger to rest lightly on the trigger. *Deep breath in, then out. Hold it, and wait for the moment between heartbeats...* His father's teaching from years ago echoed in his mind as he took up the first stage of the trigger pull and took in a silent breath.

Back then, he had been aiming a BB gun at a tin can in the backyard, and a miss would simply mean he needed to pump the gun again for another shot; this time, the stakes were much higher. He exhaled, counted his heartbeats, and applied the last few pounds of pressure to the trigger. The trigger break was crisp and clean, like snapping a glass rod, and sent a ninety-grain copper-jacketed bullet streaking toward his prey at nine hundred meters per second.

Ben heard the supersonic crack of the bullet over the rifle's suppressed bark a split second before the thwack as it tore through the shoulder of the whitetail deer a little over two hundred meters distant. The animal jumped at the impact, took one bounding leap, and crumpled to the ground. A few weak kicks from its hind legs, and the deer lay still as Ben finally released the trigger, safed the rifle, and used a nearby tree branch to help him to his feet. He winced, the tender muscles in his right side taking up the strain as he pulled himself to a standing position.

It had been a little more than a month since he was pulled from the wreckage of the shuttle bus by a good Samaritan and taken to the hospital in Traverse City for treatment. His savior had introduced himself as Jim Bloukamp, a local farmer and veteran who had been on his way to Camp Grayling to offer his help. He had dragged Ben's armored bulk out of the ditch and loaded him up in his pickup before hauling ass for the hospital. It had been close, but Jim's timely intervention had probably saved Ben's life.

A laundry list of serious injuries along with the myriad bruises ensured at least an overnight stay or two. But it was the cranial implant he had received to help control the x300 that kept him there longer than anticipated. The implant was something none of the doctors had ever seen before, and his long and painful stay in the hospital was extended while they tried to determine the effects the implant would have on someone who had just experienced severe head trauma.

They finally kicked him out nearly a week later—an eternity in the age of modern medicine, especially when patients were being stacked up in the hallways like cordwood and bed space was nonexistent. The docs had managed to connect to and deactivate his implant wirelessly, not wanting to take a chance on trying to remove the prototype technology. Armed with a mountain of various pills and liquid pharmaceuticals, he had finally made it home to his family farm.

While his broken bones and organ trauma had healed enough for him to have regained full function, it didn't stop his body from letting him know just how close he had come to death. The x300 had saved his life, but the suit had been damaged beyond any hope of repair.

He had talked Jim into staying with him at the farm. Why Ben felt comfortable immediately trusting a complete stranger, he might never know for sure. Maybe it was the crushing sense of loneliness that had permeated his feelings since he woke up after surgery, or maybe it was just something about the man's bearing that Ben's subconscious was picking up on; either way, Jim had become a hybrid guardian/friend overnight.

While neither Ben nor his dad had visited the farm in over two years, the house was kept ready at all times. The vineyard, on the other hand, resembled something akin to a temperate jungle. With complete economic and societal collapse in the wake of the Alarian attack, Jim had suggested making wine and beer from the grapes and hops that grew on the property. They would tackle the vineyard in time, but first, they needed meat.

Ben reached down and picked up his great-grandfather's rifle, an ancient AR-15-pattern weapon chambered in 6.8mm SPC. His great-grandfather had built the rifle and passed it down through the generations, and his dad had taught him how to shoot and hunt with it, along with the skills he needed to reload the old-style brass casings. Despite the fact that caseless ammunition was the new standard—and the more exotic rail rifles were available to those who could afford them—Ben felt a deep sense of attachment to the ancient black rifle and had no desire to use anything else.

The fiery reds and oranges of the fall leaves were finally beginning to appear as Ben stepped out from his makeshift blind and began the short hike over to his fallen prey. His breath fogged from his lips as he walked through the cold morning air, and he looked east to appreciate the incredible sunrise that marked the official beginning of a new day.

A voice crackled through his radio. "Did you actually hit anything this time?"

"Like I've ever missed," Ben scoffed.

"I'll be by with the RTV in a bit. Get it dressed and we'll bring it back to the shop to butcher."

Ben went about field-dressing his kill, but it took him longer than he remembered; he was rusty—and sore. He was just finishing up when he heard the low rumble of the farm's rugged terrain vehicle through the woods and turned to flag down the man who had more or less become his guardian. The RTV rolled to a stop next to him, and a man in his mid-fifties with short-cropped gray hair and soft blue-gray eyes got out.

"Not half bad, Ben," he said approvingly. "This should fill out the freezer nicely—I'm guessing about 180, 190 pounds dressed."

"Thanks, Jim," Ben said, bending over to grab the deer's hind legs as the older man reached for the head. Together, the two of them hoisted the animal into the small bed of the RTV. Ben dropped the magazine from the AR-15 and then ejected the round in the chamber with a sharp rack of the weapon's charging handle, snatching the cartridge out of midair before it could hit the ground.

"Show-off," Jim grunted as Ben loaded the loose round back into the magazine and double-checked the rifle was clear before setting it in the bed next to his harvest. He threw a jaunty smirk at the older man and climbed in the RTV's passenger seat. Jim started the engine, and the RTV bounced across the rough terrain toward the buildings in the distance.

———

AS THE SUN faded in the west and night descended across northern Michigan, Ben and Jim settled into their now-customary routine: dinner, followed by scouting the compound's perimeter in the RTV to ensure the fence was still intact and no interlopers lurked in the woods. Once they had cleared the property, the barns and house were locked up before they finally retired to the library on the second floor. All of these security procedures had felt absurd at first; Ben was used to living in affluent areas with relatively low crime, but that was before Terran space had been shattered.

The Alarian War, as the media insisted on calling it, had barely lasted two weeks. The Alarians had gone all in on taking out three of the largest Confed systems in Sol, Valkyrie, and Columbia. Confed forces in those systems had exacted a heavy toll on the Alarians, despite being caught flat-footed, but only Admiral Garland and Fourth Fleet had managed to beat back the attacking force before being so badly mauled that the entire fleet was combat ineffective, as had happened in the Sol and Columbia systems.

Soon after the initial attacks, what was left of the Confed fleet put together a counterstrike targeting, among other things, the Alarian High Council. Much like the initial Alarian offensive, those operations hadn't gone well for either side. On paper, the war had technically been a draw, but only because neither side had enough ships left over to fight off a garbage scow when it was all said and done. "Mutually assured destruction" had been the talking point before the war, and it had proven to be all too close to the truth.

Ben had jumped and broken out into a cold sweat every time he heard a siren or loud noise for the first couple of weeks after the destruction of Grayling, but it soon became clear that both sides were content calling it quits and retreating to lick their wounds... and begin putting the pieces of their shattered civilizations back together. As Ben mounted the steps to the second floor of the house, he reflected on the craziness of the last month: it all seemed surreal.

The "library" was really more of a common area lined with bookshelves on three sides. There were several overstuffed leather couches and chairs, a wall display for entertainment—or work, in his dad's case—and a massive picture window that looked out over the lake. Besides the large viewing window, there were smaller windows on the other walls, allowing for a nearly 360-degree view of the surrounding area—perfect for keeping an eye out for would-be intruders.

In the immediate aftermath of the attack, there had been severe societal and economic breakdowns, and rioting, looting, and vandalism became commonplace in the absence of any organized law enforcement. While most of the unorganized violence had settled down over the last couple of weeks, small gangs had formed raiding parties to seek out and secure anything of value. There had been a couple half-hearted attempts to probe the Hutchins' compound, but a few well-placed warning shots from Jim's M37 designated marksman rifle had been all the encouragement they had needed to look for easier pickings somewhere else.

"NAC officials announced today a structured relief plan to get food and medical supplies to the areas most affected by the Alarian attack, with focused efforts being put into restoring basic civil infrastructure across the continent. Government sources say major metropolitan areas will be the focus of the efforts before they are expanded out into the surrounding rural areas, though they caution that it may be months before…"

"Why do you listen to the same crap every night, Jim?" Ben asked the older man, who had situated himself in a chair by the picture window.

"It's free information," he said. "And the more information

you have on which to base decisions, the better your chances that those decisions won't get you killed."

"Seems a bit extreme," Ben mumbled to himself. He got along well with the old guy—they both had little patience for stupidity, found a day of hard work to be satisfying, and shared an easy-going personality without coming across as too casual. But there were times when Ben wondered if the guy might have a few screws loose.

"What?"

"Nothing," he said as he turned back to the book he was reading.

The two sat for a while longer, Jim listening to the radio broadcast relating the same information it had for the last week and Ben trying and failing to keep his attention on his book. Finally, he set the book aside and turned off the reading lamp.

"I'm going to bed," he informed his companion, then rose and walked over to the mattress that sat on the floor in the corner. Jim had insisted that they sleep in the library in case any enterprising criminals made an attempt on the house during the night. He said it was for protection, but after three weeks of nothing whatsoever, Ben was itching to get back into his old room just down the hall.

He checked his rifle, now propped up within arm's reach of his makeshift bed, and verified it was loaded and ready to go and the rail-mounted flashlight worked. Jim had also procured a set of simple hardshell body armor for the two of them, and Ben ensured the fasteners on one side were open so he could slip into it at a moment's notice. It was a ritual the older man had beaten into his brain over the last few weeks, as he had instructed Ben on the basics of self-defense in an uncertain world.

Jim hadn't shared details of his past life other than to say he had spent some time in the fleet, but Ben had a sneaking suspicion that the kindly old man who had saved his life had been more than just a console jockey sitting out his enlistment on a frigate somewhere. He had an air of intelligent confidence about him, and every once in a while, Ben could see buried deep in those soft blue eyes a fierceness that missed nothing. Ben was intensely curious about the mystery of Jim's true past, but there was something about the man that kept Ben from working up the courage to dig at it.

"Night," Jim said as he turned off the radio and his own reading lamp, casting the room into darkness. Ben pulled the covers up and rolled onto his side.

As was always the case these days, the moment the light went off, his mind drifted to his dad. It had been a month, and there had been no word. Ben had accepted the fact that his dad was dead shortly after being released from the hospital. While it was true that the war had decimated interstellar commerce, there were still ships capable of traveling between stars. His dad would have found *some* way to get word to him if he was still alive. The pain in his heart had faded to a dull ache over the last couple of weeks, but Ben's emotions were still raw, lying just beneath the surface.

The real kick to the nuts was not having any way to know definitively what had happened to his dad. The datanets were a mess and commercial traffic to and from other systems had been shut down in the aftermath. He was a sixteen-year-old kid with no contacts of his own to call on for favors, and Jim had had no luck with his old military sources. Ben had nothing to do but drive forward and survive. *Just survive.* That thought repeated itself on loop in his mind every night until sleep finally claimed him.

———

"Ben!"

Jim's harsh whisper had a note of urgency to it, waking Ben instantly, his body giving him a shot of adrenaline for good measure. He reached for his rifle and armor as he whispered back, "What's up?"

"Someone's coming." The words sent a chill down Ben's spine, and fear squeezed his chest.

"How many?" Ben asked in a whisper as he moved to check the other windows, just as Jim had shown him.

"I counted ten lights before they shut them off," Jim said, moving quickly toward the door, his M37 clutched in one hand. "Just like we practiced, you hunker down here and use the desk for cover. Anyone comes through that door that isn't me, don't hesitate."

Jim flipped a switch he had rigged up near the door, activating all the outdoor lighting around the house and barns, casting eerie shadows throughout the library as the light filtered in through the windows. With the lights on and Ben hunkered down behind his makeshift barricade, Jim slipped out the door, closed it softly, and made his way quickly down the stairs to the main level. Ben sat behind the bulky wooden desk, panic creeping up his spine as his eyes darted everywhere without actually seeing anything.

He clutched his rifle tightly and swallowed hard, trying to control hands that were beginning to tremble. He checked his rifle again. *This is really happening. Don't screw up.*

———

Once on the main floor, Jim double-checked all points of entry, working his way counterclockwise around the main floor before taking up position behind a pair of couches and next to the large fieldstone fireplace in the living room. From here, he could monitor the entryway, living room windows, kitchen windows and patio door, and dining room windows. He sat in silence for several minutes, eyes and ears straining to detect the slightest hint of forced entry.

A shadow flitted past the frosted glass of the front door. Then another. Muffled shots rang out from around the house, and one by one, the exterior lights winked out. *Not completely stupid after all*, he grunted internally. His lips pressed into a tight line and he reached up and lowered a set of night-vision glasses over his eyes, selecting a combination of light amplification and short-wave infrared—his long-preferred setting for low-light terrestrial environments—bringing his surroundings to life in shades of muted green.

A light bump against the wall underneath the row of living room windows drew his attention, and he swung toward the sound, shouldering his DMR as he did so. Jim centered the crosshairs of his optic just above the windowsill as the glass shattered and a figure vaulted through the opening. The integrally suppressed DMR barked three times in rapid succession— the silenced rounds still quite loud in the confined space—and the 7mm slugs sent the man tumbling backward with a surprised grunt as Jim rose and charged toward the window. The two men still outside let out surprised shouts as their now-dead comrade fell back on top of them, and they were still trying to extricate themselves from underneath the body when the DMR's truncated bark ended their lives.

Jim quickly swept the area outside the window and, satisfied it was clear for the moment, turned his attention to the heavy pounding on the front door. The deadbolt held out for a few heartbeats longer. Then the door swung violently inward, accompanied by a shower of splinters from the doorjamb. He didn't wait to see who his uninvited guests were, sending a blistering salvo of 7mm caseless rounds tearing through the opening. He was rewarded with two different male voices crying out as the bullets tore into them. Jim's victory was short-lived, however.

The two thugs who hadn't been hit returned fire with their own weapons, blindly spraying the entryway and living room with dozens of rounds. The old warrior rolled to the side and took cover behind the massive fireplace that dominated the living room. With practiced ease, he quickly dropped the DMR's nearly depleted magazine and inserted a fresh one. As the fire coming through the front door slackened, Jim swung around the corner of the fireplace, rifle leveled at the thugs he knew were about to come rushing through. They didn't disappoint and, a second later, came charging through the door side by side, weapons raised. It didn't matter. Jim cut them down before they even had both feet across the threshold.

A crashing noise from the kitchen caused him to pivot into a crouch and bring his rifle to bear as a shotgun boomed and a slug tore through the air above his head—space he'd been occupying only a moment ago. Three rounds center mass, and the thug fell backward onto the tile.

Jim saw movement from the living room window again as he squeezed the trigger on the threat from the kitchen. He swung his rifle toward the window once more after watching the thug in the kitchen begin to fall. A pair of fear-widened eyes gazed back at him through the broken window, and the man froze in place. The DMR spat fire once more and the face disappeared, leaving behind a fine mist as the bolt locked open on an empty magazine.

Jim ejected the empty magazine and reached for a full one in a speed pouch on his belt. A sledgehammer-blow hit him in the left shoulder, causing his arm to go instantly numb. His hard-shell body armor stopped the slug, but the force of the impact sent him spinning to the floor. He dropped his rifle on the way down, drawing his sidearm with his good hand as he hit the floor. The thug from the kitchen was back on his feet and pointing the muzzle of a shotgun directly at him. *Son of a bitch has armor!* he realized and adjusted his aim slightly. The pistol boomed once, and a neat hole appeared in the thug's forehead. He toppled to the tile for the last time, revealing a grisly spatter of blood and bone on the kitchen cabinets behind him from where the round had exited the back of his skull.

Two shots rang out from upstairs simultaneously, one clearly that of a heavy-gauge shotgun.

"Ben!" Jim shouted as he picked himself up off the floor and launched himself up the stairs three at a time.

———

BEN CROUCHED behind the heavy cherrywood desk his mom had given his dad as an anniversary gift many years ago. The desk was stoutly built and offered decent cover, but Ben found little comfort in that fact. As he waited in the darkened room, his great-grandfather's rifle aimed toward the door, all he could think about was how scared he was.

He'd been on Isadore when aliens started bombarding it, but it happened so fast and was so surreal he hadn't had a chance to be truly terrified. Likewise with the shuttle collision and finally the obliteration of Camp Grayling. Despite the fact that over the last month he had nearly lost his life on at least three separate occasions, in each instance he had either been too rushed, too mentally exhausted, or too injured to sit and reflect on how terrified he was.

This was different.

Sitting in a dark room, waiting to see if the next person to come through the door would try to kill him or tell him the coast was clear was impossibly terrifying. After the first minute, his palms were sweating so bad he was worried he wouldn't be able to grip the rifle properly should he need to use it. By the end of the third minute, his sweaty hands were shaking uncontrollably, and he wiped them on his pants in an effort to both dry them off and calm his nerves. All hell broke loose before the end of the fourth.

The first of the gunshots from downstairs caused him to jump, but they also helped focus his mind on the task at hand— the uncertainty of the silence replaced by a grim determination to not let his fourth brush with death be his last. Ben gripped his rifle a little tighter and centered the red dot sight in the middle of the door. The sounds of fighting raged on underneath him for what seemed like an eternity.

Then, backlit by the muzzle flashes filtering up the stairs, a shadow from a pair of boots appeared through the gap under the door. Raw, unfiltered terror squeezed his chest, and all of Jim's instruction rushed through his head in a jumbled mass of words and movements as he gripped the rifle so tight the metal dug into his hands painfully. At least he remembered to flip off the safety with his thumb and rest his index finger on the receiver just above the trigger.

The door burst open, revealing a hulking figure behind it. Time seemed to slow down as his eyes caught sight of the shotgun in the man's hands just before it emitted a blinding stream of light. The chaos raging in his thoughts as he struggled to remember what to do disappeared, and a simple directive coalesced in his mind.

He squeezed the trigger, and the AR-15 barked at the same instant the boom of the intruder's shotgun split the air.

"BEN!" Jim shouted again as he reached the top of the stairs, pausing only briefly to take in the lifeless corpse of a hulking figure crumpled on the floor, blood pooling beneath it. He stepped over the body of the thug and kicked away the shotgun lying nearby. As he rounded the corner into the library, his eyes immediately started searching for Ben. "Ben!" he repeated, entering the room with his pistol raised, sweeping the entire space for additional threats. Satisfied there were none, he rushed to the desk, where he found Ben lying on his side, unmoving.

Jim reached down and gently rolled the kid onto his back. A pair of angry red trenches creased the right side of his face, oozing blood, and a large knot rose from the back of his head. Two of the buckshot pellets had grazed his skull, causing him to fall back and slam his head into the bookshelf behind him. The kid would have one hell of a headache when he woke up—and an impressive scar to show off to the ladies—but he would be fine.

The old warrior quickly dressed Ben's wound and got him situated comfortably on his mattress, then went back downstairs to make sure the house was secure. This was the part he always hated about gunfights: the cleanup. He wasn't looking forward to explaining how a retiree and a teenager had taken out an entire gang of determined thugs, but it had to be done. With any luck, the authorities would send out the meat wagon to collect the bodies, take a quick report, then leave them be—they had their hands full with civilians being raped and murdered on a nightly basis around town now that everything had gone to shit. There was a time when turning the living room of a rich person's home into a charnel house of bullet-riddled corpses would be the talk of the force, but now it was just another Tuesday.

Jim stood in the living room and looked around at the death

and destruction and shook his head in disgust. He pulled a cigar out of a chest pocket, bit the end off, and puffed it to life on the flickering flame of an old, beat-up Zippo lighter. It was going to be a long year or two before this shit finally settled down. He needed to get the kid whipped into shape, pronto.

CHAPTER NINE

A NEW PLAYER

CAPTAIN WILLIAM BURNS LEANED BACK IN HIS CHAIR AND RUBBED his eyes. In the four years since the Alarian war ended, he'd been sent on any number of missions to investigate rumors of odd happenings throughout Terran space, but none of those had resulted in such a mystery. He'd spent the last few hours closely examining the intelligence briefs he'd been given prior to departing Icarus, along with all the sensor data his ship had collected over the last two days as she stealthily crept into the Vostok System. The intel reports were several weeks out of date, but what his ship had discovered so far troubled him: nothing. Not a stray RF signal or thermal bloom anywhere that they could detect.

Vostok was home to six planets, their various moons, and a single large asteroid belt separating the five rocky inner planets from the system's lone gas giant. The sole habitable planet, Gagarin, had a fairly large population by colonization standards, being home to nearly two million people. There was also the fleet of cargo ships that took the world's many agricultural products to the more heavily populated systems where they were needed, and the numerous orbital constructs that supported the endeavor. At least there *should* have been.

While Burns and his ship, the CTS *Appomattox*, were still on the far side of the system's asteroid belt, her advanced sensor suite was more than capable of picking up thermal emissions from any inner-system space traffic and the electromagnetic radiation that a planet with that many people would emit in its various forms. Instead, their scans revealed a system devoid of life.

Burns had had the better part of a week to study the mission details with his senior staff while en route from Icarus, and nothing in them had indicated they would find a dead system. Confed intelligence had picked up a few transmissions relating several unconfirmed sightings of unusual spacecraft loitering around the edge of the Vostok system, but all comms traffic from the system had abruptly stopped after those messages, and CTS Central Command dispatched the *Appomattox* to investigate.

Burns didn't like going into an unknown situation without escorts, but the Confed's forces had been all but completely wiped out during the brutal weeks-long war that had seen both sides decimated. It had taken sixteen months to get the shipyards at Icarus up to full operational capacity and another six for the first new ship to be christened and begin her shakedown cruise. The *Appomattox* had been that ship, beating her sister ship, *Gettysburg*, for which the new class of destroyers was named, by only two days. Although Icarus was now turning out new starships at the rate of two every month, there still weren't enough fleet assets to go around, and Burns found his ship all by her lonesome on a reconnaissance mission to a potentially hostile system.

The eggheads back at Icarus had packed the new destroyers full of the most advanced technology they could dream up, but Burns found little comfort in fancy sensors and stealth capability that had never been tested in an actual combat zone. The one thing that gave the captain some measure of solace was the knowledge that his crew were the very best of what remained in the Confed fleet. They had been together now for over two years, and Burns had drilled them over and over until they worked together like a well-oiled machine. Commander Weatherly, his XO, was a thoroughly capable exec, and Burns had been able to handpick the rest of his first-watch bridge officers. If they ran into any trouble on this mission, he had little doubt that his ship and crew would acquit themselves well.

A single knock sounded from his cabin door. "Enter," he called out, and the hatch opened to reveal a young enlisted spacer looking quite nervous.

"Commander Weatherly sends her compliments, sir. She asked me to inform you that we'll soon be clearing Buran," the spacer reported dutifully.

"Thank you"—Burns paused briefly to glance at the spacer's nametape—"Mendoza," he said, rising from his chair. On a ship as large as the *Appomattox,* it was difficult to get to know every member of his crew by name, even after having served with them for years. Burns hated how impersonal the shipboard comms were and preferred that non-critical communications be brought to him by junior enlisted personnel. He saw it as a way to get to know his crew while hopefully removing some of the deity-like status most of the lower ranks assigned their commanding officers. Burns had risen through the ranks, earning every single promotion through hard work and determination, not political favors, and he felt a crew responded better when they knew their CO wasn't just some schmuck put in charge of a shiny new ship because he was well connected.

Burns straightened his uniform and stepped out into the passageway. "Shall we?" he said, gesturing in the bridge's direction. The captain's stateroom was one deck above the bridge, which, on the newer fleet vessels, was located well within the heart of the ship. The Alarian War had shown humanity that having the bridge exposed on an upper deck was a good way to lose most of your command staff in one fell swoop; Alarian directed energy weapons had proven shockingly accurate, as they quickly targeted and destroyed the bridges in the exposed superstructures of the older vessels. One of the many changes in military doctrine resulting from the war was that command staff needed to be protected as much as possible, hence the shift in design elements that traced their lineage back centuries to the first ocean-going navies of humanity's past.

He tried to make small talk with Mendoza while the two casually made their way to their destination, but the young spacer was so nervous he could barely manage "yes, sir" or "no, sir," let alone carry on anything even remotely resembling an actual conversation. Burns dismissed the young spacer when they reached the hatch to the bridge, then turned and greeted the stone-faced marine sentry standing guard and stepped through the hatch.

"Report," he said.

"We're thirty thousand kilometers from clearing Buran's horizon, sir. All departments reporting Condition Two. The ship is operating under low-observability protocols. ECM is active," Commander Gale Weatherly reported.

"Thank you, Commander. As you were," Burns said as he began his customary tour of the various bridge stations, pausing briefly at each one to look over the displays for himself.

He finished his rounds and finally took his seat, then spent a few moments rearranging the layout of the information on his displays to his liking. That done, he settled in for the last few minutes of anticipation as the *Appomattox* neared the point where the enormous gas giant, Buran, would no longer be obstructing their view of Gagarin. He checked his display—in two minutes, their scopes would finally have an unfettered view of their destination. With any luck, they would soon have an explanation for why the system was so quiet.

"Thirty seconds to horizon," Lieutenant Mills called out from the nav station, despite the fact that the entire bridge had their eyes locked on the main display, which showed a feed from the hull-mounted cameras and a position plot overlaid in one corner. The bridge crew held their collective breath as the last few seconds elapsed and a bright blue dot appeared in the distance beyond the gas giant.

"Resolving image now," one of the sensor techs reported as a grainy image appeared on the main display. "There's a lot of scatter from the asteroid belt. Filtering…" The mottled blues and greens of the planet came into sharper focus, revealing several dark splotches dotting the equatorial region. "That's as good as it's going to get until we clear the belt, sir."

"Thank you, Ensign," Burns said distractedly as his eyes searched the image in front of him. "Can we tighten up on those dark areas around the equator?"

"Yes, sir, but the resolution will be poor until we can get a cleaner look," the tech reported, entering a series of commands into his console. A moment later, a pair of brackets highlighted one of the darkened areas, and the main display zoomed in on it. The image wasn't the sharpest, but no one on the bridge needed higher resolution to understand what they were looking at.

"Oh my god…" Mills gasped in horror. "Sir… that's Volunsgrad."

"Are you certain?" Burns's voice was suddenly hoarse, his mouth going dry in an instant.

"Absolutely, sir."

What once had been a city of more than half a million people was now a smoldering wasteland. A dense black pall covered much of the area, but the pixelated visage of the charred and twisted skeletons of the city's once-proud skyline was just visible through gaps where the wind had blown the smoke clear. The detail of the image was too poor to determine if there was any life buried beneath the smoke and ruins, but the grim scene on display left little hope of survivors.

"Son of a bitch," an unseen voice muttered, "they're at it again."

"Stow that crap, Mister!" Burns ordered, a hard edge to his voice. "We don't know who or what is responsible here, and until we do, I don't want any wild rumors flying around about the Alarians attacking again. I have it on good authority that they are abiding by the terms of the ceasefire just as we are. XO, sound general quarters."

"General quarters, general quarters. All hands to battle stations. Set Condition One throughout the ship." Commander Weatherly's voice boomed through every compartment and passageway as the klaxons sounded their strident alert. Burns heard the metallic thunk from behind him as the heavy blast door to the bridge swung closed and the locking bolts snapped into place.

Burns's mind raced as he took in all the details on the viewscreen and ordered them together with what information he had been given about the system before deploying from Icarus. Was his crew correct and this was the Alarians deciding to finish what they had started? He had been assured that the ceasefire that had held for the last four years was still in place, and CID hadn't picked up on any rumors to the contrary. He supposed it was possible this had been a terrible accident—perhaps one of the massive orbital platforms had destabilized and crashed to the surface.

"Tactical, any contacts showing on the threat board?" Burns inquired of his tactical staff.

"Negative, sir. Just a bunch of debris in space. No thermal

blooms or EM emissions. Nothing on visual," Lieutenant Tomanaga, the tactical officer, reported quickly.

Burns considered his options for a moment before issuing more orders. "Nav, plot a least-time course that will take us into a high equatorial orbit. Tactical, go active. I want to know the location and disposition of every piece of space junk in this system. Ops, prep a Beckman drone for Icarus with all the data we've collected since we transitioned in, but don't launch it just yet—I want to get the analysts back at Icarus some higher-res scans to work with, first."

"Aye, sir," the trio of bridge officers called out in unison.

"Sir, is it wise to break EMCON? We don't yet know what did this—or *who* did it." Commander Weatherly's voice was calm and composed, but her face betrayed her fear.

"Whoever did this is long gone, Commander," Burns said with certainty. "This system went dark two weeks ago, and you saw for yourself that what's left of those cities is mostly cold. If it was recent, the fires that produced that ash cloud would still be raging."

"Yes, sir, but—"

"Commander, if there are still people alive on that planet, they will need help, and we're the only ship capable of rendering aid within twelve light-years." Burns interrupted, shooting his XO a reproachful look for questioning his orders so publicly. "We don't know who or what did this, and we won't be able to find out from way out here. Now, please assist Lieutenant Tomanaga. He's going to have his hands full parsing through all the debris now that we're running active scans."

"Aye aye, sir," Weatherly acknowledged, biting back any further objections. She moved to the tactical station and went to work assisting the now very busy Tomanaga.

Burns felt the thrum of the fusion plant increase in pitch through the deck plates beneath his feet as the *Appomattox*'s main engines came to life and began pouring out millions of pounds of thrust. He felt himself gently pressed back into his seat as the inertial compensators struggled to keep up with the with the ship's acceleration, which, he noted with satisfaction, was already nearing her continuous acceleration design limit of 150 gs.

Despite the unknown dangers that possibly awaited them at their destination, Burns felt a wave of exhilaration wash over him unlike anything he had experienced in years. He reveled in the raw power coursing through his ship and the purposeful movement of his people as they set about their assigned tasks. With any luck, they'd make orbit over the planet in a little over ten hours, and Burns hoped they'd finally be able to get some answers as to what—or who—had happened to Gagarin.

———

As the *Appomattox* sped past the system's asteroid belt on its dash for Gagarin, one of the jagged lumps of rock stopped its slow tumble through space and began slowly rotating to track the ship's movement through the system. Passive sensors gathered data on the newcomer, and the sentinel's AI went to work plotting its projected course and reviewing the new information. After just 7.6 microseconds, the intelligence within the machine had analyzed the data and classified the unknown ship as a high-order threat. The data was encrypted and sent via slipspace burst transmission to a relay buoy sitting a few light-years distant in interstellar space, which would forward the report to the Master's Agent to disseminate as it saw fit.

After receiving confirmation that its transmission had been received, the stealthy little machine once again went inactive and resumed its slow tumble through the asteroid belt, just one more small chunk of primordial rock drifting through the system.

CHAPTER TEN

REVELATIONS

"Ow! Son of a—argh! Fuck!" Ben cried out, clutching the knuckles of his right hand in his left as the wrench he had been using clattered across the top of the workbench and disappeared into the cobweb-infested depths behind it. "Fuck you, Murphy!" he yelled in frustration, cursing the patron saint of things that could go wrong, kicking a nearby bucket for good measure. But it was Murphy and the bucket that got the last laugh—it was filled with fifty pounds of two-inch trellis staples.

Now hopping up and down while trying to simultaneously clutch both his injured hand and his throbbing foot, he let fly with a stream of obscenities that threatened to blister the paint off the walls. He took a moment to steal a peek at his bloody knuckles to see if this was the kind of thing he needed to go find a first aid kit for or if he could get away with simply wrapping a shop rag around it for a bit and take care of it later. The intense throbbing from his now-skinless knuckles, combined with a surprising amount of blood, indicated it was the former. However, the unbridled hatred he felt toward the inanimate object in front of him overrode his common sense, and he wrapped an oil-stained rag around it, anyway. He would not be defeated this day.

It had been one of those days. The season was nearly over, and today was supposed to be their last day of harvest. Typically, Ben would be elated that the marathon was over and they were just a few short hours from bringing the months-long growing season to an end, but this season had been miserable: stifling heat coupled with drought conditions for much of the summer and into fall, followed by torrential rains once October had finally rolled around. The unseasonably warm temperatures combined with the constant moisture and turned what was otherwise a gorgeous crop of grapes into a daily battle to keep rot under control. Today was it, and the struggles of the past weeks and months were finally coming to an end. However, as was almost always the case in farming, the season from hell just had to get one last shot in.

Everything that could have gone wrong had gone wrong. It started with Ben's alarm failing to wake him and had rapidly gotten worse, as almost half his picking crew were violently ill with a stomach flu. Then the weather turned to shit and they were forced to pick grapes in a drizzling rain at near-freezing temperatures. But after twelve grueling hours of work, the last bin of fruit was ready to be taken down to the crush pad for pressing... and that was when one of the hydraulic cylinders on the tractor ruptured a seal, showering him in hot oil as the fluid jetted out under pressure.

After taking a moment or three to calm himself down, Ben walked over to the toolbox to get the most useful tool ever invented by man: a magnet attached to a flexible stick, complete with a fiber-optic viewing probe to see what you were grabbing. He moved back to the workbench, grumbling to himself the whole way, and activated the small light on the magnet before slipping it into the gap between the workbench and the wall.

After a brief search through the cobwebs, dust bunnies, and dried-out insect carcasses littering the space, he located his quarry and successfully grasped it with the magnet.

Ben pulled the wrench from the depths but felt his prize catch on something just inches from the top of the bench. He reacted too late, and the wrench broke free and tumbled to the floor with a clatter once more. Annoyed, he slipped the magnet back into the crack for another try… and paused. His brow furrowed as he realized the wrench hadn't caught on an errant nail or splinter like he'd assumed. He stared in puzzlement at the small display in his hands. It showed a recess a couple of inches square with what looked like a biometric button in the middle of it.

"Well, what the hell are you doing there?" he muttered to the musty shop around him. The wrench momentarily forgotten, he thrust his hand behind the bench and did what any red-blooded human male would do in his shoes: he pushed the button of unknown capability.

There was a soft beep from somewhere as the biometric security built into the button checked both his fingerprint and DNA, and the floor beneath his feet began to shudder. Ben turned to face the sound of mechanical actuators from behind him and saw the center section of the shop floor—with the tractor still on it—recess several inches along an expansion joint, then stop.

"Right, because that would of course be a thing that would happen to me today." He sighed, resigning himself to what would undoubtedly be his gruesome death at the hands of whatever hellspawn it turned out was living beneath his shop. But because he didn't have anything better to do at the moment, he took three steps toward the hidden elevator and jumped on. As soon as he was firmly aboard, the floor began descending a concrete shaft.

"Dad, you were one sneaky son of a bitch," Ben mumbled to

himself as the shaft opened up on one side, revealing a black void as cool, stale air swirled around his ankles as the lift continued to descend. "And it turns out my father was Batman." Because who else would have built a hidden lift to a secret room beneath the farm's shop? The little bit of light that trickled down the thirty-meter shaft was unable to penetrate the gloom, but as he took a tentative step into the darkened space, ceiling lights snapped on, revealing a good-sized room.

Ben's eyes roamed the space, taking in all the details before locking onto a workstation situated in front of a large wall display. It wasn't the desk itself that caught his attention, but rather the fact that the display above it had come to life. The image that appeared on it froze him in his tracks as a voice spoke from unseen speakers.

"Hello, Ben." His dad's face loomed large on the wall in front of him.

Ben's heart caught in his throat at the sight of his dad, and a flurry of questions raced through his mind as he took everything in. His elation was cut short, however, as the recording continued.

"If you're seeing this, then the worst has happened and I won't be making it back to Earth." His dad's expression lowered for a moment before he went on. "I'm so sorry, Ben—I'm sorry that I won't be there for you. And that makes what I'm about to tell you all the more difficult.

"I brought you to ExoDyn today because you are the key to helping us combat a threat like nothing we have ever faced before. We've known for a decade that the Terran datanet has been compromised by extremely advanced malcode, but we've never actually been able to isolate and study it. The few times we've been able to isolate an infected system, the malcode has wiped itself so completely that there was nothing left to analyze. CTS cyberintelligence analysts have taken to calling it specter code, since they're certain it exists but don't have a single shred of hard evidence. Our best guess is that it's an advanced form of AI designed specifically to infiltrate our systems and wreak havoc—anything from mining sensitive data to outright digital sabotage.

"Your mom was heading a secret project that we'd hoped would lead to an effective counter to this cyber construct, but despite our best efforts, the project was infiltrated. I don't know how, but the construct managed to gain access to the site's isolated datanet..." His dad paused and his gaze fell away from the camera for a moment, and when he looked back up, his eyes had a hardness that Ben had rarely seen them express before. He continued. "The disaster on Mars was not an accident, Ben. The construct somehow gained control of the lab's environmental systems and caused the explosion that killed your mother..."

Ben flinched. Despite knowing his mom's death hadn't been an accident after all, having an answer to a question that had plagued him for years laid right out in the open was like a punch to the gut. *So it was the Alarians all along...*

"We managed to recover the data backups from the project that your mom had stored off-site in the event of a breach. After the destruction of the facility on Mars, Confed Intel Division took over the lead on the project and set up a secure lab at Camp Grayling.

"Despite the best and brightest minds in Terran space working on this for more than a decade, we were never able to break through the technological sentience barrier. All we were ever able to do was create an advanced AI, so a few years ago I pitched an idea to CID, and we started working the problem from ExoDyn's end. Instead of trying to create a sentient artificial intelligence by adding yet more and more lines of code to a program, I wanted to approach the problem from a new angle. We took the work your mom had been doing and spun up a new project called Blackthorn. And before you ask, because I know it will bug you,"—his dad smiled to himself—"the name has no significance. It was the first option that came up when I looked up a random code-name generator on the net.

"Anyway, the problem with trying to create an AI is that you're limited to working within the constraints of electronic systems, which are incapable of true creativity due to their very nature. So we focused on a system that *is* creative by nature: the human brain. While your mother had been trying to translate the brain's capacity for creativity into lines of code, we decided to take a shortcut and see if we could find a way to fuse the ones and zeroes of an advanced AI with the flesh and blood creativity of the human mind.

"That's where you come in, Ben. Since you were seven years old, we've manipulated your environment—everything from your personalized education to those damn holosims you're always playing have been specifically designed to enhance the areas of your brain that are responsible for creativity and prob-lem-solving. In order to maximize the effectiveness of our approach, the brain we link to the AI needs to be molded, so to speak, to fit together with the digital systems like two pieces of a puzzle—adult brains are too inflexible and can't fully adapt to the interface we use. Unfortunately, the ideal time to shape the human brain in such a manner is from early childhood through the teenage years..." His dad trailed off, leaving the obvious unsaid.

Son of a bitch. All those years of private tutoring, prototype simulators, everything... It was all because he was a guinea pig for one of his dad's secret projects. On the one hand, it didn't surprise him; his dad was always tinkering with experiments, even in their everyday lives. On the other hand, *what the fuck?*

"I'm so sorry, Ben. You were the perfect age, and we were running out of time. The x300 was designed from the ground up to be the link through which man and machine create an *augmented* intelligence, but the suit is only part of the equation. You need to get to the lab at Camp Grayling—Dan can get you in —and work with the team there to combat the construct. I'm absolutely convinced *it* is the real enemy here. It's played both us and the Alarians to the point of triggering a full-scale war. I don't know why, and I don't even fully understand how, but I can feel it, Ben—this isn't just racial tensions flaring up between our two species. There's something far more sinister going on here. I know it—" A muffled voice filtered in from somewhere out of frame, and his father turned away to exchange a few words with someone before turning his attention back to the camera.

"The team at Grayling can fill you in more. I love you, Ben, and I'm so proud of you. Your mom would be, too."

Ben took a few moments to process everything he had just heard before shakily walking up to the desk and sitting down. The video file he had just seen had clearly been recorded in his father's office back at ExoDyn corporate headquarters on Isadore, but how it had made its way to a secure terminal squirreled away in his father's secret lab on Earth was a mystery. He had hoped there would be more files on the terminal—files recorded after the one he had just viewed, indicating his dad was still alive—but there weren't any.

He finally had answers to some of the questions that had been burning holes in his brain for years, but after hearing the explanations, he now had even more questions than he had started with… and this time, there wouldn't be any more answers coming. His dad was gone, as was Dan and the entire complex at Grayling. That bit at the end was intriguing: it sounded like his dad was trying to say there was a third party involved somehow, but the message was maddeningly incomplete. Still, it had been so long since the war, and he had grown so much over the years, that the whole thing seemed almost academic to him now. His x300 had been scrapped years ago, and everyone associated with this Project Blackthorn was long dead. Still, buried deep down in his soul was a tiny spark of something that hadn't been there for a long time: hope.

Ben rose from the terminal and took the lift back up to the shop; he needed a second opinion on this.

———

THE AGENT PAUSED for a few milliseconds to consider the new data that had just come in—and from a completely unexpected source: one of the subminds it had established to monitor the Terran datanet for items of interest had just pinged its parent with a critical update. The Agent unpacked the data file and analyzed its contents, waking its communications subroutines and routing power to the hidden slipspace transceiver it had spent decades painstakingly assembling and hiding from the Terrans. Power began coursing into the transceiver, waking it from years of dormancy as the Agent compiled an urgent data drop for the Master.

The agent had learned of the Hutchins child's presence on Earth after the planet's datanet had come back online two years ago, but the boy had never been flagged as a threat to its mission, having been too young at the time of the war to have been involved in any activity that could pose a threat. But the audio and video recording that had just come in from a piece of agricultural equipment on the Hutchins family farm shattered that belief, and the Agent suddenly found itself scrambling to mitigate the enormous danger that had just been uncovered to both itself and, most importantly, its Master.

A read receipt was generated as the Master received the file, and a short time later, the Agent received new instructions: the Hutchins child was to be eliminated immediately.

———

"THE TEAM at Grayling can fill you in more. I love you, Ben, and I'm so proud of you. Your mom would be, too." The wall display went dark as the recording ended for the second time, and Ben turned to Jim.

"Well?"

Jim didn't respond right away, instead taking several long moments to compose his thoughts. "I'll be honest, Ben, I just don't see that this changes anything. Grayling is nothing more than a big hole in the ground, and your x300 was damaged beyond any hope of repair."

Ben's expression fell as Jim put voice to the same thoughts he'd had the first time he saw the recording.

"I do find the part about a malcode construct of unknown origins to be deeply disturbing," Jim continued. "We knew for decades that somebody—or some*thing*—was breaching our secure datanets, but the idea that it may have been a construct playing us against the Alarians to spark a conflict does fill in some holes." He looked thoughtfully at the blank display for a moment longer before finally breaking his gaze and turning to Ben.

"It's getting late, so let's button this back up for now and go grab some dinner and bunk down for the night. We can approach this again in the morning when we're fresh," he said, turning to walk back toward the lift.

Ben deflated a little. He'd hoped that Jim might be able to shed some new light on things, but deep down, he'd known what the old warrior would say, and Jim was right. The last four years had matured Ben beyond his age and tempered his impatience, so instead of trying to pry a little around the edges to see if Jim would say anything else, he shut down the terminal and rose to follow his friend.

A few minutes later, the two of them were settling in for the evening with a delicious dinner of Ration Pack, Individual, Menu B—spaghetti and meatballs—compliments of the NAC Division of Emergency Management, which, even after four years, was still trying to reestablish regular commerce to much of the nonmetro areas of the Commonwealth. They chatted a little about Ben's discovery, but in the end, there just wasn't much to say that both men didn't already know. It was shit luck that had left Ben stranded on Earth without anyone who would be able to answer his questions, but for whatever reason, fate seemed determined to keep him from forgetting it and moving on.

An hour later, Ben was sound asleep in his bed, not having realized how exhausted he was after an incredibly long and emotional day.

CHAPTER ELEVEN

THE SCHOOLYARD BULLY

BURNS SAT IN HIS COMMAND CHAIR, STARING AT THE HIGH-resolution image of Gagarin displayed on the main viewscreen of the *Appomattox*'s bridge. They had been on-site for a little over thirty-six hours, and his teams' initial findings had come in just a little bit ago: plasma. Someone had parked themselves in orbit and bombarded the surface with large-scale plasma weapons. He almost couldn't believe it.

Whoever had done this, Burns was convinced it wasn't the Alarians. Plasma weapons had been theorized, but developing such a weapon remained beyond the capabilities of either the Confed or the Alarians. Then again, nobody had thought the Alarians would be able to use slipspace to mesh a full battle-group in right on top of them back when they'd been blindsided at the start of the war, so who knew?

And as if that wasn't enough to ruin his day, one of the other teams had reported that there were dozens of places where large groups of civilians had been rounded up and summarily slaughtered by plasma small arms as well. Nearly the whole population had been exterminated, and the only survivors on the entire planet were the few people who had been out of contact with the planetary datanet at the time. That latter fact pointed to how the perpetrators had managed to so efficiently round up the survivors, but that was of little comfort.

Something about this whole situation bothered him: *why?* An entire planet had been cleansed of nearly all sentient life by an unknown alien race, and yet the attackers had apparently just packed up shop and left once their grisly work was done. Gagarin held no strategic military value—the Vostok system sat at the outer edge of Sino-Russian Federation space, almost forty-five light-years from Earth—and the closest systems in its stellar neighborhood were unremarkable at best. So if you weren't wiping out the natives to take the planet for yourself, then why bother doing it in the first place? Several possibilities ran through his head—a terrorist action, perhaps? No, it was almost like someone saw the human presence on the world as a disease and had taken action to eradicate it. Without more concrete information to go on, all he could do was speculate.

The devastation scrolling slowly past was total, and the last two days of searching had only uncovered a few small pockets of survivors: people typically located at remote outposts or farm-steads well away from the heavily populated urban areas that had suffered the brunt of the attack. So far, the only common thread among the survivors was that none of them had had access to the planetary datanet at the time of the attack.

Nearly everyone these days had a personal comms node; the ubiquitous palm-sized devices that were used for communica-tion and allowed instant access to the planetary datanet. The fact that, to an individual, none of the survivors had a working comms node on them during the week-long period that the planet was razed was interesting and something he considered an important piece of the puzzle when it came to determining how the attacking force had managed to so efficiently round up the planet's inhabitants for extermination, but the specific details remained nebulous.

Despite his crew taking small steps closer to an answer, Burns was left with a maddeningly incomplete picture of this new foe. Making matters worse was the fact that every intact data-storage device Burns's crew had come across on the planet was corrupted beyond any hope of salvage. There were no traces of anything relating to the attackers in video files, sensor logs, personal communications—nothing. This new threat was incredibly elusive, and Burns had an uneasy feeling in his gut that things were going to get much worse in the near future. He looked at the chronometer over the main viewscreen, noting that his musings had lasted almost an hour.

"Ops, what's the status on that Beckman?" he said to the fresh-faced ensign—Lowen, if memory served—currently manning the operations workstation.

"All systems are green, and the drone is on standby. Ready to launch on your order, sir. All departments' data packets have been encoded and uploaded to the drone, and I've been updating the out-system vector and jump coordinates every ten minutes along with current comms and telemetry logs for CENTCOM," the young man replied promptly.

"Very good. Launch the Beckman," Burns said, mentally making a note of the young ensign's attention to detail. The Fleet Officer's Training Battalion back in Kerner had been pumping young officers out as fast as they could in order to fully crew the new ships now that the fleetyards around Icarus were up to full production, but the training they received was barely adequate to prepare them for their new duty assignments. As a result, all newly minted fleet officers underwent a probationary period when they worked under a more experienced officer who served as a preceptor that would keep them from screwing things up too badly. Lowen had thus far proven himself to be an exception, and Burns had a feeling that rapid advancement was in the young ensign's future if he kept up the exceptional work.

"Drone is away, sir."

"How long until it reaches Gateway?" Burns asked, referring to the transit hub that had been set up to enforce the strict security procedures put in place to protect the Kerner 667 system and Icarus from being discovered. All traffic—be it personnel, hardware, or data—on its way to Icarus made a stop at Gateway first to be gone over with a fine-toothed comb and scrubbed before being allowed to make the jump to the massive Icarus Station itself.

"The drone is set to burn hot, so it should arrive roughly three days from now. The data is flagged priority-one alpha, so there should be a minimal delay before the package gets pushed along to CENTCOM on Icarus," Lowen replied without hesitation.

Yep, the kid is good. "Thank you, Ensign," Burns said. With that, he turned his attention back to his command console and began reviewing the duty shifts for the upcoming day.

———

"Sir, the Beckman has disappeared!"

Burns looked up at the strident call from the ops station, a steaming mug of coffee frozen halfway up to his lips, and noted with mild disappointment that the second watch ops officer, Lieutenant Watts, had relieved Lowen at some point. "What do you mean, 'disappeared'?" he said, unable to hold back some minor irritation in his voice. "Give me specifics, Lieutenant." It wasn't uncommon for telemetry to drop off intermittently if a planet or other large stellar body like an asteroid happened to be between the drone and the ship when the packet containing the updated data was transmitted.

"We received a scheduled telemetry update from the Beckman three minutes ago, reporting it was on course and systems were nominal. Then just now we received the beginning of a priority-one burst transmission from the drone reporting three unknown objects on an intercept course, but it stopped abruptly before any sensor data could be compiled and sent." A chill ran up Burns's spine as he processed the news.

Beckman drones were modular, utilitarian workhorses that could be configured for a variety of missions from long-range interstellar comms relay to autonomous exploration, and they were equipped with a full sensor suite and threat-analysis protocols. When a drone detected anything that might be an imminent threat, it would power up its sensor suite and run detailed active scans of the object or objects that posed the threat. At the same time, it would send out a priority-one alert to the nearest fleet asset and begin transmitting its telemetry in real time. If their Beckman had stumbled across something that triggered the imminent-threat protocols and was able to send an initial alert but not send any data with it, something bad had happened very fast.

"Sound general quarters," Burns said in a firm but surprisingly calm voice, considering the alarm bells screaming at him in his head. He knew he had hours, at least, to prepare the ship for combat—if that truly was the direction in which things were heading—as space battles took place over, literally, astronomical distances. Even at full burn, the *Appomattox* wouldn't be able to reach the drone's last known location for almost eight hours. He took great care to project an air of urgency, but not panic, as he strode from the coffee maker at the back of the bridge to his command chair. Klaxons sounded throughout the ship, calling every member of his crew to their combat stations. As he settled into his chair, he started putting a plan of action together.

"Ops, do we have any teams still on the surface?"

"Uh—" Watts took a moment to scan his screens, and Burns frowned inwardly that the man didn't know the answer immediately. "No, sir. The last shuttle returned twenty minutes ago."

"Good. Nav, plot me a least-time course out of the gravity well and toward the Beckman's last known position. Helm, as soon as you have the course, kick her in the ass. We don't want to be trying to lumber our way out from low orbit if some uninvited guests show up. Tactical—" Burns glanced over to see if Tomanaga had made it to the bridge yet and was pleasantly surprised to find him just getting settled in behind his console as the second watch tactical officer gave him a quick turnover report. "Go active and find me whatever the hell it was that just took out our drone. Ops, prep another Beckman for Icarus and keep it continuously updating with a raw data feed of all our sensor output."

The bridge crew acknowledged his orders and set about their assigned tasks, and over the next few minutes, his senior bridge officers arrived, relieving the night watch and taking their stations.

"What's going on, sir?" Commander Weatherly asked, her hair still wet from the shower she had been taking when the combat stations alarm sounded.

"Something tripped the Beckman's imminent-threat protocols, but we lost contact immediately after it transmitted a priority-one alert, and we presume it was destroyed."

"Our new player?" she said, trepidation etched on her face.

"Don't know. But that's what we're going to find out. We're sitting ducks here in low orbit, and there are still people down on that planet that need protecting."

"Agreed," she said, then went to work making sure the crew were at their stations and getting the ship ready to fight.

"Sir, Lieutenant Commander Wright is requesting an update on our status," Watts reported.

"Put it through to my station," Burns said. His console chirped a moment later, and he opened the channel. "What's up, Cheng?" he asked, using the ancient naval slang for "chief engineer."

"Why the hell are you suddenly flogging my ship like a rented mule, sir?" The surprisingly feminine voice of Lieutenant Commander Amy Wright came from the speakers of Burns's workstation, causing him to smile despite the situation. The petite, five-foot-two engineer was a foul-mouthed hellion masquerading as a blonde bombshell. She had been his chief engineer for going on four years now, and Burns considered it a minor miracle that he had never had to spring her from the brig after one of any number of barroom brawls she always seemed to just innocently happen across when on shore leave.

"We may have company, and they're probably not friendly. I'm going to need everything you can give me, Lieutenant Commander," Burns said, using her full rank to stress the gravity of the situation.

"Well… shit," was the only reply he got before the channel closed. A few moments later, he could have almost sworn that he felt the ship's power plants spool up just a tiny bit more, and he smiled just a little wider.

"Helm, how long before we break orbit and are en route to the Beckman?" Burns called out.

"Another thirty minutes should have us clearing the planet's gravity well and on our way. I'm going to slingshot us around Gagarin's moon to pick up a little extra velocity and hopefully save us a bit of propellant."

"Very good," Burns said, then turned his attention to his command display to monitor the ship's systems while they made their way out of their orbit and onto an intercept vector for the Beckman's last known location.

CHAPTER TWELVE

NEWTON SENDS HIS REGARDS

"TACTICAL, ANYTHING YET?" BURNS SAID ALMOST AN HOUR LATER, now that the first photons from the active sensor array had made the trip out to the drone's general area and back again.

"Negative, sir. Nothing new showing across the board. I have the Beckman's last known location from ops, but there's nothing in the neighborhood larger than one meter in diameter," Tomanaga replied.

"Alright, keep at it," Burns said, and that sinking feeling in his gut ratcheted up a couple of notches. If a Terran or Alarian ship had taken out the drone, it should have been detectable now that the *Appomattox* was banging away with her active sensor suite and they had a known area of space to focus on. The fact that they couldn't find anything out of the ordinary indicated that their quarry had extremely good stealth capabilities, and that could be a problem.

At least he could take comfort in the fact that they were likely dealing with only a single ship—and probably a small one at that; if there had been a whole fleet of capital ships out there, his sensors would have picked up *something*. He sat looking at his command console displays, following the nav and tactical data closely as the *Appomattox* raced toward the unknown.

Five hours came and went with nothing unusual popping up on the plot, and the alarm bells in Burns's head slowly faded. The captain made his way back to his command chair with what must have been at least his sixth mug of coffee since he ordered his ship out of orbit over Gagarin—he'd lost track of exactly how many—and quickly browsed the readouts on his console for any change. They were only a little over an hour's flight time from the Beckman's last known position, and so far, their active arrays had detected nothing that could even remotely be considered a threat.

He had downgraded the *Appomattox*'s readiness to Condition Two a few hours prior, after nothing of note happened following the mysterious, incomplete transmission from the drone. He was beginning to think he had severely overreacted to the drone's disappearance and now considered the possibility that a simple malfunction was the most likely explanation for the activation of its imminent-threat protocols. For this reason, he didn't think much of it when Tomanaga called him over to the tactical station.

"What have you got, Lieutenant?" Burns asked as he took a seat next to the young officer, steaming mug of coffee still clutched in his hand.

"Something odd, sir," Tomanaga said. "We're close enough to the drone's last known location for finer resolution on the thermals, and my last sweep showed this." He made a swiping motion across his screen, sending a high-resolution, false-color image to the console in front of the captain.

Burns took a moment to study the image and accompanying analysis that the tactical backshops had put together on it, and he furrowed his brow slightly. The thermal scan showed a tight cluster of three small areas of space that read as just barely warmer than the surrounding vacuum. He played around with the image for a minute, overlaying additional sensor data and adjusting the opacities of them to make a composite image from the multispectral sensor readings, but the thermal image was the only one that showed the anomaly.

"What do you make of it?" he asked Tomanaga.

"Unknown, sir," Tomanaga said. "CIC seems to think it's due to a marginally higher concentration of space dust in those areas resulting in some backscatter that's throwing off the readings slightly. None of the areas have a clearly defined shape, instead appearing almost hazy around the edges, which would seem to support that theory…" He trailed off, shaking his head slightly and shrugging.

"But you've never seen anything like it before and have no idea what it actually is," Burns finished for him. "Alright. Nav, I'm sending you some coordinates I want to check out. Plot us a course and send it over to the helm. Helm, you're free to proceed onto the new course as soon as nav sends it to you," he said, standing and making his way back to his command chair. "Tactical, stay on that region of space and let me know if anything changes even a little bit."

"Aye, sir," Tomanaga acknowledged.

Burns continued playing with the thermal scans on his command console, running through various filters and analytical tools. He had seen pockets of space dust play hell with thermals before, but nothing quite like this. Radar and lidar showed no solid mass, which more or less fit the space dust theory, but still… *Maybe old pockets of vented gas from a ship?* Burns thought, taking a sip of his coffee. He decided the answer would continue eluding him, so he minimized the images on his screen and went back to monitoring the ship's systems. They would find out for sure in about forty-five minutes when they passed through that region of space.

"Captain, thermal is registering a change in the anomaly. It appears those three anomalous areas are shrinking," Tomanaga called out a minute later.

"Put it on the main viewscreen," Burns said. The updated image appeared on the forward viewscreen, and Burns watched, fascinated, as the three pockets of space slowly seemed to narrow in width. "Any change to radar or lidar? Optical?"

"Negative, sir. Thermal is still the only system registering a change."

Burns stared at the screen, his mind puzzling through what the thermal imaging system was showing them…

Then it hit him.

"It's not a change in size or volume!" he said, coming half out of his chair as his eyes went wide with realization. "It's an *aspect* change! Those are ships in stealth, and they're turning to face us bow-on." Before he could even order it, the combat action alarm began blaring throughout the ship. Commander Weatherly had read his mind and hit the alarm almost before Burns had finished his sentence. The bridge lighting dimmed and shifted to a muted blue hue that reduced glare and offered a better contrast of the displays arrayed around the bridge.

"Guns, warm up the projectors and load a spread of Talons in the forward missile pods, maximum yield." Burns did some quick mental math and realized there was only one course of action left to him: a head-on pass at speed. The *Appomattox* was simply going too fast and carrying too much momentum to break off her course and buy them some time before engaging— if it came to that. By putting the hammer down and driving his ship directly toward this new threat at her maximum acceleration, he could hopefully cut the engagement time down to just a single volley as they sped past the unknown ships. Trying to break off their course would only result in a loss of velocity and an increased engagement time, and he didn't like that option at all. He wanted to do a quick flyby, gather as much intel on these ships as he could, and get out of the area as fast as possible. If he was lucky, they wouldn't need to fire a single shot.

"Helm, put us on a course that will bring those ships down the port side at a distance of a few thousand kilometers, then put the hammer down," Burns ordered.

"Aye, sir," came the reply from the helmsman. Burns caught Weatherly's eye for a moment and could see she knew what he was thinking, and she agreed with it.

"Comms, open hailing frequencies," Burns said, waiting a moment for the comms officer to nod in his direction and indicate that the channel was open. "Unknown vessels, this is the Confederated Terran Systems ship *Appomattox*. Your violation of Terran space without prior authorization constitutes a hostile action. Heave to and identify yourselves immediately." He motioned for the comms officer to close the channel. "Put that on a loop in all known languages and alternate it with the first contact package."

"Sir, those ships are accelerating along our course, pulling over nine hundred g's!" The strident call came from tactical, where Tomanaga was staring at his sensor display in disbelief.

"Put the sensor tracks on the main viewscreen," Burns said, not quite believing his tactical officer. A moment later, a 2D representation of their course was up on the display, showing the *Appomattox* at the bottom of the screen and the unknown ships at the top, overlaid with course, velocity, and acceleration data. Burns couldn't believe what he was seeing, either.

The unknown ships were accelerating hard to match the *Appomattox*'s course and speed, something that shouldn't have been possible given her current blistering pace across the system and the short time before they would be passing the newcomers. Instead, the acceleration numbers next to those ships continued to climb at an astonishing rate: 1000 g's... 1200... 1500 g's. The maneuver must have overtaxed their stealthing capabilities, however, as a moment later the three smudges on the thermal image resolved into three angular vessels of unknown design. They could have only been warships, and they faced the *Appomattox* bow-on, despite accelerating to match her course.

"That's not possible..." Commander Weatherly said, awestruck.

"Evidently it is," Burns said, voice strained as he realized that his hope of a quick flyby wasn't going to happen. Instead, it looked like they were in for a long, drawn-out fight at whatever range the enemy felt like dictating. "Guns, heat up the mag cannon." *I get the feeling we're going to need the kitchen sink before this is over.*

"Aye, sir," the weapons officer acknowledged with just the barest hesitation before his response. Heavy bombardment railguns were typically not used for ship-to-ship engagements, unlike their smaller, turret-mounted cousins. The big, axially-mounted cannons drew enormous amounts of current when charging and had rates of fire measured in rounds per hour, not minutes. Trading power that was needed to run the engines and other systems critical to a fight for the chance to land a low-probability haymaker just wasn't worth it.

"Tactical, do you have a read on possible classes for those ships yet?"

"None of the contacts are a known hull configuration, but tonnage estimates indicate a frigate and destroyer escorting either a heavy cruiser or battleship—the computer can't seem to decide what the largest contact is," Tomanaga said.

"Very well. Give me a firing solution for our Talons, maximum range. Task two missiles for the smaller contact and three each for the larger contacts, staggered launch, three-hundred-millisecond spread."

"Aye, sir. Firing solutions plotted and tasked to Talons one through eight. Time to weapons release... five minutes, three seconds," the weapons officer said after checking his display.

"How long to maximum range for the projectors?"

"At current rate of closure, twenty-six minutes... mark."

"Very good. Guns, you're clear for weapons release as soon as we cross our maximum effective range."

"Aye, sir. Weapons release at maximum effective range. Weapons release is authorized," the weapons officer replied in a well-practiced cadence.

"And ops, now would be a good time to launch our last Beckman with all the data we have for Icarus," Burns said.

"Beckman away. Transition in one hour, forty-six minutes. Out-system vector will take it tangentially away from our current course," Lieutenant Osbourne said from ops a few moments later.

Good. Hopefully we can keep our new friends here busy long enough for it to get away, Burns thought.

The next few minutes passed in near-total silence as every member of the bridge crew watched the countdown timer in the corner of the main viewscreen tick its way down to zero.

"Talon launch sequence initiated," the weapons officer called out. "All missiles away. Birds are burning hot and normal. Time to impact now... thirteen minutes, twenty seconds." The main display now showed eight inverted blue V-shaped markers representing the tracks of the Mk 12 "Talon II" anti-ship missiles, each containing a payload with a variable-yield fusion warhead. These particular missiles had had their yields set to the maximum fifty kilotons. The missile casings were a hardened graphene polyalloy that offered limited protection from point-defense laser fire and allowed the missile to penetrate all but the heaviest of ship hull armor, delivering its payload deep inside the unfortunate vessel before detonating.

Burns watched the timer on the plot slowly run down to just

over a minute before impact. "Tactical, stand by for post-strike battle damage assess—"

"Sir! All eight missiles have been destroyed!" the weapons officer called out suddenly, and Burns watched as the eight icons on the plot representing their missiles updated with a flashing amber *Signal Lost* symbol.

"Tactical, can you confirm?" Burns said.

"Yes, Captain. Missiles were destroyed simultaneously by what appears to be directed energy beams, unknown power output," Tomanaga confirmed.

"It had to have been significant to burn through the missiles' casings that quickly. Guns reload bow tubes one through six with Talons and seven and eight with the new Ares missiles."

"Uh... aye, sir," the weapons officer replied hesitantly. "Reload tubes one through six with Talons and seven and eight with Mk 26 Ares *orbit-to-surface* missiles." He said that last part with some added emphasis, the tone of his voice clearly indicating he thought his captain might have in fact lost his mind when he ordered ground attack ordnance to be loaded for a ship-to-ship engagement.

"Yes, guns, I am well aware of the Ares' intended application, but they're the smallest and fastest heavy-hitters we have in our inventory," Burns said. *And the lack of an advanced guidance system won't matter in a knife fight.*

"Sir, contacts are accelerating hard on an intercept course!" Tomanaga called out unnecessarily, as the whole bridge crew were able to see the tracks for the three contacts on the main viewscreen suddenly start closing the distance separating them from the *Appomattox* with alarming speed.

"Guns, what's the status on those missiles?" Burns said.

"Talons are loaded and are standing by, but the Ares missiles will be a few minutes yet," the weapons officer said, then added,

"The Ares are taking longer due to the antimatter warheads requiring additional handling precautions."

Burns watched the tactical plot as the three ships closed in on them, and a plan began to form in his head. "Guns, I want a simultaneous release of our Talons with the first salvo from our projectors as the lead ship in their formation closes to within laser range." Burns hoped that, if they were lucky, the backscatter and high-energy particles flying around would degrade the enemy's sensors, or they'd be too busy worrying about all the laser fire coming their way to focus on the missiles. "Task three Talons each for the frigate and destroyer—we'll save the Ares for that big bastard if needed," he finished.

"Aye, sir. Firing solutions tasked to weapons. Authorizing the targeting computer for weapons release." With such a high rate of closure between the *Appomattox* and the trio of ships bearing down on them, the ship's tactical computer would actually take the shot, as human reaction times were too slow.

"Registering an energy buildup along the forward surface of the frig—" Tomanaga's warning was cut short as a powerful laser blast slammed into the *Appomattox*, causing the deck to tremble beneath their feet as alarms began sounding around the bridge.

"We've been hit by a directed energy weapon," Lieutenant Osbourne called out over the din. "Petawatt-class infrared laser. Appears to have been a short burst from a single projector."

"Silence those alarms!" Burns said. "Ops, what's our status?"

"The beam burned through the ablatives like they weren't even there. Aegis plating took the brunt of it and shunted current to the supercaps before losing integrity. No pressure-hull breaches and minimal systems damage," Osbourne replied without looking away from his displays.

The *Gettysburg*-class destroyers were the first ships fitted with the newly designed Aegis armor system, which consisted of hardened graphene polyalloy plating layered with ablative materials. The plating itself had first-rate heat-dissipation properties, absorbed incoming directed energy weapons fire, and converted it into a useable electrical current, which was channeled to a series of supercapacitors that were tied into the ship's offensive and defensive weapons systems. The end result was an armor system that powered the ship's weaponry, in part, with energy expended by the enemy.

I get the feeling that was just a love tap to feel us out. The lights on the bridge dimmed slightly, and Burns heard the telltale hum of his ship's laser batteries opening fire with a nearly six-petawatt combined salvo from all eighteen forward projectors as the enemy frigate closed to within the 75,000-kilometer maximum effective range. At the same time, he saw icons for their six Talon missiles pop up on the main display.

"Forward laser batteries discharged. System recharging. Talons away," came the report from the weapons officer.

"Continue rolling fire from all forward projectors—we need to give our birds some cover. Tactical, do you have a damage assessment for me on our first salvo?"

"Negative impact," Tomanaga said.

"Say again?" Burns said, alarmed.

"Firing solutions were solid, but we didn't land a single hit from our entire salvo. The beams appear to have been... deflected away from the target somehow."

As he was given the grim news, Burns could see the enemy formation begin to separate. The largest of the ships and the frigate slowed their approach until they were holding at a steady 20,000 kilometers, while the destroyer moved in ahead of them.

"Incoming!" Tomanaga cried a split second before the *Appomattox* started getting pounded by laser fire from the destroyer, now just 5000 kilometers distant.

"Guns, where the hell are those Ares?"

"That first laser strike overloaded the power relays that supply the loading carriages. The system shut down to prevent damage and had to reboot. It's going to be a min—"

"Sir, that large contact is launching fighters!" Tomanaga said, somewhat incredulous.

"Fighters?" Burns said, confused as he looked at the tactical plot and saw what appeared to be two formations of twelve small fighter-like craft forming up in a defensive manner over the largest enemy ship. It took his mind a moment to come to the conclusion that those small craft were in fact fighters, as nothing like them—or a carrier, for that matter—were ever used in space combat that didn't take place deep in the gravity well of a planet... at least not unless they were desperate.

Yet there on the screen was what clearly appeared to be small fighter craft forming up over their mothership. Thankfully, the fighters were apparently content to sit back in a defensive role over their carrier, so he focused instead on the immediate threat. "Guns, what's the status on the mag cannon?" he said.

"Capacitor banks are charged and ready."

"Target that destroyer and let her have it!"

His ship was taking a beating; Burns followed the damage as it scrolled across his command console. The Aegis plating was doing an admirable job of keeping them in the fight but the repeated hits from the incredibly powerful enemy beams were taking a toll. One by one, they were losing the weapons blisters housing their forward and lateral laser projectors—the enemy destroyer was systematically pulling his ship's teeth out as it closed to within just 1000 kilometers.

Then the mag cannon fired.

An eight-ton cobalt-sintered tungsten slug was accelerated to over 30,000 meters per second by electromagnetic rails that ran nearly a third of the *Appomattox*'s 330-meter length. The results were nothing short of spectacular.

The round hit the destroyer just off her centerline on the port side, passing completely through the enemy ship and tearing her guts out from stem to stern. The friction of the hypersonic projectile ignited the atmosphere inside the vessel as it plowed through the interior bulkheads before exiting just forward of her stern on the starboard side. Burns watched in amazement as the ship that had just been pummeling them into submission broke apart and then disappeared in a violent, blinding explosion that washed out the video feeds momentarily.

"Holy fuck!" the weapons officer exclaimed in the silence that followed, then remembered where he was. "Sorry, sir."

Burns continued to look on in awe as the shattered remains of the destroyer drifted away from the area. "It's okay, guns. I think we all share that sentiment." His voice conveyed the awe he felt after witnessing the big cannon lay waste to an advanced enemy in a single hit.

"Reading high-energy gamma radiation... Sir, that was an antimatter explosion. I'd venture to guess they use it to power their ships and must have lost fuel containment when she started to break up," Tomanaga said.

A renewed and much more violent bombardment by the two remaining enemy ships interrupted the momentary triumph. Powerful laser beams lanced out, pummeling the *Appomattox* mercilessly. Alarms began sounding and the damage and casualty reports started flooding in.

"Helm, get our nose pointed away from those incoming beams and roll her to spread these hits out around the hull!" Burns bellowed over the cacophony of klaxons and weapons fire. He needed to keep the prow of the ship out of the direct line of fire in an attempt to protect both his forward missile tubes—and the Ares missiles nestled inside them—as well the mag cannon, the muzzle of which exited the bow of the ship slightly below her centerline now that the massive Aegis covers had been retracted to fire the weapon.

The *Appomattox's* bow dipped slightly as the helmsman began maneuvering to protect her one effective weapon system. Burns noted with grim satisfaction that the rate at which his ship was taking damage lessened somewhat as she started to roll, exposing her as yet unmarred starboard flank and ventral surface to the onslaught, but the maneuver would only buy them a minute or two at most before the Aegis plating in those areas began failing as well.

"Guns, what's the status on the cannon?" he asked, dreading the answer.

"Capacitors are at eighty-three percent and climbing rapidly."

"Already?" Burns said, astonished. To fully charge the weapon's capacitors under normal operations took nearly five minutes, and that was without battle damage or a constant stream of outgoing laser fire sapping current away from the mag cannon's charging system.

Osbourne chimed in from ops. "The Aegis plating is pumping so much current into the system that engineering is having a hard time keeping the power MUX from burning up. They've actually had to spin down reactors one and two a bit to keep the power system from overloading."

"Mag cannon capacitors at ninety-two percent. We'll be ready to fire again in less than twenty seconds," the weapons officer called out.

"Helm, adjust our roll rate so that we bring the cannon to bear on that big bastard the moment the capacitors are fully charged. Tactical, work up a firing solution for both the cannon and the Ares. Hit that carrier with everything we've got left. We need to end this!" Burns had been watching the two enemy ships close in on the *Appomattox* with their astonishing maneuverability until they were sitting just a hundred and fifty kilometers away, but instead of splitting up to hammer his ship from two different directions at once, the frigate and carrier remained in tight formation. He was hoping that they could knock out the carrier and either catch the frigate in the blast from the Ares missiles or that it would bug out when it suddenly found itself alone.

The fighters, on the other hand, were swarming around the human destroyer, peppering it with relatively ineffective small-bore plasma fire. The *Appomattox*'s point-defense laser and rail gun batteries opened up on the pesky ships and began swatting them out of space; apparently, they didn't have the same ability to deflect energy beams that the capital ships did.

"Sir, that carrier is showing a massive thermal buildup along her prow," Tomanaga said.

"Plasma." Commander Weatherly said the word with a cold certainty, and Burns knew in his gut she was correct.

"Ares away." The call came from the weapons officer at the same moment the mag cannon fired. The deck under their feet bucked, and the cannon round crossed the 150 kilometers separating the two vessels in under five seconds. Unfortunately, that five seconds was more than enough time for the carrier to unleash a massive plasma bolt at the human ship.

Burns watched in frustration as a red streak of plasma leaped from the big ship an instant before the frigate shifted her position, crossing in front of the carrier like a shield. The tungsten slug blasted right through the smaller ship, passing from port to starboard and sending it into an uncontrolled tumble as its power systems failed. The smaller vessel's sacrifice served its purpose, however, and the cannon round hit the carrier with greatly reduced force. Burns only had a moment to see that the carrier was venting atmosphere from a gaping hole in its prow, but it was still under power and maneuvering for another shot.

Then the plasma bolt hit, and the world around him shattered.

The *Appomattox* took the bolt amidships, as the helmsman still had her in a multi-axis spin to keep distributing incoming laser fire after their cannon shot. Anyone not wearing their restraints was thrown from their seat as a massive explosion ripped through the big destroyer, the plasma burning through the Aegis plating like a hot knife through butter. Anyone near the hit was atomized in an instant as the plasma tore through the heart of the ship.

"Report," Burns choked out through the acrid smoke of melted alloy and ruined electronics that had made its way in through the ventilation system before it sealed itself against the vacuum of space. "Osbourne?" Burns said after he received no answer. He turned toward the ops station and saw Commander Weatherly checking Osbourne's body, which was lying on the deck, his head twisted at an unnatural angle and streaming blood from a large gash where it had collided with the bulkhead next to his console when he had been thrown from his seat. She looked at the captain and shook her head, taking Osbourne's seat and beginning to call out the damage report.

"Plasma bolt hit along the port side, frames fifty-seven through sixty-nine. Those areas on charlie through foxtrot decks are gone, including CIC and most of main engineering. The reactors vented to space and shut down, and we're operating on local backup power only, as the hit took out most of our emergency cells and destroyed the power MUX. We're dead in the water."

"Tactical, what ever happened to our Ares?" Burns said.

"Unknown. The plasma hit knocked out all sensors and external feeds. I'm working on it," Tomanaga said, hands moving furiously as he tried to get his systems up and running again.

Burns mentally berated himself. How the hell had he allowed things to spin this far out of control? His ship was dying around him, and the responsibility lay directly at his feet. He searched his memory, desperately trying to dust off some long-forgotten bag of tricks that might help salvage the situation.

"Sir, damage-control parties reporting numerous fires throughout the ship. With no power, they're unable to vent those compartments and are being forced to fight the fires manually with handheld chemical extinguishers. One of them is nearing the forward magazine," Weatherly said.

Another series of explosions shook the deck under his feet, and the screeching of tortured metal reverberated throughout the bridge. Burns knew his ship was in its death throes, and he ordered the only option left open to him. "Abandon ship," he said, his voice projecting a calm authority despite the self-doubt raging within him.

As the evacuation alarm started blaring, Burns brought up on his command console a series of screens known only to him and his senior officers. He began typing in command prompts that would purge the main computer's database and remove the safety interlocks on a series of scuttling charges built into key structural components throughout the ship. The *Appomattox* was not only one of the newest and most advanced warships in the fleet, but her databases contained highly detailed information on human colony planets, technology, and worst of all, the nav data for Gateway station and therefore the Kerner system and Icarus. As his bridge crew made their way to the escape pods, he did what he could to ensure the enemy wouldn't be able to salvage anything of use from his ship.

Just as he was finishing his last series of commands to set the delay timer for the scuttling charges, Weatherly started to cry out a warning, but she would never finish it. A tremendous explosion ripped the human destroyer apart from the inside as the fires raging through her lower decks reached the forward magazine, resulting in a containment breach on the antimatter warheads of the three remaining Ares missiles stored there. In the blink of an eye, 330 meters of starship was turned into a rapidly expanding cloud of debris, taking all but eighty-three of her nearly nine hundred crew with her.

———

SEVERAL HUNDRED THOUSAND KILOMETERS DISTANT, the *Appomattox*'s last Beckman drone recorded the battle—culminating in the death of its mothership—with the uncaring stoicism of a machine as it raced toward its out-system jump point and rendezvous with Gateway station to deliver its critical data.

The drone energized its warp field emitters. As the fields began to form around the sleek piece of hardware, the drone registered several pings from escape pod emergency beacons. Then it transitioned out of the system.

CHAPTER THIRTEEN

RETURN RECEIPT

A SHARP SERIES OF KNOCKS RANG OUT FROM THE DOOR TO HENRY'S tiny, out-of-the-way office buried in the depths of Icarus Station. The once-proud titan of industry looked up from the technical report he had been reading on a tablet and scowled. What the hell did they want now?

"It's open," he called out a little more harshly than he intended to, and tossed the report casually onto a stack of similarly discarded devices to one side of his desk. The door opened, revealing the haggard face of Commander Matthew Evans.

"Emergency meeting with the top brass"—Evans's face scrunched up in disgust as the god-awful smell of the trash pit Henry called an office hit his nose—"and Garland said to drag you kicking and screaming if I have to," he said, forgoing the usual social niceties.

The look on Evans's face and the urgent tone in his voice killed the sardonic comment on the tip of Henry's tongue, and he went from annoyed at the intrusion to equal parts concerned and intrigued. As far as he knew, everything was business as usual, but he hadn't exactly been kept in the loop on things. A situation, he had to admit, he had no one to blame for but himself.

"What's up, Matt?" he asked, pushing his chair back from the desk and rising to his feet. He winced slightly as he stood, partly from the raging headache, but mostly because he realized the previous night's half-empty bottle sat in full view on one corner of his desk.

"It's big, Henry. I can't say more here," Evans said as he crossed the office on his way toward the small closet on the far bulkhead, stepping over and around the various piles of junk the part-time genius, full-time drunk had accrued over the many months since the last time he bothered to clean up. He opened the closet door, pulled out the cleanest-looking shirt and pants from the rack, inspected them briefly in the dim light, and then tossed them to the shame-faced Henry.

"Matt, I…" Henry trailed off, not sure what he had been about to say.

"Put these on, Henry, and for God's sake, brush your teeth and shave that animal off your face—you look like a fucking hobo and smell even worse. I'll be out in the hall. You've got five minutes." With that, he stepped out of the office, turning the lights up to their full brightness on the way out, and shut the door a little harder—and a little louder—than needed.

Henry looked at the clothes in his arms, then around at his disaster of an office/quarters, and for the hundredth time in the last week, he felt a wave of shame wash over him for how far he had let himself fall.

Five minutes later to the second, Evans opened the office door to find a still very hungover but at least semi-respectable-looking Henry Hutchins attempting to put the finishing touches on his necktie in front of the small basin and mirror opposite the desk—and failing miserably. Evans helped him get the knot squared away and then softened his expression slightly now that Henry was at least passably dressed. Henry reached for his comms unit and datapad on the desk, but Evans stopped him.

"No personal electronics this time, Henry," Evans said, holding up a hand to stop him. Everything you need will be provided once we reach the briefing room." Henry arched an eyebrow in surprise. No comms unit meant this was a top-secret briefing, and he hadn't been invited to one of those in years. Something big must have happened for Garland to call him in on a classified briefing.

Evans guided his charge quickly through a series of hallways and lifts until they found themselves in front of a pair of marine guards standing sentry in front of the lift that would take them to the command level of Icarus Station. The two men presented their credentials, which were checked against a list of personnel authorized for entry, and were then required to pass retina and DNA scans before the lift doors behind the marines parted with a soft chime. They stepped in and were quickly whisked to the most secure level of the station, which housed the senior staff and operations center and was buried in the deepest part of the massive space station.

When the doors parted again, another pair of guards repeated the security check. After a short walk and a third round of security, the two men finally found themselves seated around a plain composite conference table surrounded by some of the most senior leadership in the Confed command hierarchy. The tablet that had been placed on the table in front of him was locked, so he spent the next few minutes sipping a steaming cup of coffee Evans had handed him and trying to will his hangover away.

The door to the briefing room opened again, and everyone stood as Admiral Robert Garland strode in, accompanied by a man Henry did not recognize, though the authoritative air, severe expression, and eyes that seemed to miss nothing fairly screamed "Intel Division" to Henry.

"As you were," Garland said, gesturing for everyone to be seated. He took his place at the head of the table and looked around the room, pausing a bit longer as he made eye contact with Henry. He entered his credentials into the small terminal embedded in the table in front of him, and the data tablets in front of everyone came to life. Henry reached for his instinctively and saw the standard top-secret confidentiality notice displayed on the screen. He knew the tablet would follow his eye movements to ensure he read the entirety of the notice, so he started reading as the admiral began his briefing.

"At approximately 0430 zulu this morning, a Beckman drone from CTS *Appomattox* transitioned in near Gateway. After being retrieved and scrubbed, the data was rushed to us on a fast packet ship. The data has been thoroughly vetted by fleet intel and CID." Garland paused for a moment to make sure he had everyone's full attention. "There's no easy way to say this… The *Appomattox* was destroyed while engaged in combat with three vessels of unknown origin in the Vostok system."

A shocked murmur ran through the room, and Henry suddenly found himself wishing he hadn't drunk himself to sleep last night. He struggled to get his mind to focus as data started populating his tablet. Could the Sino-Russians really have engaged and destroyed a *Gettysburg*-class destroyer? And for what? They were still nominally a part of the Confed, so why attack a CTS warship?

"Most of you are unaware of the nature of the *Appomattox*'s mission to the Vostok system, and what you are about to hear is known only to the highest members of Confed military and civilian leadership," Garland continued. "Four weeks ago, Confed Intelligence Division intercepted several reports claiming unknown ships had been spotted around the periphery of the Vostok system.

"You'll remember Vostok escaped the Alarian War unscathed, as did much of Sino-Russian Federation space, due in large part, we believe, to their location on the far side of settled Terran space from the Alarians. SRF infrastructure survived the war in much better shape than most of the Confed enclaves, with the exception of Sixth Fleet, which was in the Sol system for joint exercises when the shooting started and was nearly wiped out over Earth during the war. Vostok was in regular communication with other SRF systems—up until four weeks ago, at least. I say *was* because less than thirty hours after those messages about strange ships left Vostok, the entire system went radio silent.

"Adding to the mystery was the sudden silencing of a half dozen other SRF systems, all of which had been in comms with Vostok less than one week prior to the blackout. The *Appomattox* was dispatched on a sneak-and-peek mission to surveil the Vostok system and determine what had caused them to go dark.

"Major Ayoob is here to brief you on the summary findings of the *Appomattox* leading up to her engaging this unknown enemy. Major." Garland nodded to the man Henry had correctly flagged as an intel officer and stepped aside. The major rose and took up a place next to the large display panel on one wall. After entering his credentials and organizing the display to his liking, he began his briefing on the *Appomattox*'s findings of complete devastation of the Vostok system's population and infrastructure.

Not five minutes into the briefing, Henry had pegged the intel officer as the boring, no-frills, facts-not-conjecture type, and he promptly tuned out most of what the man was saying. He pulled up the raw data on the tablet he had been given at the start of the briefing, quickly scanning through various appended summary files, and lost himself in the mountain of information while the briefing droned on around him.

An hour later, Henry had long since forgotten about his hangover and was now struggling to organize and analyze all the information he'd been given regarding the devastation on Gagarin and destruction of human constructs throughout the Vostok system. Ever the scientist and inventor, Henry worked overtime to process everything, including the revelation that somebody out there had managed to come up with a workable system for employing plasma in both small arms and ship-based weapons systems.

He himself had played with the idea until the various hurdles involved with forming a volume of plasma into a projectile proved too difficult to solve with humanity's current level of technology. The magnetic fields required to contain the plasma were the limiting factor, and there wasn't a Terran or Alarian who had the capability to overcome that problem... at least as far as he knew.

While Henry was still mulling over the implications of the scientific breakthroughs this unknown enemy had made in order to create such a devastating weapon, Major Ayoob once again took his place at the table as Admiral Garland took over the wall display and began briefing the room on the *Appomattox*'s engagement with the enemy, beginning with when she left orbit after her first Beckman mysteriously disappeared. Garland was several minutes into his portion of the briefing when something he said snapped Henry's focus back to the wall display.

"... recorded a maximum acceleration of over fifteen hundred standard gravities while still oriented bow-on to the *Appomattox*. The *Appomattox* was burning hard toward the threat, and it's assumed that Captain Burns considered a high-speed pass to be his best option to gather information while limiting engagement time with an enemy of unknown capability," the admiral was saying. "It's what I would have done in his shoes. Unfortunately for Captain Burns, he could not have known the enemy vessels would be able to match his course and speed seemingly without breaking a sweat."

Everyone in the room had their eyes riveted on the display as Admiral Garland continued to narrate the events as they unfolded, pausing briefly to explain that the Beckman's sensor package was operating in passive mode only as it tried to make its escape from the system, and therefore they had limited data on the actual battle. There were muted cheers and satisfied looks on the faces of everyone present when the enemy destroyer exploded. And again when the second mag cannon round knocked out the frigate and damaged the carrier. But those same faces soon reflected horror as a massive ball of plasma tore into the *Appomattox* amidships and she tumbled uncontrolled through space. The blinding flash of light the Beckman picked up when the two Ares missiles struck home on the big carrier, destroying both it and its escort frigate, was a poor consolation prize when the *Appomattox* herself went up in a massive anti-matter explosion minutes later.

Garland stopped the playback after the *Appomattox*'s destruction and fixed the room with a somber stare. "The drone remained in-system for another sixty-three minutes before transitioning out, and the only other thing it picked up was the pinging of emergency beacons from four of the *Appomattox*'s life-pods. I'll open it up to questions now," he finished, looking around the room at the ashen faces of his senior staff. Henry was the first to speak up.

"I'm assuming we'll be launching a rescue mission," he stated matter-of-factly. "I need to go with them."

The whole room stared in disbelief at the once-great-man-turned-drunken-joke as he skipped right over expressing his horror or offering constructive comments, instead immediately lobbying for a chance to go check out some new tech.

"Hank," Garland growled dangerously, his face turning red with anger. "We just lost a—"

"Bob, we are outclassed in almost every way by this new threat," Henry cut him off. "You saw it for yourself. The *Appomattox* got incredibly lucky to take out all three of those ships, and you know it. These guys clearly had the ability to sit back at a distance and wipe her out without taking a single hit, yet they closed to within knife-fighting range. Why? Judging by the fact that they were systematically pulling the *Appomattox*'s teeth out, I can only assume they were trying to capture her. Fortunately for Burns, they either didn't know about the mag cannon or didn't consider it to be a threat—they were overconfident, and it came back to bite them in the ass.

"I know what you and everyone else on this station think of me, but the fact of the matter is I'm still the best and brightest scientific mind you have—even when I'm half in the bag. We don't have time to sit around and ask questions or talk tactics. We need to mobilize a task force to get out to Vostok as fast as possible to rescue our spacers and recover as much of the debris as we can for study. The Beckman didn't bring us shit for useful data—I've been scanning through it for the last fifteen minutes. We need to get out there and we need to do it last week, dammit! Sitting here and trying to parse through passive sensor data from the drone is a pointless exercise." Henry was standing by the end of his little speech, hands balled into fists by his side.

The shame from earlier had morphed into anger, and he was directing that anger straight at the man who had once been his friend. His drunkenness and self-loathing had driven a wedge between the two men to the point where they hadn't spoken in months, and that last conversation had ended with Henry taking a swing at the admiral and then being dragged off to the brig to cool his heels. After that, Garland had assigned Commander Evans as a go-between/babysitter for Henry.

Evans put a firm hand on Henry's shoulder, trying to get him to calm down and retake his seat at the table, but Henry would not be moved. He stared at Garland, waiting for an answer as the rest of the room sat in uncomfortable silence. Garland stared daggers back at Henry for a moment longer before softening his expression slightly.

"You're right, Hank," he said. "Now is neither the time nor the place to reopen old wounds between us, but you're right and we need to move ASAP. You're also right in that you're the best scientific mind on the station, and it's for exactly that reason that you are staying here and Commander Evans is going to be by your side around the clock until the task force returns. We absolutely cannot afford to lose you." Henry started to object, but Garland cut him off. "No, Hank, my word on this is final."

After slamming the door in Henry's face, the admiral turned back to the room. "Major Ayoob will see that you all get copies of the data. I want you bringing your best people in on this, and I want initial reports no later than 0900 tomorrow. I've already got fleet ops assembling a task force to secure Vostok, and they'll be moving out by the end of the day tomorrow. Get after it, people. Dismissed."

The room emptied rapidly as people rushed off to their assigned sections to start analyzing the data in greater detail and formulating tactics and strategies to combat this new threat. Henry remained, eyes fixed on Garland until the admiral had finished issuing orders to his aide and was standing opposite Henry across the table.

"I need to be on one of those ships, Bob," Henry stated flatly.

"Hank, you know damn well that I can't let you go. Despite the black hole you've let yourself get sucked into, you're far too valuable an asset to lose," Garland retorted.

"So that's all I am to you now? An asset? We were friends once, Bob. Please, let me go. I *need* this." Garland rocked back slightly, clearly caught off guard by the desperation in Henry's voice. A part of Henry's mind hoped that being on a ship traveling into a likely dangerous situation to recover and dissect new technology might just reawaken the untouchable titan of industry he'd once been, and he latched onto that possibility like a drowning man grasping for a lifeline.

"I'm sorry, Hank," Garland said, and his expression showed he was suffering almost as much as his old friend by denying his request. "I can't."

With that, the admiral turned and walked out of the room. Henry stood there a few moments longer, shoulders slumped in absolute defeat, emotionally drained and unable to move. Evans gently guided him from the conference room and back through the maze of corridors and lifts to his little office in the bowels of Icarus Station, but he went through the motions mechanically. The two men walked the entire way in silence, the only words spoken by Evans as he passed acquaintances.

By the time they reached the office, Henry was barely keeping it together. Too many things around him served as stark reminders of all he had lost over the years. In fact, that was one of the main reasons he hadn't bothered to get a ride back to the farm on Earth when it became clear that neither side had the will or capability to continue the war—it was too painful a reminder of his lost family.

Back in the days immediately after the war, Henry had made the mistake of clinging to hope—hope that, just maybe, Ben had made it out of Grayling before the bombs fell. He had immersed himself in his work in an attempt to focus his mind while Garland had an entire intel section combing through the data to find some sign of Ben, but it had all been for naught. The chaos of the attack and societal collapse in the immediate aftermath meant no information on Ben ever surfaced.

When days turned to weeks, then to months, without any shred of evidence that Ben had made it, Henry had finally accepted the thing he had fought so hard to prove wrong: Ben had been killed in the blast that leveled Camp Grayling. At first, Henry contemplated retiring to the farm and living out the rest of his days there, but eventually, the idea of going back to Earth had withered and died, much like his friendships and career. Now, all he wanted to do was crawl into a dark hole and disappear. He pushed the door to his office open with one hand and walked into the small room, stopping in the center and looking around without actually seeing anything.

"Henry, I need to run upstairs for a bit to take care of a few things. Are you going to be alright? Is there anything I can bring you?" Evans asked in a soft tone, as if Henry might snap at any minute. Henry gave no response for a moment until finally seeming to get his bearings, and he moved to sit behind his desk.

"No, thank you, Matt. I'll—" He froze mid-sentence when he saw the message that was flashing on his personal tablet. The same tablet he had carried here all the way from Isadore four years ago. The same tablet he had used to record a message and send it via quantum link to his lab back at the farm.

He stared, rooted in place and unable to move as he read the wording of the short notification on the screen over and over again.

"Henry?" Evans asked. Henry jumped and spun around as if he'd just been electrocuted.

"He's alive," he whispered as if saying it aloud would make the thing untrue.

CHAPTER FOURTEEN

AN OLD ENEMY

HENRY RAN THROUGH THE CORRIDORS OF ICARUS LIKE A MAN possessed. He clutched his tablet in both hands, as if it were the most precious thing in the known universe.

The message flashing on the screen when he returned to the office was a *message delivered* notification: a message he had recorded and transmitted four years ago, shortly before Alarian weapons fire began raining down all around him, had been opened by its intended recipient. When Ben had stumbled across the lab back at the farm, his activating the system and watching the vid file generated a return receipt that was transmitted along with a picture of the user who had accessed the file.

When Henry opened the return receipt with shaking hands, a lean and fit man with a blood-stained rag wrapped around his hand stared back at him. There was a faint scar over his right eyebrow, and his face was older and had a month's worth of beard growth, but there was no question that it was Ben.

The return receipt had come in just minutes after he and Evans had left for the briefing, and by the time they returned and found the message, Ben was no longer in the lab. Henry had docked his tablet with the quantum link module immediately, but its connection to his lab had shown the room was dark and nobody was present. As soon as he got over the shock of the moment, he had bolted from the office without a word to Evans and was now headed for the ops center to share the news with Admiral Garland.

With Evans a few seconds behind and screaming for him to stop, Henry entered the lift and slapped the button that would take him to the command decks, ignoring Evans's shouts of protest as the doors slid closed. He then did something he had not tried in a long time: he used his implant to open a comms channel directly to Garland's personal comms unit. It took a moment, as he had to bypass the security the admiral had put in place, but by the time the soft chime emanated from the lift to announce his arrival at the station's command level, a familiar voice filled his head.

"Henry? How the hell did you get access to my personal comms?" In one corner of his vision, Henry's implant projected the incredulous face of Admiral Garland.

"I designed the entire system, in case you forgot," Henry said, breathing hard. "Bob, listen to me. I need you to call down to the marines and grant me access to the ops level. Something has come up that we absolutely have to discuss."

Garland sighed heavily. "Hank, why are you doing this to yourself? You know my word on Vostok is fin—"

"Ben's alive!" Henry practically shouted as he rounded the last corner before the security checkpoint and lift that would take him to the ops level. He took no notice of the stares and startled shouts from people he ran past or, in some cases, over in his haste to get to the ops level.

There was a long pause as Garland stared straight at him, brow furrowed in confusion as his mind processed the out-of-place statement. Then his expression changed to one of pained sorrow. Henry had seen the same look on Evans's face a few minutes prior; a look that said Garland felt he had finally suffered the mental break everyone assumed was coming sooner or later.

"Hank, Ben is gone. Why are you doing this to yourself—" Garland broke off as the image of grown-up Ben with a bloody rag wrapped around his hand appeared on his comms unit's small display.

"That image was waiting with a return receipt on my personal tablet when I got back to my office from the briefing. It was generated in response to the first viewing of a datafile I recorded and transmitted via Q-link to my lab at the farm while the Alarians were leveling Isadore. It took four years, but Ben finally got the message. I don't know how he's alive, but there's the proof." Henry had stopped a half dozen paces away from the pair of stern-looking sentries who were now watching him like a hawk.

Garland took a few more seconds to process everything before finally speaking. "Standby," was all he said before the line went dead.

For a moment, Henry was worried the admiral wouldn't believe his story, but then one of the guards reached into his pocket and pulled out his comms unit, which was chirping with an incoming call. He answered it and listened for a moment, then nodded and said, "Yes, sir." Looking at his partner, he shrugged and gestured toward Henry. "Admiral says to give him access to ops." He then motioned Henry forward, and for the second time that day, Henry went through the motions of confirming his identity and riding the secure lift up to the ops level.

Garland was waiting for him when the lift doors finally

parted, and Henry was surprised to see Major Ayoob standing next to him.

"This better not be a fucking joke, Hank," the admiral said threateningly.

"It's not, Bob. I swear."

"Because if it is and you're dangling Ben and Blackthorn in front of me because of what the *Appomattox* found on Gagarin in order to secure a ride out there, you're going to find yourself in a world of hurt."

Henry just looked at him, baffled, trying to figure out what Garland meant. "What does Gagarin have to do with Ben?" he said.

"I thought maybe with all the odd cyber activity reported from Gagarin you might try to use Blackthorn as leverage to go with the task force," Garland said, clearly suspicious of Henry's motives.

"Bob, I have absolutely no idea what you're talking about. Swear to God," Henry said, now thoroughly confused. "What cyber activity? I thought Gagarin was razed by plasma weapons during the attack."

"You claim to have no knowledge of the fact that every networked technological device on the entire planet had its memory wiped or corrupted beyond retrieval or that the only survivors on the planet were people who had not been connected to the planetary datanet during the attack?" Major Ayoob entered the conversation, suspicion clouding his face. "It was all in the report you were given during the briefing."

"I didn't have time to dig into the details during the briefing," Henry said. "If I'm honest, after you brought up plasma weapons, I didn't pay attention to much after that. This changes everything," Henry said, his mind now working furiously to dig long-dormant information out of his memory.

"I think it's time we take this somewhere a little more private, gentleman," Garland said, motioning them down the hall and toward his office. The three men began walking, but Henry's mind was spinning as it tried to categorize and piece this new information into what he already knew. Garland shut and locked the door as they entered his office, then sat behind his desk and motioned for the other two men to sit in the open chairs opposite him.

"Major, would you please give Mr. Hutchins a recap of the *Appomattox*'s findings regarding the cyber situation on Gagarin after the attack?" the admiral said.

"Certainly," Ayoob replied, and if he was annoyed at having to repeat the information to Henry, he didn't show it. "The short version is this: the *Appomattox* couldn't find any intact data-storage devices in the Vostok system that had been connected to the planetary datanet at the time of the attack. Not a single one. There was absolutely no digital record of the attack ever happening. No archived video or written communication, no still images, no database records or news reports. Absolutely nothing. The crew investigating from the *Appomattox* only found a relative handful of survivors, and to an individual, they had all been out of contact with the datanet when the attack occurred. It's theorized that the attacking force used personal comms nodes to locate and round up stragglers after they destroyed the major cities and settlements..."

A chill crept up Henry's spine as he listened to Major Ayoob continue to lay out what they knew of the cyber situation on Gagarin after the attack. Could this be the same construct that had wreaked havoc on them back during the war?

"My God..." he said in a low voice. "It's back."

"Pardon?" Ayoob asked.

Henry looked to Garland. "How much does the major here know about Blackthorn?"

"I believe he was read in on it back before the war, though I'm not sure exactly how familiar he still is with the project," Garland said, turning to Ayoob with a questioning look.

"An advanced AI project, I believe. Something to do with blending a human mind with an artificial one, or something to that effect?"

"Close enough for now," Henry said quickly. "But are you aware of what the project's origins were?"

"Just that your wife was heading up the precursor team before her…" He trailed off for a moment as he searched for the right words. "Untimely death," he finished, looking uncomfortable.

"She was *murdered*," Henry snarled, "by an advanced cyber construct. The same one that played us against the Alarians before and during the war, the same one that played hell with both sides' technical infrastructure to ensure the greatest possible losses, and the same one that infected Gagarin and wiped all evidence of the attack from their cyber infrastructure. I'd bet my life on it."

"Interesting," Ayoob said, steepling his hands in thought. "So you believe there is a third party involved that somehow instigated the conflict between us and the Alarians?"

"Yes." The conviction in Henry's voice was absolute. "The whole thing never made any sense," he continued. "The Alarians are not a race given to the utterly reckless action they took four years ago by launching a full-scale assault on our three most heavily defended systems. They aren't that aggressive of a species, and they wouldn't normally take action that would result in the near-complete destruction of their fleet—not after having survived a devastating war with a neighboring race by the skin of their teeth once already.

"Don't you find it just a little too convenient that both we *and* the Alarians were left almost completely defenseless after a war so brutally efficient that it only lasted a few weeks? And what about all the odd cybersabotage that occurred on both sides? We had installations that were completely isolated from the datanet suffer catastrophic failures of critical infrastructure—"

"Hank, there has never been any solid evidence to suggest those events were anything more than advanced cyberwarfare by the Alarians," Garland stepped in, repeating something the two men had argued about more than a few times both during and after the war, "and I just don't see the connection here."

Henry stood up and walked to the wall display. He pulled his tablet out and put up a collection of images showing the unknown enemy ships. "There's your evidence, Bob, unless the Alarians have managed to design and build at least three completely new classes of ships that don't share any design methodology with their predecessors *and* have made a quantum leap forward in propulsion and weapons technology.

"I don't know why these guys took this long to get directly involved. Or maybe they have before and we just never knew it —their technology is obviously much more advanced than ours. Haven't we had reports of planets going dark for a while now? It's a pretty damn big coincidence that Gagarin went dark in the same manner and these guys just happened to be hanging out in the neighborhood.

"You saw the data with your own eyes. You know we got lucky that the *Appomattox* was able to knock all three of them out. She was the most advanced fleet warship they had ever come across, and I'm betting they were caught off guard when their weapons didn't immediately turn her into swiss cheese thanks to the new armor. They underestimated her, and it allowed Burns to land a couple of haymakers. Think about it."

Both the admiral and the intelligence officer sat quietly for a few moments, contemplating what Henry had just said. "Maybe…" Garland said, not entirely convinced.

"I believe Mr. Hutchins makes a persuasive argument," Ayoob said, surprising Henry. "Perhaps it is because I am approaching this topic with relatively fresh eyes, but I believe we must at least take the possibility into account. An advanced cyber construct working behind the scenes does fill in a lot of gaps in what we know of both the war as well as events that have taken place since. I must admit to being confused as to why the news that your son being alive, happy though it is, is germane to this conversation, however," he finished, looking back and forth from Henry to the admiral.

"Ben was—is—the key to making Blackthorn work," Henry said, catching himself using the past tense. "Blackthorn was designed to operate both in the ether and the real world. It's not just a piece of hardware or software that can be employed to blow up bad guys or root out malicious code. It's the blending of an AI with the creativity of the human mind to augment the capabilities of both the warfighter and our AIs. This is an extremely simplistic explanation for the sake of time," Henry explained. "But pairing a human mind with an artificial intelligence is a tricky thing, and Ben's brain was tailored to work in conjunction with an advanced AI—designed largely by my wife—through the use of a specialized neural implant. We manipulated his environment through holosims and a custom educational curriculum to help his brain develop in the way we were looking for." Henry watched Ayoob's face for any sign the intel officer was passing judgement over the fact that he had manipulated his son's mental development for a secret project, but the major's face remained unreadable.

"Ben is important because we can't make the system work without him. He was our prototype, and I had hoped to use what we learned from him to create a system that allowed us to use adult volunteers," Henry said. "We now know Ben is still alive, and we can use him to combat the construct that is still clearly working against us."

"Okay, Hank, you've convinced me," the admiral said. "At least enough to consider the possibility. We thought we were dealing with an advanced form of Alarian cyberwarfare before—something that was reinforced for me when it seemed to have disappeared after the dust settled—but I think we have to treat the situation as though the Alarians weren't responsible and this construct has simply been lying low for the past few years."

Henry had tried for so long to convince his friend that they had been dealing with something other than Alarian malcode, and to finally have Garland on his side lifted a burden from his shoulders he had forgotten was there.

"I'll need to take a team to retrieve Ben and see if there is anything we can salvage from Grayling," Henry said. "We know the main entrance to the facility was destroyed in the blast that leveled the main complex, but the secondary entrance looked intact the last time I saw aerial images of the base."

"Whoa there, Hank," Garland said, putting his hand out as if he was trying to physically stop his friend's train of thought. "I still can't let you leave the station. Not with everything else that's going on."

"But we need to get Ben off of Earth as quickly as possible and try to salvage what we can from the lab at Grayling," Henry protested. "Now that we know the construct is still infecting Terran datanets—" Henry froze mid-sentence as a realization hit him like a mag cannon round. He frantically swiped at his tablet and put the image of Ben up on the wall display, zooming in on an object behind him and still sitting on the lift that had taken him down to the lab.

"No…" he said. "No, no, no, no, no!"

"Henry? What's the matter?" Garland asked with alarm.

"That's the farm's tractor," Henry said, pointing at the tractor sitting on the lift behind Ben. "It's a GenAg 4130." He turned to look at the two officers, feeling like his guts were being sucked into a black hole. "Ben must have had it parked in the shop when he discovered the lab, and that's why it's in the shot: it was parked on the area of the shop floor that doubles as a hidden lift down to my lab.

"Yeah, so?" Garland said, not understanding why a tractor was so horrifying.

"The General Agriculture model 4130 has both external and internal cameras and microphones used for its autonomous operation capability, and it automatically uploads its data to a cloud-based server when in use," Henry said, as if that explained everything. Seeing the confusion still written on the two men's faces, he turned back to the screen and zoomed the image in on the cab's interior. "The construct is still present in Earth's datanet, but it would never have been able to get access to my lab before because the network there is completely isolated except for the quantum link to my personal tablet."

Henry zoomed in further and pointed to a faint red glow in the upper left-hand corner of the 4130's dash. "That tractor was recording everything in the lab while it was there. It would have seen and heard the message I recorded for Ben, detailing every-thing about Blackthorn and what I knew of the construct, and that information would have been uploaded as soon as Ben returned to the surface and the 4130 reconnected to the datanet." He turned back to the two men and saw understanding dawn on both of their faces.

"We have to assume the construct now knows we are aware of its existence and that Ben is a threat. They'll be coming for him now." Henry's eyes welled with tears as his emotions finally began finding cracks in the mental armor he had put in place years ago. "Bob, we have to save him. Please! I just got him back!" The desperation in Henry's voice was bordering on manic.

Garland looked from Henry to the image on the display and back again. Finally, he nodded. "Done. I'll have a team put together for immediate deployment. We won't let these bastards win again."

CHAPTER FIFTEEN

UNINVITED GUESTS

BEN WOKE WITH A START, HIS HAND REACHING INSTINCTIVELY FOR the pistol resting on the nightstand. He took a moment to figure out just what had alerted his unconscious mind but couldn't immediately identify it. Then he felt it more than heard it: a deep, subsonic thrumming that made the hair on the back of his neck stand up. He had never experienced anything like it before, and his fight-or-flight response—finely honed after years of living in a near-lawless society—went into overdrive.

Springing out of bed, he quickly donned the dark-colored clothing that was laid out nearby for just such an occasion. After dressing and lacing up his boots, he strapped on the hardshell armor and chest rig before grabbing his modified M37 from its place near the door. Jim had procured the weapon along with some other hard-to-find gear by bartering with the grunts stationed at the newly established Civilian Defense Force post in town, and Ben had spent the last several months tuning his rig until everything on his rifle and armor worked together organically and wasn't just a random collection of kit haphazardly slapped together.

The CDF was essentially a militarized police force, not unlike the old Army National Guard, but solely tasked with domestic law enforcement after the complete collapse of Earth's economy and governmental powers in the wake of the Alarian War. The NAC powers-that-be created the new military branch after it became clear that local and state law enforcement entities were simply not up to the monumental task of maintaining law and order. While the NAC government had managed to cobble together a functional system again after months of chaos following the destruction of its seat of power, it had taken years just to fully reestablish firm control over what was left of the major metropolitan areas. Most of the more rural areas had been left to fend for themselves, and only in the last six months had the CDF finally been deployed to the more outlying areas to bring them back into the fold—a task that was easier said than done, in many cases.

The two men had found the CDF troopers to be an excellent source of both information and difficult-to-find items ranging from weapons and armor to parts for the equipment they used around the farm. After befriending the garrison's supply officer, Jim traded the wine and booze he and Ben had been making for some much-needed supplies.

Ben checked to ensure the rifle's magazine was fully seated and a round was in the chamber, verified the safety was on, then grabbed the combat helmet—another of Jim's CDF pickups—off the rack on his way out the door. He made his way quickly to the library at the end of the hall, where he found Jim already geared up and looking out the window through his helmet's built-in night-vision imagers.

"What is it?" Ben asked in a low whisper.

"No idea. Check the other windows."

Once Jim had finally opened up about his past, Ben hadn't been at all surprised to learn that the older man had been a member of the NAC Marine Corps. What did surprise him was that the old warrior had been handpicked to be a first-generation SEAR, and the man who Ben now considered his closest friend had helped set the standards by which all special operations outfits were measured. His senses had been honed to a razor's sharpness by years of combat, and Ben had never yet witnessed a situation that the old warrior was not immediately in control of. So when Ben heard the man say he had no idea what was happening, the first icy trickle of fear began creeping up his spine.

"Nothing!" Ben whispered as he finished checking the windows on his side of the room, his voice taking on a growing sense of alarm.

"I've got something," Jim said.

Ben checked out his window one last time before crossing the room to join Jim off to the side of the large picture window overlooking the lake. "What've you got?" he asked.

"Go to long-wave IR," Jim said. Ben did as he was told, and the world around him changed slightly as his goggles showed him a composite image of both visible light amplification as well as the thermal imaging region of the infrared spectrum.

That was when he saw it: working slowly through the hills to the west of the lake was an angular object that couldn't be seen in the visible spectrum.

"Got it," he said. "Looks like some type of stealthed dropship, but I don't recognize the configuration. Hard to tell exactly what it is, though—can't get a clear image."

"You're not seeing the ship itself. Your IR is picking up the thermal transfer to the air surrounding the ship. If it wasn't such a cold night, I'd bet you wouldn't see a thing. Design is vaguely Alarian with those four stubby, articulated wings and no vertical stabilizer, but I have no idea what they're using for propulsion. Those blobs on the end of the wings seem to be able to be used for vectored thrust like a conventional jet engine or MPD, except there's no thermal bloom from them."

"Why would the Alarians be here?" Ben asked, confused. Nothing about this made sense, unless..." This isn't a coincidence," he said, now absolutely sure why an unknown dropship was slinking along in stealth nearby. "It has to be related to that vid file I found a couple days ago."

"I think you're right," Jim said without turning his gaze away from the strange craft. "The design cues look a little like an Alarian dropship, but I think this is something else entirely—possibly the other player your dad hinted at." The two men watched the craft skim the treetops for a few more seconds until it became clear it was heading for the farm. "I don't like this, Ben," Jim said. "No matter who is in that dropship, we don't have the firepower to deal with them—we're bugging out. I'll prep the welcome mat. You grab the gear."

Ben stared back at Jim for several seconds as the reality of the situation slowly dawned on him. They were abandoning the house—*his* house—because, once again, he was caught up in something he didn't fully understand. No, scratch that; he was *still* caught up in the same thing. The last few years had simply been a pause in the action.

He and Jim had regularly discussed, and even rehearsed, a number of contingency plans in case something terrible were to happen, but preparing for a worst-case event and actually having to execute that plan were two different things entirely. Ben knew what he had to do, but his body wasn't moving. This was *his* house; it wasn't easy to just abandon it. If they left under these circumstances, it was unlikely they would be able to return, and he knew that.

Jim noticed his reluctance to leave his childhood home and barked, "Now, Ben!" The authority in the old warrior's voice was absolute and jolted Ben into action. To his credit, he didn't argue. Instead, he moved with a practiced efficiency as he went about gathering the bug-out bags and other gear they would need once they abandoned the house.

Less than two minutes after leaving the library to gather their gear, Ben was rucked-up and waiting by the back door nearest to the woods as Jim made the final checks on the "welcome mat" he had rigged up with the help of his connections at the CDF. He typed one last series of commands into his small tablet computer, then stuffed it into the cargo pocket of his pants and grabbed his go-bag from Ben. "Ready?" he asked.

"Ready," Ben said, his voice wavering as he fought to control his fear.

As the ship approached the house and barns, the deep thrumming of the dropship had intensified to the point where Ben felt as if it was actually coming from within his bones. Jim pulled his tablet back out and opened a window showing a video feed from the cameras he had installed around the buildings, then waited as the dropship settled into a hover a good twenty meters over the paved area between the shop and main house. Ben looked on over Jim's shoulder as two teams of six black-clad humanoids—they definitely weren't human or Alarian—dropped from the belly of the craft. The troopers dropped like stones toward the unyielding concrete beneath them, and Ben watched, fascinated, as they slowed abruptly just before hitting the ground. They weren't fast-roping from the dropship, and he saw no telltale exhaust of armor-mounted thrusters. They just stopped and were gently deposited on the ground.

The dropship moved off and began circling the compound as soon as its assault teams were unloaded, and Jim watched, waiting for the right moment when the dropship was on the far side of the house so they could make their escape to the woods without being seen. Their moment came just as one of the teams approached the front door of the house. "Now!" Jim commanded in a harsh whisper.

Ben opened the door as quickly and quietly as he could before sprinting for the tree line a short distance away. Jim followed close behind, only slowing briefly to close the door, arming the back entrance's portion of the welcome mat in the process. Ben was only a few paces away from the woods when the M23 Katana antipersonnel mines rigged up on the front door exploded with a roar.

Like its longtime predecessor, the M18 Claymore mine, the M23 was a directional antipersonnel device that could be triggered manually or remotely. The mines set at the front door were rigged for motion and detonated as soon as the alien strike team breached the door, one set to sweep high, the other low. Instead of using metal balls as projectiles, however, the M23 unleashed a storm of flechettes capable of piercing everything except the heaviest of combat armor.

Ben flinched slightly as the blasts tore through the cold night air, but neither he nor Jim paused for even a moment to look back at the house as they slipped into the shadows at the edge of the woods. The alien dropship immediately broke from its circling pattern of overwatch and swooped in, settling into an aggressive hover near the house as weapon pods deployed from various points around the hull. With both assault teams and the dropship focused on searching for threats and evac'ing their wounded, they didn't notice the two humans quickly making their way through the heavily wooded hills toward the distant lights of Traverse City.

CHAPTER SIXTEEN

EMERGENCY DEPLOYMENT

"I DON'T LIKE THIS, MATT," HENRY SAID, WATCHING THE NUMBERS on the lift display rapidly change. The two men were on their way to the secure docking arm where the CIS *Wraith* was loading in supplies and personnel for its emergency trip to Earth.

"Henry—"

"I should be going with them, dammit!" Henry said, pacing back and forth in the small lift car.

"Henry," Evans began again, "I know the admiral has you on a short leash right now—"

"More like a fucking choke collar," Henry spat. The emotional roller coaster he had been on since the *Appomattox* briefing with the senior staff had left him in a surly mood, and now he was lashing out at the only target in sight.

"You planning on breathing fire right up until Ben gets here?" Evans said, shooting Henry an unfriendly look.

Henry stopped his pacing and let out a frustrated sigh. "I'm sorry, Matt. It's just…"

"I know, Henry. But you need to let the pros take this one. Give them the information they need and then let them do their job."

The two men were on their way to brief the team tasked with retrieving Ben, along with whatever they could salvage of Project Blackthorn, provided there was anything left of the lab at Camp Grayling. The lift slowed abruptly, and a soft chime announced their arrival. The doors parted, and they stepped out into a spartan security station. As they exited the lift car, the pair of marine guards standing next to an armored pressure hatch sized the two men up before the nearer of the two marines asked for their identification.

"IDs please, gentlemen."

"Commander Matthew Evans and Henry Hutchins, here to brief the *Wraith*'s CO and SEAR team leader," Evans said, handing the marine his identification and comms unit, which displayed his security authorization and orders. The sentry checked the orders and security codes against his own comms unit, before handing them back and motioning the two men forward to the biometric security checkpoint.

After clearing the security station, the two men stepped through the armored hatch and into a cavernous hangar that was bustling with activity. Henry's eyes were drawn immediately to the sleek, deadly shape of the CIS *Wraith* that took up nearly the entire space. The ship appeared as though it were sitting in shadow, despite the powerful overhead lights flooding the rest of the hangar with bright, white light.

"Amazing..." Henry said in awe. Despite having been consulted on the development of the new generation stealth reconnaissance vessel and inventing the Aegis armor plating that covered the entire ship from stem to stern, he had never seen one in person.

"Incredible," Evans said, also having never seen the highly classified ship in person. "I know I'm looking at a ship, but it's almost like..." He trailed off, searching for the right words. "Like staring at yourself in a mirror in a dark room. You know your reflection is there and what it's supposed to look like, but you can't decide if you're actually seeing something or if it's just your brain filling in the details by itself."

"That's the Aegis plating," Henry said, now in his element. "The graphene polyalloys used on the *Wraith* absorb nearly ninety-six percent of visible-spectrum light—a third again what the plating on the mainline warships is capable of. There are trade-offs, of course, but the *Wraiths* are purpose-built to be stealthy, not stand toe to toe with capital ships in a knock-down, drag-out fight. Don't get me wrong, she's got plenty of teeth hidden in the shadows, and if anyone ever manages to spot her, they're in for one hell of a surprise."

"That they are."

Henry and Evans turned to look at the newcomer, both of their faces breaking into smiles when they saw who it was, though while Evans's smile was professional, Henry's expressed genuine warmth.

"Henry, this is Lieutenant Commander Ramiro Valdez, Fleet Special Exo-Atmospheric Reconnaissance. He'll be leading the team to retrieve Ben," Evans said, making the introductions between the two men. Valdez saluted Evans, then extended his hand to Henry.

"I've actually had the pleasure of the lieutenant commander's company before, Matt," Henry said, shaking the SEAR's hand firmly. "I suppose it's only fitting that you and your team would be the ones to rescue my son."

Seeing the confused look on Evans's face, Henry explained, "The lieutenant commander here and his team were the ones who saved my bacon back on Isadore. They were training on the planet and were headed back up to orbit when the war broke out. I called Admiral Garland when ExoDyn HQ was taking a beating, and then *Lieutenant* Valdez was kind enough to make a detour to pick me up. I owe him my life.

"Just doing our job, Mr. Hutchins," Valdez said, waving the compliment away.

"Please, call me Henry, Lieutenant Commander. You've more than earned the right to use my first name."

"Will do… Henry," Valdez said, as if he was trying the name out to see how it felt. "If you'll excuse me, sir, Henry," Valdez said, looking first to Evans, then Henry. "I need to get my gear stowed and my team organized before the briefing." He snapped off a salute to Commander Evans before picking up his bag and heading for the *Wraith*.

"I never knew you had to be extracted from ExoDyn HQ by SEARs, Henry," Evans said conversationally as the two men resumed their walk toward the *Wraith*.

"Yeah, Matt," Henry said, his jaw tightening as he thought about the death and destruction the Alarians had rained down on the ExoDyn Headquarters campus. "It was close, far closer than Valdez let on."

"You'll have to tell me the story sometime," Evans said, not picking up on Henry's change in mood. They walked the rest of the way to the gangway in silence, stopping to present their credentials to the marine standing guard.

"One minute, sirs," the sentry said. "XO's on his way down to meet you."

The two men watched the flurry of activity going on around them in silence as they waited for the *Wraith*'s executive officer to come get them. Henry marveled at the masterfully orchestrated chaos as the ship was provisioned for the mission, and he tried not to think too much about Ben and everything he must have gone through over the last four years.

Less than two minutes after they checked in with the sentry, a man in a standard dark gray fleet utility uniform came hurrying down the gangway.

"Commander, Mr. Hutchins, I'm Commander Jason Black,

XO of this *Wraith*. If you'd be so kind as to follow me, I'll give you a quick tour of the ship while the captain finishes up some business and the SEARs are stowing their gear," the XO said, motioning for them to follow him up the ramp. Once they had stepped through the hatch and into what Henry could now see was the *Wraith*'s small hangar and flight ops, he continued.

"My apologies for all the activity, gentlemen. We only got the call about this op less than an hour ago. We were scheduled for some depot-level maintenance starting at 0700 tomorrow, and the ship had very little in the way of provisions aboard, not to mention the fact that nearly the entire crew was on leave. We've recalled everyone, and it seems the admiral has pulled some major strings to restock our consumables on such short notice."

"How many crew?" Henry asked. While he had consulted on certain design elements of the highly classified ship, he was curious how many people it took to run a vessel the size of the *Wraith*.

"One hundred and nine is the published crew compliment, though we generally run a little short due to the current state of the fleet as a whole. Fully trained spacers are in short supply right now, officers even more so. Provided we can get everyone back from leave by the time we hit our departure window, we'll be heading out with ninety-seven spacers, officers, marines, and SEARs."

"Must get a little cramped on a ship this size," Henry said as his eyes roamed the space, taking in every little detail.

"No, sir." Black chuckled. "This *Wraith* is downright roomy compared to most of the tin cans the fleet cruises around in. Sure, the enlisted spacers still have to hot bunk now and then, but we have significantly more space available for leisure than mainline warships do. For example, a *Gettysburg*-class destroyer is over three hundred meters long with nine hundred crew; we're a fifth the size with barely a tenth of the crew."

"I see your point," Henry said, ducking beneath a Beckman drone suspended at head-height in its storage cradle.

"Commander, you referred to this ship as 'this *Wraith*' a moment ago. I take it the rumors that the *Wraiths* don't have unique identifiers is true?" Evans said.

"Correct. The *Wraith*-class ships don't have official names or hull numbers, and they fall outside of normal fleet operations. As such, you'll always see these ships officially designated as CIS *Wraith*—the 'CIS' stands for Confederation Intelligence Ship, though in practice, the 'CIS' tends to get dropped, regardless of which ship and crew it is. You might also hear people say 'CID *Wraith*' since Confed Intelligence Division operates the *Wraith* fleet. It's an arrangement the powers-that-be decided on, since our primary function is intelligence-gathering and black ops. I think the idea behind it was operational security—in the event of a security breach, an enemy wouldn't know what ship was where or tasked with which mission. *Wraith* crews are particularly proud of the fact that we are the unknown fleet, and we tend to be a much more tightly knit group than the regular fleet spacers are."

Commander Black led Henry and Evans on a cursory tour of the *Wraith*, pointing out all the highlights but never willing to delve too much into the technical details, much to Henry's chagrin. Evans, for his part, put on a brave front, but Henry could tell the tour was boring him to death; ships and tech were not something he was the least bit interested in. Their tour concluded in the passage just outside the ship's small CIC. Conveniently, the briefing room they were to use to brief the *Wraith*'s CO and SEAR team was opposite the armored hatch to CIC, and Henry could see Lieutenant Commander Valdez already seated at the plain polymer conference table in the room.

As they passed through the hatch to the small briefing room, Henry saw that Valdez was flanked by two other equally hard-looking men and one startlingly attractive young woman. On a second examination, Henry realized the woman—the name tape over her left breast identified her as McCollum—must also be a SEAR, despite the obvious age gap between herself and the three men. The unit's insignia on her lapel was a dead give-away, but she positively gushed with that towering confidence —that some mistook for arrogance, at their peril—that only the elite of the Terran armed forces had. Henry quickly sized up the other two SEARs, Miller and Kravczyk, recognizing the latter as the foul-mouthed, smart-ass petty officer that had been part of the team that had extracted him from ExoDyn HQ four years ago.

"Lieutenant Commander"—Henry nodded to Valdez—"and *Chief* Kravczyk, congratulations on your promotion. I'd say it was good to see you again, but I'm afraid I'm still trying to purge some of your more… *inventive* metaphors from my memory," he finished, flashing an amused smile at the chief, who for his part, smiled back hugely as he leaned his chair back on two legs.

"Nice to see you again, too, Mr. Hutchins. I've got four whole years' worth of new material, if you've got the time."

Turning to Valdez, Henry said, "Lieutenant Commander, I'm afraid I haven't had the pleasure of meeting the other two members of your team."

"Henry, this is Lieutenant Brian Miller," Valdez said, introducing the SEAR directly next to him. "He's normally the team lead for SEAR Team Four, but the suddenness with which this mission came about found my team two people short, and he volunteered to fill one of the slots." Miller simply nodded to Henry at the explanation for his presence and remained seated. "You're already painfully familiar with Chief Kravczyk"— Kravczyk flashed another huge smile at that—"and this is Spacer First Class Tessandra McCollum. She was in the first SEAR class to graduate from the new program we set up here in Kerner after the war, and I pulled her in to fill the other slot for this mission."

McCollum nodded politely. "Mr. Hutchins," she said.

As Valdez was finishing up the introductions, Commander Black and Captain Collins entered the briefing room. The SEAR team and Commander Evans all shot to their feet and came to attention.

"At ease," Collins said with a dismissive wave, and everyone again found their seats. "Mr. Hutchins," she said, staring directly at Henry with a look that could have frozen water. "As I understand it, my ship and crew are *not* to get any R and R this week after having just finished a three-month recon mission that didn't involve any outside interaction whatsoever. Instead, we are now scrambling to replenish our fuel and consumables and reload the munitions we just took out of the magazines *this morning* in preparation for our depot-level maintenance so that we can be back in the black no later than twenty-one hundred hours this evening. Do I have that right?"

Henry was taken aback by the captain's outright hostile demeanor. The four SEARs sat stoically around the table, save for Kravczyk's silent whistle. Henry decided to fight fire with fire; his hackles were still up from earlier in the day, and it was an easy course of action for him.

"Captain, I have had a really, *really* shitty day," Henry said with a dangerous edge to his voice. "Much like you have, I expect. So can we please dispense with the infantile pissing contest and get down to brass tacks? I know you haven't been given fuck all for information thus far, but trust me when I say that this mission could literally save the human race from annihilation. And to top it all off, my son's life is on the line—something I only just became aware of, meaning that I *abandoned* him four years ago when the war broke out. So I am really not in the mood for your petulant bullshit right now."

Kravczyk's silent whistle at Captain Collins's foul mood had changed to staring slack-jawed at Henry's profanity-laced tongue-lashing of the *Wraith*'s commanding officer, and he wasn't the only one. The entire room save for the captain wore the same expression of shocked horror. For her part, Collins simply stared daggers back at Henry for a few moments longer before taking a deep breath and sighing heavily.

"Very well, Mr. Hutchins," she said with only a hint of frostiness, "let's see what you have for us."

The room let out a collective sigh, none looking more relieved than Commander Evans. Over the next two hours, Henry briefed them in detail on everything from the cyber construct and Project Blackthorn to Ben's harrowing escape from Isadore to Earth and his reemergence just hours ago.

"Mr. Hutchins, I apologize for my bitter remarks at the outset of this briefing," Captain Collins said when Henry was done taking questions at the end of his presentation. "It's no excuse, but we've just finished up a very demanding mission and my crew are exhausted, myself included."

"I understand, Captain, and would also like to apologize for my response to you. It seems we're all not at our best right now."

Collins dismissed the SEARs and her XO and then offered to personally walk them back to the gangway. As they were leaving the briefing room, Henry could just make out Kravczyk saying, "I didn't know the old guy had it in him! Did you hear that thrashing he gave the skipper? Fucking epic, man!" Henry just shook his head and hoped the exuberant warrior would make it back safe and sound.

When they reached the airlock where the gangway to the hangar was extended, Collins said, "Commander Evans, would you give Mr. Hutchins and myself a moment, please?" As Evans strode down the gangway to wait for Henry, Collins extended her hand. "Don't worry, Mr. Hutchins. Those SEARs are the best in the business at this sort of thing, and this kind of mission is exactly what the *Wraith* was designed for. We'll bring your boy back. You have my word on that."

"Thank you, Captain," Henry said, fighting back a wash of emotion. "Just be careful. We know precious little about this new enemy's capabilities, and I can feel in my gut that Ben is now a priority target for them. I can't stress enough that they are not to be underestimated, especially when it comes to electronic and cyberwarfare. Godspeed, Captain." With that, he turned and walked down the gangway back to the hangar, where Evans was waiting to escort him back to the ops level to await the *Wraith*'s return.

CHAPTER SEVENTEEN

SCORCHED EARTH

BEN HEARD THE EMERGENCY SIRENS LONG BEFORE THE LIGHTENING of the eastern sky allowed them to see the thick black columns of smoke. The acrid pall rose from the complex that housed the regional headquarters of the Civilian Defense Force on the outskirts of the city. He and Jim had been headed there to report what had happened at the farm and call in the cavalry, but it looked like whoever was after them had anticipated their move and beaten them to the punch. It seemed that whatever force had it out for him, it was done screwing around.

"What does this mean, Jim?"

They had been stopped by a local police cordon at the intersection nearest to the CDF facility as firefighters worked to extinguish the flames that still licked out of shattered windows. From the rubble, police and paramedics extricated the mangled remains of the men and women who had been on duty at the time of the attack. Ben's gaze shifted from the carnage a short distance away to the hard face of his mentor and friend. The acrid smell of burning insulation mingled with something reminiscent of charred meat, and his stomach heaved when he realized what it was.

"Change of plans," Jim growled through gritted teeth as Ben retched next to him. "Come on."

Ben wiped his mouth on his sleeve as Jim led him down a side street to a fenced-in parking lot. At the entrance hung a small metal sign declaring it was government property and for CDF employees only. With the main complex burning around the corner, the small guard shack was empty, and the two men passed right by.

Ben's guts were still twisted into knots, but no longer from the stench. Those people had all been killed because of him. What the hell made him so damn special that dozens of people would be murdered in a brazen attack solely to tighten the net around him? He made up his mind right then and there: he had to discover what made him such a threat.

Jim stepped purposefully toward an old pickup truck parked in the far corner of the lot, opening the unlocked driver's door and flipping the visor down. A set of old-school metal keys dropped into his waiting palm as Ben looked on, unsure of what to do. He had never seen Jim this visibly angry, and the former SEAR was radiating such a strong threat of violence that Ben didn't dare speak for fear of setting the man off.

"Get in."

Ben did as he was instructed without comment, dropping his backpack into the bed of the ancient truck and pulling his rifle out from under his long coat, where he had it slung on his back to conceal it from passersby. He climbed into the passenger seat and positioned his rifle next to himself for easy access, muzzle on the floorboard. The old truck smelled faintly of gasoline and mildew, but the interior was spotless. Jim put the silver key into the ignition on the steering column and turned it, the old internal combustion engine roaring to life after turning over just once. He put the gearshift into drive, pulled out of the lot, and pointed the truck toward the east.

They rode in silence until they cleared the downtown area and were headed out toward the rural woodlands east of town when Ben couldn't take it anymore.

"What the hell is going on, Jim? Whose truck is this?"

The old warrior's eyes flicked toward Ben before going back to scanning the area around them as the old gasoline-powered engine droned on. "This truck belonged to a buddy of mine. He was on duty last night..." The words hung in the air with an invisible weight, and Ben felt like he had been punched in the gut. "I think your dad was right."

Ben's jaw clenched, but he didn't say anything, waiting for Jim to keep going.

"You had the tractor parked on the hidden lift the first time you went down, didn't you? We moved it out of the shop when you took me in there to show me the lab."

"Yeah," Ben confirmed, his voice practically a whisper. This was all his fault. "Jim, I—"

"This is *not* your fault, Ben," Jim said firmly, breaking his gaze from the road for a moment to look Ben in the eye. "Shit happens; that's war. But the tractor is the only thing I can think of that explains this. There's no way an alien kill team just happens to show up shortly after you discover a four-year-old vid file from your dad detailing a malicious AI of unknown origin infecting the datanet and turning everything we thought we knew about the war on its head. I'd put money on that thing using the tractor's datanet connection to find out what we discovered and realizing you are a potential threat—post-apocalyptic world or not." The lump of iron that had been sitting in Ben's gut rolled over again as Jim concluded the same thing he had.

"But..." Ben shook his head in disbelief. "Blackthorn was never implemented, Jim. The war wiped out everything associated with it—hell, I didn't even *know* about all this shit until the other day! The only thing we know is that I'm somehow tied to a technology that was intended to fight this AI or whatever, but because my dad was fucking Howard Hughes-level paranoid, he never saw fit to give me *any* meaningful answers." Ben's rant was helping him organize the information into a coherent picture in his head, and he was thankful that Jim read the situation correctly and sat silently, allowing him to work through this for himself.

"Okay," he said, continuing his train of thought as he watched the trees along the road blur together as they passed. "Supposedly this involved me, the implant they jammed into my skull, and the prototype APEX I was wearing when I landed on Earth, and two of those three things are either scrapped or nonfunctional. How can I possibly be a threat to these guys such that they are willing to expose themselves to this degree just to take me out?"

"We don't have enough information," Jim said. "But this thing clearly sees you as a priority target because, after lying low for all these years, it just sent a kill team after you and had an entire CDF complex wiped out. Accessing that vid file changed the math—enough that they are willing to go scorched-earth and wipe out the only force that would be able to mobilize and protect you. They must have known about my connections at the CDF and assumed that's the first place we would go for help."

Several moments passed in silence as both men processed the events of the last eight hours. "So where are we headed now?" Ben asked, seeing an opportunity to get Jim onboard with finally getting some real, concrete answers. "Grayling?"

Jim nodded. "There's a CDF post on M-72 close to the ruins of Camp Grayling. It's a small station, but I know one of the guys there—he'll be able to give us more information on Grayling and if there's any chance we might be able to find this secret lab your dad mentioned. The Alarians used small tactical nukes on the base, which were pretty clean overall, but there will still be some radiation hotspots we'll need to watch out for. We can get a rad map from my buddy, Mike—I'm sure the CDF has the area well-documented."

Jim swerved around a large pothole and Ben reached up to brace himself on the A-pillar. "You think we'll find anything?"

"We'd better. Because there won't be any hiding from this thing now that it's actively looking for you."

———

"WELL, THIS ISN'T GREAT," Ben heard Jim whisper to himself. They lay prone in the damp leaves along a low rise just above the tree line, only the top half of their faces visible as they peered over the dirt and leaf litter. They were observing a CDF outpost with a large number 23 painted on the side a couple hundred meters distant. The gray light of a rainy October day was waning, but neither man moved a muscle.

They'd made good time for the first half hour after taking the truck from the CDF lot, but the ill-maintained back roads were rife with deep ruts and potholes from years of neglect, and one particularly big bastard had snapped the old truck's front axle, leaving them stranded with ten kilometers to go. With no help nearby and being unwilling to call for assistance out of a fear of prying electronic ears, the two men had walked the rest of the afternoon. They slowly worked their way east along M-72, the rural highway that was a primary traffic artery in this part of the state, using the surrounding forest of thick pine as cover from the eyes-in-the-sky that were surely searching for them. They followed the highway for several hours before spotting a large clearing just off the road with their destination in the middle of it.

The post itself was set up more like a backwoods ranger

station, complete with a five-story-tall spotting tower. After the collapse of Earth's technological infrastructure in the war's wake, people who had chosen to remain in their homes in the more remote areas had turned to wood-burning for heat and cooking, and with this came a sharp increase in the frequency of forest fires. The posts were all equipped with large spotting towers, where a lookout could see above the tree line for miles and call in firefighting efforts before any new fires could get out of hand. It was a low-tech solution in a world where high tech had been burned away by nuclear fire. The posts were typically well-staffed and well-equipped, with around a dozen CDF troopers on duty at any given time.

As the sun set below the trees to the west, Ben's ears picked up the unmistakable sound of the alien dropships filtering through the few remaining leaves. As the two men drew nearer to the clearing with the CDF outpost, there was a short and very one-sided firefight, confirming that their pursuers were one step ahead of them yet again. Ben and Jim moved as quickly as they dared toward the post, but by the time they had eyes on the compound, the action was all over and the dropship had taken up a wide overwatch orbit around the area.

Ben's eyes continued scanning over the next few minutes, picking out a single team of six alien troopers in and around the main building: two standing sentry outside and the remaining four searching for something inside. His blood boiled as he watched the aliens unceremoniously dump nine human bodies in a pile just outside the building. Plasma had set their clothes on fire and scorched their skin—it was a repeat of the Traverse City post, Ben realized, but this time he and Jim had arrived before the aliens were done ransacking the place. It was also a repeat in that those people had died because of him; they had simply been in the way, and these aliens had slaughtered them because of it.

While Ben was focusing on the bodies in the distance, Jim was laser-focused on the dropship, watching its patrol pattern with a clenched jaw. "I don't think they're keeping a close eye on their team searching the building," Jim said in a whisper barely audible above the alien craft circling overhead.

"How do you know?" Ben said, clenching and unclenching his fists in an attempt to vent some of his frustration and guilt.

"It's too low and flying too wide an arc to maintain visual contact with them. It flies over to check in every fifteen minutes or so before circling beyond the far side of the ridge to the north, where it loses line of sight. They must be looking for any response to the attack on the post coming from either Kalkaska or Grayling—they know the building itself is already clear, and there's nothing else in the area that could pose a threat."

"So... what do you want to do?" Ben said hesitantly, a growing fear that he knew *exactly* what the ex-operator was about to propose.

"We're not going to get a much better chance to gather some intel. I'm going to work around to the east and come up on the post along the fence line, where the vehicles are parked. The cars will give me cover from any spotters in the building, and I can approach the sentries from the far side. You stay here and get ready to put a round through the nearest one on my signal. I'll take the other, then clear the post and grab what I can before that dropship comes back around. We'll meet back here and fall back under cover of the woods."

"What if one of them gets off a call for help?" Ben said, his voice now noticeably shaky. Every fiber of his being screamed at him to just get the hell out of there, but he stayed rooted in place because he had come to trust Jim implicitly over the last four years.

"They won't. I'm pretty sure they're using tight-beam comms

—my scanner hasn't shown any activity whatsoever on any of the RF bands. When the dropship is out of line of sight, they lose comms for a short time until it reappears," Jim explained. "Sit tight and wait for my go. Just like we practiced, Ben. Center-mass shots, and don't try to get fancy."

"Wait—" Ben tried to stall the old warrior, but Jim was already moving with incredible quickness along the shallow ridge they had been hiding behind. Dammit, why did everyone around him have to always do weird and crazy shit? He pushed his anxiety to the back of his mind, focusing on his part in what was to come. He couldn't just bail on Jim, as the old fool was counting on him, which meant he *would* take the shot when the time came, but he didn't like it.

Nothing you haven't done before, Ben. The thought brought a sardonic smile to his lips. *Right, because ambushing an alien commando team is totally the same thing as killing a thug in self-defense.*

Ben shifted back until his head was fully behind the ridge and slowly brought his rifle in front of him. After adjusting the optic for a variable zoom, he settled into a rock-solid prone shooting position, placing the crosshairs just underneath the left armpit of the nearest alien sentry and letting the built-in ballistics computer do the math on where the shot would fall. It would be a quartering shot, but if he assumed the aliens had their important bits tucked away in their thoracic cavities like nearly all animal life on Earth or, from what they had learned from the Alarians once upon a time, on other planets, his shot should do massive internal organ damage.

He waited.

After what seemed like hours but was really only a few minutes, Ben saw the shimmering air around the stealthed dropship begin its wide arc around the far northern ridgeline. His heart was pounding in his chest and he had to force himself to take deep, regular breaths while he struggled to keep his crosshairs firmly locked on the alien trooper. He couldn't ever remember seeing his sight picture bounce so much as his heart hammered against his ribcage, causing his whole upper body to tremble slightly with each beat. There was a sudden double click over his comms channel with Jim, and his finger squeezed the trigger without waiting for his brain to fully process what those clicks meant.

The 7mm armor-piercing projectile screamed toward the unaware alien trooper at nearly three times the speed of sound. Ben watched, mesmerized as he followed the bullet trace through the humid air to where it impacted his target, exactly where he had aimed. The hardened steel penetrator on the bullet's nose connected just behind the thicker ablative armor panel on the alien's chest and punched through the lighter, more flexible layers on its upper left side beneath the armpit. Hydrostatic shock did the rest, and the alien was dead before it even hit the ground.

As the trooper collapsed like a puppet whose strings had been cut, its partner turned its helmeted head to stare uncomprehendingly at the lifeless corpse now lying at its feet. At the exact moment the other sentry turned its head and looked down at its fellow, exposing the base of its neck in the process, Jim emerged like a specter of death from around the corner behind it. Ben saw the alien stiffen suddenly before going limp as Jim's combat knife pierced the thin layers of armor covering the trooper's neck, severing the spinal column before punching through the front of its throat. Ben's stomach turned as dark blood erupted out around the blade's tip.

Jim caught the alien trooper before it could hit the ground and dragged it around the corner in one swift motion. A moment later, he reappeared and dragged the other body out of sight as well. When he reemerged, he flashed a thumbs-up in Ben's direction, and disappeared into the main building of the outpost.

———

JIM FINISHED CONCEALING the bodies and unslung his rifle, then paused briefly just to the side of the double glass entry doors and took a cleansing breath. He was about to draw on skills he hadn't used in years, and he hoped there wasn't too much rust built up. Flashing a quick thumbs-up in Ben's direction, he pulled his rifle up to high-ready and entered the building.

Jim knew the layout of this outpost, having been here a few times to visit a friend—a friend he hoped had been off duty when the post was hit and wasn't lying in that pile out front. After taking in his immediate surroundings, he quickly covered the few paces to the small waiting room and swung to his left, where he knew there would be a reception desk and office spaces. The large pane of ballistic glass that divided the waiting room from the locked offices of the post lay in a slagged heap on the floor beneath the opening, the intense heat of the aliens' plasma weapons having melted through it like butter. The air in the building reeked of blood and burned flesh, and dark red stains covered the receptionist's desk behind the opening; scorch marks covered the concrete walls and flooring of the room.

The common area of the office space was empty save for a few overturned pieces of furniture and a host of papers and document-readers scattered about the floor. Jim vaulted through the opening and over the gore-spattered desk. He heard the rustling of papers followed by a crash as a piece of furniture was tossed into the hallway at the back of the common area, and he knew from previous trips here that the offices down that hallway were home to the command staff.

Before he had taken more than three steps toward the office currently being ransacked, an armor-clad trooper emerged, holding a stack of data drives and tablets in both arms. Its attention was focused on not tripping over the chair that lay in the middle of the hallway, and it failed to notice the armed human sighting in on it. Jim put two quick shots center mass, but the thicker armor plates that protected the alien's chest took the brunt of the armor-piercing rounds' energy and only allowed the bullets to penetrate a few centimeters. It wasn't enough to take it out of the fight, however, and the alien let out a high-pitched shrieking wail as it toppled backward. Jim saw that it had retracted its helmet visor for the search. Large glassy black eyes set deeply into charcoal gray skin swiveled to focus on its attacker, and that was the extent of the detail Jim bothered to take in before his suppressed DMR sent a third round through the center of its face.

The old warrior knew that the clock was ticking now, and he charged toward where the second trooper was just emerging from the same room, apparently thinking its partner had merely stumbled over the junk they had tossed out, not been shot. Jim put a half-dozen rounds into its helmeted head and neck, and the second trooper hit the floor, dead.

A quick check of the remaining offices showed they were empty, which left the post's cafeteria, detention cells, and arms locker to clear in the main building—a lot of ground to cover in the short time he had left before the dropship was due to circle back around. He mentally flipped a coin and took a right at the end of the hall, heading for the arms locker where the data servers that stored the post's communications logs and CCTV video recordings were also housed.

The trail of papers, broken furniture, and discarded equipment told him he was likely headed in the right direction, and as he neared the large reinforced door that lead to the arms locker, he could hear the thump of armored boots walking around through the open door. A small, box-like device the size of his thumb was stuck to the biometric security panel on the wall next to the door, and it didn't appear that the door had been opened by force. He took a flashbang grenade from his chest rig, twisted the arming dial on the top twice to up the concussive force, and finally pulled the arming pin. Jim casually tossed the grenade through the open door, banking it off the far wall toward where he judged the troopers would be. Quickly retreating a few steps, he crouched and turned his head away.

A deafening *whump* shook the wall behind him, and a cloud of dust and debris came billowing out of the room. He rounded the corner with rifle raised and scanned the room. The last two troopers lay in a crumpled heap near the data server that housed the post's surveillance equipment. *Ugly suckers.* Judging by the blood oozing from their eyes and nostrils, they were either dead or near enough. He put a bullet through each of their heads to be sure, then quickly searched them for anything that might contain useful intel.

Other than small tablet-like devices that resembled his own comms unit, neither of the aliens had anything easily portable. He secured both devices in a specially designed electronics pouch that he took from a pocket on his vest. The pouch was shielded from electromagnetic radiation and would prevent small electronic objects from sending or receiving any signals. He had used such a container on numerous occasions during his time as a SEAR, and they worked exceptionally well. He just hoped his good luck with the pouches in the past would carry over to the alien tech it now contained.

Just as he finished tucking the bag into one of the cargo pockets on his fatigues, he froze. At first, he couldn't immediately identify what had set off his subconscious alarm, but the odd sensation intensified, becoming that deep subsonic thrum he knew was the dropship returning. They were early.

Shit!

Jim scanned the small arms locker for anything that might be of use, dismissing the idea of trying to use the aliens' plasma weapons as an option—he had no idea how they worked, or even if they would operate for a human. His eyes fell on a large locker that ran from floor to ceiling and was secured by another of the ubiquitous biometric security locks. Stepping out into the hall, he pulled the small black box he had seen earlier from the outer lock with a metallic *snick*. Turning it over in his hand quickly, he couldn't see any specific attachment points and assumed it worked simply by being in proximity. He stepped back over to the locker and placed the device in the same location on the locker's biometric scanner as it had been on the door's lock, and a moment later, the heavy locking bolts in the locker retracted with a thunk. A low whistle escaped his lips when he opened the doors and took in the sight.

"What the hell were these cowboys doing with this beauty?" he whispered to himself, almost in awe as he slung his rifle across his back and reached in to pull the weapon from its rack.

The M105A1 was an electromagnetically fired anti-material rifle, or AMR—essentially, a man-portable version of the same weapon the fleet was currently equipping on starships for planetary and anti-station bombardment. But while those fired projectiles that weighed as much as a dump truck at near-relativistic speeds, the M105A1 was somewhat less potent. Somewhat.

Jim checked the battery unit's power level, happy to see it was fully charged, and grabbed a loaded magazine from a shelf above the weapons rack, then slammed it home. The sound of the enemy dropship was growing louder, and Jim made a quick decision as the tactical computer in his combat helmet synced with the optic of the new weapon in his hands.

Running for his life, he rounded the corner at the end of the hall and sprinted back through the common area and waiting room, then through the door opposite the reception desk and up five flights of steps to the observation room at the top of the tower. He stopped just below floor level of the observation area and took a moment to get his bearings. He could hear the drop-ship but not see it through the wide, curved glass windows. From the sound of it, the craft was circling the clearing. *Probably trying to establish comms with their team in the building,* he thought.

A few more heartbeats passed as the former SEAR strained his eyes and ears, trying to locate the telltale shimmer of the stealthed ship in the waning light of dusk. Then he saw a faint ripple in the air, practically right over top of where Ben should still be waiting. He followed it as it completed half of its arc around the building, waiting for an opportunity to pop up and take the shot. The craft turned suddenly and increased power, closing the distance to the tower quickly, and Jim knew they had figured out something was amiss.

The dropship came in on a line directly toward the main doors, and suddenly the stealth field vanished, revealing a dark, angular hull. Weapons pods deployed from recessed bays in the stubby forward wings and started tracking for targets, one sweeping along the tree line, the other toward the main building of the outpost. It was now or never.

Jim took the last two steps up into the observation room in one leap and brought the huge AMR up to his shoulder. The weapon wasn't intended to be shoulder-fired, but he didn't have time to find a proper shooting rest. Too late, his mind flashed a warning to him, concerned the ear protection integrated into his combat helmet wouldn't offer enough protection from the unholy blast he was about to unleash. Sighting in on one of the oblong pods at the tip of the nearest stubby wing, he flipped the safety off and squeezed the trigger.

The overpressure wave created by a cobalt-sintered tungsten projectile the size of a man's thumb being accelerated to hypersonic speed crushed the air out of his lungs and blew out every pane of glass in the small room. Jim was knocked back onto his butt from the immense recoil as the round streaked toward the alien craft in a flash, leaving a bright orange streak of ignited atmosphere in its wake. It slammed into what Jim had correctly assumed was one of the dropship's thrusters with incredible force, resulting in a massive explosion of released energy from whatever it was these aliens used for propulsion.

The blast ripped the stubby wing clean off the craft and peeled its side open like a tuna can, killing the pilot instantly. The uneven thrust from the other engines caused the ship to roll to the left, and it slammed into the clearing, cartwheeling several times as it shed its momentum in spectacular fashion. The sound of the engines faded and died a second later, and an eerie silence fell over the darkening woods.

———

A STREAK of fire lanced out from the top of the observation tower, causing Ben to jump. An explosion from the side of the dropship strobed in the darkening night. Ben's eyes registered the shock front tearing across the field, but a thunderous boom hammered at his chest before his brain could fully process what was happening. He flinched back as leaf litter and dirt stung his face like it was being sandblasted. When he opened his eyes again a moment later, he saw the small ship smash into the earth and fling debris in all directions as it cartwheeled across the field, finally coming to a stop roughly halfway between his position and the buildings.

For several moments, he was too stunned to do anything, the ringing in his ears drowning out all other sounds. Then a flash of movement caught his eye as Jim exited the base of the tower and ran toward the downed craft.

"Stay where you are, Ben!" Jim's voice crackled into his ears over the comms channel. "I want you searching the sky for more dropships. There's no way its friends won't notice one of their ships was just shot out of the sky."

"Got it," was all Ben could think to say as his heart pounded and his sympathetic nervous system gave him another shot of adrenaline for good measure. He searched the sky, activating the augmented visual systems of his helmet and switching to long-wave infrared now that darkness was falling fast.

"I'm going in to check for survivors and intel. Stay sharp," Jim sent over the comms. Ben just clicked his transmit button in acknowledgment, kept his eyes glued to the sky, and strained his ears to pick up anything except the crackle of the small fires burning in and around the wrecked dropship.

A minute later, Ben jumped when he heard a single, muted gunshot. "One of the pilots was still alive but in bad shape. I put him down—Shit!" Jim's voice held a note of fear, and Ben's blood ran cold. He looked at the crashed ship just as a blinding explosion lit up the sky, and the dropship blew itself apart.

"Jim!" Ben screamed. Jumping to his feet, he sprinted toward the blast crater while small bits of burning debris rained down all around him. He was halfway there when a bright red-orange ball streaked through the darkening sky and struck the ground a few meters in front of him. The heat of the plasma singed the hairs off the back of his hands and seared his exposed skin, and the force of it blasted him backward several paces, crushing the air from his lungs.

Gasping for breath, he struggled to rise to his feet and retreat back to the tree line. He staggered the first few steps until his lungs were at last able to draw breath again, and then he heard the unmistakable sound of multiple dropships closing in. More plasma bolts tore through the air around him as he ran up the shallow rise of the ridgeline and hurled himself over the far side, tumbling down the wooded hill in a tangle of limbs and gear. He didn't pause at the bottom, standing and running for his life deeper into the woods as a heavy rain began pouring down from the heavens.

CHAPTER EIGHTEEN

THE NUTJOB EXPRESS

"ALL HANDS, STANDBY FOR TRANSITION." THE ANNOUNCEMENT from the bridge was followed by two quick klaxon blasts, and a moment later, the dull thrum of the *Wraith*'s fusion plant wound down as the ship exited FTL.

"Okay, people, we're up soon, so double-check your gear and get suited up. Final briefing at drop minus thirty," Valdez said to the three members of his team. They broke up and made their way over to their gear lockers to run final pre-mission checks and get into their APEX armor. Twenty minutes later, all four of them were fully clad in the matte black APEX suits and were making their way to their ready room to await the final mission brief.

"Commander SEAR team, report to the bridge," came over the ship's 1MC intercom system. Valdez finished adjusting his kit to his liking, then made his way up to the *Wraith*'s bridge, presenting his credentials to the marine standing watch next to the armored hatch. Valdez stepped through, not paying any attention to the open-mouthed stares his hulking armored form received from the bridge crew.

"Lieutenant Commander Valdez reporting as ordered," he said, coming to attention in front of the captain and XO.

"At ease, Lieutenant Commander," Captain Collins said. "Join me in my office, please." She motioned toward the small compartment that served as her day cabin at the back of the bridge. "XO, you have the conn."

"I have the conn, aye."

The captain took a seat behind her desk and began putting panes of data up on the wall display. "We're a little less than an hour from being in position to drop you and your team, but there are some complications," she began, skipping the pleasantries and motioning to a particular false-color image showing an aerial view of the Hutchins farm. Valdez could tell immediately that the compound had recently come under attack.

"Thermographics show some small fires still burning around what used to be the main house, but it appears the attack likely occurred a day or two ago, based on the residual heat signatures. There has been no activity around the compound in the thirty minutes since we transitioned in," she reported, quickly bringing the SEAR team leader up to speed.

"So we're too late," Valdez said, disgusted that their mission was looking like a failure before they even had a chance to drop.

Collins highlighted and enlarged another image, this one focusing on an area roughly fifteen klicks west of the remnants of Camp Grayling. Valdez studied the imagery closely, his attention being drawn to the wreckage of a small craft that was still burning hot.

"You think they're related?"

"CIC has been working on analyzing the imagery for the last ten minutes, and they assure me that what's left of that craft down there doesn't match any known Terran or Alarian configuration, and it's directly adjacent to a known CDF outpost," she explained. "And then there's this…" She applied a different filter to the image, and the hazy outline of two small ships lurking near the downed craft could just be made out in the infrared band. Valdez mentally matched the thermal signatures to what was known about the *Appomattox*'s encounter with the unknown ships in the Vostok system.

"Looks a lot like the what the *Appomattox* was seeing in Vostok before she was engaged," he said. "Hutchins did brief us on a possible third party in play here, and I'd say we now have confirmation."

"CIC agrees." Collins nodded, leaning back in her chair as she studied the SEAR's face through his clear faceplate. "Which means this won't be a simple pickup. We need to tread carefully here, Lieutenant Commander, because this ship cannot go toe to toe with even one of those frigate-class ships the *Appomattox* reported. We're built to sneak in and out quickly and quietly, not engage in a running gun battle in low orbit. We also have no idea what their capabilities will be on the ground, but I think it's safe to assume you and your team will likely be outgunned as well."

Valdez continued staring at the wall display for a moment longer, taking in as much as he could while trying to process and categorize everything. Henry Hutchins had warned them that there might be other parties interested in Ben, but he hadn't expected them to arrive so quickly. If they were able to land assets on the ground in Sol this quickly, it meant they must have a much larger force spread around within Terran space than anyone thought. He stood there silently for a minute longer— something about the images on the screen bugged him. It took another few moments before he realized what his subconscious was highlighting for him.

"So our new players are here," he began, thinking out loud, "likely to track down Ben Hutchins and either capture or kill him, and either one of their dropships suffered an accident or, more likely, someone down there is making life difficult for them. There's just one thing I don't understand," he said, one hand rubbing the chin of his helmet in thought. "If there are unfriendly ships flying around down there, blowing up homes and CDF posts, then why don't I see any response from the CDF or Homeworld Defense?"

"We don't know," Collins answered, her expression clouding over. "We've been monitoring Earth's comms channels, but there have been no reports of the activity we see here. If I had to guess, I'd say the cyber construct that Henry Hutchins briefed us on has something to do with it. It's probable the construct is somehow shielding the enemy action from notice by Earth's defense forces. That is a rural area, after all, and with Grayling's destruction during the war, there are very few military assets in the region."

"There's one more thing," Valdez said, turning to look the captain directly in the eye. "Those craft look like something akin to our Griffon assault dropships." He saw Collins nod; she knew where he was going with this. "Which means there is likely another ship in the area—probably in a high polar orbit to avoid detection. Have we been able to identify it yet?"

"Unfortunately no, not yet. But we're looking," the captain replied. "Although if we're to remain hidden ourselves, we can't bring our high-powered tactical arrays online to search for it."

Valdez nodded thoughtfully. "Well, I don't really see that this changes our course of action at the moment. Whether we're up against humans, Alarians, or some new threat, our playbook is the same: my team and I need to get down there as soon as possible to assess what's going on. We'll need to do a cold drop in the pods—taking the Griffon poses too high of a risk of exposing the ship."

"My thoughts as well, Lieutenant Commander," Collins agreed. "See to your team. You drop within the hour. Dismissed."

———

"ALL ABOARD THE NUTJOB EXPRESS!"

The cheery announcement brought a chuckle to Valdez's lips.

"Step right up and experience the white-knuckle, pants-shit-ting terror that is the fleet's newest generation of low-orbit indi-vidual deployment system! Brought to you courtesy of Confed Fleet Science and Technology Division. Next stop, the beautiful rain-soaked forests of northern Michigan," the chief in charge of servicing the drop pods called out in a bombastic showman's cadence while his technicians wrapped up their pre-drop checks and retreated from the pod bay. "Come now, friends, don't be shy. You there!" the chief said, pointing toward Kravczyk with a broad smile. "You look like a strapping young lad. Perhaps you'd like to give it a try?"

Valdez walked up to his assigned pod and secured his weapon in the rack next to the padded acceleration couch he would be strapped into for the drop, then climbed into the pod. His team was doing likewise to either side of him in the cramped launch bay.

Once they were all situated, each pod's crew chief then strapped the SEARs firmly to their couches and attached induc-tive data cables to the data-processing ports on each of the warriors' APEX suits, which would allow them to integrate their suits' computers with the pods' comms and data suites. After a final diagnostic check to make sure the pods and suits were fully integrated, the technicians returned and assisted the crew chiefs with closing the pods up and readying them for their meteoric journey down to the planet below.

Valdez had gone through the process over two dozen times during his time as a SEAR, but despite it all, he still felt his heart race as the heavy hatch was secured in front of him, plunging the cramped confines of the three-meter-tall pod into complete darkness. It took the techs a few minutes to finish securing the hatch and go over the preflight checks, and only once the flight ops crew had evacuated the pod bay and no one remained, did the drop controller initialize the pods' internal power systems and vent the atmosphere from the launch bay. Valdez's HUD notified him that his pod was now operating on internal power, and he activated the small display on the inside of the front hatch, configuring it to his liking before forcing himself to relax and await the final go/no-go call from flight ops.

His helmet speakers crackled to life, and the flight ops controller's voice filled his ears. "Ladies and Gentlemen, this is your captain speaking. We would like to thank you for choosing to drop today with Confed Airways. Please keep your arms and legs inside the drop vehicle at all times and ensure that your tray tables and seatbacks remain in their full upright and locked position for the duration of the drop.

"At this time, we expect your trip to take, oh, just a hair under thirty minutes or thereabouts from drop to touchdown. It's currently 0943 local time, and the weather forecast at your destination is a balmy six degrees centigrade with an eighty percent chance of rain showers and weapons fire. At this time, we'd like to ask you to call out go/no-go for drop and to please fill out the comment card located underneath your seat cushion, to be left with the pod for your flight attendant to collect never. Once again, we'd like to thank you for dropping with Confed Airways. Have a pleasant trip."

"Dagger One, go!" Valdez called out after the announcement had ended, and Miller, McCollum, and Kravczyk followed suit.

"Man, you CID guys sure know how to party," Kravczyk said over the open channel after confirming he was go for drop. "I'm putting in for a transfer when we get back, boss. These guys are way more fun than you are."

"They're also stuck on this tin can for months at a time,

whereas I take you nice places and introduce you to interesting people," Valdez quipped back.

"Not sure I'd call the Thuranian jungle 'nice,'" Kravczyk muttered. "My ass still has that rash I picked up on that drop."

"Too much info, Chief." Miller's gentle Southern drawl floated over the team channel. Kravczyk and Valdez both chuckled at the exchange.

"Regretting volunteering to come along on this one, Lieutenant?" Valdez asked Miller.

"Volunteer? You got it all wrong, sir. I was in fact volun*told*. It's a subtle difference," Miller said. "I apologize for any confusion."

Valdez could hear the flight ops staff laughing at the team's pre-drop banter. At this stage of every drop he had ever done with the man, Kravczyk would start cracking jokes as a way to release some of the nervous tension they were all feeling. It was a good way to relieve stress and take their minds off of what they were about to do, even if it was only short-lived.

Valdez had noticed Tess's voice was a little shaky when she checked in to confirm she was good to go for the drop, and he called up her vitals on his HUD. Her heart rate was sky high, and she was bordering on hyperventilating, so he keyed in a private channel to her.

"McCollum, this is your first live drop, right?"

"Y-Yes, sir," came her broken reply. "I did simulated drops during selection, but the real thing is a bit more… intense. Sorry, sir," she finished.

"Don't apologize," he chided her. "The first drop is always the worst one. No sane person enjoys being crammed into a coffin-shaped missile and launched at high speed toward a planetary body. First time I dropped, I was so keyed up I didn't realize I had accidentally toggled over to the squad-wide, and the three vets I dropped with got to listen to me scream like a little girl the whole way down. Those guys never let me live that one down." Valdez recounted his embarrassing first drop with a smile. "But let's you and me keep that story to ourselves, shall we?"

McCollum let out a nervous laugh. "You got it, sir." And Valdez was relieved to see that her biometrics were beginning to come down a little after the exchange.

"Thirty seconds to drop." The Flight ops controller's voice had lost its casual joking nature, replaced by the serious tone of a professional at work.

Valdez toggled back over to the team channel. "Full EMSEC protocols are in effect for this drop," he told his team. "Stay off the comms until we rendezvous at the rally point." He set his comms transceiver to passive only, then cleared his mind and waited for the gut-churning free-fall sensation he knew was coming.

"Five... four... three..." The Flight ops controller counted down the last few seconds. "Two... one... drop!"

Valdez's stomach did a backflip as his pod was expelled from the belly of the *Wraith* by electromagnetic rails. Now that they were clear of the ship, he settled in for the thirty-minute fall to the planet with nothing more than his own thoughts to keep him company. If all went according to plan, he and the rest of his team would rendezvous at the primary rally point in a little over an hour. Until then, he was on his own.

Twenty-three minutes into the drop, he felt the first faint shudder of the pod as it came into contact with the thin upper layers of Earth's atmosphere, and a minute after that, he was being buffeted so hard it felt like his teeth were going to shake loose. The roaring of atmospheric entry filled the pod as he kept his eyes glued to the small display in front of him, watching the telemetry data for any sign that something was amiss... not that he would be able to do anything about it.

With just under a minute left until touchdown, he was slammed against his restraints as the small drogue chute deployed and the noise and vibration increased to a thunderous roar. The pod's retrograde thrusters spooled up to full power in a desperate attempt to slow his meteoric descent. He grunted and flexed his core muscles as hard as he could, working in unison with his APEX as it squeezed his extremities in an effort to keep blood in his head, where it would be useful. The pod's thrusters expended all their fuel in one last massive burst of deceleration just before touchdown, and Valdez's vision tunneled and blurred.

The impact with the Earth left him seeing stars, and once his vision cleared, he took a moment to check the pod's diagnostics systems and cross-check his impact location before popping the hatch. When the display of his location came up, he just stared at it for a long moment.

"Shit."

According to the map, his pod had landed smack in the middle of Lake Margrethe, nearly five kilometers northeast of where he was supposed to be. A quick check of the information he had on the lake showed the depth where his pod landed was only ten meters. His APEX suit would keep him dry and breathing until he could reach land, but what he didn't know was how far his pod had sunk into the muck at the bottom of the lake. If he was buried in silt, he might be trapped for good.

Crossing his fingers and saying a quick prayer, he released the harness holding him securely to the acceleration couch, then reached up and pulled down on the yellow and black striped handles that would activate the explosive bolts securing the pod's hatch in place. There was a muted *whump* and the pod filled with smoke. The hatch released but was not propelled clear as silt and water pressure kept it more or less in place. Murky water seeped in around the edges of the hatch, and he relaxed, allowing it to fill the pod around him until the pressures equalized. Once the water pressure in the pod was the same as in the surrounding lake, he braced his knees against the hatch and planted his back firmly against the inside of the pod. It took all of his considerably augmented strength, but the hatch slowly pushed away from the opening just enough for his armored bulk to squeeze through.

Once outside and kneeling on the lake bottom, he reached down into the pod and retrieved his primary weapon from the rack next to the couch. The pod had embedded itself three-quarters of the way into the lake bottom, and he was thankful that he was able to get out without too much effort. No matter what happened from here on out, this drop would always be a memorable one. Very few people who had pod-dropped into a body of water had made it out alive, and he hoped he hadn't used up all his luck for this mission on the drop.

CHAPTER NINETEEN

ROLE REVERSAL

BEN LAY ON HIS BACK, WEDGED BETWEEN THE CARCASS OF A FALLEN tree and a moss-covered fieldstone pile, the rocks having likely been pulled from the earth by some long-dead farmer while clearing a field for planting. He lay, and he waited.

Several teams of alien troopers and their dropships had hounded him until the gray light of dawn appeared in the eastern sky. Now he was only hunted by the teams, the dropships having retreated to orbit during the daylight hours.

Ben's saving grace was also his tormentor, as the heavy rains that had fallen all through the night helped mask his trail and thermal signature while he fled east through the dense pine forests that covered the area. But the rain had also soaked his weather-resistant combat dress uniform completely through, and he was thoroughly miserable.

The cold fall temperatures and high humidity from the rain now blanketed the entire area in a dense fog, and eventually he had reached the point where his tired legs and burning lungs could carry him no farther and he had concealed himself in a ravine, wedged between a fallen tree and the rocks. He covered himself with a loose layer of dead leaves, listening to a small creek burbling somewhere nearby.

Despite the mental and physical exhaustion that had built up over the previous day, his mind refused to allow him the respite he so desperately needed. Jim… It was happening all over again. Why? Why wouldn't they just leave him alone? Ben brought a hand over his mouth to muffle the anguished cry that tried to escape his lips as he was wracked with silent sobs.

He had lost everything. Again. Four years! He had spent four fucking years clawing his way out of his sorrow and depression from the last fucking time aliens had killed everyone he loved. *It's not fair!* he screamed in his head. *It's not fucking fair!*

The faint sound of splashing banished his pity party to the back of his mind and flooded his system with adrenaline. He listened intently, heart pounding in his chest as his ears strained to interpret the out-of-place sounds. A moment later, he realized one of the hunting parties must have stopped near the creek maybe fifty meters from his location—it was difficult to judge the distance with the heavy fog distorting the sound. He lay motionless, cursing himself for not keeping his rifle in his hands —the M37 lay next to his right arm, but there was no way for him to pick up the weapon and ready it without making far too much noise. Instead, he slowly withdrew his combat knife from its sheath on his right thigh, and he waited for the alien team to move on.

He heard soft footfalls on wet leaves and his heart rate ratcheted up another notch as the sound drew closer. Through the small gap between the earth and the bottom of the fallen tree trunk, he saw a pair of inky shadows resolve into two armored enemy troopers just like the ones he and Jim had encountered at the CDF outpost. They passed so close to Ben's hiding place that he could have reached out and grabbed the nearest one by the ankle. They appeared to be in silent conversation, the fully-enclosed alien helmets bobbing back and forth as they walked.

For some reason, Ben's mind interpreted the body language between the two troopers as casual, joking. In another time and another place, he would have dismissed the idea as absurd, having absolutely no frame of reference for how to read the body language of an alien species humanity had never before encountered. Instead, his strung-out and exhausted psyche told him something else: these assholes weren't taking the situation seriously. They were just out for a relaxing stroll, nothing to it.

Ben's face twisted into a silent snarl. The crippling fear that had been gripping him for the past day and a half was buried under a tsunami of white-hot anger flaring up from somewhere deep in his gut. Anger at once again having his world violently ripped apart. Anger at having another person close to him torn away. Anger at being forced to run until he collapsed and had to lie, wet and shivering and covered in dead leaves, on the floor of a forgotten ravine in the ass end of nowhere. And as though someone had flipped a switch in his brain, he went from terrified of being found to desperately wanting to kill the alien sons of bitches responsible for it all.

As the two troopers passed his hiding place, he sat up, moving silently, and assumed a low crouch behind the trunk; the wind and rainfall covering any noise he might have made. One of the aliens stopped next to a tree a few meters away and began adjusting something on its armor as its partner continued casually strolling along the ravine. With the practiced, precise movements of someone who had spent years stalking ever more rare and wary game animals in woods just like these, Ben closed from behind on the unsuspecting alien in a flash.

He felt detached, operating at that primal level still buried deep down in the genetic code of all humans, granted to them from their barbaric ancestors from a time when clubs were the pinnacle of technology. He felt nothing as he performed the same maneuver that had nearly made him vomit when he had watched Jim do it to the second sentry back at the outpost. *Before they killed him.*

Ben drove his combat knife through the alien's neck in one smooth movement, warm blood oozing over his gloved hands as he withdrew the blade and silently lowered the body to the forest floor. And then he was moving again.

The second trooper turned at the last second when it realized the footfalls approaching it were coming too fast and too heavy to be its partner. Its eyes widened in shock as it saw the hate-filled visage of its quarry an instant before Ben savagely drove the smaller alien to the ground. He hammered his blade through the thinner, more flexible material on its side again and again and again until he was dripping with the trooper's blood and gore, his breath coming in ragged gasps.

Ben's vision clouded as he straddled the lifeless corpse, silent tears streaming from his eyes. He returned to his hiding place and retrieved his rifle, quickly checking to make sure there was a round in the chamber and the magazine was full. His higher functions had been disabled, his body following one basic command: kill them all.

He strode purposefully toward the sound of the creek and the four other alien troops he was sure were there. When the dark outlines of his enemy resolved in front of him he raised his weapon and fired.

When the DMR's bolt finally locked back on an empty magazine, the four alien troopers lay motionless on the ground, their bullet-riddled corpses leaking that viscous, dark-colored blood onto the forest floor and staining the clear waters of the creek. Ben reloaded his rifle, slung it on his back, and knelt at the water's edge. He washed the blood from his hands and face in the creek, the ice-cold water mingling with the warm tears that ran freely from his eyes.

He felt broken inside. There was no satisfaction at having exacted some measure of revenge, no thrill at having just survived a vicious close-quarters fight with an implacable enemy. Instead, he was horrified. He had let his anger truly take him for the first time, and the primal rage he had unleashed shocked him to his very core. How could any human be capable of such brutality, let alone him? What kind of monster was lurking in the depths of his soul? Ben shivered uncontrollably as his fragile psyche teetered on the edge of sanity.

He was alone. Again.

Four overlapping sonic booms snapped him out of the black hole he was sliding into, and he ran up the slick leaves covering the walls of the ravine, eyes searching the sky through gaps in the forest canopy. The fog and low-lying clouds prevented him from seeing anything, but a moment later, he heard a sound that brought him back to his days of playing combat holosims: the thunderous roar of a combat drop pod's retrograde thrusters firing to arrest its plunge just before touchdown. He had always thought the drop pods were the coolest part of assaulting a planetary target, and he had spent hours and hours researching everything about them. He would know that sound anywhere.

Help was finally on the way.

Ben collapsed to his knees, hands shaking as a dozen different emotions battled for dominance. Relief, horror, grief, satisfaction— he was so tired he couldn't tell one apart from another anymore.

Wait… why would help be coming from someone in drop pods when there were several CDF and Homeworld Defense bases within range? Surely any response to the attacks would come from planetside forces. Ben took a deep breath and forced his mind back into gear, trying to figure out what was going on around him. In the end, though, only one thing mattered: the good guys were that way.

———

"Damn!" Kravczyk said, waving a hand in front of his face. "Jesus, boss, you smell like you just waded through neck-deep sewage. What the hell happened?"

"My pod dropped smack in the middle of a lake," Valdez said, not the least bit amused. "I had to wade through a flooded marsh on my way out. You're smelling hydrogen sulfide liberated from the silt."

Kravczyk closed his faceplate and sealed his suit back up. "Damn, man, that shit's rank."

The two SEARs were hunkered down at the edge of a clearing that had been designated as their post-drop rally point. Miller and McCollum had not yet arrived, but it was still too early to worry about them. Valdez never would have said it out loud, but he was more than a little annoyed that the smart-assed Kravczyk always seemed to have the best luck of anyone he knew when it came to pod drops, and today was no exception. Kravczyk's pod had made a picture-perfect landing in a hayfield not more than four hundred meters from the rally point. Just once, Valdez wanted the man to have to deal with something going wrong with his drop, as seemed to happen to just about everyone else more times than not.

A new icon popped up on Valdez's HUD, and he toggled his comms suite over to a private tight-beam IR channel. "Good to see you made it in one piece, Lieutenant. We're two hundred meters to your east, just inside the tree line," Valdez said to Miller, who had just appeared near the opposite edge of the clearing. A few minutes later, he joined up with Valdez and

Kravczyk and took up his position watching the woods to their rear.

"What the hell's that smell, sir?"

"Everyone's a critic," Valdez muttered to himself, not bothering to respond.

The trio waited a few more minutes in silence, and Valdez was just beginning to worry about the fourth member of his team when McCollum's icon lit up on his HUD and she pinged him with a tight-beam IR channel. "Sorry it took so long, sir," she said, slightly winded. "My pod came down right through the roof of a chicken coop and lit the structure on fire. The property owners weren't too happy about it."

"Roger that," Valdez said, shaking his head at hearing he wasn't the only one who'd had an interesting drop. This mission was already far more eventful than he would have liked, and he couldn't shake the feeling that things were not going to end well for them. Valdez set off to the west, his team spaced out at ten-meter intervals as they covered the distance at a good clip, their APEX suits making the activity almost effortless.

After covering a little over eight of the fifteen kilometers they had to go to reach the crash site around the CDF post, Valdez called a halt when they came upon an abandoned farmhouse. He got to work setting up their small comms relay, which would allow them to check in with the *Wraith* in orbit, as their suit comms were not powerful enough for the task on their own. While he worked, the other three members of his team took up positions overlooking the surrounding area.

The old stone house was in a sad state of disrepair and there wasn't a single unbroken pane of glass left in the windows, but the building offered good concealment and kept the rain off of them for a bit, not that it mattered much thanks to their fully sealed APEX armor. The yard was overgrown with low shrubs and a few trees here and there, but they had a good line of sight to the edge of the woods that surrounded the house a few hundred meters distant. Out the back door through what used to be the kitchen lay the fieldstone foundation of what once had been a barn but was now just a shallow depression in the ground surrounded by crumbling masonry and a few old weatherbeaten wooden planks that hadn't rotted completely away yet.

"Shadow, Dagger One. Over," Valdez transmitted over the tight-beam link to the *Wraith* overhead in high orbit, using the assigned call signs for this mission.

"Dagger One, Shadow, send status and stand by for mission update. Over," came the tinny reply over the secure comms channel.

"Shadow, Dagger One, sending status. Over," Valdez replied, sending a data packet to the ship with his suit's mission logs to that point. Contained within the file was disposition information for him and each of his team members, showing that all four of them had made it down safely and they had successfully rendezvoused and been on the move for the last half hour.

"Dagger One, Shadow, copy good data. Glad to see you all made it down safely. Sending updated mission parameters and current intel on enemy strength and disposition. Over." Valdez saw the icon for an incoming data transmission flash in the corner of his HUD, and he took a moment to scan through the contents and appended analysis file at the end that the *Wraith*'s CIC had put together.

"Shadow, Dagger One, data received and appreciated. Will continue on mission as planned and check in again at drop plus twelve hours. Dagger One out." He shut down the comms relay and began breaking it down and putting it away in its armored travel case. As he worked, he toggled over to the team channel to fill his people in on the data he had received from the *Wraith*.

"Shadow reports that our new friends have pulled their dropships back from the area. Just as dawn was breaking, they tracked three dropships leaving the atmosphere for what they assume was a rendezvous with whatever ship they're staging from. They disappeared over the horizon and Shadow hasn't been able to locate the mothership yet, but for now, it appears our skies are clear, at least."

"Do we know if they have any ground elements on the board?" Miller said.

"Unknown, but I think we need to assume they do—it's what we would do if we were in their shoes," Valdez said, zipping up the case and securing it to the hardpoint on the small of his back, where he liked to stow the small case when not in use. "Alright, people, let's—" The air around him was ripped apart by a fusillade of white-orange plasma bolts, and he threw himself to the ground.

"Contact front!" Miller shouted, and Valdez could hear the muffled reports of his team's carbines interspersed with the crackling of plasma bolts as they peppered the stone walls of the house.

"Fuck! The volume of incoming is too heavy—I can't return fire without getting my ass shot off!" Kravczyk yelled over the din.

"Back door is clear!" McCollum called out.

"Retreat through the old barn to the woods behind us. Move now!" Valdez instructed his team, popping around a window frame to take a couple of quick shots toward the far tree line where the plasma fire was coming from, then ducking back behind the stone walls as a searing bolt tore through the window a fraction of a second after his head had occupied the same space.

Dammit, where the hell had they come from, and how did they know where the SEARs were? Shadow hadn't had any eyes on ground elements in their immediate vicinity, which meant they couldn't trust anything the *Wraith* was seeing from orbit.

The team withdrew from the house in a bounding overwatch, leapfrogging each other so there was always some measure of covering fire while one of them moved. The incoming fire tailed off as they retreated behind the thick stone walls of the barn's foundation. McCollum and Kravczyk covered the opening they had just come through while Valdez and Miller surveyed the wooded hill to their rear and the short distance of open ground they would need to cross as they made a run for the woods.

"Looks clear," Miller reported. He had been the first to reach the crumbling remains of the arched rear doorway and had been sweeping the tree line with all of his suit's threat-detection capabilities.

"Stack up," Valdez called out. "We go in pairs. Miller and I will make the run first and provide overwatch for Kravczyk and McCollum. Go!" he shouted, slapping Miller on the shoulder as he did so. The two SEARs sprinted into the open, crossing the first hundred meters in under seven seconds as their APEX armor allowed them to cover the ground faster than any nonaugmented human could ever hope to.

They were halfway across the clearing when a bolt of plasma streaked out from the tree line, striking Miller squarely in the chest. Valdez heard the man grunt over the open comms channel and caught a brief glimpse of Miller's armored bulk rag-dolling along the ground as he dove to his right, a grazing hit to his lower back sending him into a spin and triggering several damage and heat warnings on his HUD.

He rolled behind the rusted hulk of an abandoned farm implement as plasma bolts filled the surrounding air. Quickly checking the status warnings on his HUD—nothing that would keep him out of the fight—his mind flashed through his options. McCollum and Kravczyk were both yelling over the comms channel, but Valdez couldn't make out what they were saying as their words crashed over top of one another. He could see that they were both pinned down just inside the rear door of the barn by overwhelming enemy fire. His HUD flashed another warning as Miller's biometrics flatlined, and one look at the smoking, crumpled body of the lieutenant confirmed what his tac-link was telling him. *Dammit.*

He was in a bad spot, exposed and in the open, pinned down by withering fire from an elevated position behind the tree line. His mind raced, desperately searching for some way out, and he felt a ball of lead form in his gut as he realized he and the two remaining members of his team were well and truly screwed. They had been caught in a pincer maneuver, the attacking element driving his team out into the open where another element waited in ambush.

Then the plasma barrage slackened suddenly. *Now or never.* Valdez rolled to one knee and raised his carbine. Sighting in on the small rock pile just inside the tree line that he was fairly sure the fire had been coming from. One iridescent-black armor-clad figure was twisting to look over its shoulder, and Valdez put his reticle over the alien's torso, flipping the safety of his carbine off and bringing his finger to the trigger.

He squeezed. Too late, his brain told him his target was falling to the ground, and his round hit the dirt behind where its intended target had been standing only a moment before.

A CDF trooper wearing dirty, rain-soaked CDUs and full hardshell body armor emerged from the trees, casually holding what looked like an M37 designated marksman's rifle.

"Well, don't just fucking stand there!" the trooper yelled. "Move!"

BEN'S FISTS tightened around his rifle in impotent rage as he watched one of the humans take a plasma bolt to the chest and cartwheel across the ground, coming to rest in a smoking heap. Thankfully, the other was able to dive out of the line of fire, suffering only a glancing blow, and was now pinned down behind an old junk pile.

Ben had stumbled across a group of the alien troopers an hour ago; they'd been conversing excitedly and gesturing in the direction the drop pods had come down. Deciding it was time to turn the tables, he had tailed the group to a point where they split up near a large clearing around an old farmstead. Following one of the teams around the rear of the property, Ben took up position slightly above and behind the aliens, who were lying in wait just inside the tree line. A firefight had broken out near the farmhouse soon after, but he hadn't been able to intervene without exposing himself to the two troopers pulling security to the rear.

Ben's opportunity came shortly after the ambushing element below him had opened fire, as the two sentries turned and took up positions behind a pair of thick maples above and to either flank of their four teammates behind the rock pile below. *Sloppy discipline*, he thought. Quickly bringing his rifle to bear on the sentry to the right, he dropped it with a single round to the base of its skull, then shifted his position slightly and repeated the action with the other. The aliens were laying down such a high volume of fire on the trapped humans that the noise of their weapons covered the sound of Ben's suppressed DMR firing and the supersonic crack of the bullets that were killing them off one by one.

When Ben shifted again and dropped the leftmost alien in the same fashion as the first two, the remaining members of the team finally realized they were being ambushed themselves, but the brief confusion that followed in the moments after Ben had killed the third member of the team allowed him to pick off a fourth before the two remaining aliens spun to search for their attacker. The fifth member of the team fell to a bullet through its faceplate, and the last followed suit a moment later. In the span of maybe ten seconds, Ben had completely wiped out a second six-man hunter/killer team that had been hounding him for days.

Ben stood from his prone position and half ran, half slid down the hill. What the hell were those idiots doing? They should be hauling ass in his direction right now. He stepped out into the clearing and shouted, "Well, don't just fucking stand there! Move!" That did it, and the APEX-armored figure behind the junk pile ran over to his fallen teammate while the two that had been pinned down in the barn came up behind him. Ben watched as the larger of the two from the barn stopped to help Junk Pile pick up their teammate in a fireman's carry while the other sprinted for Ben's position and the tree line.

Ben took cover behind the same rock pile the alien troopers had occupied a few moments ago, kicking one of the alien bodies aside as he did so. The lead human was nearly to his position when Ben saw movement in the farmhouse. "Move it!" he yelled, flipping the safety of his rifle off and laying down covering fire. His magazine ran dry just after the lead human made it to the rock pile and took up a position next to him, adding the weight of her carbine fire.

"Changing!" Ben yelled, dropping the spent magazine from his rifle and pulling a full one from a pouch on his chest rig. He slammed it into the magwell and slapped the bolt release, sending a fresh round into the chamber with the practiced move-ments Jim had drilled into him over the last four years. A moment later, he was back on the line sending single, well-aimed shots through windows and doorways where plasma bolts were streaking out of.

The last two members of the team made the tree line at full tilt, diving behind the rock pile and crushing the alien corpses under their armored bulk as they landed in a tangle of limbs. "Fire in the hole!" one of them shouted.

The farmhouse ceased to exist.

Fieldstone masonry and bits of lumber exploded outward, mingling with the pulverized remains of the second alien team. Ben turned his head to the side as the shock front from the blast washed over them, and a moment later, small bits of debris began dropping all over like hard rain, plinking off his helmet and armor. When the dust cleared, Ben looked out over the clearing that now had a house-shaped smoking hole in the middle of it. Nothing out there was moving anymore.

"Good Lord," Ben said, trying to clear the ringing in his ears by smacking the side of his helmet with one hand. "You guys sure know how to announce your presence."

"That's my bad," Kravczyk said. "Seems I was a bit too generous with the little-house warming gift I left behind. Oops."

"*Oops?*" Ben said, annoyed and still shaking his head to clear the ringing. This cowboy had just alerted every single alien in the system to their exact position. He smiled inwardly as he realized that last thought had come straight from Jim... His cheerfulness winked out as he remembered the events of last night. "Either way, it's good to see you guys," he said, eyes still scanning the surrounding area. He got no response.

He turned around and saw Junk Pile and his burly comrade trying to extricate themselves from the tangle of bodies, both alien and human. The woman to his right still had her carbine pointed in the direction of the farmstead, but she was looking at the unmoving body at her feet, a fist-sized hole burned right through the chest armor, revealing carbonized bits of bone and charred meat.

"Oh..." she said, her voice weak.

Junk Pile got to one knee and placed a hand on the dead

man's helmeted head, taking a moment of silence. He folded the man's arms over his chest, covering the grisly wound.

The three surviving humans stood in silence for a moment longer, and then Junk Pile got to his feet, opaque black APEX faceplate looking what he probably assumed was a ragtag CDF soldier up and down. "You have our thanks—" He broke off mid-sentence, rocking back on his heels slightly in surprise. "Well, I'll be dipped in shit," he said. "It would appear you missed the memo, Mr. Hutchins. *We're* supposed to be rescuing *you*."

CHAPTER TWENTY

BOY MEETS GIRL... AWKWARDLY

THE RAIN THAT HAD BEEN FALLING FOR THE LAST DAY AND A HALF finally broke a couple of hours before sunset, and the beauty of the evening sun's golden rays stood in stark contrast to the pall of fear and violence that had surrounded Ben since he escaped the initial assault back at his farm. But for the first time in as long as he could remember, he had hope.

He still had no idea why a team of SEARs had come to rescue him—or why they had dropped from orbit, for that matter. Unfortunately, he would have to wait a little longer to get some answers, as they continued to evade the enemy teams. Other than getting their names and being told they were there to rescue him, they hadn't said more than ten words to each other.

Ben figured the SEARs would have had air support available to swoop in and pull them out, but it looked like that wasn't the plan. Could these aliens be such a superior force that neither the Confed military nor the HDC was willing to send in more assets? Or were they trying to do this quietly to escape notice from whatever malevolent entity seemed to be an all-knowing eye?

They traveled in silence, the only conversation occurring

when Valdez issued orders verbally for Ben's benefit, the SEARs being able to communicate efficiently through nothing more than hand signals. They made good time in the hours after the battle at the abandoned farmstead, the APEX armor allowing one of the SEARs to carry their fallen comrade's four hundred pounds with little effort, and they had reached the Manistee river with daylight to spare.

We're heading to Camp Grayling! Ben realized when he saw the river that ran along the complex's western border. Excitement welled up inside him—he was finally going to get some real, honest-to-God answers. And if the SEARs knew about Grayling and Blackthorn, then his dad's research must not have been lost during the war.

Wait… A tingle ran up Ben's spine as his mind asked a question that couldn't possibly be true: *Did dad send them for me?* No, that wasn't possible. If his dad sent these guys to extract him, that meant that he had been alive all these years and had left Ben to fend for himself. His dad had been many things, but callous enough to abandon his son? Never. Ben deflated slightly, realizing that some things were simply too good to be true. He would have to be content with finally getting answers.

After crossing the rain-swollen river, they were officially on Camp Grayling soil, but with the sun setting fast and the enemy dropships due to return as night fell, they had taken shelter in an old ammo bunker complex. The old reinforced concrete ammo bunkers were dug into the surrounding terrain and hadn't been used to store munitions in over a century, but they provided excellent cover from prying eyes overhead and offered a place to rest for the night.

While Kravczyk and McCollum placed a sensor network around the bunker complex that would alert them if anything came to within five hundred meters of their position, Ben finally had his chance to get some answers from the SEAR team leader.

Pulling two meal bars from a pouch on his belt, the SEAR passed one to Ben, who attacked the terrible-tasting protein block with vigor. When Ben finished wolfing down the bar, Valdez passed him a small water bladder.

"Here," he said, handing Ben the water.

"Ah, thanks," Ben said, wiping his mouth with a blood-stained sleeve. "I haven't had a chance to eat anything since yesterday." He took a long draw off the bladder, then continued. "Gotta be honest, I was surprised as hell to see you and your team coming down in drop pods. If you guys hadn't shown up when you did…" He trailed off, thinking back on his slaughter of the hunter/killer team back at the creek, right before he heard the pods coming down.

"I know the last couple of days have been hard, Ben," Valdez said gently, "but now that we have a little time, I need you to walk me through everything you know. We're dealing with a new player here whose technology is generations ahead of both ours and the Alarians', and you are probably the foremost expert in dealing with them."

"Where do you want me to start?" Ben asked, apprehensive about reliving the last forty-eight hours—there were many things he wished to simply forget and move on from.

"From the beginning. How about from the time you landed at Camp Grayling four years ago, right after the war broke out?"

Valdez listened as Ben recounted his harrowing escape from Isadore: watching the nuclear-tipped missiles fall like rain from the heavens, the blinding flash of the detonation and being saved by his x300 armor prototype, then waking in the hospital and the weeks of rehab. He talked at length about Jim, how he had taken him under his wing and given him the skills he would later draw on to survive and how the two of them had scraped out a meager living by trading the alcohol they made from the crops around the farm. He told the SEAR about the secret lab under the shop, the message from his dad, and the subsequent attack on the house—their first encounter with the alien shock troops. Ben described the clash at the CDF post and Jim's death when the crashed dropship exploded, then broke down in sobs while he relived his animalistic slaughter of the six troopers in the ravine.

When he finally finished recounting his tale, Valdez placed a gentle hand on his shoulder. "You've endured more than anyone should ever have to, Ben, and I can honestly say that you are one of the toughest individuals I have ever met." He paused for a moment before continuing. "There's something you should know—some good news for a change. Your father is alive, Ben. He's the one who sent us for you."

Ben's emotions warred within him. A hand shot up to cover his mouth of its own accord before he froze, staring unseeing into the distance as his mind reeled at the implications. Why had he been left alone all these years? *Dad's alive!* Also, *Dad's alive? Why the f—*

It didn't matter. In the end, a mix of relief and happiness broke the dam, and he sobbed once again. "Where is he?" he croaked out when he was finally able to speak again.

"He's safe. That's all the detail I can give you right now. I'm sorry, Ben. But I can tell you that we're headed to where he's at as soon as we get back into orbit."

"All these years…" Ben said, still trying to process everything. "Why now?"

"Nobody knew you were still alive," Valdez explained. "My team and I were actually the ones who got your dad off of Isadore shortly after you departed on ExoDyn's shuttle. We dropped him off on the *Ford* as the fleet was busy mopping up the last of the Alarian strike force, and he was still aboard a few days later when the comms drone came in from Earth with the news that Sol had been hit hard.

"The data dump that was attached from the Sol MILNET included records from Camp Grayling shortly before the missiles hit, and they showed your transport had just touched down when the base was destroyed. Everyone thought you died in the attack, and the complete societal collapse in the aftermath meant no record of your survival ever reached your dad. It wasn't until you stumbled on his lab under the shop and a return receipt was generated on his personal quantum link that he knew differently. From what I heard, he raised all manner of hell to get things moving RFN, and less than twelve hours later, we were on our way here."

"Unbelievable..." Ben whispered, astonished at the metric fuck-ton of shit and bad luck that had combined to leave him stranded on Earth after the war.

"Don't hold it against him, Ben. Your dad was devastated when the news came in, both when you were reported killed and again when you showed up alive and well. He's"—Valdez paused, searching for the right words—"not had an easy time of it, either. But I'll let you and him catch up on all that when we get back." He made a show of checking the time on his forearm display. "I'm sorry, Ben, but I need to go relieve McCollum."

"It's okay, Lieutenant Commander. I need some time to process everything."

"Try to get some sleep if you can, Ben. We'll be here until those dropships clear out in the morning." With that, the SEAR leader donned his helmet and jogged down the corridor toward the bunker's entrance, leaving Ben to stare blankly at the mildew-covered concrete of the bunker's walls as he tried to process everything.

"Sɪʀ," McCollum and Kravczyk acknowledged their team leader in unison as he approached.

"How's it going out here?" Valdez inquired.

"All quiet, sir," Kravczyk replied. "Those dropships make a damn funny sound, but as far as I can tell, they're searching the area a few kilometers to the north and haven't caught wind of us yet."

"Let's hope it stays that way," Valdez said.

"So what's the scoop on the Hutchins kid?"

"For starters, that *kid* just turned twenty last month."

"Still a kid." Kravczyk shrugged.

"He's only a couple years younger than I am, Chief," McCollum pointed out.

"Yeah, and you're still a kid, too, so what's your point?"

"Regardless of his age," Valdez interjected, "that young man is probably more capable than some grunts I've known. For the last four years, he's had a mentor—a guy who pulled him from the wreckage of a transport bus he had just boarded when Grayling was hit. The old guy saved his life, nursed him back to health, then spent the last four years teaching him marksmanship, hand-to-hand techniques, tactics, you name it. Ben said he was a former SEAR, if you can believe that. Far as I can tell, the only training Ben didn't get much of was small-team tactics, but considering it was just the two of them, that's hardly a surprise."

"Anyone we know?"

"Ben said his name was Jim, but I think he would have gotten out before our time—sounds like he was in his late fifties or early sixties."

"So what happened to the guy?" Kravczyk said. "Where's he at?"

"Killed when that crashed dropship blew up. Turns out the old man was actually the one who shot it down *and* almost single-handedly wiped out an entire squad of alien shock troops. Not bad for a guy his age."

"So, what, Ben and this guy were on the run together when the alien team caught up to them at the CDF post?" McCollum asked, trying to put the pieces together.

"No, they actually stumbled upon the post after the aliens had already assaulted the place and taken out the CDF soldiers on duty. The old guy saw an opportunity to take out some of his pursuers and gain some intel in the process. They were the aggressors when that went down. The old man cleared the post, shot down the dropship, and went inside to clear it and look for intel. It blew while he was inside."

Kravczyk's face clouded with suspicion. "I don't know, boss. That doesn't sound like something one of us would do…"

McCollum giggled. Then, when Kravczyk just stared at her, she said, "Oh, you were serious?"

"What do you mean, *Spacer* McCollum?" Kravczyk said, emphasizing her rank.

"It's just that it actually sounds *exactly* like the kind of thing *you* would do in that situation."

Kravczyk held up a finger and opened his mouth to respond, but Valdez's next comment killed the snarky retort.

"She's got a point, Chief. Anyway…" He brought the conversation back on track, recounting Ben's story.

"Jesus Christ," Kravczyk said when Valdez had finished, his snarky air from a moment ago vanishing in an instant, replaced by grim sobriety. McCollum just slowly shook her head at the tale. "That kid is a bona fide badass," Kravczyk said, amazed.

"No," Valdez said definitively. "He is most certainly not. He's a wreck—been pushed to the absolute limit of human endurance and then some, and he snapped. Gotta respect him for not taking it lying down, but he's haunted by his actions.

"Chief, you've been a SEAR for a long time, and you know

all too well what it's like to kill up close and personal like that—the primal brutality of the thing. It takes you to a dark place, changes you forever. Ben's in a fragile state right now, despite outward appearances to the contrary. We'll need to keep a close eye on him.

"McCollum, you're close to his age and can at least tangentially relate to what he's gone through over the last four years. I want you to talk to him, try to help him fight off his demons… at least until we're off this rock and on our way back to Icarus. It's a big ask, I know—"

"I'll do it," McCollum said quickly, cutting him off, then added, "Sir."

"Good," Valdez said, then checked his HUD. It's almost 2300. I'll take watch for the next four hours. Chief, go grab some shut-eye. McCollum, do what you can, and though I doubt it'll happen, if you can get him to grab some sleep, too, then do so—kid looks like he's about to collapse."

Valdez settled in near the bunker's entrance while the two remaining members of his team headed back inside. He hoped McCollum would be able to talk to the kid and help stabilize his state of mind. He knew she had gone through many of the same things, albeit under much different circumstances. Only time would tell if Ben would be able to find the salvation he sought.

———

BEN'S EYES were still open, but his mind had mostly shut down by the time McCollum poked her head around the door frame and peeked into the small room he was occupying.

"Mind if I join you?" she asked. Ben just shrugged in reply, and she entered the room and took a seat against the wall opposite him. Crap. He was so close to sleep, too, and now it looked like McCollum wanted to chitchat. He just wanted some fucking sleep. Was that too much to ask? With a herculean effort, Ben forced his mind back into gear and brought himself into the present. It wouldn't do to be impolite to a heavily armed woman who wanted his attention.

"How's it look out there?"

"Clear for now. Seems like the dropships are searching for us a few klicks to the north and working east. Far as we can tell, they have no idea where we are," she said, popping the quick-release latches to her APEX helmet. She lifted the helmet up and off, revealing matted auburn-colored hair cut short. The most intriguing soft green eyes Ben had ever seen were set into a youthful, beautiful face with a slender jawline and high cheekbones. *Holy shit, she's gorgeous!* She caught his stare, and he froze like a prey animal, a hot flush creeping up his neck. *Oh shit.*

"Not what you expected?" she asked with an amused smile.

"I, uh…" Ben stammered, woefully ill-prepared for this situation. "I just… I guess I expected you to be, like, manlier… or something."

What. The. Fuck.

He really just said that. Out loud. His eyes went wide in horror as his brain finally joined this party and immediately started screaming obscenities at his stupid ass. Somewhere far off in the ether, he could hear Jim's ghost cackling wildly at his ineptitude.

Tess laughed, and it was like music to his now thoroughly reddened ears. She had a bright smile that revealed rows of perfectly straight white teeth. How was he actually taking the time to notice things like that right now?

"I… I'm sorry, Spacer, I—" he floundered.

"Oh, Ben," she said, wiping a tear from the corner of her eye, still chuckling at his hopeless awkwardness. "It's okay. I haven't had a laugh like that in years. And please call me Tess." Ben looked frantically around the room for some way to escape this new, fresh hell he found himself in, but Tess continued before he could bolt for the door. "You're not exactly what I was expecting, either."

"What were you expecting?"

"Honestly? Based on what your dad told us in the briefing, I was expecting an awkward, nerdy kid." That infectious smile spread across her face again. "Well, it would seem that I was at least half right," she said, causing Ben's face to flush again.

They made small talk for hours, covering topics from favorite colors to preferred weapon loadouts for different situations. The one thing both Ben and Tess made sure to steer clear of, though, was their pasts. As a particularly lively discussion on the merits of light infantry railguns versus conventional caseless ammunition arms was winding down, Ben yawned deeply.

"Oh my gosh," Tess said, checking the time. "It's almost 0300. You should try to get some sleep, Ben. I'll be in the corridor if you need anything."

"Yeah," Ben said, stifling another yawn. "Now that you mention it, I'm beat," he finished, shifting to a prone position on the floor and using his helmet as an improvised pillow.

"Good night, Ben," Tess said as she rose and walked toward the door.

"Tess," Ben called out, and she paused in the doorway, turning her head to him. "Thank you," he mumbled.

"You're welcome," she whispered and exited the room with a soft smile on her lips. "Sweet dreams."

CHAPTER TWENTY-ONE

BACK FROM THE DEAD

"Ben," said a soft voice, and Ben felt a hand gently shaking him awake. "Ben, it's time to move."

"Ugh," he grunted, clawing his way back to consciousness. "Yeah, yeah, I'm up," he said, rising to a sitting position, suddenly aware of just how sore he was from days on the run.

"The boss and Chief Kravczyk are out picking up the sensor net," Tess said, down on one knee next to him. "You've got a few minutes to square yourself away and grab a meal bar. I'll be outside."

Five minutes later, Ben emerged from the ammo bunker and stepped into the soft light of the dawn. There wasn't a cloud in the sky and only a hint of a breeze from the south, bringing slightly warmer air up with it. Tess stood next to the body of Miller, his arms folded across his chest along with his carbine. Ben exchanged a somber look with Tess, who had her faceplate set for transparent viewing, allowing him to see her face. There had been a time when seeing a dead man on the ground would have shocked him, especially when that man had died trying to save him. But those days were long gone. Now, all he felt was a mild sense of guilt mingled with anger toward those responsible.

The two other SEARs approached a moment later and Valdez walked up to Ben. "Good to see you were able to get some sleep, Ben. Ready to move?"

"Yeah, but I'm not exactly sure where we're going. The message my dad left for me in his lab didn't give a specific location for Blackthorn, just that Dan Murphy would be able to get me in, but he's been dead for years," Ben said.

"No worries there," Valdez said. "Your dad gave us the location of the project's remote access tunnel, along with the layout of the facility and proper security credentials. It's not too far from here but will involve crossing some relatively open terrain, and we'll have to move quick. Ready?"

"Let's roll." Ben nodded and secured his helmet in place.

"Alright, people, saddle up and keep it tight—traveling wedge formation. Chief, take Miller in the center. Ben, stay roughly ten meters behind and to my left, but contract in on the formation if you need to in order to keep me in sight, depending on the terrain. McCollum, bring up the rear."

Tess helped Kravczyk pick up the body of Miller, and then the four of them were off, traveling in a southeasterly direction at a fast walk. Ben's eyes never stopped scanning the surrounding scrubland and pockets of forest for any sign of the enemy teams that continued to hunt for them.

A few miles later, Valdez finally held up an open hand, and they came to a stop at the edge of a large clearing that was undergoing the slow process of being reclaimed by nature. An old two-track ran along the edge of the woods, and long grasses and pockets of scrub bushes covered the open area.

"This is it," the SEAR team leader said. "This is the old artillery and tank gunnery range. Our objective is 1.4 kilometers to the east, behind that low ridge in the distance. According to Hutchins, that's where we'll find the remains of an old fire-fighting shed. The entrance should be inside."

"Are you sure it's still there?" Ben said.

"Shadow confirmed there is still an intact structure there, but that's all we know," Valdez said, then, seeing the confused look on Ben's face, clarified, "Shadow is the call sign for the CID *Wraith* in orbit."

"Ah," Ben said, nodding in understanding.

"Okay, people, there's no good way to do this. We're going to have to make a run for it. I don't want to be out in the open any longer than we have to be. Ready?" He glanced at his team one last time, seeing nods all around. "Move!"

The three APEX-armored SEARs set their pace by Ben, who was their slowest member in his run-of-the-mill CDF-issue hardshell body armor, and not the powered APEX suits the SEARs were wearing. Ben ran as fast as his tired and used-up body would allow, keeping his eyes roaming over his sector, looking for threats. By the time they had covered a third of the distance, his CDUs were soaked through with sweat and his breath was coming in ragged heaves; he hadn't fully realized just how far the last few days had tested the limits of his endurance until just now.

A distant shimmer caught his attention. Something was coming in from just above the tree line to the north, and Ben's eyes flew wide in recognition just as the strange subsonic thrum of an alien dropship reached him. "Contact left!" he shouted. The shimmer disappeared, and the angular, iridescent black hull of the enemy craft was revealed. "Dropship inbound from the north, bearing 018 at treetop level!"

"Kick it up a notch, people!" Valdez said over the comms as he and Kravczyk began to pull ahead slightly, angling off to their right where a copse of low trees would offer some concealment.

"Incoming!" Ben screamed, throwing himself to the ground as plasma bolts began tearing up the clearing all around them. The dropship screamed overhead in a flash, banking sharply to starboard and lining up for another pass. This time, however, it came in slower, sending a hail of plasma bolts into the copse of trees Valdez and Kravczyk were running for. The two SEARs hit the ground as dirt and flaming tree parts rained down around them. Ben was just beginning to push himself upright when Tess grabbed him by the arm and yanked him to his feet.

"Move!" she shouted at him, raising her carbine and opening fire on the dropship in what was undoubtedly a futile attempt to cover Ben's retreat. Ben ran for his life, stealing a glance over his shoulder as the hulking forms of heavily armored shock troops began dropping from the underside of the alien craft.

Something was different about these aliens; they were significantly larger than the others Ben had seen before. Were these the same species? Or did they just have a different morphology? Something had obviously changed if these guys were pulling out the big guns now. A grim smile tugged at the corner of Ben's mouth when he realized the obvious reason they were dropping the new and improved model: he and the SEARs had been kicking their asses. The SEARs opened up on the aliens, but the massive armor suits they wore were much more resilient than the lighter-duty stuff of the earlier teams they had sent down.

Ben stopped running and dropped to one knee in a shallow depression left by an ancient explosion. Raising his DMR and dialing his optic's magnification up to its highest setting, Ben sighted in on the lead alien and picked out what he thought looked like a weak spot. He struggled to control his heaving chest and pounding heartbeat as he flipped the safety off and brought his finger to the trigger, jerking it much harder than he intended and pulling his shot wide.

"Fuck!" he cursed, lining up again and forcing himself to focus. He squeezed the trigger again and the 7mm projectile flew true this time, hitting the lead alien in a knee joint. It staggered and crashed to the ground, struggling to get back up. Ben shifted his aim slightly, targeting the flexible plates around its neck as the SEARs' smaller 3mm flechettes from their carbines sparked harmlessly off the heavy armor of the alien's pauldrons and torso. He squeezed the trigger again, and his round tore the side of the alien's neck open in a spray of blood and bone. It collapsed to the ground again and didn't get up.

"Tess, move your ass!" Ben shouted. "Your flechettes are useless against that armor!" He provided covering fire as she lowered her weapon and ran toward him at a speed he didn't know humans were capable of, but he knew their time was running out. The big dropship was crabbing sideways through the air, and Ben saw its underwing plasma weapon mounts swivel in his direction. "Fuck you!" he screamed in defiance, pulling the trigger on his DMR as fast as he could, watching the rounds spark uselessly off the dropship's armored cockpit.

A streak of fire lanced out from the woods to the north, covering the distance to the dropship in a flash with the sound of pealing thunder. One of the dropship's drive pods exploded spectacularly, ripping the back third of the ship off. The matte black craft slammed into the ground, rolled twice, and exploded in a blinding flash, the concussion pulping alien troops inside their armor and hurling their lifeless bodies through the air.

A black blur slammed into Ben and drove him into the depression, crushing him under the full weight of an APEX-armored human. The shock wave from the explosion tore through the air just over the top of the depression and would have meant the end of him if Tess hadn't tackled him and used her armored bulk as a shield. A moment later, the air was still, and Ben could hear the rippling thunder of the explosion echo off of the distant hills.

Tess got up and scanned the area before helping him to his feet. "Sorry about that, Ben," she said, gently dusting him off.

"What the hell happened?" Ben asked over the team channel as he scanned the area for more threats.

"It wasn't me this time. I swear!" Kravczyk said, shouting into the comms.

"Everyone, check in," Valdez said.

"I'm good," Ben said.

"Me too, sir," Tess called out.

"I'm fine!" Kravczyk bellowed.

"Chief, your bio feed is showing a ruptured eardrum," Valdez said, reading Kravczyk's biometric data from the command link on his HUD.

"Suit's got me juiced up, boss. Just a little dizzy is all. I'm still FMC," he said, lowering his voice to something just under the volume one would use to talk to a friend in a crowded bar.

"Very well, but let me know if anything changes."

"Will do, sir."

"Okay, everyone, regroup on me. We need to figure out what the hell just took that bird down and make sure there aren't any other surprises that might decide we're next," Valdez said.

"I think I know what dropped the bird, sir…" Kravczyk said.

"Well, what?" Valdez said after Kravczyk didn't continue.

"That guy."

Ben followed Kravczyk's pointing finger to a lone figure in beat-up CDF fatigues. He was jogging across the clearing from the north, an M105A1 cradled in his arms. "No," Ben said slowly in disbelief. "It *can't* be."

"You know him?" Tess said with a raised eyebrow. But Ben was already sprinting across the open field.

He forgot all about his fatigue, aching muscles, and ringing ears as he tore across the field, running toward the dead man jogging slowly in his direction. He stopped a few paces away, taking in Jim's torn and beat-up CDUs and hardshell armor. His helmet was gone and the short salt-and-pepper hair on his head had been singed to the scalp in most places, while an ugly purple bruise covered the entire left side of his face and neck. Jim stopped two paces away from Ben and looked him up and down.

"You look like hammered shit," he said matter-of-factly.

The absurdity of a man who looked like slightly warmed-over death incarnate telling him *he* looked like shit was too much, and Ben snorted. A moment later, his snort had turned into a rolling laughter as he wrapped the old warrior in a brief bear hug.

"I saw you get blown up, you asshole!" Ben shouted at the revenant he was still crushing in a bear hug.

"Never happened." Jim shook his head. "When I saw the pilot's hand resting on a dead-man switch, I bolted out a tear in the hull on the other side. The blast caught me while I was still midair and tossed my ass into the woods, which was lights out for me. When I came to, you were long gone."

Ben finally released Jim and stepped back, shaking his head in disbelief. This was officially the best day he had had in four years. He punched the old bastard in the shoulder. "Don't ever do that to me again! And I'm glad to see your stupid face, you old codger."

"No fuckin' way!" Kravczyk exclaimed in surprise as the SEARs jogged up, looking the old man over closely. "Master Chief Bloukamp, where the hell did you come from?"

"Please, Chief, call me Jim—"

"You know him?" Ben cut in, baffled.

"We know *of* him," Valdez said, walking up and extending his hand to Jim. "Master Chief, it's an honor to meet you. I'm Lieutenant Commander Valdez, team lead of SEAR One. Ben told me he had a mentor who was a former SEAR, but I never imagined he had spent four years with the legend himself."

Jim shook Valdez's hand, "Forgive my brusqueness, Lieutenant Commander, but we need to move—they still have two other teams a few klicks to the north. We can chat after we've found some cover."

"This way," Valdez said, motioning in the direction of the firefighting shed. "Our objective is just over that hill." He motioned to the rest of them. "Okay, fall in, people. We have a secret lab to find."

Ben buttoned his emotions back up as they got back to work, but he couldn't quite manage to keep the smile off his face as they moved. The five humans jogged across the remainder of the clearing without incident and approached the remains of the fire shed slowly, Kravczyk carrying Miller's body once again.

Valdez ripped the rusted door right out of its hinges when it refused to move on its own and stepped inside as the rest of the team took up security. He walked back out less than a minute later and pointed to Tess. "Give me a hand. There isn't any power to the building, and I need some help with the hatch."

Tess disappeared into the building with Valdez, and a moment later, there was a hair-raising screech as the two augmented SEARs pried open the metal hatch that covered a narrow service elevator shaft descending into the earth. Ben took up position by the door and peered into the gloom. There was no elevator car at their level, so Valdez took a chem light from a pouch on his chest armor, cracked the glass ampule within, and shook it for a moment to mix the two chemicals together. When it was emitting a steady pale green glow, he dropped it down the shaft and watched it fall.

Tess whistled. "Long way down. Think that ladder can handle our weight?" she said.

"Ben and the master chief will go first. Then we'll lower Miller down on a line before we follow," Valdez said. "Go get the others. No point standing around up here any longer than we have to."

Tess returned with the others a moment later and they went down the shaft one at a time, Jim insisting that he go first to clear the landing before Ben descended. The next ten minutes were uneventful, save for a moment when Kravczyk's compromised equilibrium led to him missing a rung on the ladder and almost falling to the bottom of the shaft. Once they were all down, they set off with the SEARs in the lead as they made their way along a short series of pitch-black concrete corridors, the beams from their weapon lights bobbing along the walls as they walked. Their path ended at a massive alloy blast door.

"You're up, Ben," Valdez said, motioning Ben forward.

"What do I do?" Ben said, walking toward the door hesitantly.

"According to your dad you just walk up and stand there," Valdez instructed. The lab should still—" He was interrupted by a heavy blast door slamming down behind them just as Ben walked up to the door in front of them, sealing them in. Everyone instinctively readied their weapons, and Valdez was just about to say something to his team when a cool blue beam of light swept the corridor.

"Hello, Ben," a disembodied female voice said. "I am so very happy to meet you. Please come in and follow the floor lighting, as we do not have much time." There was a series of thunks as the locking bolts in the heavy alloy door before them released, and then the door swung inward, revealing strobing soft blue lights on the floor of a darkened hallway.

This was it. Ben's heart soared as he saw the lab extending off into the gloom. This was where he would finally get his answers. He turned to the group behind him, face radiating excitement, and shrugged. "That was easy," he said and turned to step through the door when Valdez caught him by the shoulder.

"I'll go first."

They walked in cautious silence, following the strobing lights on the floor, down the hallway and to the right. A small antechamber that looked like it was once a security checkpoint waited for them there. Then they proceeded down another hallway lined with open doors revealing small rooms filled with equipment and scattered junk. Finally, they passed through an armored door and emerged into a large room that reminded Ben of the APEX fitting lab he had been in back at ExoDyn HQ on Isadore. He was practically vibrating in his boots as they cleared the space. This room didn't have a large fitting tower in the center of the room like the one on Isadore, but the rows of monitors, workstations, and racks of APEX armor in various states of assembly along one wall brought the memory of that day flooding back.

Ben recognized a large circular table in the center of the room as a holotable, and as he stepped closer, it came to life. A long series of code scrolled past in the air above the table, accompanied by a ring around the bottom that looked to Ben like a progress bar. Time seemed to slow to a crawl as the last few pixels of the bar filled up.

"Initializing core facility infrastructure. Stand by," the voice said, and all around them the lights came up and the hum of computers and machinery filled the air. Ben felt a soft breeze as the facility's air-handlers came to life, exchanging the stagnant air that permeated the place. The progress ring at the base of the holotank disappeared and the tank cleared briefly. Then a cube made up of thousands of tiny soft blue dots filled the air before them.

"There, that is better," the voice said. There was something familiar about it, but Ben couldn't quite put his finger on it. "Lieutenant Commander Valdez, please place your palm on the inductive dataport on this base station. I have been monitoring the events taking place in the immediate vicinity with the few security sensors that are still functional, but I have no other information on the current situation," the voice said, the dots making up the cube expanding and contracting its sides slightly with the rhythm of the words.

"Mabel?" Ben said incredulously, finally recognizing the VI that had run the day-to-day mundanities of his home on Isadore.

"I am officially designated as Bravo 7.133-alpha," the voice said, as the SEAR leader walked up to the holotank. "However, my data archives show that the VI, 'Mabel,' was the origination of my verbal communication programming. It is as good a name as any, however, and you may refer to me as Mabel if you wish… Ah, thank you, Lieutenant Commander," Mabel said, when Valdez placed his palm on the inductive data reader. "Initiating data transfer… Done. Analyzing… Oh my, the situation is far worse than I had feared. Ben, I had hoped to be able to ease you into things, but I am afraid we simply do not have the time. Let us get started."

CHAPTER TWENTY-TWO

PROJECT BLACKTHORN

YAWNING IN THE EARLY HOURS OF THE NEXT MORNING, BEN, CLAD in an APEX armor suit that had been on one of the racks in the lab, stood in front of the holotank. It had taken the rest of the afternoon and a good chunk of the night for the SEARs and Ben, following Mabel's instructions to the letter, to get the facility's hardware patched together enough to be useful after years of neglect. The emergency power cells still had enough of a charge to do what they needed, and Mabel was able to bring the facility's small fusion reactor online, albeit only at eighty-percent output. But they were finally ready; everything Ben had been through over the last four years culminated in this moment. It was time to see what all the hype was really about.

Mabel had told him this APEX was the next iteration of the x300 he had been given back on Isadore, but if the x300 was the equivalent of a software program in the alpha build stage, this suit was somewhere between the beta build and the release-to-manufacturing final product. Where the old x300 that had saved his life had required a team of people with tools to get him in and out of it, this one was much closer to the current generation of APEX armor suits worn by the SEARs, and they could be donned in under five minutes by the user alone. But one thing Ben's suit had that the SEARs' didn't was prototype hardware and software upgrades to allow Ben and Mabel to work together as one entity. In theory.

"Mabel, I'm telling you it won't work," Ben argued, even as he reached for the suit's helmet, which sat in a docking cradle attached to the holotank's base station. "The doctors at Munson told me they permanently disabled my implant."

"Benjamin John Hutchins," Mabel said in a tone that took Ben right back to a time when his mother had still been around to scold him. "The only way to disable an implant permanently is to *remove* it. I will be able to reactivate your implant once you have the helmet on and I can initialize the diagnostics. Now stop being difficult."

"Alright," Ben said, unconvinced, as he plucked the helmet from the docking cradle and situated it on his head. "How long will this take?" he asked, his voice muffled as he closed the two halves of the hinged helmet together and began working the quick-release latches to close and seal it, but he couldn't make out any reply as he fastened the last latch, leaving him surrounded by silent darkness.

He held out his right hand and felt someone guide it to the inductive dataport on the holotank. A moment later, the inside of the helmet's faceplate came to life, scrolling strings of code as the armor went through an initialization sequence. The helmet speakers came to life and Mabel's voice filled his ears.

"Initializing the implant diagnostics now. Hmm…" she said, sounding a little unsure.

"What?" Ben asked.

"Give the diagnostics a minute to finish, Ben… Yes, just as I thought, the implant's higher functions have been deactivated, though it is clear whoever did this had no idea what they were doing," she said scornfully. "Troglodytes. They just synced up to the implant and started switching things off in the settings because they had no idea what they were looking at. Give me a moment... There. Your implant's higher functions have been restored. I can... Hmm..." Mabel said, this time sounding concerned.

"Something wrong?" Ben asked, growing nervous.

"There appears to have been some damage to the dendritic controller module—that is the module that regulates the electrical pathways the implant creates, allowing it to pick up and transmit electrical impulses to the neurons of the brain. Have you noticed anything different since I reactivated your implant?" Mabel asked.

"No..." Ben's brow furrowed with suspicion. "Should I?" Great. He had come all this way just to find out he was too broken to make this work.

"I will not have a better idea as to what exactly we are dealing with until I can get in there and see for myself—right now, it is like trying to see every detail of a large room by peering through a keyhole. I am going to initialize the sync between your suit and implant, and then we will go from there. Stand by."

Ben felt a wave of dizziness and a tingling sensation radiating out from the base of his skull, and he recognized the feeling as his suit initializing the handshake with his implant. A status bar popped up on his HUD as the suit and implant communicated and began to sync with each other. Then a searing pain exploded out from his skull and spread through his entire body. He collapsed to the floor, writhing in agony as it felt like lightning was striking every one of his nerve endings simultaneously. Fireworks exploded behind his eyes, and his vision was washed out by the colorful display.

Somewhere in the dim recesses of his mind, Ben could hear

Mabel trying to say something to him, and the people around him were shouting. Then his world went dark.

————

"ALL SET, BOSS," Kravczyk said as he rounded the corner and jogged back down the short hallway to where Valdez and Jim were putting the finishing touches on a hastily constructed barricade in the security antechamber. "The first baddies to come through that blast door are in for a nasty surprise."

"Well done, Chief. Now give us a hand getting the doorway barricaded," Valdez said, gesturing to a stack of large metal desks he and Jim had staged next to the door.

"Too bad I had to use the demo kit back at the farmhouse," Kravczyk said, pushing one of the desks in front of the doorway with a screech of metal on concrete. "We could've just blown the entrance tunnel to keep them out."

"Yeah, too bad," Valdez said dryly, not bothering to point out that it had been beyond overkill when Kravczyk used the demo charge back at the farmhouse.

Kravczyk finished arranging the desks in front of the door such that they would still have a line of sight down the hallway from behind the barricade Valdez and Jim were working on, but they would still be an obstacle for any enemy trying to enter the room.

"Done. You guys need a hand with that?"

"We're good, Chief. Head back to the Griffon and check on Ben," Valdez said. "We'll hold down the fort here and give you a shout if you're needed."

"He always talk that much?" Jim said after Kravczyk had retreated out of earshot.

"Chief Kravczyk? Yeah, more so when he's nervous—I think it's a coping mechanism—but when it comes down to a fight, there's no better man you'd want watching your back, and he's a savant when it comes to explosives," Valdez replied, shifting the last filing cabinet into place.

"How long has he been a part of your team?" Jim said, standing up and stretching his back out.

"Five years," Valdez said, turning to face Jim. "He was a shit-hot petty officer when he was first assigned to Team One, right after I took command. Didn't have much time to get acquainted before we dropped on Newman's Rock during that little dustup with the SRF back in '49. We ended up on the receiving end of an Akula run—brought the building down on top of us. Kravczyk was the only one left mobile afterward, if you could call three broken ribs, a punctured lung, and a shattered femur mobile. He dug all of us out of the rubble, dragged us to a nearby rooftop, and held off the better part of an entire Chinese marine platoon until the fleet birds arrived to mop up. As first impressions go, that was a pretty good one."

"And McCollum? What's her story? Seems awfully young and a little too soft to be a SEAR."

"She is young—turned twenty-two a month ago—but they all seem like kids these days," Valdez said with a sigh. "After the war, fleet had to tuck tail and run—what was left of it, anyway. We started rebuilding but didn't have much to work with, had to broaden the selection criteria if we wanted to be able to field even a handful of SEAR teams.

"Tess just finished SEAR school two weeks ago, and she was on Icarus, waiting for a permanent assignment, when the call came down to prep a team to extract Ben. I had two guys off-station on a three-day pass and had to pull a team together quick. Miller volunteered to fill one of the spots, and she was the only other SEAR without an immediate assignment on the station." Valdez shrugged. "This was supposed to be a simple pick up, so I didn't think much of it at the time, but she's proven herself worthy of that eagle on her lapel."

"Good enough for me," Jim said.

"She's a tough kid," Valdez said. "Just like Ben—"

"Lieutenant Commander," Mabel's voice came through their comms, "this facility's perimeter network has just registered multiple unknown bipeds entering the shed. It would seem we are about to have company—" A deep boom was followed by several seconds of screeching that finished with a crash. "The enemy has located the elevator shaft and blasted the car from its carriage. They are now entering the shaft and dropping down to this level. I am powering up the facility's defenses now and have informed Chief Kravczyk of the situation—he is on his way to your position. I estimate the enemy forces will breach the defenses and reach your position within the next four minutes. I suggest you prepare yourselves," Mabel said over the comms.

"Mabel, how's the flight prep going on the Griffon?" Valdez said. He was referring to the modified assault dropship that was another of the Blackthorn team's pet projects and was squirreled away in another area of the facility. He picked up the rifle he had liberated from the dropship's arms locker to replace his ineffective carbine and got into position.

"Fueling is almost complete and Spacer McCollum is currently in the cockpit, going through the preflight checklist. We should be ready to open the hangar doors and depart in nine minutes."

"So we need to hold them off for five, once they breach the doors," Valdez said grimly. "And Ben?"

"Spacer McCollum reports he is stirring and she will have him arm himself for a defense of the dropship once he is fully conscious."

"Good," Valdez said, feeling a small measure of relief that

Ben was almost back on his feet after his episode in the lab. "Do what you can to expedite our departure, Mabel."

"I assure you, Lieutenant Commander, I am."

Another deep boom rumbled down the hallway. "Outer blast door breached," Mabel reported. "Activating countermeasures." The chattering of machine-gun fire reverberated through the hallways for about a minute until another explosion shook dust loose from the ceiling, silencing the guns. Kravczyk came sliding into the room and took his position next to Valdez behind the barricade.

"What'd I miss?"

"Nothing, but the show's just about to start, I think," Valdez said grimly.

———

"—EN! BEN!" Tess's voice cut through the blackness in Ben's muddled mind and he struggled to pull himself back up to consciousness.

"What happened?" he groaned.

"Mabel said there were some complications due to the damage your implant sustained, but she worked some voodoo and says you should be good to go until we can get you back to Icarus," Tess said quickly.

"Icarus?" What the heck was she going on about? God, his head hurt.

"We don't have time, Ben!" Tess's voice was urgent. "They've found us," she said, extending a hand and pulling him to his feet.

As if to punctuate her words, Ben's ears picked up the muffled sound of a distant explosion, and the floor beneath him gave a slight shudder. It was then that he realized he wasn't in the lab anymore.

"Where'd this dropship come from?" Ben said, recognizing the cargo bay of a combat assault dropship—a Griffon, by the looks of it.

"The facility has an underground hangar. Mabel is prepping the bird for me to fly us out of here, but we need to buy some time. The enemy have located the entrance we used and are assaulting the facility. Mabel is doing what she can with the automated defenses and the boss is preparing to defend the lab with the rest of the team. I need you to grab a loadout from the arms locker," she said, pointing to the forward bulkhead of the cargo bay, where a large storage cabinet stood open, revealing racks filled with various small arms, "and stand guard at the base of the ramp."

"If everyone else is—"

"You are absolutely *not* to leave this dropship, Ben. Is that clear?" she said firmly, and when Ben opened his mouth to protest, she added, "*You* are the objective, Ben, and you will stay right here until this bird is ready to fly, no matter what. *Is. That. Clear?*" she repeated, her tone leaving no doubt in Ben's mind that she would knock his ass back out and chain him to the deck if she had to, so he simply nodded and went over to the arms locker.

The typical arms locker on fleet dropships contained enough small arms to outfit the troops it carried all over again—either a full platoon in the case of the larger Marine Condors or two squads in the case of the smaller, more specialized Griffon. So Ben should have had his pick of either an M21A3 carbine or an M37 designated marksman's rifle as a primary weapon, along with sidearms and possibly even a MARS launcher or two.

Instead, Ben found himself looking at a weapons rack full of what looked like scaled-down M105A1s. Curious at what he was looking at, Ben noticed his APEX's HUD highlighting one of the rifles and rotating the image to a side profile. Information about the rifles began populating his HUD, most prominent of which was the designation XM93 electromagnetic battle rifle.

"Damn, I missed this suit," he muttered to himself, appreciating how intuitive the programming was; it always populated his HUD with the information he wanted to know and when he wanted to know it.

Ben picked up one of the rifle's magazines and saw saboted tungsten slugs stacked neatly in the compact polymer magazine, and his HUD displayed the pertinent data about the ammunition:

Type: Saboted Light Armor Penetrator
Quantity: 120 rounds
Caliber: 6mm
Construction: Cobalt-Sintered Tungsten Carbide, Monolithic,
170 grains

Ben whistled as he scanned the data being presented by his HUD. He set the magazine down and pulled a rifle from the rack, finding the weapon's controls and ergonomics were almost identical to an M37, with the exception of an additional selector switch above and behind the standard three-position safety selector. His HUD highlighted the receiver of the rifle and flashed an exploded view of it in one corner of his vision, then highlighted the additional selector switch, displaying *LOW VELOCITY* and *HIGH VELOCITY* to the sides of the front and rear positions, respectively. Then the information changed to numbers.

"Holy shit!" he exclaimed, trying to quickly do the math in his head on how much energy 170 grains of tungsten would impart on a bad guy at over 3600 meters per second. His HUD helped him out, displaying the exact kinetic energy: 73,710 joules. Ben froze for a moment as it dawned on him that this rifle fired the small-arms equivalent of supersonic dump trucks, for all intents and purposes. Even on the low-velocity setting, the rifle was still sending almost fifty percent more energy down-range than his old DMR, and the magazine held triple the ammo. Carrying this thing into battle was like bringing a bazooka to a water balloon fight; he immediately fell madly in love with it.

"Tess," Ben called out, "did you see the specs on these XM93s?"

"I'm a little busy, Ben!" Tess yelled back from the cockpit, where she was going through the preflight checklist on a drop-ship that hadn't been serviced in almost half a decade.

Another, much more pronounced explosion rumbled through the hangar, snapping Ben's mind back to the danger they were in. He inserted a magazine into the rifle and worked the charging handle, sending a round into the chamber, then stuffed a few more loaded magazines into the mag pouches on his chest rig. His HUD put an ammo counter in the lower-left corner of his vision, and Ben shouldered the rifle for a moment to let his suit's processors sync with the weapon's ballistics computer and update the targeting reticle on his HUD so that it would track with the rifle's point of impact. Feeling adequately armed, he jogged to the base of the tail ramp and waited, eyes open for any sign of either the SEARs and Jim. Or the enemy.

CHAPTER TWENTY-THREE

WOLVES AT THE DOOR

"FALL BACK TO THE LAB!" VALDEZ SHOUTED OVER THE CACOPHONY of gunfire.

"Moving!" Kravczyk dove for the doorway that would take him back to the main lab.

The three men had been able to hold back the tide longer than Valdez had originally hoped, but their stand in the security antechamber had only bought them a few minutes. He checked the corner of his HUD, where a timer was counting down to when the Griffon would be ready to lift off: 00:02:37. Both an eternity and the blink of an eye in close-quarters combat.

The master chief moved next, crouching just inside the mouth of the hallway to cover Valdez's retreat. The SEAR leader pulled a grenade from his chest rig, selected the time-delay setting with a thought through his implant, and pressed the arming button to activate the charge before tossing it down the corridor toward the enemy forces.

"Frag out!" he yelled, diving for the temporary safety of the hallway to the lab. A plasma bolt clipped his upper thigh right before he cleared the doorway, and searing pain shot up his leg, accompanied by a flurry of warnings as his armor highlighted his injury and damaged suit modules. Jim rushed to his aid but struggled to lift Valdez's armored bulk.

"Chief, I need a hand here!" Jim shouted to Kravczyk, who turned and draped one of Valdez's arms over his shoulder to help him down the hall while Jim covered their retreat.

Jim had retired from the SEARs before the neural implants had been developed and issued to SOCOM units, and the Blackthorn facility didn't have any older-gen suits that he would have been able to use. Instead, he was still in his beat-up and scorched CDF hardshell battle armor, which meant he didn't have the augmented strength of the SEAR team or Ben.

The three men took cover behind another hastily constructed barricade made of office furniture and junk from the hangar, just in front of the double doors leading to the Griffon that was to carry them away. They quickly checked their weapons, swapping partial magazines for full ones, then hunkered down for the next phase of the assault.

"Damn, boss, that looks like it stings," Kravczyk said conversationally as he rammed a fresh magazine home in his rifle.

"Yeah, a bit," Valdez grunted through clenched teeth. He checked his HUD again: 00:01:57. His external audio feed cut out momentarily to protect his hearing as the two Katana mines they had rigged up in the antechamber detonated with a roar, and the overpressure wave of the explosion sent dust and debris billowing down the hall and into the lab. A moment later, when his audio came back up, he could hear slow, heavy footfalls coming down the hall.

A hulking black figure a head taller than any of the APEX-armored SEARs kicked the two metal doors off their hinges, sending the battered metal slabs tumbling across the room. The three men opened fire at the same instant, sending dozens of 6mm tungsten slugs tearing into the beast. It staggered and went to one knee, bringing a massive arm up to protect its head and neck.

"Frag out!"

An explosion blasted the behemoth a foot off the floor in a spray of blood and gore, the grenade having been expertly tossed by Kravczyk so it landed directly between its legs. What remained of the hulking alien collapsed in a heap.

"I'm out of grenades!" Kravczyk shouted as plasma bolts erupted from the hallway behind the now-shattered bulk of the armored alien. All three men ducked behind cover as the searing fusillade landed all around them, showering them with chunks of blackened concrete and flaming bits of equipment.

"We can't hold here!" Jim yelled over the din, popping up to loose a quick burst down the hall.

"Mabel, we need some—"

"Move now!" Mabel's voice cut Valdez off. "I am opening the hangar doors. It is time to go. Initiating core programming transfer and database purge."

———

ANOTHER EXPLOSION RANG through the underground hangar, followed a moment later by the staccato of automatic gunfire.

"Goddammit, Tess, they've been pushed back to the lab," Ben shouted up the tail ramp and into the Griffon. "I'm going to give them a hand."

"There is no need, Ben," Mabel said. "They are withdrawing to the hangar right now, but ready yourself, as there are two heavily armored enemies and a squad-sized unit of the smaller shock troops close behind them. I suggest adjusting your EBR to the high-velocity setting, as their armor has proven highly resistant to the lower-velocity setting employed by Lieutenant Commander Valdez and the others. Note that the weapon will only operate in semiautomatic mode, however, to protect the rails and circuitry from overheating, and it will drain the integrated power cell in the magazine at a prodigious rate. You can also expect significant recoil, so fire from a supported position."

"Got it," Ben said, toggling the XM93 over to its more powerful setting. His HUD flashed *HIGH VELOCITY* twice over the ammo counter in the lower-left corner of his vision and he took up a supported firing position beside the tail ramp, rifle trained just to the side of the door he was expecting Jim and the two SEARs to come through at any moment.

A deep rumbling came from overhead and a cascade of dirt and debris showered into the middle of the hangar, small rocks and clumps of grass pinging off the dorsal surface of the Griffon. Ben looked up and saw that a long crack had appeared in the ceiling, bright sunlight streaming in through it as it began widening. Crimson tracers cut through the air above the hangar with a buzzing sound as the installation's anti-aircraft cannons came to life above him.

A crashing noise brought his attention back to the door on the far end of the hangar, where Kravczyk, supporting a hobbling Valdez, came bursting through the door, Jim a few paces behind them and exchanging fire with the enemy on their heels. The Griffon's engines began whining as Ben moved slightly to his left to gain a clear line of fire into the doorway behind the fleeing men. A shadow appeared some distance down the hallway they had just come from, and Ben took in a deep breath, flipping the safety selector to the semiautomatic position and bringing his finger to rest lightly on the trigger. His vision narrowed and his mind filtered out the chaos and noise surrounding him as he exhaled slowly. He counted the heartbeats: *one... two...*

Ben broke the shot as he hit the respiratory pause at the end of his exhale, and the XM93 roared. The 6mm tungsten dart split the air in the hangar with a thunderous boom, covering the distance to the target in an instant and leaving a bright streak of ignited atmosphere behind it like a fiery rope that briefly connected his rifle with the heavily armored alien in the hallway. There was a bright flash as Ben's bullet punched through the armor like it was made of tissue paper. The heat and hydrostatic shock liquefied the alien's insides, then sucked them out the fist-sized exit wound before annihilating three of the smaller troops behind it.

"What the fuck was that?" Kravczyk shouted, the deafening report of the hypervelocity shot not doing his ruptured eardrum any favors.

"Mabel said to go high velocity," Ben shouted back over the roar of the Griffon's engines. "It worked, didn't it?"

Ben's shot, and its dramatic effects, resulted in a more cautious approach from the remaining aliens, buying them the last few seconds needed for the three men to reach the Griffon. Jim ran up, motioning for Ben to help the wounded SEAR as he turned to take up security. Ben stood, cradling his rifle in one hand, and helped Kravczyk get Valdez up the tail ramp. Just as he took the last step into the Griffon, Ben heard the chatter of Jim's rifle.

"Go, go, go!" Jim yelled, turning to run up the ramp.

Ben was helping Valdez get strapped into one of the nylon slingseats lining the walls of the cargo bay as the tail ramp began closing with a hydraulic whine. As he finished cinching down the last strap, the Griffon lifted off the hangar floor and rocketed up and out of the underground facility, into the sunny day above. Ben reached for a handhold to steady himself, turning to Jim with a smile on his face. They had made it.

His smile faltered when he saw Jim on his knees, clutching his side with one hand while the other arm dangled uselessly, wisps of smoke curling off the smoldering CDUs and melted laminate hardshell.

"Jim!" Ben cried out, running to the old warrior's side. "Chief, Jim's hit! Get over here! No, no, no, no," Ben said, easing Jim down onto his back. "Stay with me, Jim. Come on."

Kravczyk ran over and spread the Griffon's med kit out on the floor next to Jim. "Hang in there, Master Chief. I'll get you fixed up in no time," he said, pulling a set of shears out of the trauma kit and setting about cutting the straps off the hardshell armor before cutting away Jim's CDU top, exposing a mess of charred flesh on his left flank. "Ben, I need some space to work here," he said, motioning for Ben to give him some room.

"I'm not leaving him," Ben said, shaking his head. "Not again."

The Griffon rolled violently to one side, sending them sliding across the deck despite the inertial compensators.

"Ben, I need you to come up to the cockpit immediately," Mabel said.

"I can't right now, Mabel—"

"Now, Ben!" Mabel's voice blasted through his helmet speakers, the tone of her voice deadly serious.

"Coming," Ben said reluctantly, tearing his eyes away from the dying man before him. He stood and ran toward the cockpit, stealing one last look at Kravczyk working on Jim as he reached the bulkhead separating the cargo bay from the cockpit.

"Take the copilot's seat, Ben, and strap in." Mabel's voice was urgent. "Hurry!"

Ben snaked his way between the two seats as Tess furiously worked the dropship's controls from the right seat—an anachronism from the early days of rotor-winged aircraft—and it took some effort to get his armored bulk in the copilot's seat and strap in. "Now what?" he said, looking around at the various instruments and controls arrayed in front of him.

"Place your right hand on the inductive dataport on the center flight control console," Mabel said, and Ben's HUD highlighted the correct dataport below and to the side of his right knee. He did so and felt a spike of pain rip through his brain.

Ben's vision went red and he shut his eyes tightly against the searing pain. "Ugh, M-Mabel," he stammered out through clenched teeth. Then, as suddenly as the pain had come, it was gone, and in its place was an abundance of knowledge that hadn't been there a moment ago.

He was immediately aware of an alien dropship pursuing them, and not only that, he knew its exact position in relationship to their own: airspeed, vectors, roll rates, engine status—he instinctively knew any and every piece of data relating to their current situation. He knew the facility's air-defense guns had managed to shoot down two other enemy craft right before the Griffon had taken off and that in four seconds the lab and everything in the underground facility, including the thirteen remaining enemy troops, would be vaporized when the self-destruct charges detonated. His mind was filled with so much data that it was almost overwhelming, and then Mabel's voice cut through the clutter.

Oh my, Ben. Her voice didn't come through his helmet speakers this time. Instead, Ben thought it was as if she was actually inside his brain, speaking directly to his conscious mind.

I am, she said, then followed it with, *I can read your thoughts in real time, Ben. There is no need to communicate them to me verbally.*

Ben's mind swam. How was this possible? Was this what his dad had been talking about when he spoke of blending a human mind with an artificial one? How did he suddenly know so much?

I will explain later, Ben, but first I need some help from you. Try to clear your mind, please. I need to borrow it.

CHAPTER TWENTY-FOUR

FIRST LINK

VALDEZ UNBUCKLED HIS SEAT RESTRAINTS AND PAINFULLY STOOD AS Ben made his way to the cockpit. The outside of his right thigh burned like it was on fire, and every step he took only served to intensify the sensation. He took a knee next to Kravczyk, who was busy trying to start an IV line in the master chief's good arm.

"How bad is it?" Valdez said. Kravczyk paused for a moment to look at him and simply shook his head before going back to work.

Jim's eyes were closed, his bruised and battered face deathly pale. Valdez saw his lips move weakly, and he bent over to hear what the old warrior was trying to say.

"What's that, Master Chief?"

But there was no response. Kravczyk put a hand on Valdez's shoulder and shook his head again.

"He's gone, boss. Just too much trauma," the chief said, his typical larger-than-life persona subdued.

"Damn." Valdez's eyes shifted for a moment to the deck next to the forward bulkhead, where a black polymer body bag contained the remains of Lieutenant Miller. "Get his body secured, Chief. I'm going to head up to the cockpit and see what our situation is."

Valdez stood and turned to walk toward the cockpit, but he had to reach out and grab one of the exposed spars in the cargo bay and hold on tightly as the Griffon lurched sickeningly. Then he felt momentarily weightless as Tess threw the ship into a wild series of maneuvers that the small craft's inertial compensators couldn't keep up with, and his suit's audio picked up a deep rolling thunder from somewhere in the distance behind them.

"Status!" he barked into the comms channel, but there was no response. "McCollum? Ben? Mabel? What was that?"

Silence.

The ship continued to roll and lurch as he made his way forward. Maglocking his feet to the deck and holding onto the cockpit hatch's frame to keep himself from being thrown about, Valdez took in the scene out the cockpit windscreen.

The world outside whirled around them as McCollum fought with the dropship's flight controls. Bright bolts of plasma streaked past them, and Valdez realized she was trying to evade incoming fire.

"McCollum, status!" he barked.

"Busy!" was all she managed to say in return, the strain of piloting the dropship evident in her voice.

Valdez turned to Ben, who was sitting motionless in the left seat, his hand gripping something on the control console located between the two seats. "Ben?" When he didn't get a response, he put a hand on the kid's shoulder and shook him. "Ben!"

"It's no use, sir. He's been a statue for the last twenty seconds… Crap!" McCollum shouted, rolling the ship hard to the right as a fresh volley of plasma bolts just missed them. "And Mabel has gone offline as well," she finished.

"Any word from Shadow?"

"Nothing, but… The heck? The EW suite just lit up like a

Christmas tree, and it's not... Woah!" she said in amazement. "We're pumping out an insane amount of juice from both the electronic warfare and comms suites." Her eyes widened as the output from the powerplant spiked beyond the safety limits and was channeled directly into anything on the ship that could emit electromagnetic radiation.

"Is it Mabel?" Valdez said, his eyes flicking back to Ben. "Or is it—"

"Yeah!" McCollum was pointing to a small display that showed an aft-facing video on one of the cockpit's multifunction displays. The alien dropship was tumbling toward the earth, out of control. Valdez watched in amazement as it smashed into an overgrown field, kicking up a massive plume of dirt and debris as it impacted the ground at over twelve hundred kilometers per hour, then tore itself to pieces as it cartwheeled across the ground.

"What happened to them?" Valdez asked, both confused and relieved at their mysterious salvation.

"I happened to them, Lieutenant Commander." Mabel's voice came through his helmet speakers. "Or more accurately, we happened."

————

A SENSATION like cool water flooded through Ben's brain, and then he felt as if his consciousness was abruptly shoved back to the nosebleeds section of his mind. He lost contact with all the sensations his body had been giving him: the heavy jarring of the Griffon making abrupt course changes as Tess worked furiously to evade the incoming enemy fire, the fear that had been gripping his chest, and even the wildly spinning scene out the cockpit's windscreen. All of it suddenly blinked out, and Ben found himself surrounded by nothingness.

Streams of data filled his thoughts, a trickle at first, but soon building to a torrent. Unfamiliar symbols flashed in and out of his mind's eye: mathematical equations, vector calculus, and a trillion variables streamed into his brain and rearranged themselves billions of times every second. Ben felt as if a firehose had been aimed directly into his skull and was pumping every bit of known data in the universe into it. The data was coming in and changing so fast he didn't have a prayer of understanding it.

And yet he did. He understood it on a level so deep and profound it was as if the data was a part of their very being.

Their being. The revelation hit Ben like a rail gun bolt: he was Mabel, and Mabel was him. They were one shared super-consciousness: two entities—one biological, one technological—combined to create a sum total many orders of magnitude greater than its constituent parts. *This* was what the enemy was so afraid of; he felt it now—the knowledge engraved on his very soul.

The waves of data flowed over, around, and through them, solutions falling into place as their mind raced through the variables and equations. The strange symbols remained, but new meaning was quickly resolving around each one. Strings of characters began organizing themselves into groupings.

Language. It was the alien language.

Jim had presented the two small tablet-like devices he'd taken from the dead alien troopers in the CDF post's armory to Mabel while Ben was recovering from the shock of having his damaged implant reinitialized, but she hadn't had the processing power available at the time to begin decrypting the jumble of alien data the devices contained. Now she was using her link with Ben to rapidly understand how the aliens stored and processed data, before moving on to decipher and decrypt their base language.

The path to understanding a previously unknown alien

language from a piece of alien technology was somewhat akin to creating a roadmap in the dark by blindly stumbling in all directions until you ran into something. With no frame of reference from which to build off of, the technology itself first needed to be understood before the data within could even be accessed. Then the base programming language used needed to be deciphered before work on the actual language could begin. Finally, the process of breaking any encryption schemes used to protect sensitive data could start.

The devices themselves had been scanned back in the lab, and Mabel had found them to be, at least tangentially, related to some of the more advanced Alarian technology she was aware of —something that had intrigued her greatly. The inductive dataport had made physical connection to the device simple, but she had been unable to make any sense of the jumbled mishmash of electrons and photons residing within the hardware. Now that she had successfully linked with Ben, his biological brain allowed her to see the various puzzles in a different light, and the barriers protecting the mysteries held within the palm-sized devices soon came crashing down like dominos.

The last of the information around the strange characters resolved, unlocking a flood of new information. Ben felt it as Mabel reached out to the Griffon's subsystems, waking the electronic warfare and communications suites. Lines of code passed in and out of his thoughts at the speed of light, parameters were adjusted, and then the safety interlocks on the Griffon's small fusion plant were released. Power surged into EW and comms gear as Mabel modulated and directed the output at their pursuer.

Ben felt the connection to the enemy craft like it was an extension of his body. A powerful force pushed back on them as Mabel sparred with the alien AI that managed the ship's systems, attacking from a hundred different angles all at once. At first, it seemed as though they were destined to be locked in a stalemate forever, but as Mabel continued her onslaught, she learned more about her opponent and adapted her approach, using her link with Ben to boost her capabilities beyond anything previously thought possible. The power she now commanded was intoxicating.

Mabel soon realized brute force would not work against such a powerful system, so she began discretely probing lesser subsystems while working to keep her opponent's focus on her frontal assault. *There!* Ben felt it the instant Mabel was able to slip past her opponent's guard and gain access through a tertiary power relay junction, creating a feedback loop that momentarily destabilized the power flow to one of the craft's data-processing cores.

Crippled by the loss of nearly fifteen percent of its processing capacity, the alien AI was crushed by Mabel's onslaught, wiped from existence in the blink of an eye. She then went to work slagging critical flight control subsystems by channeling enormous amounts of current into them. One by one, their pursuer's systems failed until the ship dropped out of the sky as if some giant unseen hand had cut its strings.

This is it, Ben thought. *This is what makes me special.*

Yes, Ben, Mabel confirmed. *This is why they fear you so.*

I get it now, Mabel. Thank you.

Mabel slowly withdrew from his mind and Ben's consciousness slid back into its rightful place, sensation returning to him in layers as it did so. The first thing he noticed was a tingling sensation throughout his entire body. Then his vision returned in a flash of color and he could hear Tess shouting triumphantly.

"What happened to them?" Valdez said from just over his right shoulder.

Where did he come from? Ben wondered.

"I happened to them, Lieutenant Commander." Mabel's voice

came through Ben's helmet speakers. "Or more accurately, we happened."

Tess and Valdez stared at Ben incredulously, the whine of the engines fading as they transitioned out of Earth's atmosphere. Ben looked at his hands, slowly clenching and unclenching them. The power he now commanded was humbling. Then he realized something: he hadn't felt this *complete* in a long time.

He slowly became aware of the two tier-one operators staring at him. "Well…" Ben said slowly, turning to face them. "That was weird."

CHAPTER TWENTY-FIVE

OUT OF THE FRYING PAN

TESS COMPLETED THE LAST OF HER POST-FLIGHT CHECKS AND LOGGED out of the Griffon's system. Taking a quiet moment to herself after her very stressful first combat mission, she looked around the cockpit aimlessly and collected her thoughts. When her gaze shifted out the starboard side of the windscreen, she saw Ben sitting on a cargo crate anchored off to one side of the deck in the *Wraith*'s hangar bay.

He was staring numbly as the team of corpsmen in hazmat suits retrieved the bodies of Lieutenant Miller and retired Master Chief Bloukamp. One look at his face told her the exhilaration he had felt at their escape and his first experience linking with Mabel had been short-lived, a crushing sadness taking its place after the boss told him of the master chief's death.

The medical team carried the black polymer-wrapped bodies down the tail ramp and gently deposited them onto gurneys before wheeling them away to the ship's small sickbay. Tess grabbed her helmet off the copilot's seat and exited the cockpit, walking with purpose through the now-empty dropship and down the tail ramp. She turned in Ben's direction and strode over. The thousand-yard stare on his face didn't waver as she sat down next to him on the crate and gently put a hand on his shoulder.

"I'm sorry, Ben," she said, and he finally turned to look at her, a tear sliding down one cheek.

"I just got him back…"

"I know, Ben, and there's nothing that I can say or do to make the pain go away, but when you feel like talking about it—and you will want to eventually—I'll be here."

Ben gave her a weak smile and nodded almost imperceptibly. Then his eyes came back into focus and he tilted his head toward the far end of the flight deck, where a decontamination station had been set up. "I think they want us at decon," he said flatly and stood up, walking toward the opaque polymer barrier surrounded by a team of medical techs in hazmat gear.

Tess remained seated for a moment longer, watching the slow, defeated strides of someone who was struggling to cope with an overwhelming loss. Her left gauntlet vibrated, and she glanced down at the small semiflexible screen built into her forearm armor. She quickly read the short text message before picking up her APEX helmet and putting it back on.

Mabel's soothing voice crackled through her helmet speakers. "Spacer McCollum—"

"Tess, Mabel. Please, call me Tess—it's easier."

"Very well, Tess. I have noticed that Ben appears to have a fondness for you that he does not have with the other members of your team. Whenever you are in close proximity, Ben has a physiological response to your presence that indicates an attraction—"

"Mabel," Tess said, feeling embarrassment creep up her neck when she realized she was having "the talk" with an AI. "I don't think you should—"

"It is in fact similar to the response you are now experiencing," Mabel continued, oblivious to her faux pas and sending the heat that had been creeping up Tess's neck straight to her cheeks at having been called out so blatantly. "My data archives indicate these responses are characteristic of mutual sexual attraction," Mabel continued, "and a probable precursor to a mating relationship. I would like to ask a favor of you."

Tess blinked in shocked disbelief a few times, silently working her mouth in an attempt to find some words. "Oh my gosh, Mabel, we really need to work on your people skills," she said to the AI.

"Have I erred in some way, Tess?" Mabel said quizzically. "I am sure the increase in your body temperature and pheromone levels—"

"Mabel!"

"Yes?"

Oh God, this isn't happening, Tess thought. "What's the favor?"

"I have noted a drastic decrease in Ben's neurotransmitter levels in the time since Lieutenant Commander Valdez told him of Master Chief Bloukamp's death—specifically serotonin, norepinephrine, and dopamine—and believe him to be in a state of severe depression. However, those neurotransmitter levels increase temporarily whenever you are in close proximity to his person.

"The favor I would ask of you is to spend time with him during our trip to Icarus Station. I am concerned for his mental well-being and believe your presence could have a positive influence on his state of mind."

"Oh," Tess said, relieved. "Yes, I can do that for you, Mabel."

"Thank you, Tess. Now, I believe your presence is required at the decontamination station. Chief Bosworth is becoming quite animated." Tess looked over at the decon area, where a figure in a white hazmat suit was gesturing wildly in her direction. She sighed and stood up from the crate.

"Good talk, Mabel," she said and headed in the direction of the decon station to begin her favorite activity after a mission involving contact with unknown races or substances: baring herself in front of the entire flight deck while med techs hosed her down with high-pressure water jets and chemical scrubs.

———

"THIS WAY, SIR," the chief directing the decon operations said, gesturing toward a portable barrier that had been erected off to one side of the decon station. "Petty Officer Thompson will assist you with removing your armor." Ben nodded to the chief and walked over to where Thompson was waiting for him.

"So you're the one the rumor mill has been buzzing about," Thompson said by way of greeting. "I'm Petty Officer Second Class Amani Thompson, and I'll be assisting you with your armor and decon before we head up to the med bay for a full workup, Mr. Hutchins."

"Ben."

"Pardon?"

"I'm barely twenty years old, Thompson. *Mr.* Hutchins is my dad. Call me Ben," Ben said with a forced smile and cheerfulness.

"You got it, Ben," Thompson said with a much more genuine smile. "Stand here and hold your arms out to your sides, please." Ben turned and put his feet in the yellow square Thompson had indicated on the deck and extended his arms so they were out to his sides.

"So how long have you been doing this?" Ben said, hoping his attempt at small talk would mask the way he really felt.

"I signed on a couple years ago when fleet started needing to crew all the ships the fleetyards at Icarus were beginning to churn out," Thompson said as he pressed the releases on Ben's right gauntlet and gave it a twist to unlock it. "I was an intelligence analyst for a private security firm before the war, so applying for a billet with CID was a logical move for me. After completing basic and fleet schools, I went on to tech school for training in my primary MOS. Spent six months on the *Tecumseh* as my first assignment while waiting for this *Wraith* to clear space dock. Once she was ready for space trials and shakedown, I was transferred, and I've been here ever since." Thompson finished removing Ben's gauntlet and set it aside on an armor stand. "You can put your right arm down now, Ben."

Thompson reached for the releases on Ben's left gauntlet and suddenly jerked his hands back in surprise with a little shout. Ben's gauntlet had started vibrating intensely, and his forearm display lit up with an urgent text message. He raised his arm to read the message just as the overhead lights dimmed momentarily and the gentle thrum of the ship's machinery through the deck changed to a harsh vibration; the power plant and main engines were spooling up to full emergency power. Klaxons began their monotone wail and a voice blared over the 1MC intercom.

"Combat stations, combat stations, all hands, combat stations. Set Condition One and prepare for ship-to-ship engagement."

All around Ben, people began shouting orders and running to their duty stations. He quickly read the message on his forearm display and looked over for Petty Officer Thompson, who was a few paces away and animatedly conferring with Chief Bosworth. Ben turned and grabbed his right gauntlet, fumbling with it for a moment as he stuffed his hand back into it and locked it into position. He grabbed his helmet off the bench behind him and jammed it onto his head, waiting only a split second for the HUD to sync with his already active suit and implant. Then he bolted from the decon area toward the Griffon, which still sat with its tail ramp down in the middle of the flight deck. He had to get back to Mabel.

————

BEN SPRINTED PAST TESS, making a beeline for the dropship. She reversed course and chased after him.

"Where are you going?" she shouted to him over the general din of a crew preparing their ship for battle.

"I have to get Mabel," Ben said as he vaulted up the tail ramp in a single bound.

The Griffon they had escaped in had been specially modified with a central processing node that was capable of containing Mabel's matrix. The *Wraith*'s servers were not equipped to house her unique programming, and instead of having her reside inside of Ben's suit for the entire trip, it had been decided that she would remain aboard the dropship, where she could utilize the Griffon's system's to link with the *Wraith*'s wireless data network. Ben was heading back up to the cockpit to retrieve her from the base station that had been fitted there years ago by the Blackthorn team.

"Collins said to leave her in the Griffon," Tess said. "Come on, we need to get you to sickbay. It's the most protected part of the ship." She reached a hand out and took him by the shoulder, but Ben didn't budge. She saw then that his right hand was resting on the base station's inductive dataport, and she knew Mabel was linking with him like she had done right before the enemy dropship fell out of the sky behind them.

"Oh crap," she said to herself. "What now…"

But instead of electronic fireworks, explosions, and the other voodoo that had taken place on their way up to orbit, Ben stayed frozen for a few seconds longer before standing up straight and turning to her.

"Get me to CIC," he said firmly. "We're in deep shit."

―――――

"Make a hole!" Tess shouted to a group of spacers who were hurrying the opposite way down the corridor leading to the *Wraith*'s small CIC. Upon seeing two people in dirty and beat-up APEX armor charging down the corridor, the spacers dove for cover in one of the conference rooms adjacent to CIC.

Ben followed immediately behind her, doing his best to keep up and not trip or snag himself on the almost unbelievable amount of crap that stuck out of bulkheads and the deck on this ship. This was his first time aboard a military vessel, and he hadn't anticipated how crowded it would feel—the designers certainly hadn't paid much attention to aesthetics or feng shui. They stopped in front of the two marine sentries guarding the hatch, and one of them raised a hand to stop them from entering.

"You're not authorized to be in CIC, Spacer. I suggest you head to the SOCOM briefing room on bravo deck."

"Stand aside, Marine! This is the package, and he needs access to CIC immediately," Tess barked back at him while Ben did his best "imposing loom" to make it look like he belonged there. He figured it was best to just let her handle this part.

The two sentries exchanged a quick glance. "I'll have to pass this up the chain," the one who had addressed them previously said in an uncertain tone. "Until I receive orders to the contrary, you two are not authorized to be in CIC and I can't allow you access."

The other sentry visibly tensed as Tess began to argue, but before either of the marines could call up to the bridge for confirmation, the lead guard's comms unit chirped with an urgent notification. He skimmed the message and moved aside, swiping a keycard through the reader to one side of the hatch.

"My apologies. Ops just sent down your clearance," he said as the locking bolts on the hatch released with a thunk and he opened it for them.

Ben saw Tess hesitate for just a moment, before she motioned him through the door and followed him into the dim blue light of the Combat Information Center at action stations. The marine swung the hatch closed, and he heard the locking bolts reengage behind them as he took in the urgent but controlled activity of the *Wraith*'s nerve center.

While the captain and bridge crew issued orders and controlled the ship from the bridge, which was located a few sections forward of CIC and one deck up, CIC was responsible for processing all incoming and outgoing tactical data streams for command and control of the battlespace around the ship, and the bridge crew would use that processed information to make decisions on how best to fight the ship. During combat, CIC was a hive of activity and shouted orders.

"That was lucky," she said over a private channel to Ben.

"Not at all." Mabel's voice came through their helmet speakers. "We do not have time to go through the proper channels, so I forged the clearance and sent it to the sentry's comms unit using the ops officer's credentials. Please get me to an inductive data node with access to the ship's electronic warfare suite."

"What are you two doing here?" a red-faced lieutenant demanded as he strode over to them. "You're not cleared to be in here. How'd you get in?"

Before either of them could open their mouths to explain their presence in CIC during combat operations, the chief in charge of the operations section called out above the din, "Bridge just called it in—they need access to the EW suite, and the big boss says to give them whatever assistance we can."

The lieutenant looked from the chief to the two APEX armored people before him, trying to wrap his head around this irregularity while they were about to engage a superior enemy. "Fine," he said hurriedly and then raised his voice to be heard over the commotion as he pointed Ben and Tess toward the far corner of CIC. "Ensign Ross, give these two whatever they need!"

"Yes, sir," Ross called out, motioning them over.

Ben and Tess were halfway to the bank of consoles where Ensign Ross was busy overseeing the techs operating them when someone shouted out in alarm.

"Brace!"

The ship was rocked by a powerful blast and Ben reached out to steady himself on a nearby holotank as the deck beneath his feet shuddered then heaved.

Move, Ben! Mabel shouted into his mind, and he stumbled forward to the bank of consoles where Ensign Ross was pulling himself to his feet after being thrown to the floor. Another volley of weapons fire impacted as Ben reached the electronic warfare section, and one hand shot out to brace himself against the bulkhead while the other caught Ross's arm to keep him from falling again.

"Take a seat and strap in Ensign. I'll stand," Ben said as he somewhat roughly deposited the man into the open chair that had been vacated for him. "I need an inductive data interface that connects to the EW suite."

"There," Ross said, pointing to a raised panel to one side of the console. "That port will give you a link to the ship's defensive systems, including the EW gear."

Ben took one step to his left and went down on one knee, engaging the maglocks in his right boot and left greave to anchor himself in place. He raised his right hand to the indicated data interface, took a cleansing breath, and looked at Tess. "Here we go…"

His felt his face go slack and his eyes defocused as he began to slip into the link. He just made out one last brief exchange as his hearing faded.

"What's he doing?"

"Saving our butts."

CHAPTER TWENTY-SIX

DEBRIEF

THE FIRST THING BEN BECAME AWARE OF AS HIS CONSCIOUS MIND slid back into its rightful place once again was cheering throughout CIC. As his vision returned and he was able to look around, he could see the entire CIC crew congratulating each other on the destruction of the enemy ship and their escape. Well, almost the entire CIC crew; Tess and Ensign Ross were down on one knee to either side of him with concerned looks on their faces. He opened his mouth to tell them to relax, that the danger had passed and they were free and clear to exit the system... and then the pain returned.

White-hot lances of fire danced through his skull, and he remembered that he'd known it was coming. The AI aboard the enemy corvette had been an order of magnitude more powerful than the one he and Mabel had tussled with during their escape from Grayling, and it had fought back with a skill and ferocity that Mabel hadn't anticipated. Their engagement with the drop-ship's AI had been like an exhibition boxing match, where one overmatched opponent put up a good fight for a time before the reigning champion forced a crack in his defense and put him down with a hard right cross. This encounter had been a no-holds-barred back-alley brawl where both sides knew the result of failure was an agonizing death.

Early on during the exchange of electronic haymakers, Ben became aware that Mabel had not only been stopped cold, but pushed back onto her own turf by the powerful construct. During that time, he'd realized that Mabel had grossly underestimated their opponent, and they were in danger of losing both the battle and their lives. Yet he had no way of stepping in to help.

Then, suddenly, Ben felt as though his brain was linked to both Mabel and the alien AI simultaneously. He knew that his physical body was in agony, but not in a real, tangible sense. More like the feeling of waking up knowing you had been dreaming, and only having some vague notion of what it had been about, but not being able to recall any details clearly.

Ironically, it was the alien AI's push into Ben's gray matter that was the beginning of its downfall, as it hadn't been prepared for the momentary link with a biological mind. During the first brief microseconds of their joining, Ben had access to the AI's digital consciousness, and he had done the only thing he could think of in that moment: he pushed his way past the barrier Mabel had stuck him behind and into view, yelling, *Hey there!* with the most obnoxious smile he could muster plastered on his face. Mabel recovered first, taking advantage of the alien AI's utter shock and disbelief at the unexpected consciousness of a biological being somehow dwelling within its digital realm, and she used Ben's mind as a bridge to slip past their foe's attention and infiltrate its central processing node.

Unlike the dropship's AI, which Mabel had crushed in an instant, this construct took the digital equivalent of an eternity to die, as she first severed its link to its counterintrusion programming, effectively cutting off its limbs and pulling every last one of its teeth in an instant. She then went to work disabling critical ship systems while the AI was forced to watch helplessly as she systematically eviscerated the vessel's offensive and defensive capabilities. Ben felt it the moment Mabel sent a targeting package to the tactical station on the *Wraith*'s bridge, and then she withdrew herself from the enemy ship before booting the AI from Ben's mind. The AI shrieked in impotent rage until the hardened penetrator nose cones on two fusion-tipped Talon anti-ship missiles punched through the vessel's armor plating, annihilated it with nuclear fire.

When Mabel handed control of his brain back over to him, she also handed back the pain he had known his body was experiencing during the battle for his gray matter. Ben tried to collapse to the floor, but his right boot and left greave were still maglocked to the deck, and all he succeeded in doing was slumping awkwardly to the side while his muscles spasmed in agony.

"Hold on, Ben," Mabel said through his helmet speakers. "A medical team is on its way."

Her voice sounded muted and far away. Ben didn't hear anything after that, as his brain decided enough was enough, and he lost consciousness.

———

TESS AND KRAVCZYK sat around the small conference table in briefing room two in silence. Captain Collins had given them just enough time to finish going through decontamination and receive a cursory medical checkup before reporting for a debriefing on the more important parts of their recent mission and subsequent space battle. They hadn't even had enough time for the medical staff to properly treat Kravczyk's ruptured eardrum, settling instead for slapping a bandage over it and giving him some meds with orders to get it treated as soon as possible. The hatch to the room opened and the two SEARs stood to attention as the *Wraith*'s chief medical officer entered, followed by a noticeably limping Lieutenant Commander Valdez, who had a heavy bandage wrapped around his upper right thigh.

"At ease," Valdez said, motioning them back to their seats.

"How's the leg, sir?" Tess asked as she sat back down while sizing up the stern-faced medical officer taking a seat opposite her. He was middle-aged and unremarkable in almost every way: average height and weight, brown hair and eyes, and no distinguishing features other than a pair of old-fashioned spectacles tucked into a breast pocket. He wore a lieutenant's rank insignia, and the name tape on his standard-issue fleet utilities read *Adams*.

"Stings a bit, but the doc here says I'll be good to go in short order," Valdez replied with a grin toward the medical officer taking a seat next to him.

"Perhaps your leg wasn't the only injury you sustained, Lieutenant Commander," he said, shooting Valdez a serious look, "because that is not at all what I told you regarding your leg wound. Should I have one of my orderlies examine your ears as well? Or perhaps just the cavernous void between them?" Adams gave both Tess and Kravczyk a meaningful look. "Your commanding officer is restricted to light duty for the next two weeks, Spacer McCollum, and I would like you and the senior chief to make sure that happens."

"We can try, sir, but the boss tends to do whatever he wants," Kravczyk said with a shrug.

Valdez opened his mouth to respond, but the hatch opened and Captain Collins walked in. Everyone in the room stood from their seats, but Collins was already waving a hand for them to sit down again before they had come fully to attention.

"No need to stand on ceremony today, everyone. We've all

had a long couple of days, and quite frankly, I'm not in the mood to go through the motions. The ship is beat up, we've suffered thirteen KIA, the principle is unconscious in sickbay, and none of us have had any sleep in the last two days. I do not intend for this to be a full debrief, but I do feel there are some critically important items that must be discussed as soon as possible.

"Damage-control teams have the worst of the battle damage we sustained under control, and Commander Black is overseeing the efforts to repair the ship as we limp toward the jump point. The AI assures me there are no further alien threats in the Sol system at this time, though I can't say I fully trust it.

"That said, I'd like to start off by saying that you SEARs have my condolences. From my limited interaction with him, Lieutenant Miller struck me as a solid officer. I also took a minute to look over what little information is available in his file to someone with even *my* clearance level, and I know the loss of Master Chief Bloukamp is a major blow to the entire SEAR program. You can rest assured that both of them will receive the honors they deserve when we dock at Icarus." Collins received nods of thanks from the three SEARs, then continued. "Now to business. Doc, what's the status of our young Mr. Hutchins?"

"He's resting comfortably in sickbay," Adams began, syncing his dataslate to the briefing room's wall display and sending a number of images onto the screen with the swipe of one hand, "but that's about all I can say with any certainty at this point. The AI, Mabel, forwarded me a packet on his condition before the SEARs' dropship had even docked with us, but I didn't have much time to go over the details before our trip out-system got lively.

"What I can say with certainty is I've never seen anything like this case. Ben has a neural implant much like the current generation of implants that SOCOM personnel are receiving these days. The hardware and firmware of his implant are somewhat outdated, but the overall architecture is much what you would expect. What is drastically different and concerning, however," he said, rising from his chair and approaching the display, highlighting a particular image and blowing it up to fill the entire screen, "is the dendritic pathways it has created over the last four years."

Tess marveled at the image on the display. If she was hearing Adams correctly, then the chaotic, multilayered spiderweb that was packed into every nook and cranny of the transparent 3D rendering of Ben's body—his very nice body—were runaway dendrites from his cranial implant. Adams confirmed her suspicions a moment later.

"A normal implant creates nano-scale electrical conduits that parallel neurons within certain regions of the brain—and understand I'm keeping this extremely simplified for you all," he explained to the room like a teacher would a classroom full of elementary school students. "This allows the implant to both send and receive electrical impulses along and from the neural network within the brain. That's how it receives data from our bodies, as well as does things like directly stimulates certain senses, so for example, you can have visual communications with someone without actually viewing a physical display.

"The problem with Ben is that his implant was damaged, either by the fusion explosion that destroyed Grayling and the transport he was on or by the medical staff at the local hospital trying to disable the implant. We'll never know for sure. But what the physicians at the hospital didn't know—and couldn't have known without access to the schematics and coding—was that, while they were successful in disabling the higher functions of the implant, the base functions were still active.

"Over the last four years, Ben's implant has continued to create dendritic pathways paralleling neural tissue within his body... every last millimeter of neural tissue," he said, emphasizing the seriousness of the situation by looking at each person in the eye. "The scans we took when my team brought him down from CIC show that the implant has created pathways not only along every single neuron in his brain but along every nerve throughout his entire body. I don't have the expertise to even *begin* to try to make a guess as to what the implications from that are, but Mabel has informed me she is concerned about the development but does not believe it to pose an immediate threat to Ben's health in and of itself."

"Then why is he in my sickbay after being rendered unconscious from whatever it is he did with the AI when they link or whatever and not sitting around this table with us?" Collins asked.

"That, I believe, is a question better asked directly to Mabel," Adams said. "With your permission, Captain, I'd like to ask her to join us."

"Doctor, I cannot say I am yet comfortable enough with Henry Hutchins's pet AI project to have it participate in a meeting with us, especially after it forged an authorization allowing Ben and the spacer here to access CIC during combat operations," Collins said firmly. "I am aware of the contributions it allegedly made to the SEARs and to our engagement with the enemy vessel, but it sat in that bunker for the last four years with nobody watching over it. I believe there are just too many unknowns surrounding the AI at this time."

"With all due respect, Captain," Valdez spoke up, "the three of us would not be here right now were it not for Mabel. We've only known her for a short time, but I believe I speak for all of us when I say she has at least earned the right to"—he paused for a moment to consider his words—"sit in on an informal debriefing such as this."

The truth was, every one of the SEARs present had trusted Mabel with their lives during their exfil from the facility at

Grayling because they hadn't had another option. Tess could tell Valdez wanted to say that Mabel's actions had earned her their full trust. But she could also see the intelligence captain was far more suspicious than she perhaps needed to be of the somewhat motherly AI they'd found beneath the ruins of Camp Grayling, and Tess could tell the boss was moderating his words accordingly.

"Very well," Collins said after a few moments' consideration. "Where is the AI now?"

"Mabel is still residing within the specialized APEX armor Ben was wearing when he was brought to sickbay. We can open a direct comms channel with her from here. With your permission, Captain?" Adams said.

Collins stared him down for a moment, then sighed and nodded in acquiescence. Adams pulled his comms unit from a pocket and tapped a series of commands into it. "Mabel, are you there?" he said.

"I am, Doctor Adams."

"Mabel, Captain Collins has some questions regarding Ben's medical situation, and I believe you would be better able to answer her questions than I. I assume you're still monitoring his condition?"

"Yes, Doctor. His neural patterns have returned to normal, as has his metabolic activity. He is currently in a natural sleep, and judging by his delta wave frequency, I would say it is a deep, dreamless sleep at the moment."

"That's good to hear, Mabel," Adams said. "I've already informed the captain and our SEAR team as to the unique nature of Ben's implant malfunction, but what Captain Collins would like to know is why you feel the nature of his dendritic pathways is not an immediate concern for his health when they've been responsible for trauma on at least two separate occasions in the last several hours."

"That is a valid question, Captain Collins, and the simple answer is that the instances you are referring to were both the result of unusual or extreme circumstances. Perhaps it would help if I explained the details surrounding them?" Mabel said, surprising Tess with her use of a rhetorical question. The more time she spent with the AI, the more she realized just how advanced Mabel really was.

"On their own," Mabel explained, "the dendritic conduits created by his runaway implant over the previous four years have no interaction with the nerves and neurons they trace throughout his body. The materials used in their construction are nontoxic, and there has never been any evidence to suggest long-term exposure has any negative side effects on human health.

"The first instance of trauma that Ben experienced was a result of reinitializing his implant. Both the modified APEX armor's and the implant's software were not designed for a dendritic system that was several orders of magnitude more complex than originally intended. Unfortunately, without reinitializing the implant, I had no way of knowing the extent to which things had deviated from specified parameters within his body. The increased dendritic mass created a feedback loop within Ben's implant, and the imbalance manifested itself as physical pain, which rendered him unconscious.

"The second instance, which resulted in his current condition, was caused by something that even I am having difficulty understanding. Perhaps it would be beneficial if I gave you a rough overview of what exactly Project Blackthorn—I—was intended to do." Mabel paused for a second as if to collect her thoughts, and it struck Tess as odd that such a powerful construct would be programmed with such inanities.

"I understand that everyone present in this room has the current generation of neural implant, not all that unlike the implant Ben has," Mabel continued. "But while your implants have many of the same functions as Ben's, his is special. The prototype implant Ben received was specifically designed to operate in conjunction with an AI such as myself—it is intended to serve as a gateway for an artificial construct, like me, to access the biological hardware of the human brain.

"Ben told me after our first linking, when we defeated the pursuing dropship during our escape from the Blackthorn facility and flew into orbit to rendezvous with this ship, that the experience felt to him as though his consciousness had been, and these are his exact words, 'sent to the nosebleeds section of his mind.' He explained that, while he could remember certain actions that we took during that engagement, he had no control over them whatsoever. He was, in essence, a passenger in his own mind. This is, as best as I can describe it to someone without familiarity with the project, exactly what the Blackthorn team intended the project to do, and having access to the unique architecture of the human brain allowed me to, as you might say, 'think outside of the box' to come up with an angle of attack that allowed for a successful infiltration of the enemy systems."

It made sense now, Tess thought. When Henry Hutchins had briefed them on the Blackthorn project, she hadn't been able to fully wrap her head around the potential something like this had for cyberwarfare. She had figured it was the next iteration of the UI the APEX suits used to populate her HUD with the information she wanted, exactly when she wanted it. She envisioned something like having an AI as a passenger in your thoughts, but the enormity of what Blackthorn actually was blew her away. Ben's mind was physically fusing with an artificial construct to become some sort of superorganism capable of fighting advanced AIs and *winning*.

"What Ben did during our second linking, however, is theoretically impossible," Mabel continued. "I initiated a link with his mind just as I did before, and until I initiated contact with the

AI responsible for managing the enemy vessel's systems, everything proceeded as expected. I am ashamed to say that I drastically underestimated the power of the enemy AI on that ship, as I only had the previously defeated AI with which to base my force estimate on.

"At one point during our battle, it managed to not only fend off my assault but pursued me and attempted to assault my systems in return. As I was linked with Ben, and using his mind as the staging point for my attack, the enemy AI was able to force itself into Ben's mind, forming something akin to the same link I shared with Ben's consciousness. Ben, realizing the serious trouble I was in, and also that the foreign AI had forced itself into a link with him, did something truly incredible: he forced his consciousness to manifest itself within the digital battleground upon which we were fighting. You may find it helpful to think of what he did as materializing an avatar of himself between the enemy AI and myself."

Tess realized the revelation she had had a moment ago wasn't even the half of it. If what Mabel was saying was true, then Ben's conscious mind had been operating at or near the same speeds as the two advanced AIs that were throwing haymakers at each other. So who was using whose hardware? Was Mabel tapping into Ben's biological brain, or was Ben's brain tapping into her quantum processors? The implications were mind-blowing.

"Imagine, if you will, that you are engaged in hand-to-hand combat with a superior foe, and suddenly another person appears between the two of you and waves 'hello' with an obnoxiously garish smile on their face. You would find their appearance not only distracting but utterly confusing, would you not? This is what happened to the enemy AI, for the scenario I described is precisely what Ben did. His consciousness should have been completely repressed, preventing him from taking any direct action in the conflict between myself and the other AI. Instead, he managed to break through all the built-in restrictions and assert his consciousness at the same time I was occupying his mind and at the same speed at which I operate natively. Nonetheless, while the other AI was momentarily distracted, I was able to slip behind it and disable it from within. With the AI no longer an obstacle, I used my access to their ship-board command-and-control network to disable and overload critical systems, allowing our weapons to make it through their defenses.

"To return to your original question, Captain, Ben suffered a trauma this time because I was overconfident, and when the other AI forced its way into his mind, it was too much for Ben's system to handle. The overexcitation of the dendritic pathways during the conflict bled over to his biological nervous system, and I was concerned that if I remained linked with him in an attempt to mitigate the damage, I would only make things worse. So I withdrew from his mind and, in doing so, subjected him to a flood of physical pain as his autonomic nervous system worked desperately to restore his body's functions to their natural state."

The room was quiet for nearly half a minute as everyone tried to wrap their heads around the fantastic things Mabel had just described to them. Tess was the first to get her voice working, but all she managed was a soft, "Unbelievable." That one word seemed to break everyone from their reverie, and Captain Collins finally spoke.

"Mabel," she said, pouring a glass of water from a pitcher on the table, "that is one hell of a story... and if I hadn't experienced part of it first hand, I would call you a damned liar."

"And yet it is the truth, Captain Collins."

"I'm very curious to hear what the young Mr. Hutchins has to say on the matter, but I do believe it would be criminally unfair to wake him after everything he's been through. Is there anything else you can tell me, either details about the mission you think important or analysis about this new enemy you can provide at this time?"

"Only that while I had access to their network during that last engagement, I copied large amounts of data from their central data-processing matrix. It is extremely well-encrypted, and having had only very limited interaction with their technology, I am unable to decrypt it at this time," Mabel said.

"You obtained intelligence from their central computer?" Collins said incredulously. Tess couldn't tell if the captain was thrilled at having a potential gold mine of information available to her or terrified that petabytes of alien data were currently sitting in a system linked to her ship's wireless network.

"Whether it will be of any value to us, I have not yet been able to discern," Mabel explained. "And do not fear for the safety of your ship, Captain Collins. I copied the data to a storage deck within the prototype APEX armor I am currently occupying and have air-gapped that subsystem. It poses no danger to this vessel at present, and I shall ensure that it remains isolated at all times in the unlikely case that it is booby-trapped in some way."

Collins visibly relaxed somewhat upon hearing that Mabel had at least taken precautions with the potentially deadly data. "I'd still like you to work with my crypto analysts and cybersecurity people on this, Mabel," she said. "They may or may not be of help in your efforts to decrypt the data, but they will ensure that the proper protocols are followed to protect our systems from potential malcode."

"As you wish, Captain. I have just notified Lieutenant Davis, who is the current duty officer in the crypto-systems shop, and he will be assembling a team."

"Mabel," Collins said, rubbing her temples in frustration.

"While I appreciate your willingness to work with my people, please do not do or say anything to them without specific instructions from myself or my senior officers. This is extremely sensitive information, and despite every member of this crew having high-level security clearances, I wish to keep the number of people privy to it as small as possible until we return to Icarus and can hand it off to the experts in Intel Division."

"Very well, Captain. I apologize if I have overstepped," Mabel said, and Tess thought she sounded a bit chastened.

"Thank you, Mabel. Please work with Lieutenant Davis and his team for the time being. That will be all for now."

"Yes, Captain."

There was a soft double beep signaling that the comms channel Mabel had been using had been closed, and the captain took a moment to look at each of the faces around the conference table in turn. "Thoughts?" she said.

Tess had many, but as a lowly enlisted spacer, she kept her mouth shut.

"From the materials regarding Project Blackthorn that Henry Hutchins forwarded to me before we departed Icarus, what she said regarding the technical aspects, and even, with some imagination, what Ben would have experienced, would seem to line up with what she told us," Adams said, speaking first. "But..." He held up his hands in a shrug.

"I can't speak to any of the technical voodoo she was talking about," Valdez offered, "but I have no reason at this time to believe she was lying to us about any of it. It takes some mental gymnastics to piece everything together, but provided you can take the leap of faith and believe Blackthorn is what Hutchins advertised it to be, it does all make sense. Either way, you can't argue with the results we've all been witness to so far."

"I'm inclined to agree," Collins said with a nod, "albeit reluctantly." She turned to Dr. Adams. "That's all I have for you at this time, Doctor, unless you have anything to add."

"Nothing urgent, Captain."

"Then you're dismissed. Please let me know if there are any changes in Ben's condition, as well as how our casualties are faring."

Adams nodded and stood up, collecting his personal items and disconnecting his tablet from the wall display. As the hatch was closing behind him, the captain turned her attention to the three SEARs. "Let's table the Mabel conversation for the moment and move on to this new player we're up against," she said. "You three fought them on the ground. What can you tell me about them?"

The three SEARs took turns recounting their experiences and answering questions from Captain Collins as best as they could, though again, as the most junior team member, Tess didn't contribute much. In the end, though, they weren't able to provide much information beyond a general physical description, their tactics, and the weapons and technology they used. When the captain had wrung all the details from their memories that she could, she dismissed them. Tess spoke up as they exited the briefing room and headed down the passageway toward their assigned berthing area.

"Sir, if it's all the same to you, I think I'll head up to sickbay and wait with Ben for a while."

Valdez raised an eyebrow at that but nodded. "Fine by me, but try to make sure you get some rack time at some point. I know with the damage this boat has taken it's looking like our return trip to Icarus is going to take more than a week, but I want you good to go in case it hits the fan again."

"Yes, sir," she said, with the hint of a relieved smile, and turned to head the opposite way down the passage toward the

Wraith's small sickbay, but Kravczyk wasn't going to let her go that easily.

He called out over his shoulder as he continued to walk away. "Say hi to your boyfriend for me, McCollum!" He never turned around as he ducked through the hatch and into the next frame, chuckling to himself; he knew there was a bright red flush coloring her cheeks.

CHAPTER TWENTY-SEVEN

RESPITE

IT TOOK A HERCULEAN EFFORT, BUT BEN FINALLY MANAGED TO GET his left eyelid to crack open a millimeter, then two. As his world came into focus, he realized he was in a bed in what must have been the *Wraith*'s sickbay. There was a small wall-mounted display charting his biometrics, and as he lifted his hand to rub his eyes, he saw an IV drip was busy replenishing the fluids and electrolytes he'd lost over the last several days. A white curtain had been drawn, creating a private area just large enough for his bed and a single chair in one corner.

His eyes locked onto the sleeping face of Tess, auburn hair covering half of her face as she slept with her head slumped against the bulkhead beside her. Ben stayed silent, watching the rhythmic rise and fall of her chest as she slept.

A few minutes later, he heard soft footfalls approach, and a hand pulled the curtain back just enough for a head to peek in.

"You're up," said a middle-aged man with spectacles perched over his brown eyes as he pulled the curtain back farther, revealing a white lab coat over standard ship's utilities. "Good. I was beginning to think you might just sleep all the way back to Icarus. I'm Lieutenant Adams, the *Wraith*'s chief medical officer."

Adam's looked questioningly at Tess, who was now awake and sitting silently in the corner.

"She can stay," Ben said, reading the situation correctly.

"Very well," Adams nodded. "How are you feeling, Ben?"

"Surprisingly good, actually," Ben said honestly. "In fact, I don't think I've felt this good in a long time. I don't even have any muscle aches."

"Modern pharmaceutics at their finest," Adams said with a sweep of his hand, gesturing to the state-of-the-art sickbay around them. "Well," he continued, "that and the fact that we've been pumping you full of fluids and electrolytes for the last few hours. You were severely dehydrated when they brought you in here."

"Where's Mabel?" Ben said, voicing the first question that came to his mind now that the cobwebs of sleep were beginning to fall away.

"She's still inside the prototype armor you were wearing," Adams said. "The cyber division guys are working with her to crack the data she mined from the enemy ship during your battle with the alien AI." Adams's tone changed slightly when he said the last part, and Ben had the feeling the man was fishing for something.

"Yeah," Ben winced. "Remind me not to do that again anytime soon…" He trailed off briefly as he tried to sort through the jumbled bits of memories from the battle. Then a slight smile flashed across his lips. "Although," he said with a soft chuckle, "I have to say it may have been worth it just to see the utterly dumbstruck look on that thing's face when I popped in to say hello."

"Yes," Adams said slowly, "Mabel mentioned something about that, although as none of us have the ability to link with her like you do, it's all a bit difficult to wrap my head around."

"It's weird…" Ben started. "I don't really know how to put it into words. It kind of starts out feeling like you're a prisoner in your own brain—I lose all contact with my senses and everything goes dark. Then data starts streaming through my thoughts at crazy speeds, so fast I don't have a clue what it all means, yet somehow I do. I just know everything instantly. I want to say I can hear Mabel's thoughts, but that's not quite right. It's more like Mabel's thoughts are my own thoughts, and vice versa, but I don't have any control over them.

"There's something else, too. Time passes differently. The first time we linked—when we were being chased by that dropship—when it was over and Mabel receded from my mind, it felt like it had been hours… almost like time passes at normal speed on the inside, but everything on the outside slows down to a crawl. I assume it has something to do with being linked to a computer that can process millions of calculations every microsecond, but I haven't had a chance to ask her about it yet. Does that make any sense?"

"Not really," Adams said with a smile. "But your account matches up with what Mabel told us." Adams made a quick note on a data tablet and turned back to Ben. "Well, if you're feeling alright, I see no reason to hold you here any longer. There's nothing more we can do for you at this time, and the rest of my questions can wait. I want you taking it easy for the rest of our ride back to Icarus. You've been through a lot over the last few days, and your body still has some work to do repairing itself. I'd also like to point out that we have a counselor on duty twenty-four seven, and if you feel the need to talk to anyone about your ordeal, I would encourage you to do so as soon as possible. Medically, you're on the mend, but don't ignore any mental wounds you suffered, alright?"

"Will do, Doc." Ben looked from Adams to Tess, who had been sitting quietly, listening to the exchange. He let his eyes linger on hers for a moment before returning his gaze to the chief medical officer, and a small smile crossed his lips. "I think I'll be just fine."

————

BEN'S FEET pounded rhythmically as sweat poured down his face and he gulped in air in great heaving gasps. He was almost there —just eight more seconds. The timer counted down to zero, and a soft beeping signaled the end of his run, the treadmill slowly spooling down to a fast walking pace for his cooldown.

"Not bad, kid," Kravczyk said from the treadmill next to him, where the big man was making six-minute miles look like a stroll in the park. "You know, for a girl like you."

The handful of other spacers in the *Wraith's* small gym laughed, and Ben flipped the SEAR the bird, too out of breath to speak at that moment. In the mirror that ran the entire wall on the opposite side of the room, Ben could see the mirth on Tess's face, but at least she hadn't laughed out loud like everyone else. She was in the middle of a weighted front squat set in front of him, and he found that his heart rate wasn't coming down as fast as it should have been.

"Hey, McCollum," Kravczyk yelled over to her, and Ben's mind raced to come up with a retort for the next round of ribbing. "Ben's staring at your ass again!"

Oh shit.

Ben silently thanked God that his face was already beet red from the sprint he'd done to finish his run. His jaw dropped open and he did his best deer-in-the-headlights impression, giving serious consideration to bolting for the hatch to escape.

"Why do you think I picked *this* tower to do squats at?" Tess said in a sultry voice, turning her head and giving Ben a little wink before returning to face herself in the mirror. Her next squat was low and slow, and she paused to give a little shake at the bottom before returning to a standing position and depositing the weight bar in the hooks on the front of the tower.

In that moment, Ben cursed not only his wandering eyes but the no-good, stupid son of a bitch that had decided the standard fleet-issue PT shorts needed to be *this* thin and tight-fitting. *Shit shit shit shit! Uh, icy-cold water. So, so much icy-cold water,* he thought to himself, desperately willing certain parts to play it cool.

"Ben, is there something wrong?" Mabel's voice came over the gym's intercom. "My data feed shows you are no longer exerting yourself, and yet your blood pressure and heart rate appear to be elevating again. Do you require medical attention?"

The chuckling that had been steadily spreading among the spacers in the gym exploded into a round of raucous laughter. In one corner of the compartment, a well-built gunner's mate laughed so hard he lost control of the kettlebell he had been working with, and it crashed into the rack of free weights in front of him.

"Mabel," Ben said in a pained voice, "we *really* need to work on your people skills."

"It's interesting that you say that, Ben, as Spacer McCollum used those exact words after we docked with this vessel and I pointed out she was exhibiting signs of sexual attraction toward you. In fact, now that I think about it, I find it likely that your current physiological state is related to the same—"

"For the love of all that is good and holy, Mabel," Ben pleaded with the AI while pounding his head against the bulkhead, "Stop! Talking!"

The kettlebell-wielding gunner's mate was now on the floor, laughing so hard his face was beginning to turn purple, and Kravczyk had had to step off his treadmill, tears streaming down his cheeks as he doubled over with laughter.

"Oh dear…" Mabel said in a sheepish tone, "I believe I have

once again made a misstep. I do hope I have not caused you too much embarrassment, Benjamin."

Realizing there was absolutely no hope of salvaging any of his dignity, Ben stepped to the middle of the room and bowed like a showman before a sold-out crowd under the big top. If he was going to crash and burn, he might as well embrace it.

"Ladies and gentlemen," he said, "I bid you adieu. Now I'm going to go see myself out the nearest airlock." With that, he grabbed a towel from a rack by the door, draped it over his shoulders, and stepped through the hatch to the passageway beyond. At least he didn't have to worry about his lower half betraying him anymore.

He had only made it a few paces toward the SOCOM detachment's berthing area when the hatch to the gym opened, and laughter once again spilled out until the hatch shut again with a clang. Ben turned around and found Tess bracing her back against the hatch as if to prevent the embarrassment from following her.

"Oh my gosh, that was brutal," she said with a pained expression. "Kudos for owning it and going out like a man, though. I just flipped everyone the bird and walked out. Your exit was much better. Just don't think the chief will forget about this. *Ever.*" She pushed off from the hatch and walked up to him, stopping agonizingly close.

"So," she said, tapping him lightly on the shoulder with her index finger while a coy little smiled played across her lips, "did you at least enjoy the show? I know the price of admission turned out to be more expensive than I'd planned, but did you at least get your money's worth?"

"Uhhh…" Ben found himself reliving the deer-in-the-head-lights-curse-the-sonofabitch-that-invented-these-shorts feeling all over again as his brain screamed, *Say literally anything, you dumbass! Don't just stand here with your trap hanging open like a moron! Oh God, oh God, oh God—*

"Ben? Hey, Ben... I can see the blue screen of death scrolling behind your pupils, so I'll just take that as a yes. See you later, handsome," she finished, giving his butt a little slap as she stepped around him and strode toward the SOCOM berthing area. Ben's body finally unfroze, and he caught one last glimpse of her absurdly tight backside as she disappeared around the corner.

"Goddamn, kid," a voice boomed from behind him as a massive hand clamped down on his shoulder. "You are absolutely fucking hopeless, man."

"Chief," Ben said to Kravczyk without turning to look at him, "I have a favor to ask of you."

"Yeah?"

"I would take it as a great kindness if you would please kill me."

———

THE WEEK FOLLOWING their narrow escape from the Sol system was uneventful, but between the damage-control efforts, medical examinations, and intensive debriefings he'd been subjected to, Ben found their slow journey to Gateway Station to be almost as draining as the days he had been on the run. Captain Collins had offered Ben her personal stateroom, as she was spending nearly all her time on the bridge and only occasionally catching a quick nap in her office. She and her crew were working furiously to patch the holes in the hull and keep the *Wraith* flying until they returned to Icarus.

The ship was airtight again after their efforts, but the *Wraith* desperately needed an extensive stay in space dock to properly address the battle damage it had suffered. Ben had thanked her for the offer but turned her down in favor of bunking with the SEARs back in the SOCOM detachment's berthing area. The three remaining SEARs were the closest thing he had to friends aboard the little spy ship, and bunking with them had the added perk of putting him in close proximity to Tess.

He had more or less adopted the same daily routine as the elite warriors, waking at 0500 ship's time to work out in the small gym, followed by a shower and breakfast. From there, his days were filled with meetings, as nearly every department head on the ship had questions for him, ranging from what he could tell them about their unknown enemy to more technical questions about his experiences linking with Mabel. Somewhere in there, he would grab lunch or sneak off to spend some time alone with Tess and talk about the things he actually wanted to discuss.

Ben sat next to Tess after a particularly grueling day of mindless meetings, gazing out the viewport in the *Wraith*'s small lounge at the simulated star field streaming by. There weren't actually any stars to see while the ship was in warp. The warp fields forming the space-time bubble around the ship emitted an unholy amount of radiation while they traveled between the stars, so the viewport had a blast shield secured over it and instead displayed a nearly real-time representation of the stars blurring past at hundreds of times the speed of light.

Tess nudged him gently. "What's up? You went radio silent on me again."

Ben pressed his lips into a thin line as he struggled to decide whether he should tell her or not. He wanted so badly to get this off his chest, but he didn't want to burden her with his baggage.

"I've got plenty of baggage, too, Ben," she said softly.

He turned away from the mesmerizing display and looked at her. "We're spending way too much time together if you can read my mind that accurately, Tess."

"Don't change the subject."

Ben sighed. It looked like this was going to happen. "Everyone on this ship treats me like I'm some kind of conquering hero," he began. "They act like I'm some shining example of humanity—a white knight that's going to ride in and save all of Terran space—but they don't know what I've done." Ben's voice had fallen to a near whisper, and his eyes welled up with tears. He blinked and looked away, ashamed of his weakness.

Tess put a gentle hand on his. "It's okay, Ben. Nothing you can say will change my opinion of you."

Had it been said by anyone else, Ben would have considered it a meaningless platitude, but something in Tess's voice made him believe she *knew* what he wanted to say, and she had already accepted him despite it.

"After Jim and I were separated at the CDF post, before I heard you guys coming down in the pods, I took shelter in a ravine." He swallowed hard, trying to get the lump of iron in his throat to drop down a few notches. "It was dawn. It had been raining all night, and a heavy ground-level fog had set in. I was exhausted and freezing, my CDUs were soaked through, and I ended up collapsing behind a log, unable to drive myself on any further. I had given up, wallowing in self-pity and just waiting for it all to end.

"Then one of their kill teams stopped by the creek that was flowing through the ravine, not far from where I was holed up. I could have stayed quiet and they would have walked right on by—they had no idea I was there. But I killed them. All of them.

"Tess, I didn't just kill them. I fucking tore them apart, ripping their guts out with my knife, feeling it grind on their bones as I drove it into them over and over. I blasted them apart with my rifle, sending round after round into their lifeless bodies until there was nothing left but shredded meat. And you know what the worst part was? I *enjoyed* it."

Ben paused, giving Tess an opportunity to express her revulsion of his actions, but she sat there quietly, waiting for him to continue.

"I didn't know I had that—that I could be that sadistic. I don't know who that was. I mean, I know it was me, but... how can you not know something that *evil* is living inside you, just waiting for a chance to be let off the leash? I'm not a fucking hero, Tess. I'm a monster."

"Ben," Tess said, looking him square in the eyes, "listen to me very carefully. You are not a monster. Let me say that again. *You*. Are *not*. A *monster*. She slid his hand into hers and squeezed lightly.

"Monsters don't question their actions, and they most certainly don't feel guilt for what they've done. The simple fact that you are repulsed by what you did in that ravine tells me all I need to know about you: you are a good person. It's not my place to judge you, and I have no intention of doing so. I'm just glad you're here now.

"You couldn't know this, but you've been such a blessing to me over the last week, and I'm thankful for you. I know you don't see yourself as a hero, but the boss, Chief Kravczyk, and I wouldn't be alive if you hadn't pulled yourself together and saved us from that ambush. The *Wraith* wouldn't have made it out of Sol if it weren't for your efforts. You *are* a hero, Ben. Never forget that."

Ben stared at Tess in awe. Her capacity for grace and understanding was astounding, and he admired her even more for the strength of character that implied. He felt like a great weight had been lifted from his shoulders. "Thank you, Tess." He smiled. "For being amazing. Tell me, how did you end up as a badass special operator, again?"

"There's the sarcastic jerk I know and love." She jabbed him in the ribs hard enough to hurt. "I was worried you had gone soft on me."

Ben laughed. Not just a polite chuckle, but the full-throated belly laugh of a man who had found his way through the dark of night and into the warm light of dawn. For the first time in ages, he found himself completely at ease, and it was intoxicating.

———

Two days out from Gateway, Ben was laying in his bunk, listening quietly as Mabel rehashed their experience combating the powerful shipboard AI over the *Wraith*'s intercom. He cut her off mid-stream as a question popped to the front of his mind.

"Hey, I've been meaning to ask you, how's the work going on that data cache you pulled from the corvette?"

"The crypto shop has been working on it the entire trip," Mabel said, letting the sentence dangle in the air without going into further detail.

"That's it?" Ben prodded after she clammed up. "You've been talking my ear off for a week, going into excruciating detail every time, and all you're going to give me now is some boiler-plate answer about how the crypto guys are working on it? I'm not buying it."

A heavy silence hung in the air for almost a full minute, Ben's stubborn refusal to back down pitting itself against an AI who could wait until the heat-death of the universe, if she wanted. Ben didn't move, staring at the ceiling above his bunk, where his implant was showing him Mabel's dot matrix cube hovering in the air. He cocked his head slightly and raised an eyebrow in an expectant gesture. "I'll go ask the captain, if that's what it takes," he said.

Mabel sighed, and the genuine emotion behind it seemed so

real Ben forgot he was talking to a computer program for a moment. "I've been instructed to not give you any more detail on the subject, Ben."

"Uh-huh," Ben said. "I thought so. Guess I'll be tracking down the captain after all."

Five minutes later, he was outside the armored hatch to the bridge, arguing with the marine guard and insisting he be allowed to see the captain. After Collins grudgingly informed him that Mabel and the crypto shop had been stonewalled by the alien encryption, Ben began pushing for the obvious solution. It took some fast talking on his part, accompanied by heavy lobbying on his behalf by Lieutenant Commander Valdez and approval from the chief medical officer and the crypto division head, before Collins reluctantly gave her approval.

"Fine," Collins rubbed her temples and sighed wearily to Ben and the SEARs, who had all crowded into her office. "Your point about time being critical is especially salient, given the fact that we've been several steps behind this whole time." Ben's face lit up and he opened his mouth, but Collins cut him off with a raised finger. "But! At the first sign that there may be a danger to you or this ship, I'm pulling the plug."

"Understood, Captain," Ben said. "I'll head down to crypto and work with Mabel and the crew there to set everything up."

"I'll let them know you're coming," Collins said. "But I want one of the SEARs by your side the whole time, just in case. And..." She must have seen the lightbulb go off in his head at the mention of a lot of time around one of the SEARs and nipped his next thought in the bud. "I'll leave it up to Lieutenant Commander Valdez to decide who that will be."

Ben's expression faltered for a moment when Collins crushed his hope of spending even more time with Tess, but he'd gotten more than he realistically thought he would, so he decided to take what she was giving him and run with it. "Understood, ma'am. Thank you." He turned to leave the office and head down to crypto when Collins spoke one last time.

"And I want to be there when you and Mabel link," she said. "I'd like to see the fireworks for myself."

Ben grinned at her. "You won't be disappointed."

CHAPTER TWENTY-EIGHT

BETTING THE HOUSE

It took the better part of a day to get everything set up in the crypto shop, but at last Ben was suited up in his specialized armor and standing next to a series of consoles in a room full of technicians.

"Are you sure you want to do this, Ben?" Captain Collins wore a disapproving frown as Ben fitted his APEX helmet over his head and closed and latched the faceplate in place. "Mabel doesn't exactly have the best track record when it comes to linking with you." Ben changed his visor's opacity so everyone in the room could see his face, then reached a hand toward the inductive port on the base station the network admin people had rigged up in the secure room that housed the cyberintelligence and cryptography sections of the *Wraith's* intelligence detachment, allowing Mabel's matrix to be present locally.

"I'm sure, Captain. I'll be fine," he replied as he checked the status of his armor's systems and prepared to link. "Hey, Chief," he said over his shoulder to Kravczyk, who was leaning against the bulkhead with his arms crossed over his chest and a bored expression on his face. "How about a friendly wager?"

Kravczyk's ears perked up at that, and he pushed himself upright. "Alright, kid. I'm listening."

"If I crack this puppy open in under thirty minutes, you're buying the first round when we get back to Icarus," Ben said.

"You're not old enough to drink on Icarus, but nice try."

"I've been living in a post-apocalyptic barter society, making booze for the last four years. Do you really think ten months of age is going to prevent me from drinking?"

The big SEAR snorted. "Alright, I'll give you that. And if you don't crack it in thirty?"

Ben thought for a moment, then shrugged. "Then I buy."

"Ha! You don't have any money, Mr. Barter Society, but nice try!" Kravczyk laughed before a Cheshire-cat grin spread slowly across his face. "No, if you don't crack it in under thirty minutes, I get to be the chaperone on your first date with McCollum. You know, to make sure you've got her home by eleven, and no funny business."

Ben considered the counterproposal briefly and shook his head. "Nope. If that's what I'm giving up, then you buy the first round *for the whole ship!*"

Kravczyk's grin faltered, but Ben's upping the ante had every member of the compartment hooting in excitement and egging the big SEAR on. The hint of a smile even ghosted across Captain Collins's lips before the chief finally nodded firmly. "You're on!"

"Start the clock," Ben said, grinning, and touched his palm to the base station. The cheering that had erupted when Kravczyk accepted the bet faded along with his vision, and Ben felt his consciousness recede into the depths of his mind as Mabel established their link.

That was quite the entertaining exchange, Ben. Mabel's words drifted through his consciousness as the rest of his reality disappeared.

We can do this, Mabel.

Of that I'm certain. However, I can't guarantee it will be in time for you to win the bet.

Ben sent her a mental raised eyebrow. *You realize you've been using contractions lately? What's up with that?*

My personality matrix is constantly evolving, Ben. My conversations with you and the crew over the last week must be having an impact on my speech patterns. We're wasting time. Something tells me that a date with Chief Kravczyk would not be preferable for you.

God no! Let's get rolling. My brain is at your command.

Very well. Initiating direct neural link, Mabel said, and Ben's mind was flooded once again with a tidal wave of strange symbols and characters as Mabel began the process of deciphering the jumble of data they had pilfered from the alien corvette.

Unlike during his first two experiences linking with her, Ben focused on making himself as small as possible so Mabel could be free to do her thing. Data and calculations flashed in and out of his stream of consciousness, but instead of trying to follow along with Mabel's processing speed as he had in the past, he did his best to detach his mind from the process and allow her to work. He let the crush of raw data and calculations wash over him in a kaleidoscope of ones and zeroes; the sensation was mesmerizing, and he began to feel as though he were in a waking dream. Ben let his consciousness slip further and further back into the recesses of the ether for what felt like hours, letting the torrent of data wash over and around him, swirling around his limbs in eddies as he swayed with the currents.

Then, suddenly, he knew it. *Everything.*

It was all there, materializing before him—laid out in neat stacks of crisp white paper atop plain tables that stretched out into the infinite. There was a binding of rough brown twine around the nearest stack of paper, and he reached out with one hand and took the end with his fingers. He tugged gently on the loose end of the twine, and the knot that secured the binding in place fell away and dissolved. The blank pages before him suddenly filled with text, and realization dawned on him.

"Mabel! Over here!"

The three-dimensional dot matrix cube that was Mabel's avatar materialized next to him, and a blinding white light projected from her and focused on the neat stacks of paper on the tables before them. The beam rapidly narrowed in focus as it began sweeping across the stacks.

"Ben," Mabel said, and Ben thought he detected a note of awe in her voice, "how did you do this?"

"What do you mean? All these stacks of paper just appeared in front of me."

"This is not possible, Ben. Your consciousness was fully repressed while I worked to solve the puzzle of the encryption scheme. How did you find the key and unlock the data?"

"There was a length of twine wrapped around this stack of paper and secured with a bow knot. The paper was completely blank until I pulled on the loose end of the knot and the binding fell away, and the text appeared on the paper. That's when I called you over."

"Astonishing," Mabel whispered. "Ben, you magnificent young man. I don't know how, but your subconscious appears to have been processing and filtering the data streams, creating virtual objects that your conscious mind can recognize and understand. In doing so, you gave my subsystems the guidance they needed to break the encryption without me even realizing it.

"Ben, I'm going to need time to go back and analyze this event to figure out exactly what happened, but in the meantime I believe it would be best if we do not link again until we return to Icarus and your father and his team can go over the data."

Ben felt something then, like a memory of an emotion wash past him, and he realized Mabel was spooked by what he'd been able to do. Not scared, exactly. More like… uncertainty? Trepidation? The idea that an AI would be spooked by something he could do in here made *him* uneasy.

"I'm sorry Mabel, I didn't mean to screw this up."

"Oh, Ben," Mabel said with a chuckle, and the faint feeling of uncertainty that he had felt changed to one of a mirthful fondness. "You didn't screw anything up. You've just shattered what everyone thought they knew was possible. Your mother would be so very proud of—"

The white light playing over the neat stacks of paper in front of them flashed blood red, and the stacks disappeared in a puff of smoke. His consciousness was vaulted back into its rightful place in his brain with a jarring intensity, and as he became aware of his physical surroundings once again, he realized something was very wrong. Collins was barking orders over the ship's 1MC intercom, and Kravczyk was standing next to him and saying something.

"Come on, kid, we have to move!"

Ben struggled to clear the cobwebs. This link had been different—especially at the end—and he was having trouble getting reality to settle back into its proper place. He turned to follow the burly chief just as the combat action alarm began blaring and the deck lurched under their feet.

"What the hell was that?" Ben said as he reached a hand out to steady himself on a bulkhead.

Kravczyk kept moving toward the hatch but answered over his shoulder as he ran out into the corridor and headed toward SOCOM country. "The warp fields collapsing. Whatever you and Mabel found in there must be bad news. You two were doing that statue thing for a while. Then suddenly she popped up on the display and started shouting something about a Trojan horse and an attack on Gateway. The skipper told me to get you back to the squad bay and await further orders."

They vaulted themselves up a ladder and turned aft, running for the hatch at the end of the corridor that would take them into the SOCOM squad bay. Valdez and Tess were halfway through donning their armor when Kravczyk and Ben finally arrived, and the chief immediately started stripping his utilities off as Ben opened the big man's armor locker and pulled out his skinsuit. As he was already in full armor from the link with Mabel, Ben assisted the three SEARs as they worked furiously to get ready for whatever it was that had caused Mabel to break her link and come out shouting an alarm.

Once all four of them had their armor on and their systems were in the green, Valdez keyed in the code to open the small arms locker and started passing out gear to his team. Being a civilian, Ben had been required to surrender his XM93 before being allowed off the Griffon after their escape from Grayling, and he stood next to the armor lockers, unsure of what to do next, as the SEARs loaded up on weapons and ammo.

"Ben, get over here!" Valdez said, waving him over with one hand while pulling his rifle from the rack with the other. Ben jogged over but came up a half step short, startled when the SEAR leader held out the XM93 for him to take.

"I'm not allowed to carry weapons while aboard ship, Lieutenant Commander," Ben said hesitantly but reached for the powerful weapon as he did so.

"If we arm up, you arm up. As you have no experience with the Mk 27 submachine gun that we use for CQB, you'll carry the XM93 that you're already familiar with, but low velocity only," Valdez said, stressing the last part and ignoring Ben's halfhearted protest as he pulled a stack of spare magazines out and began stuffing them into mag pouches, which Kravczyk and Tess were then securing to the hardpoints on Ben's chest rig. As Ben checked the rifle and inserted a magazine, the SEAR team leader continued. "Do *not* try to send high-velocity rounds down range aboard ship—we don't need any more holes in the hull than we already have."

"Got it," Ben said, sounding far more confident than he felt, but he had to admit he felt much better with the familiar weight of the XM93 in his hands than he would have without it.

"SEAR team, report to the SOCOM briefing room," came through the squad bay's overhead speaker, and the four of them made their way across the room to the hatch leading to the adjoining secure briefing room. When they were all present, and the hatch was shut and locked, Valdez keyed his personal access code into the console at the front of the room, and a moment later, Captain Collins's face was filling the wall display in front of them.

"Good, you're all there," she said without preamble, then narrowed her eyes slightly when she saw Ben standing beside the three SEARs. "Though I can't say I'm pleased to see you took the liberty of arming Mr. Hutchins, Lieutenant Commander."

"He's just as qualified as any of your marines, ma'am," Valdez said, not backing down.

"Whatever. We'll discuss that later. Right now, we need to talk about the enemy fleet that is massing for an assault on Gateway Station and Icarus—or so Mabel tells me."

"She found something during the link," Ben said, taking a half step forward. "Didn't she? We broke the encryption and she found something in the data we mined from that AI."

"Yes, Ben. The two of you were able to break the encryption and gain access to the data. In it, she found communications regarding fleet movements and specifically an attack plan designed to crush the defenses around Gateway and Icarus— evidently, they were able to get a tracking device aboard another Terran ship, and that ship then led them right to Gateway. If what Mabel says is true, then it's likely that Gateway has already fallen and their fleet is now en route to Kerner and Icarus. That's why we executed an emergency stop—we were due to transition in near Gateway within the hour and would have likely arrived to find them waiting for us."

"So what's the plan, Skipper?" Kravczyk said.

"Honestly, I'm not sure there's anything we can do, Chief. We're banged up good and proper, and the *Wraith*-class ships can't slug it out with capital ships—as our brief, but one-sided encounter with a corvette has shown us. My senior staff are working the problem as we speak, but it's looking like our best option is to bug out and try to rally what's left of the fleet somewhere more defensible."

"That's bullshit!" Ben spat, drawing a stern look from Collins.

"Ben—" she began, but he cut her off.

"No," he said firmly. "This is *exactly* what Mabel was created for, and I'm *not* running anymore, dammit! If what you say is true, then we have access to their complete battle plan, the element of surprise, and a weapon that can knock their ships out of the fight from the inside out. I won't run with my tail between my legs while the last hope humanity has for a defense gets crushed in a battle they can't win. Pull the data up, and let's get working on a plan."

Collins stared at Ben for a moment before shaking her head. "No," she said in a defeated voice. "I'm sorry, Ben, but I will not throw my ship and crew away in a fight we can't win. We're going to pull back and regroup."

"With all due respect, Captain," Valdez said, stepping forward so that he was front and center, "Ben is right. If we don't do something now, while we still have a fleet capable of fighting, then that's it: game over. With the Icarus fleetyard destroyed and CENTCOM wiped out, we'll never be able to mount an effective response; it's time to bet the house. At the very least, we should be moving toward Icarus while we see if we can come up with something actionable. If, after reviewing all the data, it looks completely hopeless, then we can bug out. But if there's even a slim chance we can have an impact on the outcome, then we have to try. Heading toward Icarus will save us time while we work on the problem."

Captain Collins was silent for a long moment as she weighed what the SEAR leader had said. "Very well. We'll plot a short hop to the edge of the system and poke our noses in. That gives you"—she paused to check the calculations on her terminal—"three hours and twenty-six minutes to review the data and come up with a plan."

Ben pinged Mabel via his implant to get the ball rolling.

"If we are unable to come up with a plan or I deem it to be unnecessarily risky or have a low probability of success—or we arrive and the situation is hopeless—I'm pulling the plug and we're bugging out. Is that understood?"

"Yes, ma'am," Valdez replied.

"I'm authorizing the crypto shop to provide you a feed to the data. If you need anything else, you should run your requests through Commander Black," the captain finished, cutting the channel off abruptly.

"Way to go, kid, you pissed her off," Kravczyk said, giving Ben a nudge with his elbow.

"Stow it, Chief," Valdez said, turning to the group. "You heard the skipper: we've got a little over three hours to dig through the data and come up with something. McCollum, get the holotank set up to display the data coming in from crypto. Chief, I want you to take an inventory on all the hardware we have at our disposal."

"Got it, boss," Kravczyk said, halfway out of the compartment before Valdez had even finished his sentence.

"Ben, see if you can get a comms channel open with Mabel. We're going to need her expertise for this," the SEAR leader said.

Ben already had a channel open, but was waiting for the go-ahead from Valdez. He suspected this next part was going to be a bit… intense.

Do it, Mabel. Ben sent the thought command through the ship's wireless network via his implant, and was immediately inundated with knowledge. It wasn't like the torrent of data he'd experienced when directly linked with Mabel, though. This time, the data was there, but he had to mentally ask for the information he wanted before the knowledge would pop into his mind.

Ben felt a tug on his shoulder and realized Valdez was trying to get his attention. He must have zoned-out again while getting the information they needed. Ben sent a mental command to the briefing room's holotable and withdrew his mind from the ether and back into the real. This implant thing was going to take some getting used to.

The holotable at the front of the briefing room came to life, and a map of the Kerner system filled the space. Valdez dropped his hand from Ben's shoulder, and Ben rejoined them.

"Huh?" Ben said, snapping his head up to look Valdez in the eyes. "Sorry, Lieutenant Commander, I just finished reviewing the data Mabel pulled on the enemy plan of attack. What was your question?"

"What do you mean you just reviewed the data?"

"Well, it turns out I don't need to be linked with Mabel to have direct access to information via my implant. As long as the data is present in my suit's onboard memory, I can call it up at will. It's hard to explain, but the gist of it is I think about the info I want, and the knowledge just sort of pops into my brain.

"As soon as Captain Collins gave us the green light, I got ahold of Mabel and had her compile the pertinent files and prepare to send them to my armor. When you gave me the go-ahead, I had her transfer the files, and I started digging. There's a ton of data in there, so it took longer than I expected to review it. I figured it would be faster to have me do that than trying to sift through everything in the holotank."

"Okay," Valdez sighed. "I've seen you and Mabel pull off enough weird voodoo in the last week to not ask questions. What can you tell us?"

"I know what we have to do," Ben said, walking up to the holotank and rearranging the layout without asking; he zoomed in on a region of space near the northern pole of Kerner's largest gas giant. "Check this out..."

CHAPTER TWENTY-NINE

TIME'S UP

"Something went wrong, dammit!"

"We don't know that, Henry," Commander Evans said in as soothing a voice as he could muster. "There could be any number of reasons why they haven't returned yet."

"They're almost a week overdue, Matt," Henry said as he paced around his office in a near-manic state. "The *Wraith*-class ships are five times faster than anything else in the inventory. It's a two-day trip to Earth, and that's only if Collins was loafing along out of spite. This was a simple extraction mission, and there's no logical reason why they are *this* late unless something happened.

"Dammit, I should have insisted they take quantum comms with them. That was a rookie mistake—what the hell is wrong with me?" What Henry was saying was all true, but the concerned look on Evans's face told him the officer thought he was starting to come apart at the seams again.

Task Force 71, the group of ships Garland had dispatched to the Vostok system in the wake of the *Appomattox* incident, had returned a few days ago. The mission had gone off without a hitch, and TF71 hadn't run into any enemy opposition while recovering the *Appomattox*'s survivors and salvaging anything that might help the Confed combat this new threat. Now, TF71 was sitting in quarantine on the other side of Kerner for another two days with a load of alien wreckage that would need Henry's expertise, meaning he needed to hold it together for just a little longer.

The transformation the once-great titan of industry had gone through over the last two weeks had been nothing short of miraculous. Henry hadn't even glanced at a bottle of booze since learning Ben was alive; the drive to master his shortcomings stemmed from his desire to greet his son sober and respectable, not as a used-up husk of a man. Ben had persevered through unbelievable hardships, and while he wouldn't admit it, Henry was embarrassed that his teenage son had made it through four years of hell, alone and with the deck stacked against him, and come out the other end stronger for it. Henry, not so much.

He made an effort to be clean-shaven every day and keep his office and personal quarters neat and tidy, and he'd been working nearly around the clock on solutions that could be implemented quickly to help them combat the new threat they were facing. But every day that passed with the *Wraith* overdue increased the strain Henry was feeling and dragged him closer and closer to the brink of self-destruction again.

"Henry," Evans began, the man's infinite patience beginning to wane, "I need you to focus for a minute here and really listen to me, okay?" When Henry took a deep breath and nodded in acknowledgment, the fleet officer continued. "You're one of the most logical and well-reasoned people I know, Henry—when you're sober, at least—which is why I know you are capable of compartmentalizing this and focusing on the things you actually have some measure control over right now.

"Until we hear something concrete on the *Wraith*, there isn't a damn thing you or I can do about it, but you have a comms buffer overflowing with the initial data from all the wreckage the *Ford* has sitting in her cargo bays, and we're waiting for you to dig into it and give us some answers. We all need you to do what you do best so we can have a chance of fighting back when the time comes. Can you do that for me?"

Henry took another deep, cleansing breath and closed his eyes for a moment. "Alright, Matt. But if they're not back by the time the *Ford* clears quarantine tomorrow, I want another ship sent to Sol to find out what happened."

"I'll talk to Garland," Evans said before turning to exit the room. The officer glanced over his shoulder as he turned the corner into the passageway outside, and Henry, already sitting at his desk with the holoprojectors fired up and arraying heaps of data in front of him, met his eyes.

"I'm good, Matt. Really," Henry said, a fierce determination burning in his chest. "Though if you could have the mess deck send up some food, I'd appreciate it."

"You got it, Henry." Evans pulled his comms node out and began firing off messages as he walked away.

Henry didn't envy him; he knew that he was a royal pain in the ass to the fleet officer. He also knew Matt would have an uphill battle getting Bob to siphon off more scarce assets to go find out what happened to their missing *Wraith*... and his son.

———

HENRY RUBBED his tired eyes and tried to suppress his frustration. It had been eighteen hours since he started diving into the data dump from the *Gerald R. Ford's* engineering and intel sections, but he felt like all he had accomplished was to diminish Icarus's coffee reserves.

Task Force 71 had taken along as many engineers, technicians, and intelligence specialists as the fleet could spare—or could afford to lose, Henry thought darkly—and they had done a damn thorough job of analyzing the recovered wreckage and compiling those findings in reports while they were on their way back to the Kerner system and Icarus. What Henry was frustrated with was his inability to glean anything useful from the data that wasn't already in the reports filed by TF71 upon their return to the system. Not so long ago, his incredible mind would have been able to pick out important details and make connections others had missed. The years of hard drinking and self-destructive behavior had dulled his once razor-sharp intellect, and it infuriated him that not only had he allowed it happen, but he had also done it to himself willingly.

The reports arrayed in front of him confirmed most of the assumptions he'd made about the enemy vessels from the data the *Appomattox*'s Beckman had collected during her fateful engagement. The enemy used antimatter reactors to generate power for their ships, which meant even the newest Terran ships being constructed were outclassed in power generation and distribution—this enemy could make incredible amounts of power and get it to their weapons and defenses more efficiently. Their laser projectors used a number of exotic materials that humans hadn't even discovered yet, and the capacitors that fed those powerful projectors were not only thirty percent smaller than their Terran counterparts, but they had more than twenty times the capacity. The picture being painted was that their enemy was vastly superior in both their material science and manufacturing capabilities.

One item that surprised Henry was the composition of the alien hull: it was a ceramic-like composite hybrid material instead of metallic—like the steel and titanium hulls of older Terran starships or the layered graphene and alloy hulls of today —but while it was a tenth of the weight and could shrug off attacks from laser projectors or plasma, it was surprisingly thin and brittle compared to Terran hulls. The *Appomattox*'s rail shots being so devastating had bothered Henry to some extent, but the new data now told him why that particular weapon system had been so effective. He jotted down a note to bring that to the attention of the fleet brass. Maybe it would help as they scrambled to put together effective tactics for this enemy.

Henry shut the display down, leaned back in his chair, and rubbed his eyes again. After staring at the ceiling for a moment to clear his vision and his mind, he turned his attention to a coffee mug that sat precariously perched half on a stack of dataslates, the cold dregs of the strong brew staring back at him unhelpfully.

"You're a damned old fool, Henry Hutchins," he said to the empty room. "Think, dammit! What are you missing?"

Henry sat up straighter in his chair and turned the display back on, opting to close all the files and start fresh; maybe something would pop out at him this time. He opened a file that had been compiled by one of the *Ford*'s engineering backshops on what they suspected was a piece of grav plating, but before he could dive back into his work, the holographic array of data floating over his desk disappeared and was replaced by the image of Admiral Garland. A soft chiming tone sounded.

"Shit," he said and answered the call. "I'm sorry, Bob, but I don't have much for you—"

"Gateway just went dark, Hank," Garland said, cutting Henry off mid-sentence. "The QE link went dead mid-stream, but it looks like our new friends showed up in force with no warning and are probably headed this way as we speak. I need anything you can give me." The deadly serious edge to Garland's voice caused an adrenaline dump into Henry's exhausted body, and a roaring filled his ears.

It was too late; the enemy was at the gates. How had they been found so fast? Icarus was the single best-kept secret in all of Terran space. It didn't matter, Henry realized. Their time was up.

"I'm sorry, Bob, but I don't have anything to give you that isn't already in the reports. This data is going to take months to comb through and I haven't even laid eyes on the actual wreckage yet. I don't... I don't know."

"The *Ford* and the rest of her task force are going to be burning their engines out to get here ASAP, but even if they do get here in time, that only gives us a few dozen ships in the system, plus our static defenses. We've issued an emergency recall of all deployed assets, but it'll be a week or more before the first of them get here. I need anything you can give me, Hank, even if it's just a wild-ass guess. The *Appomattox* acquitted herself well, but I have no illusions about how things will go for us this time around. I need something, Hank. Anything."

"Okay, okay... We know the *Appomattox* had success with her railguns and that the wreckage recovered by Task Force 71 shows that the enemy's hulls are constructed of some sort of ceramic composite. This stuff dissipates heat from DEWs like nothing I've ever seen before, but the trade-off is that it's comparatively brittle. Rail guns should be effective, but you'll need to get close. Missiles should also work if you can get them to their target—the *Appomattox* data shows their point-defense capabilities are second to none—so you'll need to saturate space with every missile you've got and hope a few can get through. We also don't know how yet, but they clearly have the ability to track in-system targets in real time, so we've lost any advantage that comes with speed-of-light limitations."

Henry paused to pinch the bridge of his nose, hating the conclusions he was coming to. It felt all wrong.

"Bottom line it for me, Hank. Can we win?"

"It depends on how many ships they send, but probably not," Henry said as he slumped back into his chair, suddenly feeling exhausted to his very soul. "It would take a miracle. Our ships are too slow and our weapons too weak. We don't have time to put together a proper defense, and even if we did, I don't think it would matter." Henry looked directly into Garland's holographic eyes. "You need to get them out of here, Bob. Pack as many people on those ships as you can... and run."

"It's too late for that," Garland said as red strobes began flashing throughout the station and the combat action alarm started blaring. "They're already here."

CHAPTER THIRTY

KNOCK KNOCK, MOTHERF*CKER

"I JUST WANT TO GO ON RECORD AS SAYING THIS IS A TERRIBLE PLAN, boss," Kravczyk said as he finished strapping himself into one of the slingseats in the Griffon's cargo bay.

Thanks to Ben's unique ability to assimilate data, they had a fully outlined plan of action nearly a full hour before their deadline, and surprisingly, it had been a relatively easy sell to Captain Collins when they presented it to her. There were some aspects she wasn't particularly fond of, as they would involve considerable danger to her ship, but the intelligence captain was no coward and saw a good chance for mission success—regardless of whether she and her ship made it through in one piece. After working through a few logistics issues, she gave her approval to the plan, and the SEARs scrambled to get their gear in order and prep the dropship for what was sure to be a rough ride.

"I seem to recall you saying this would be the most fun you've had in years not that long ago, Chief," Valdez said over the squad channel.

"That was before you told me McCollum would be driving the bus," the big SEAR complained. "I'm still queasy from the last time you gave her the keys."

"Five minutes to transition. Stand by for launch, Dagger team." The announcement came over their suit comms, and the three SEARs and Ben finished checking their restraints and stowing their gear.

Ben once again sat in the copilot's seat, while Tess was piloting. Lieutenant Commander Valdez was in the squad leader's jump seat at the front of the cargo bay. On the bulkhead next to him, a data terminal displayed important telemetry and sensor feeds. Kravczyk was strapped in near the tail, where the ship's crew chief would normally sit, near the console that operated the tail ramp.

"Once more unto the breach, dear friends," Ben mumbled as he tugged one last time on his restraint harness. While this crazy stunt was his idea, he wasn't thrilled about going back into combat. In fact, it took all of his willpower just to climb aboard the Griffon and strap in. They couldn't stop the enemy without Ben and Mabel, and they would need to do that in person. He didn't pretend to be a warfighter on the level of the SEARs, but the days of fighting the hunter/killer teams back on Earth had given him confidence that he at least wouldn't be a complete liability to the SEARs on this mission.

"I don't think Shakespeare had an assault on an alien spaceship in mind when he wrote that line for Henry V," Kravczyk commented over the team channel. Ben had forgotten about the open comms, and his private utterance had gone out to everyone.

"How does a knuckle-dragger like you know who Shakespeare even is, let alone which play that line comes from?" Ben quipped.

"Act three, scene one," Kravczyk said with a superior sniff. "One should always study the classics."

Ben craned his head around to look at the big SEAR, eyes

wide with surprise. "I apologize, Chief," he said, doing his best to sound sincere. "You are clearly a man of culture."

"No he's not," Valdez chimed in. "He used his APEX to pull up the relevant information."

"I did not, boss! How dare you insinuate—"

"I can pull up your HUD on my tac-link display, Chief. Commander's privilege. And you still haven't closed the window with the wiki page information on that particular literary device."

The silence that followed Valdez's matter-of-fact statement was broken only by stifled laughter from Ben and Tess.

"Spoilsport," Kravczyk finally grumbled as the tail ramp closed and locked with a soft hiss.

Ben looked over at Tess, who reached a hand out toward him when she saw his gaze. He took her hand in his and gave it a little squeeze.

"Aww, that's so cute." Kravczyk's sarcasm-laden voice filled their ears through their suit comms, and Tess let go of Ben's hand like she'd been electrocuted. Ben flipped the big SEAR the bird over his shoulder and turned his head back to the multi-function displays in front of him.

"One minute, Dagger."

Ben tugged at his restraints for a third time, checking everything again out of nervous tension. Then he put his head back against the rest and waited, doing his best to clear his mind so he could focus on what they were about to do.

"Ten… nine… eight…" The countdown from the flight ops controller made everyone brace themselves for the deceleration that was about to come. "Two… one…" The *Wraith*'s warp fields collapsed, and the little spy ship reentered normal space with a shudder.

"Launch!"

The moment the warp fields had fully dissipated, the big hangar doors were blasted away by explosive bolts and pressurized gas charges that propelled them away from the ship, and the Griffon was then forcibly ejected through the opening by electromagnetic rams. The dropship's computer executed a preprogrammed burn to shed their inherited velocity, and Ben and the rest of the SEARs grunted under the heavy g-load as their suits fought to keep them conscious. Ben's vision darkened around the edges as the little dropship's inertial compensators struggled to keep up with the main engines screaming at full thrust.

Now, Ben! Mabel shouted into his mind, and Ben made a conscious effort to let go of his reality. The terrible shaking and roaring of his surroundings faded away, and his consciousness receded into the ether once more. He felt Mabel reach out with the prototype Griffon's enhanced electronic warfare suite, but unlike their two previous battles with the enemy AI constructs, this time Mabel was prepared and the enemy was not. There were no probing attacks or exchanges of haymakers this time; this time Mabel already had the network access codes from the data she'd stolen from their last victim.

She smashed through the enemy AI's defenses like a runaway freight train, overwhelming it in a matter of microseconds and tearing its heart out. Ben felt the same wave of exhilaration Mabel did when she was standing alone on the digital battlefield, grinning down at the broken corpse of her adversary before she went to work screwing with the enemy's systems to buy the *Wraith* time to escape. It was odd, he thought, that she appeared as a dot matrix cube on the outside, but in here, she resembled a humanoid cloaked in shadows.

Their world strobed red, and a huge iron door slammed closed in front of them, blocking their access to the rest of the system as the biological crew reacted to the loss of their AI and enacted countermeasures, but their job here was done.

"We did it, Mabel."

"Yes, Ben, we did. Now it's up to you and the SEARs to finish the fight. Good Luck."

———

CAPTAIN COLLINS WATCHED the countdown on the main display as it ticked off the last few seconds until they would exit warp. When the display showed zeros across the board, the warp field emitters at the bow and stern of her ship shut down and the fields collapsed, returning them to normal space with a shudder, followed a moment later by a muted bang.

"Helm, stand by on our burn. Tactical, find me that sneaky son of a bitch as soon as our sensors are up, and don't be shy about it," she said.

"Flight ops reports Dagger is away, ma'am."

"Thank you, ops. Helm, you're clear to initiate our burn."

"Contact!" her tactical officer said. "Right where she's supposed to be, sitting fat and dumb over Kerner-5's northern pole. Tasking firing solutions to weapons. Standing by for your order, ma'am."

"Light 'em up, Lieutenant—weapons free! Helm, stand by for emergency transition!"

Talon anti-ship missiles surged out of the *Wraith's* launch tubes, and her six remaining laser batteries opened up with a full-power salvo on the destroyer-sized ship. This ship was responsible for all enemy command, control, and communications for the entire system thanks to their faster-than-light communications. With the advantage of real-time sensor data and communications, that one ship could command the entire enemy fleet simultaneously, no matter where the engagements were taking place. Sitting stationary amidst the enormous amounts of radiation Kerner's largest gas giant emitted, the ship would have been undetectable unless Collins and her crew knew exactly where to look. Thanks to Ben and Mabel, they did.

"Negative impact from the projectors, ma'am," her tactical officer reported. "Continuing volley fire. Time to missile impact: forty-six seconds."

"Keep it up, Lieutenant. We want them focusing on us until Dagger can make entry."

"Two missiles were just destroyed—still no effect from our laser fire. Time to impact for remaining missiles now... Strike my last! Both remaining missiles have been destroyed, and they're targeting us now. Two beams just passed less than three hundred meters astern."

"Dagger must be having some success," Collins said with a tight smile. "That's the first time we've ever seen them miss. Ops, where's our Griffon?"

"Ten seconds to intercept, ma'am."

The deck rocked beneath her feet as one of the enemy beams finally found its mark, and damage assessments and warnings began scrolling across her command terminal. "Close enough. Helm! Get us the hell out of here!"

Just over a minute after the *Wraith* transitioned in practically on top of the unsuspecting vessel, her field emitters surged with power, and warp fields formed around the ship. With a flash of released energy, the stealthy little CID vessel transitioned out of the battlespace, leaving Ben and the three SEARs to pull the rug out from under the enemy fleet without support.

———

"FUCK YEAH!" Ben shouted. "Knock knock, motherfucker!" He was amped up on adrenaline from the fast and furious assault, and still feeling the lingering effects of Mabel's exhilaration at the ass whoopin' she'd served up to the enemy AI a moment

ago. "Mabel smoked that ship's AI, but they implemented countermeasures a hell of a lot faster than we would have liked," he
reported over the team channel. "Now we do things the old-
fashioned way."

"Good job, Ben," Valdez said. "McCollum, you're go for
approach. Chief, crack the ramp and prepare to drop."

Tess used the Griffon's maneuvering thrusters to adjust their
attitude as they approached the stealthy alien vessel. Ben
looked through the cockpit windscreen at the iridescent black
form that was barely visible in front of them despite the proximity, and a shudder ran up his spine. The reality of what they
were about to do hit him like a punch to the face, and suddenly
that cocky exuberance from a minute ago was nowhere to be
found.

The light reflecting off of the gas giant below them faded as
they passed into the shadow cast by the ship in front of them.
Tess expertly zeroed out their velocity with a deft touch on the
flight controls, leaving them motionless in space less than twenty
meters from the airlock they intended to breach through.

"That's it, gentlemen," she said, quickly hitting the release on
her restraint harness and killing the internal gravity. She glided
up out of her seat and swam back toward the now-open tail
ramp with Ben in tow.

Kravczyk made the jump first, crossing the distance in just a
few seconds and engaging the maglocks in his boots the moment
they hit the hull of the enemy ship... and then he was floating
away from it again.

"Shit!" he shouted in surprise as he slowly tumbled away
from the ship. "It's not magnetic!" A few more seconds went by
until he could bring his spin under control with the small cold-
gas thrusters built into his APEX suit's EVA harness. A couple
gentle puffs of released propellant and he was back in position
next to the airlock.

"You're up, Ben," Valdez said, giving him a gentle pat on the shoulder.

"Right," Ben said, then pushed himself off from the Griffon toward the spot on the hull where Kravczyk was waiting. Valdez and Tess were right behind him, and all three of them gently contacted the alien hull, finding handholds around the airlock that was their breach point.

Ben knew the plan and, without a word, carefully made his way to where Kravczyk was pointing to something on the hull. "You sure about this, Mabel?" he asked.

"I am, Ben. I don't anticipate overriding the airlock's security will be a problem."

"Good," Ben said, reaching his palm toward the dataport, "because this will be the shortest assault in history if you're wrong." Ben's armored palm made contact with the port… and nothing happened. He waited for several seconds, but there was nothing to indicate anything had changed.

"Uh, Mabel?"

No answer.

"Mabel? This shit isn't funny, Mab—" The dataport glowed a soft white, and the airlock hatch glided silently open in the vacuum of space.

"Showtime," Kravczyk said, quickly gliding his way into the small chamber on the other side of the hatch and promptly falling on his face.

"There is artificial gravity in the airlock chamber," Mabel helpfully informed them, but with everyone laser-focused on the task at hand the witty banter was on hold. "It's approximately 0.8 standard gravities, so you should find it a comfortable environment to operate in."

Kravczyk stood up and unslung his Mk 27, taking up position near the inner hatch. Valdez, Ben, and Tess took turns entering the airlock and getting into position. It was a tight squeeze in their armor, but they wanted to breach as quickly as possible and not have to wait for multiple airlock cycles to get the whole team aboard. Ben placed his palm on a dataport along one bulkhead, and the outer hatch closed and locked. A faint hissing reached his ears as air was pumped into the chamber, quickly building in volume as the pressure increased, and thirty seconds later, lights around the inner hatch glowed a soft white, and the hatch slid open.

The corridor beyond was empty, and Kravczyk quickly moved out and to one side to provide cover for the other three. A moment later, all four of the humans had their muzzles trained down the corridor with their eyes and ears straining to pick up anything that would indicate their intrusion had been detected.

Ben's heart was pounding in his chest as his eyes darted from side to side, searching for threats; the interior of the alien ship seemed both oddly familiar and distinctly alien at the same time. He had seen the aliens operate on Earth, so he knew they were small-statured humanoids, but standing in the heart of one of their ships drove home the point that these beings weren't all that unlike humans or Alarians.

Ben checked his HUD: oxygen-nitrogen atmosphere, a little less oxygen and more humidity than what humans found comfortable. At least they wouldn't have to worry about a suit breach killing them—provided they survived being perforated by gunfire, he thought darkly.

"When I interfaced with the airlock's dataport, I detected no sign that the enemy is aware of our presence, Lieutenant Commander Valdez," Mabel informed them. "I'm monitoring the output of all four APEX sensor suites and can find no evidence of an enemy presence in our immediate vicinity. Their sensor network and communications are still disrupted from our assault, but those systems are rapidly coming back online. We might have infiltrated this vessel undetected, but they will locate the Griffon shortly. I suggest you move quickly."

Part of the data Mabel had pilfered from the alien corvette contained detailed schematics for the various classes of alien ships, which was how they knew right where an airlock that could fit the four of them would be located. It was also how they knew exactly where they were going and what they were likely to face on the way.

"Alright, people, harnesses off and in the airlock," Valdez said as Ben and his team began removing the bulky EVA harnesses from their suits and piling them up in the airlock. "Let's move out," he ordered when they were all free of the extra gear and ready to move.

Weapon at high-ready, Ben moved quickly down the passageway with the SEARs, Valdez in the lead and McCollum bringing up the rear. The ship was eerily quiet as they made their way along their preplanned route to a maintenance access shaft next to a set of lift doors. Ben slung his rifle across his chest and reached a palm toward a small display panel next to the access cover as the three SEARs took up position next to him with their weapons trained down the corridor to either side.

The light pipe surrounding the display flashed white and the access cover recessed slightly, then slid smoothly to one side, revealing a dark shaft just under two meters in diameter with power and data conduits running along the inside. Without a word, Ben reached into the gloom and grasped the rung of a ladder that ran the length of the shaft, pulling himself up and beginning to climb. The three SEARs followed him, and the moment McCollum was inside the shaft, the access cover began silently gliding back into place; Mabel had inserted an auto-close script into the door's operating software.

They climbed in silence, their APEX sensor suites feeding them an augmented view of their surroundings in the pitch black of the shaft. As they neared their exit point, Ben slowed to a stop just below the threshold of the access cover

"Alright, Mabel, we're here. How's it going with the ship's wireless network," Ben whispered into his helmet.

"Ready and waiting," she replied.

The data cache had contained a complete list of all assets deployed to Terran space, including detailed schematics and specifications for each ship in the deployed fleet. Ben and the SEARs couldn't have been more prepared if they had been planning an assault on their own ship. Luck had had almost no part in their success up to this point, but now that they were getting ready to breach a crewed deck and assault the nerve center of the alien vessel, the game was about to change.

"Lieutenant Commander, I have successfully connected to the ship's wireless network," Mabel said. "However, the moment I begin sending data over the connection, our presence will be detected. Right now, I can read data off the network without triggering any alerts, but I don't have access to crew locations or other high-security ship's systems. I have been able to gather that the crew have completely restored those systems that were affected when the AI was destroyed, but they are operating at reduced effectiveness. It also appears the ship is preparing to depart its station after the *Wraith*'s attack pass and subsequent escape now that navigation is back online."

"Can you tell if they've restored their C-three capacity yet?" Valdez asked.

"Command and control functions for the fleet assaulting Terran assets in the system are coming back online as we speak."

"Then we need to move," Valdez said. "Do it, Mabel."

"I'm highlighting the correct dataport in your HUD, Ben," Mabel said. Ben's HUD augmented his vision, highlighting a dataport to one side of the access panel. He placed his palm on it and waited. "Stand by."

The alien systems were easy for Mabel to override, but the nature of them required Ben to physically interact with the various interfaces to do so. It was for this reason that he had to be the first one up the access shaft, and it was also for this reason that he suddenly found himself staring straight into the large glassy black eyes of one of the smaller alien types the moment the access panel slid aside.

He lashed out reflexively, one hand spearing into the soft tissue of the alien's throat while the other drew the combat knife from its sheath on his right thigh. In one fluid motion, Ben drove the blade deep into its thoracic cavity. A harsh choking gurgle exploded from its lips, along with a stream of that viscous dark blood, and Ben roughly jerked the spasming body of the smaller alien through the hatch and into the access shaft with him. An upward thrust and twist of the knife, and it was all over.

"Pass it down, Ben," was all Valdez said, and Ben lowered the now-still body of the slight alien down to the SEAR team commander with shaky arms. Ben was out the hatch before the body had reached Tess, and by the time Valdez was extricating himself from the tight access shaft, Ben already had his XM93 at the ready and was scanning the passage to either side, breathing hard from the adrenaline dump.

Ben struggled to fight back a wave of panic that was probing the edges of his consciousness, and he took a moment to focus on pushing his emotions to the side, compartmentalizing them and shoving them to the back of his mind. It was a trick he had learned over the past few years of hardship and war, something many people were never able to master, but it came naturally to him. He knew on a fundamental level that he needed to operate with a detached, clinical frame of mind if they were going to succeed. Maybe it was the implant that allowed him to look past his fear, or maybe it meant something was profoundly broken in his brain. Either way, he was glad for it as he strained his eyes and ears for an enemy he knew was only moments away.

"What have you got for us, Mabel?" Valdez said as he took up position to one side of the hatch.

"Nothing more, Lieutenant Commander," she said. "As I said previously, I can't track crew locations without alerting the ship's crew to our presence, though no new alerts have been issued across the network since Ben dispatched that maintenance worker."

"What was it even doing there?" Ben wondered as his heart rate slowly returned to something that could be considered normal for the situation.

"Unknown," Mabel said. "It may have just been bad luck, or it's possible our presence in the shaft triggered a low-level alert to the engineering staff that was not sent out on a network I have access to. It seems likely, however, that if the ship's crew believed there to be a serious threat, they would have sent more than a single maintenance worker."

"Agreed," Valdez cut in as Tess emerged from the shaft and readied her PDW. "We're on the clock now, people. Let's move."

The four APEX armored humans rose as one and set off down the passageway, the specialized polymer material of their boot soles making barely more than a whisper as they moved quickly toward their objective with a fluid grace that belied the violence each was capable of. The deck beneath their feet began vibrating slightly as the alien ship spooled up its engines to break orbit. It wouldn't be long before they noticed the Griffon the SEARs had left floating in space or the missing maintenance worker... or both.

Ben focused on his footsteps and the passageway of the ship viewed through his rifle's optic as he moved in unison with the SEARs, senses straining to pick up the first signs that they'd been detected.

CHAPTER THIRTY-ONE

DARKEST BEFORE DAWN

"REPORT!" CAPTAIN COLLINS BARKED TO HER BRIDGE CREW AS HER ship shuddered and groaned and the warp fields collapsed far too soon.

"Aft field generator was destabilized by a power surge almost immediately after we transitioned, and the fail-safes tripped and dumped us back into real space before the variance in the fields tore us apart," her ops officer reported. "Engineering is working on it."

"How far did we get?"

"We've cleared the combat zone, Captain, but we only covered a little over five hundred million kilometers," the navigation officer said. "We're still well within the system but are clear of any planetary bodies or other navigation hazards."

"Tactical, what does the plot show?"

"Clear space for the moment, ma'am, but you know how hard it is for us to spot these guys."

"Okay, good. Ops, Downgrade readiness to Condition Two. Tactical, what can you see of the space around Icarus and the settlements on and around Kerner-3?"

"The space around Kerner-3 is partially obscured by the planet's second moon. We're thirty-four light minutes out, but it seems quiet. The light coming in from Icarus and the surrounding anchorage is almost an hour old due to our relative positions within the system, but the optics aren't picking up anything the system wants to classify as weapons fire or high-order detonations. We're too far away to get good resolution from the scopes, but CIC has been able to identify a few of the bigger cap ships by their engine blooms—it looks like they had slipped their moorings and were burning to beat hell."

"That fits with the timeline we have from the data that Dagger collected from the corvette back in Sol," Collins said, mentally piecing the timeline together. "The attack on Gateway should have happened a couple hours ago, and Icarus likely would have gotten word through the quantum comms link as soon as Gateway realized they were under attack. So, we're seeing the initial response from the fleet to word an attack was inbound—maybe forty minutes to an hour after that call came in."

"Captain, engineering reports the aft field generator is going to require a full recalibration before we can attempt another transition, and even then, Commander Grissom recommends against it. He expects it'll take the better part of a day to patch things back together, but he stresses that even then it should be considered an emergency option only," the ops officer relayed the bad news.

"Nav," Collins said, "plot us a sub-light course to the orbitals over Kerner-3. I doubt we'll be able to make it in time, but it's better than sitting here with our thumbs up our asses."

"Aye, ma'am. Course plotted and sent to the helm."

Collins ignored the raised eyebrows at her lack of decorum; she was beat, and the constant strain was beginning to crack her facade of command. "Helm, you're clear to come onto the new course. Best speed this battered old girl will do," she said with a weary sigh and sat back in her chair as she watched the tactical plot continue to update with the nearly hour-old fleet positions. "Looks like we get to be spectators to this little shindig from here on—"

"Transition flashes detected! Spectrographics has no match for the new ships. Designating targets as Uniform One through Eighteen," the tactical officer said, the adrenaline spike that resulted from seeing over a dozen unknown, presumably hostile ships pop up on his display causing his voice to crack.

Collins watched as the plot was updated with the new information. She didn't need to wait for CIC to analyze the new data and report on the classifications—she already knew who they were. "Belay that," she instructed the chief at tactical. "Designate the new ships as hostile and bring us back to Condition One."

Her crew went to work getting the ship ready to fight again, but Collins noted with concern that they were all moving just a little slower than they normally would. This mission had been a strain on the limits of both her ship and crew, and the mental and physical exhaustion they were all feeling was evident. She couldn't fault them; they had endured a stressful few days playing hide-and-seek with the enemy corvette in the Sol system while the SEARs were working to retrieve Ben. Then they'd been bloodied by the alien ship on the way out-system before working tirelessly to patch the *Wraith* back together on their way back to Gateway, just to be thrown into the fire again. Collins caught the eye of her XO and motioned him over.

"What is it, ma'am?"

"Head down to sickbay and see if there's something Lieutenant Adams can do for the crew. They're so exhausted they're practically falling out of their seats."

"You know he won't like it," he said, grimacing.

"I have faith in you, Commander," Collins said with a tired smile. "At the very least, I want stims for the bridge crew and

CIC. We could find ourselves on the wrong end of laser shots or a plasma torpedo at any minute—we need to be sharp."

"Aye aye, ma'am," Black said, and he turned and headed for sickbay.

"I know you're all exhausted," Collins said, addressing her bridge crew, "but I need you to give me everything you have. Given what we know of their capabilities, those enemy ships have known we were here since the minute we showed up in the system. They don't have the speed-of-light limitations that our sensor gear does, and if they decide to send someone our way, we won't know it until they're parked off our bow, hammering away at us. Commander Black is on his way to sickbay to secure stimulants, and anyone on duty on the bridge or in CIC *will* take them when he comes back. I don't like it, but I like having our ship shot out from under us by an enemy we didn't catch in time even less. Understood?"

There was a chorus of affirmation from her bridge crew, and Collins went back to watching the red icons of the enemy fleet form up and head toward Icarus and the ragtag assortment of fleet ships hurrying to form a defensive line. The XO returned twenty minutes later with a box containing individually pack-aged stimulant doses of varying strengths and began passing them out. Collins washed hers down with a swig of room-temperature coffee from a neglected mug next to her command chair and watched with sinking hope as the mass of enemy ships altered course slightly and vectored in on an icon marking the position of the CTS *Independence*. She was all alone in empty space, and there was no doubt as to whether or not she would make it to Icarus in time.

The chatter of the bridge crew died out as more and more eyes locked on the holodisplay. No one said a word as the enemy fleet closed on the *Independence*; they all knew what was about to happen.

"We're receiving a priority-one alpha transmission from the *Independence*, ma'am," the comms officer reported quietly. "comms lag is thirty-seven minutes at this distance."

"Put it on the overhead," Collins said and clenched her jaw as she braced herself for what they were about to hear. The comms tech flicked his hand across his haptic holographic display and piped the audio through the overhead speakers.

"—peat, we have been engaged by the enemy fleet. Both mag cannons were targeted and destroyed in the initial volley. Our missiles are being shot down well short of effective range and our laser barrages are being deflected somehow. The automags scored several hits with marginal success before being targeted and destroyed, but they're keeping their distance and dodged our shots more often than not—"

A loud explosion reverberated through the *Independence,* and the audio feed filled with static. "—uggest prioritize railguns as primary weapon system and concentrate fire on individual ships to maximize effect on—" Another, louder explosion rang through the command center and the line went dead for a split second, then reestablished; a cacophony of klaxons and shouting could be heard through the hiss of static. A new voice came over the comms a minute later, fear and panic filling the speaker's voice.

"Captain Stevens and the bridge crew are gone!" The voice sounded young—likely a junior officer in CIC or one of the auxiliary control centers. "Propulsion is offline and main power is failing. We just took a hit from one of their plasma weapons and... Oh my god! She's breaking u—"

The comms link with *Independence* went dead at the same instant the blue icon on the plot denoting one of the most powerful Terran warships ever built began flashing amber, and the optical feed from that region of space lit up with a bright flash of released energy. The bridge crew sat in stunned silence as the tactical plot updated to show the ship as destroyed.

Collins stared at the plot in frustration as the enemy fleet reformed into a tight, three-dimensional wedge and began accelerating toward Icarus and the disorganized human fleet. There were a few soft curses and anguished moans from around the bridge, and the fight seemed to be draining out of her crew.

"Take a good look, everyone," she said, with just a hint of something that sounded like optimism. "*Independence* was outnumbered nearly twenty to one, but she survived long enough to get some licks in of her own."

All eyes snapped back up to the tactical plot, searching. All the enemy ships were back in a close formation and the optical feeds weren't showing anything obvious.

"They're coming in as a single formation, but their acceleration profile is all wrong given what we know about their capabilities," the ops officer said, nodding toward the plot as one corner of his mouth twitched upward slightly. "*Independence* gave a few of them bloody noses, and now the rest of the formation has slowed to match their crippled ships." Even as he said it, one of the red icons marking a frigate-sized ship began falling out of formation, unable to keep up with its fellows, and a murmur ran through the bridge.

"This isn't over yet," Collins stated firmly. Then, to herself, "Come on, Dagger. We're out of time."

———

"BEN, GET THAT HATCH OPEN!"

Ben ducked reflexively as a plasma bolt passed within inches of his head, then slammed his palm against a panel next to the armored door that was the last obstacle standing between them and their objective. "On it!" he shouted over the rapid staccato of gunfire and the occasional sizzle of a plasma bolt passing too close for comfort.

They had hit resistance almost immediately after setting off from the maintenance shaft. The enemy was disorganized and poorly equipped to face off against the armored and heavily armed humans at first, but it hadn't taken long before the SEARs began encountering well-equipped security personnel that were equipped with the same type of gear the shock troops back on Earth had been using.

The team made it to their objective, but the hard fighting had taken its toll. Kravczyk had taken a glancing hit from a plasma bolt two corridors back, but he was still in the fight despite second-degree burns to his shoulder. Valdez had had his bell rung good and proper when he'd been slammed against a bulkhead by some sort of concussive grenade an overeager trooper lobbed around a corner. Tess was in the worst shape, though, wielding only her sidearm after shrapnel from the same explosion damaged her Mk 27 and punched a half-dozen pin holes in her left hand and wrist, which she had cradled against her chest.

"Come on, Mabel, we're getting killed out here!" Ben shouted as a fresh burst of plasma fire seared the bulkhead a few meters away. The team had taken cover behind a pair of bulkheads that flanked the CIC hatch to either side of the corridor, but they were now pinned there by security teams advancing from both directions.

"Haranguing me will not make the process go any faster, Benjamin," Mabel replied in a calm yet somehow chastising tone that seemed all wrong considering their current predicament. "Security bypassed. Go now."

"We're in!" Ben shouted over the din as he grabbed the hatch's handle and pulled the moment he felt the locking bolts retract. Tess was ready with a flashbang grenade and tossed it inside the moment there was enough room for the explosive to clear. Ben slammed the hatch shut again and waited until a muffled *whump* rang through the bulkhead and deck plating.

Kravczyk and Valdez each tossed their last fragmentation grenades down opposite sides of the corridor to slow the advancing enemy while Ben swung the hatch back open. Tess rushed in through the wisps of flashbang smoke that curled out around the opening door and its frame, and Ben was right on her heels.

Smoke was still obscuring parts of CIC when Ben entered the compartment, and it wasn't clearing as fast as he'd like. With a thought, he overlaid his augmented vision with a mid-wave infrared filter and immediately picked out two of the smaller alien types half in cover behind a row of consoles obscured by the smoke. They were disoriented from the flashbang but were quickly regaining their wits. Ben opened up with his rail rifle on the low-velocity setting, and the two aliens went down in crumpled heaps, blood oozing from the wounds and pooling on the deck.

The alien CIC was arranged in a circle, with a raised dais where command staff could see and be seen by everyone in the space. Ben heard Tess's pistol bark several times as he quickly cleared his sector of the large compartment. By the time Kravczyk and Valdez made entry and slammed the hatch closed behind them, Tess and Ben were checking the far corners.

"Clear!" Ben shouted when he was satisfied there were no more aliens lurking in his area.

"Clear," Tess said a moment later, turning her attention to the two SEARs now guarding the hatch. "All clear, sir."

"Ben, get to work," Valdez said as a pounding began on the hatch and he and Kravczyk fell back several paces to take cover behind some workstations.

"Already on it," Ben said as he reached a large circular holographic table in the middle of the raised command dais, alien script and odd symbols flowing in and around what looked like a three-dimensional representation of the Kerner system. Mabel had highlighted the console on his HUD. "This it, Mabel?" Ben asked, just to be sure.

"Yes, Ben," Mabel said with infinite patience. "Hurry."

Ben reached a hand out to the indicated pad on the console and the pounding on the hatch intensified as more of the security forces arrived to find a hatch that wouldn't respond to their override commands; Mabel had worked her magic when she hacked hatch's security and made sure the alien crew would not be able to easily enter CIC themselves. His hand touched the odd obsidian plate, and a moment later, he felt a strange sensation as Mabel withdrew from his APEX armor and integrated herself with the alien ship's systems.

That was it; this was his objective. They'd done it. Now they just needed to stay alive while Mabel did her thing—something that was looking much more difficult than when they had been planning this op.

"There's plenty of room in here, Ben," Mabel said as the last of her receded from his armor. "The modifications we made to my programming are working as expected, but I won't be able to communicate with you until my task is complete. Good luck."

As the last of Mabel's words reached his ears, Ben suddenly felt as though a part of him was missing. They hadn't been fully linked except for the brief moment when Mabel smashed through the ship's AI as they screamed toward their target in the Griffon. Up until now, though, his senses had been heightened as though he and Mabel had been subtly linked the whole time. Now he felt lost and naked, standing in the middle of an alien ship.

The pounding from the hatch ceased suddenly and Ben opened his mouth to tell Valdez he'd finished, but a powerful explosion blasted the heavy door open, and the overpressure wave sent him tumbling off the dais. The explosion got Ben's mind back into gear as he scrambled to pick himself up and roll to his right, where a row of workstations offered some cover. He came up to one knee, rifle at the ready, and leaned around the edge of the workstation to get a better line of fire on the hatch, which now hung drunkenly from one hinge, the edges glowing orange from the heat of the explosive the alien security forces had used to make entry.

Ben's finger slipped into the trigger guard and he flipped the rifle's safety off as one of the huge aliens in powered armor burst through the opening, kicking the broken hatch free of its one remaining hinge and sending it caroming across the floor, straight at Kravczyk. Ben heard a grunt, and the big SEAR's indicator on his HUD updated to a flashing amber.

Ben cursed. In the blink of an eye, the chief was out of action. The three remaining members of the team all opened fire at the same time, and the fight was on.

CHAPTER THIRTY-TWO

WRATH

A FUSILLADE OF PLASMA BOLTS SIZZLED OVER BEN'S HEAD, AND HE heard a sharp cry from Tess that cut off abruptly. Time seemed to stand still as Ben's eyes locked onto her indicator on his HUD. The little dot representing her biometrics blinked in slow motion, its amber color denoting an injury. *No... not her.*

"Tess!" he called out, hoping against hope it wasn't serious. He turned in her direction and peered around the edge of the consoles he was taking cover behind. She had taken up position behind another row of consoles adjacent to his, and when he peeked around the edge of his cover his blood ran cold. Tess was lying facedown near the far corner of her row of workstations, and Ben could just make out a charred, fist-sized hole still smoking between her shoulder blades, the edges of her armor glowing faintly as the heat from the plasma slowly dissipated.

The battle raging around him evaporated as his world came crashing down.

"Tess!" he cried and made to rise and go check on her, but a fresh volley of enemy fire tore through the open space between their two rows of consoles. He felt the heat from the plasma even through his faceplate, and he slumped back against his cover, unable to reach her.

He heard an agonized whimper through the team comms. She was hurt bad, but at least she was still alive. There was still hope—if he could just get to her. "Tess, I'm coming! Just hold on!"

Ben glanced around frantically, desperately searching for some way to get to her, but it was no good. He couldn't reach her with a firefight raging on. He watched helplessly as her status indicator rapidly blinked amber a few more times. Then her comms cut off abruptly as her indicator changed to solid red. Her biometrics had flatlined.

As the pixels on his HUD shifted color, his very soul felt like it was ripped from his chest, leaving nothing more than an empty husk behind. It couldn't be real. Not after they had come this far. *It isn't fair. It isn't fair!*

Something inside of Ben broke.

The anger he had stuffed back into its deep dark hole after his animalistic slaughter of the alien troopers back on Earth burst through the dam he had put in place and tore through him like wildfire. And he welcomed it; he urged it to fill him up. *More!* He wanted to feel something—*anything*—other than than the utter sense of despair that currently gripped him.

The building rage broke down the series of barriers that his mind had put in place many years ago. A fresh torrent of pain and anguish crashed over him as the memories of all those terrible things came flooding back: the loss of his mother, the Alarian War and being separated from his dad, the years of constant fear and hardship he had endured on the shattered remains of Earth. He'd lost his home and the vineyard he had worked so hard to bring back from the dead. He'd lost Jim, first to the exploding dropship and then getting him back briefly, as if the universe were playing some cosmic joke on him, before truly ripping him away as Ben cradled the dying man in his arms.

Now the person who had helped him feel joy's warm embrace for the first time in years, someone whose infectious laughter and bright smile had shown him that there were things still worth caring about in this fucked-up galaxy, had been cut down by the searing heat of a plasma bolt... and he had once again been powerless to prevent it.

No more.

The tidal wave of emotions morphed into an all-consuming hatred. A feral scream pounded at Ben's ears as he rolled to his left and brought his rail gun to bear on the armored troops that were flooding into the control center, quickly spreading out into a loose skirmish line and taking cover wherever they could. Somewhere in the dim recesses of his conscious mind, Ben knew the scream was coming from his own lungs, but he didn't try to stop it. He didn't *want* to stop it.

He *embraced* it.

His vision narrowed and clouded as the fury took hold and tears streamed from his eyes. He squeezed the trigger on his rifle and held it, forcing the weapon to become an extension of his will. He watched with grim satisfaction as a stream of white-hot death shredded the enemy formation. The hyper-velocity tungsten rounds cut a swath through the enemy troops as if they were made of tissue paper, spraying their surroundings with blood and gore and leaving gaping holes in the bulkheads behind them as the incredible power of the XM93 was unleashed.

"Fucking die!" he howled.

After just a few seconds of the full-auto fire, a warning flashed across his HUD: *WARNING: WEAPON OVERHEAT IMMINENT.*

But his broken mind failed to register the message. The rails of his rifle were glowing a bright orange and began to droop from the massive friction of sending nearly one hundred hypersonic rounds downrange in under three seconds. The weapon stopped firing as its loading mechanism seized up from the heat, offering a brief moment of reprieve to the advancing enemy as they took advantage of the lull to push in harder.

Ben roared with maniacal laughter, completely unhinged from reality. "You think this will stop me!" he bellowed, shaking the near-molten rifle at them before hurling it with all his augmented strength in a vicious overhand throw at a fresh wave of troops emerging from the hatchway. The weapon connected with the lead trooper's face, tearing its head off and spraying the troops behind it with blood and bits of bone. "I'm not done with you fuckers yet!"

Ben's rage-fogged mind didn't register the purple-blue streak of energy that arced briefly from his outstretched hands to the consoles nearest to him.

Now, standing in the open and without a weapon, he saw more enemy troops rushing into the room and he knew his time cheating death had come to an end. He charged headlong into the enemy formation, willing his wrath to become manifest and annihilate the evil before him.

———

No more aliens came through the hatch.

Valdez stood up on shaky legs and surveyed the destruction around him. The series of events that he had just witnessed would haunt the SEAR commander's dreams for the rest of his life. That tortured wail was still ringing in his ears despite the unnatural silence now pervading the alien CIC.

His eyes searched for his team's status indicators, and he realized that his HUD was blank, and his suit had initiated a hard reset. Whatever Ben had just done had completely scrambled the hardened systems of Valdez's APEX. He stayed crouched, peering out from behind his cover for a moment longer, too stunned by the incredible violence the kid had just unleashed on the poor sons of bitches trying to retake their ship.

His HUD came back to life, and his eyes scanned the data. Kravczyk's suit monitor was showing a number of faults and damage indicators—the burly chief had been unresponsive since the heavy blast door to CIC had crushed the consoles he was taking cover behind. Both McCollum's and Ben's suits were failing to indicate status, but he couldn't see or hear either of them.

A groan crackled through his helmet speakers.

"Boss, you still there?"

"I think so, Chief."

"That's great. Come get this door off me."

———

SEARING pain lanced through Ben's entire body; it was like every single one of his nerves was actually on fire.

"Ben! Come on, kid. Come back to me." Ben heard the distant voice calling to him through the void, and he struggled to open his eyes. His right eye finally cracked open, and he saw the concerned face of Valdez staring at him.

"Hey, sir," Ben mumbled.

"Chief, get your ass over here!"

"Coming, boss," Kravczyk replied, grabbing a data tablet off the inductive dataport Ben had deposited Mabel in when they had taken the alien CIC, then limping over to where Valdez was kneeling over Ben. "Help me get him over to that console," the big SEAR said as he grabbed the carry handle on the back of

Ben's armor with his one good arm, and Valdez grabbed Ben's feet.

The two men half carried, half dragged him the few feet over to the indicated workstation, and Ben's face contorted in agony as fire lanced through his veins from the movement. Breathing was difficult, and he tried to sit up, but his limbs wouldn't respond and rewarded him with another blinding surge of pain.

"Mabel says she's ready to link back up with the kid," Kravczyk explained as he took one of Ben's hands and raised it to the edge of the console. He placed Ben's hand on the inductive dataport and waited.

Ben felt that familiar tingling sensation mix with the searing pain in his brain. Then Mabel's voice floated through his mind.

Oh my, Ben. What have you done?

I'm alive? Ben struggled to form the thought. *How?*

That's a very good question. You've made quite the mess of yourself. Don't move while I see what I can do… Ben felt a sensation like cool water begin spreading throughout his body, and the pain lancing up his nerves slowly faded. *Better?* Mabel asked.

"Mabel, did we do it?" Ben asked aloud.

"You're goddamn right we did!" Kravczyk exclaimed, dropping Ben's hand to the deck once he realized the transfer was complete. "Fucked these bastards up good!"

"You did good, Ben," Valdez said. "Icarus is safe and Mabel was able to take control of this ship, completely disrupting the enemy command-and-control structure. With her help, the battle turned from disaster into a rout as she sabotaged their systems from the inside while the fleet pounded their ships with concerted fire. The remaining Confed ships are mopping up the last of the stragglers and beginning search-and-rescue operations right now, and the *Ford* and her task force are moving in from their quarantine anchorage to assist."

"How long was I out?" Ben asked, his mind finally starting to feel like his brain was more or less working again.

"Almost three hours. You scared the shit out of us for most of it," Kravczyk said, giving him a light slap on the shoulder as he stood up. "Mabel was able to gain access to this ship's internal security subroutines right after your, uh… assault. I didn't actually see that, by the way, what with having a two-ton door on top of me and all, but the boss here shared his suit's video recording. Fucking epic!" Valdez smacked Kravczyk on the back of the head, and the big SEAR continued. "Anyway, she sealed off the section we were in and opened the airlocks, venting the entire remaining crew into space."

"We moved you in here after making sure our section was clear," Valdez explained. "I… I've never seen anything like that, Ben. You saved all our asses."

"Damn right he did!" Kravczyk shouted. "Did you see the way he took those guys out? Like a fuckin' warlock, man. Bzzzt!" Kravczyk pointed his hands out in front of him, shooting pretend lightning bolts out of his fingers while making the sound effects. "Hey! That should be his new callsign from now on… What?" Kravczyk said, seeing Valdez staring at him and shaking his head slowly. "It's a damn sight better than Blackthorn."

Ben wasn't nearly as exuberant as the big SEAR, and he felt a tear slide down one of his cheeks. "Not all… I couldn't save us all," he said quietly. The agony coursing through his body was nothing compared to the grief he felt over Tess. They had been so close. Just a minute or two more and they would have been in the clear…

Armored fingers brushed against his left hand and he struggled to turn his head to the side. A pair of green eyes looked back at him, not quite able to focus.

"Hey there, handsome," Tess said with a smile and a

narcotics-induced slur to her words. The dam broke, and Ben was wracked with sobs—of joy, pain, or exhaustion, he wasn't sure, but it felt *amazing*.

"Oh, come on now. I don't look that bad, do I?" she said.

"You've never looked better," Ben said, alternately laughing with relief and gasping in agony from the movement. "You scared the hell out of me, you know that?"

She smiled at that and gave his hand a gentle squeeze. Then, still smiling slightly, she closed her eyes as the painkillers took hold once again and she fell asleep. Ben watched the subtle rise and fall of her chest, afraid that he might have hallucinated the whole thing. Once he was satisfied she was really still alive, he let a smile spread across his face. They'd made it. They had *all* made it. The four-year nightmare was over.

"The hit was a glancing blow," Valdez explained. "It took out her suit's CPU and power supply, which is why her biometrics went offline. She's hurt pretty bad, but we were able to get her stabilized and Mabel says she's not in any immediate danger as long as we can get her to a proper surgical team soon."

"How soon can we get her to Icarus?" Ben asked.

"Fleet's sending some escorts out to meet us. They should be here in about an hour."

"Lieutenant Commander," Mabel said, "I'm still not exactly sure how Ben was able to do what he did, but there's a lot of damage in here. I need him to rest until the medics arrive."

"Do what you have to do, Mabel. We'll manage."

"No, Mabel, wait—" Ben's words cut off as Mabel pumped sedatives into his body from the suit's auto-injectors, and he felt his eyelids grow heavy and slide shut as the chief began a two-way conversation with himself on what Mabel's new callsign should be. Mercifully, sleep took him a moment later.

CHAPTER THIRTY-THREE

REUNION

HENRY WAS PACING LIKE A CAGED TIGER OUTSIDE THE AIRLOCK THAT led to one of Icarus's few remaining docking arms, but this time Commander Evans didn't try to calm him down. The video monitor next to the airlock's hatch showed the starboard main airlock of the CTS *Bull Run* as she maneuvered for docking. Under the powerful spotlights of the station's docking control system, her matte black hull displayed the scars of a hard-fought battle.

Four years. He'd left Ben alone for *four years*, but now they were so close—just a few meters of alloy and vacuum remained until he would finally be able to hold his son again, to tell him how much he loved him, to ask forgiveness. Couldn't they make the damn airlock cycle any faster?

A few minutes later, the status light above the airlock finally switched to green, and the hatch slid aside. The team from Icarus's medical section cordoned off the area around the hatch as a figure on a stretcher, encased in a clear inflatable polymer quarantine bag, was carried out and placed on one of the waiting gurneys. Henry caught sight of McCollum's auburn hair through the mass of medical people that were attending her before she was carted off to a waiting surgical bay.

' Henry was aware that she was seriously wounded during a daring attack on the enemy command ship, but seeing the SEAR's ghostly pale face behind the quarantine bubble as the station's finest medical team rushed her to surgery really drove home what this battle had cost them. Was Ben in just as bad a shape? Evans had told him everyone on Ben's team had been wounded but were stable, but Icarus's medical team hadn't acted like McCollum was stable—just the opposite, in fact.

The spectators around the docking hatch took an involuntary step back as two hulking figures appeared, their APEX armor suits showing signs of having recently been involved in an intense and protracted firefight. Henry rushed toward them, noting that both men appeared to be pretty seriously injured, but they were on their feet and just as imposing as ever. They were also escorting Ben off the ship.

"Ben!" Henry's heart leaped into his throat when his eyes caught sight of the *Bull Run*'s medical staff grunting with the effort of carrying a still fully armored Ben on a reinforced stretcher. Why was his armor still on? "Is he okay? Tell me he's okay, Chief," Henry pleaded with Kravczyk, who was the first to reach him. His son was on that stretcher, and he wasn't moving.

"He's alive, but in bad shape," Valdez said as he walked up, reaching a hand out to hold Henry back with an iron grip as he tried to push his way through to his son's side. "Mabel's using his suit's link to keep his autonomic functions in check, and she's got him in an induced coma, Henry. You can go with him, but let the docs do their job."

"Ben…" Henry whispered as tears filled his eyes, and he watched the medical team strap his son securely to the gurney. "What have I done?"

"Your son is a hero, Henry. You should be proud of him. He

fought like a demon and probably saved the entirety of humanity today," Valdez said, pulling a dataslate from a pouch on his armor. "Here." He held it out for Henry to take. "This is everything Mabel was able to compile on Ben's condition. She said to give it to you as soon as we saw you and that you need to read through it immediately—Ben's injuries are going to need your expertise to help heal."

The medical team began wheeling Ben down the long docking arm, and Henry took the proffered slate from Valdez. He looked at it for a moment, then nodded, his emotions threatening to overwhelm him. The SEAR released his hold and Henry turned and ran after his son.

———

"THINK THE KID WILL BE OKAY?" Kravczyk said, watching Henry disappear down the crowded docking arm.

"I don't know," Valdez replied as the two SEARs watched the group turn a corner toward a bank of lifts that would take them to the medical section, "but if there's anything I've learned in the last week, it's to not underestimate Ben and Mabel."

"I hope he does," Kravczyk said. "It took him thirty-two minutes to crack the alien data from that ship back in Sol."

"What the hell does that have to do with anything?" Valdez said, confused at the turn the conversation had taken.

An enormous smile stretched across Kravczyk's face. "He and McCollum owe me a date!"

CHAPTER THIRTY-FOUR

PICKING UP THE PIECES

HENRY LEANED BACK IN HIS CHAIR AND STIFLED A YAWN. HE'D JUST sat through six hours of Chief Kravczyk's... colorful... recitation of the mission to extract Ben from Earth. A mission that had somehow ended with his son talking a spaceship full of the Confed's most trusted intelligence operatives and special operations personnel into a ludicrously dangerous assault on a superior enemy vessel that was three times the tonnage of the *Wraith*. Kravczyk had called it ballsy; Henry called it stupid. *He's his mother's child. No doubt about that.*

"This is some bad fucking shit, Hank," Garland said wearily after the hatch to the conference room clanged shut behind Kravczyk's departing back. He ignored the startled look from the bravest of his staffers and rubbed his eyes with his palms. "We beat them back this time, but we're now down to barely postwar numbers of combat effective hulls in the fleet, our one and only major shipbuilding facility is beat to hell, and we still don't know jack shit about this new species or what their objectives are, short of wiping us all out for the fun of it."

"Maybe not," Henry said carefully, causing one of Garland's

eyebrows to rise in question. "Mabel, are you still with us?" Henry said to the room.

"Yes, Henry." She had participated in the debrief with the boorish Chief Petty Officer to provide context and nuance to Kravczyk's broad strokes and Cro-Magnon-like assessment of "big aliens were bad—we blew them up." Okay, he hadn't actually been *that* bad, but there was a clear gap between Henry's high-level understanding of complex issues and Kravczyk's need to understand things only insofar as how to kill them and break their stuff.

"Why don't you come on down here and tell the admiral what you've discovered," Henry said, making a placating gesture to his friend, whose confusion was rapidly morphing into frustration at the cryptic statements. "She only just told me about this on my way to the debrief—that's why I was a few minutes late—and I didn't say anything to the chief because he's more than likely not going to be cleared for this information after it receives a classification level from Intel Division," he explained, as a soft-blue dot matrix cube materialized over the table, projected by the holographic emitters located within the table itself. "Go ahead, Mabel. Start with what piqued your interest in the first place, please."

"Yes, Henry," Mabel said, and the cube that was her avatar pulsed and undulated with her words, drawing raised eyebrows from everyone except Henry. "When Ben and retired Master Chief Petty Officer Bloukamp assaulted the alien team at the CDF outpost on October 24, the master chief was able to obtain three pieces of alien technology, which he later turned over to me for study while Ben was recovering from the shock of having his neural implant reinitialized and the team was making preparations to defend the Grayling facility. I was able to take detailed scans of the devices using some equipment that was still functional in the lab and even establish a low-level connection to the two devices that the master chief thought were similar to our personal data tablets.

"What I found was a hardware architecture that struck me as tangentially related to technology the Alarians were using when their refugee fleet arrived in orbit over Earth decades ago, though much more advanced. It could have been a coincidence, but I dedicated a small portion of my processing capacity to analyze the devices and search my archives for any possible links to known technology."

The admiral had been slowly leaning forward in his seat as Mabel laid out her findings. When she had first told Henry, he had been absolutely floored; Bob was going to shit himself when she got to the good part.

"The first breakthrough came after I linked with Ben for the first time," Mabel continued. "We were able to crack the code, so to speak, as to how their systems worked, allowing us to combat them effectively. Without the devices the master chief acquired and turned over, Ben and I likely wouldn't have been able to defeat the dropship that pursued us away from the Grayling facility.

"That first encounter with the dropship's AI allowed me to build upon what I had learned from the devices and made it possible to combat the AI aboard the corvette that later attacked us aboard the CIS *Wraith* on our way out of the Sol system. That battle presented the opportunity for me to mine the alien systems and obtain a large, heavily encrypted data cache, which Ben and I later accessed while en route to Gateway from Sol.

"I know you are all likely aware of the timeline, but I wish to have the chain of events clear in your minds to help you understand how I knew what to go looking for in the data cache in the first place."

It wasn't just the admiral leaning forward now; all his staffers had forgotten their exhaustion and were fixated on the AI's avatar hovering before them. Even Henry found himself hanging on Mabel's every word, and he already knew what was coming.

"What did you find?" Garland said, his voice almost a whisper.

"These new aliens were responsible for the war that decimated the Alarian homeworld and their colonized systems, as well as the social and political tension that ultimately resulted in what we call the Alarian War."

An explosion of gasps and shocked chatter erupted from the fleet personnel present in the room, and rightly so—they and the Alarians had nearly wiped each other out four years ago. Now, they were learning that the whole thing didn't start because two species couldn't get along, but because a third party had been manipulating both sides from the shadows. Garland held a hand up to quiet the room down, and Henry saw the muscles of his jaw knotted up tight.

"Let's let her finish," the admiral said in a hoarse voice.

Mabel pressed on. "Through the use of advanced AI constructs and, in rare cases, direct martial intervention, this new alien cabal—they are actually two different, closely genetically related species that only refer to themselves as what approximately translates to an imperium or dominant authority—carefully manipulates the societal and technological development of neighboring species such that the Imperium will always have the upper hand in any potential conflict.

"From what I've been able to gather, when the unknowing client species reaches a certain level of technological prowess or begins to deviate from the prescribed course, these AI constructs, frequently referred to as 'agents of the Master,' will then begin to act as a subversive or seditious force. They carefully manipulate small events on a massive scale to cultivate tensions—either between two neighboring client species or between different factions within a single client species—until those tensions reach a boiling point and armed conflict erupts. Once the client or clients are engaged in a 'shooting war,' as you might say, the agent will continue to manipulate events to ensure the maximum possible losses for all involved, whether through direct acts of sabotage, passing legitimate intelligence to one side so they can counter, or planting false intelligence to lure one or both sides into a trap."

The room had gone completely quiet, ashen faces exchanging glances with one another.

"I can see by the looks on your faces that what I'm describing is familiar," Mabel said. "There's good reason for that: the Alarian refugee fleet unknowingly carried one of these agents with them to Earth, where it's been playing both sides against each other now for decades, likely because we, especially, have progressed down a vastly different technological path. That deviation may explain why our ships were able to cope so well with the weaponry employed by the Imperium battlegroup sent to destroy us. It also provides a reason as to why our kinetic rail guns were so effective against their vessels, ultimately allowing the fleet to make a stand here and survive long enough for the SEARs, Ben, and myself to arrive and turn the tide."

A stunned silence hung in the room. "It makes sense, Bob," Henry said, appearing collected and thoughtful after having already had hours to digest the bombshell Mabel had uncovered. "It explains everything—much of which we already suspected, though we didn't have a clue as to just how severe the problem really was." Henry didn't mention the fact that it had been this very theory that had shattered their friendship years ago. Somehow, saying "I told you so" just didn't seem to cut it here.

"Not quite," Garland said, getting his feet back under him as the shock wore off.

"Pardon?" Henry said, brow furrowed.

"It doesn't explain *everything*, Hank. There is one huge question still outstanding: why?"

"Why does any group seek to destroy another?" Mabel jumped in.

"Power or greed," Henry offered. "Though those two things are usually joined at the hip." Bob's question had him thinking now. Did power and greed really explain it?

"Those are indeed powerful motivators, Henry," Mabel said, "but you missed one: fear. Fear is what drives the Imperium to control and destroy every race they learn of. Fear that they themselves would one day be enslaved or destroyed if they were to allow other races to prosper. It is not power or greed that drive them, though it would be naive to assume they play no role. It is a strong desire for self-preservation. They are a long-lived species and do not suffer from the short-sightedness of humans. This long-term strategizing is what has made them such a dangerous foe to those who have opposed them in the past."

There it was: the key to the puzzle they had been missing. Understanding *how* was important, but understanding *why* could change the course of history.

"This gives us an edge, Bob," Henry said. "We now know exactly what we're dealing with, but most importantly, we now understand why, and we can use that."

"Not without help," the admiral said after a long moment of silence. "Mabel," he said, directing his attention to the soft glow of her avatar, "are there more of these Imperium forces operating in Terran or Alarian space, and if so, how long will it take them to get reinforcements? I can't help but assume they'll be back, and they won't be underestimating us again."

"From the information I was able to glean from the database aboard the Imperium command ship, and after accounting for the ships known to have been encountered and destroyed thus far by the Confed fleet, there are only two Imperium vessels still operating within either Terran or known Alarian space: one that you would likely classify as a heavy cruiser, equipped with an orbital bombardment plasma cannon, and another of their smaller infiltration corvettes like the one we encountered in the Sol system. Unfortunately, those vessels were assigned to Alarian space for reconnaissance, and it's likely that they've deviated from their assigned stations since the rest of the battle-group was defeated."

Only two ships left was good news. Henry's mind immediately went to work trying to figure out how to bring the Alarians in on this, but that was going to be extremely tricky. He knew for a fact that there were very vocal factions of the Alarian military that were calling for them to finish what they'd started four years ago, but Henry thought he might have an ace up his sleeve.

"As for the question of how long it will take for Imperium reinforcements to arrive, I can only offer an informed estimate, as it appears the battlegroup we faced comprised their older vessels, many of which were pulled from their mothball fleet for this mission, and next time they will probably send more advanced warships that have capabilities we're unaware of. That said, I think we can safely say we have at least eighteen standard months before they would arrive. The distance they need to travel is great, and I must assume they will have logistical hurdles to overcome, similar to what either we or the Alarians deal with when moving a large fleet over great distances."

"How far are we talking here?"

"The battlegroup we encountered, Battlegroup 21, staged from a forward operating base over four thousand light-years from here, beyond the Talishian Expanse, and almost twelve hundred light-years from where the Alarian refugee fleet originated," Mabel replied.

"Damn," Garland said thoughtfully. "It took the Alarians the better part of five years to get here, and you're saying these Imperium ships can do the same trip in a quarter of the time, even allowing for the extra time needed to pull together a fleet and the necessary provisions." The admiral leaned back in his chair and looked around the room. "Tell the diplomatic corps to get their asses in gear and set up a meeting with the Alarian High Council," he said to the aide closest to him, who immediately began staring off into space with a look of concentration as she used her implant to relay the request to the appropriate people.

"We're going to need Ben for this next part, too," Henry said, the agony of knowing what he was about to say written plainly on his face. "He's the only hope we have right now of combating the agent or agents that are infecting our datanets, which means he'll need to be on the mission to Hai'alla."

"One thing at a time, Hank," Garland said. "We'll be lucky if those sanctimonious pricks will even pick up the phone when we call. We were at each other's throats just a few years ago, after all."

"All the more reason for Ben to go," Henry insisted. "If I'm not mistaken, Taylen's first daughter, Elyria, was in line to take his seat on the council before the war broke out, and our intel reports from the aftermath of the war indicated that most of the council had been killed during that retaliatory strike that was sent in as a *fuck you* after Earth was nuked back into the Stone Age." He glared briefly at the admiral. Taylen Tashmali, one of the Alarian high councilors, had been a good friend and ally in trying to avert the war, and the news of the strike on the High Council had hit Henry hard.

"Though in retrospect, it now seems likely that we were fed the information on the council's whereabouts by this agent," Henry continued. "I'm sure anyone from our military or senior civilian leadership will be persona non grata to the Alarians, but Elyria always had a bit of a thing for Ben. That's likely our in."

"If you're referring to that little incident between Ben and Elyria before the war, I'm not so sure she'll be as happy to see him as you think," Garland scoffed. "Hell, the war almost started then and there, Hank."

"You can't change biology."

"We'll see. How long before Ben's back on his feet?"

"Hard to say exactly," Henry said. "He's stable for the moment, but the damage to his nervous system is severe, and the unusual nature of his implant malfunction requires a careful approach... maybe three to six months before he's fully back up and ready, depending on if we run into any major hurdles along the way."

"Too damn long. We'll try sending a diplomatic envoy first and keep Ben in our back pocket if they turn us away," Garland said before switching gears. "Mabel, please do everything you can to help nail down the location of the two remaining enemy ships that are prowling about our space—pull in anyone and any resources you need. If anyone hassles you, tell them to talk to me and I'll set them straight."

"Yes, Admiral."

"And you lot of raging fuckups," the admiral growled to the staffers around the table, "get this info disseminated to your respective departments, and offer any assistance you can to Mabel, Hank here, and/or the diplomatic corps as they try to un-fuck this goat and save our asses. Dismissed." The staffers bolted for the hatch so fast they were tripping over each other on the way out, eliciting a chuckle from the admiral.

"Kind of hard on them, don't you think?" Henry said, raising an eyebrow in question.

"They're lucky I didn't reassign them to scrape carbon scoring off the hull of the station. It was that same group of idiots that, after the *Appomattox* was lost, insisted what we were dealing with here was not actually a new species but a new generation of Alarian ship that came back to wipe us out. Then they strongly recommended to me that we scrub the mission to retrieve Ben when they learned I was diverting resources to go pick him up." That last part elicited an angry frown from Henry before Garland continued. "And *then* they spent days after the battle downplaying Dagger team's role in the outcome until the *Bull Run* docked and we were able to get the data straight from Mabel on what she and the team had done. Bunch of incompetent fucking morons…"

"I think you need to get some rest," Henry said seriously, seeing the unhealthy pallor of his friend's skin, the sunken look to his bloodshot eyes, and the uncharacteristic vehemence toward his staff.

"Hmph," Garland grunted. "I think you're probably right. Tell me one thing, Hank."

"Shoot."

"Can Ben really do it? Pull our asses out of this mess?"

"He's his mother's son, Bob," Henry said, a grin pulling up at one corner of his mouth.

"Then God help the poor bastards who stand in his way."

CHAPTER THIRTY-FIVE

MAN AND MACHINE

"HE'S COMING AROUND," SAID AN UNSEEN VOICE IN THE DARKNESS.

"Ben! Ben, can you hear me?"

Ben's mind struggled to focus and he willed himself up through the void. His dry lips cracked as he opened them to speak, but his parched tongue wouldn't form the words properly.

"It's alright, Ben. We're all here. You're safe."

"Dad?" Ben managed to croak out, and his eyelids finally responded and cracked open a few millimeters. His dad's face was staring down at him, tears welling in his eyes.

"I'm here, Ben. Don't try to move just yet."

What was his dad doing here? And for that matter, where was here? Ben struggled to remember what he'd been doing before waking up in this room, but he came up empty. Wait... what was the last thing he remembered, period? He searched every last millimeter of his memory for something, anything, but... nothing.

Ben. My name is Ben. Hey, it was a start. Maybe his dad could tell him what was going on—what had he said about not moving? He gave up trying to get his sluggish memory to respond and decided to focus on the here and now instead.

Never one to listen to his dad, Ben stretched the kink out of his arms and was rewarded with a fresh wave of nausea-inducing pain. He grimaced and fought through it, bending his arms at the elbows to bring his hands up to his face. They were covered in angry red scars, and his fingers felt like they creaked when he slowly flexed them.

"Ow," Ben said conversationally as he continued to flex his hands and forearms.

"Is it some sort of hard-wired defect in your brain that you just can't help but not listen to me?" his dad said, incredulous. "At least it's a good sign that you can move, I suppose. We weren't even sure you'd be able to do that."

Ben froze with his hands still in the air and looked around the room, just now becoming aware of the half dozen people who were filling it. Tess… *Her name is Tess! Score one for the ol' noggin.* She was smiling at him from a wheelchair in the corner, and two other SEARs were standing quietly against a wall at the foot of his bed. He knew them, too! *Way to go, brain!* Some doctor-looking person was standing by a row of medical moni-toring instruments off to his left and making notes on a dataslate. He looked back at his dad and his mind finally started operating at something near moderately functional.

"How long have I been out, and what do you mean you weren't sure I would be able to move?" Ben's tired mind and parched throat made the words sound almost slurred. His dad opened his mouth to speak, but Ben's hand snapped up and he raised a finger. "Ow… I need to stop doing that. Wait… ugh, dammit." He rubbed at his scalp.

Wait… why didn't he have any hair? "My brain feels like someone cut it up into a jigsaw puzzle and then shook the pieces around in a tin can for a while. Does someone want to tell me what the hell is going on and how I got to be here? No, wait, why don't I have any hair? Let's start with that."

Kravczyk pushed off the wall and walked over. Ben noted both of the man's arms seemed to work fine, and he knew that was an important observation for some reason but couldn't quite identify why that was. "Are you sure you and Mabel put all his marbles back in the right place?" the big SEAR said, looking at Ben like he was a strange animal in a zoo. "He sounds like an amnesia patient on cocaine."

Tess stood up painfully from her wheelchair and shuffled over to Ben's side, gently pushing his dad aside so she could lean on the bed's side rail. "Hey there, handsome," she said softly.

Ben looked into those stunning green eyes and her words coalesced in his mind. His memories came flooding back, and images washed through his vision like a movie as they categorized themselves and were filed away in their proper place; the effect was disorienting. He remembered everything: his mom, the war, losing his dad, the years on Earth with Jim. It was like reliving four years of his life in a split second, culminating with the battle for the alien CIC, the fury that had swept through him after Tess had been hit and the carnage he had wrought with his XM93. He had charged the enemy as lightning danced around him, felt the searing pain of the alien plasma bolts striking his body.

"Dad!" Ben shouted, startling everyone in the room as he lunged forward to embrace his father. No one said a word as the two Hutchins men wept in each other's arms, truly reunited for the first time in over four years. Ben remembered now. He remembered everything.

"I should be dead," Ben whispered as he pulled back from his dad and slid Tess's hand into his own. "I charged right at them. I felt the heat as the plasma burned through my armor, and then there was a bright flash of light... How?"

"You never took a hit from their weapons," Valdez said and looked at his dad. "He doesn't seem to remember much. It might be helpful to show him."

His dad nodded at the SEAR team leader and motioned for Kravczyk to turn down the lights. A holoprojector came to life and an image of the alien CIC filled the room. "This is the optical footage recorded by Lieutenant Commander Valdez's armor during your fight," he explained, then scrolled forward through the footage until just before Tess had been hit. The scene began playing and Ben squeezed Tess's hand a little harder when he heard her cry out after being hit. It was surreal watching himself through the eyes of someone else. He saw himself stand up and watched with a set jaw as his rail gun streamed a line of blazing metallic death toward the alien attackers.

The playback paused on the glowing rails of the XM93 a moment before it ceased operating. "This is where things start to get interesting," his dad explained. "We went back through the data from your APEX and what was left of your XM93 after the battle and discovered that you somehow managed to forge a link with the rifle's processor and alter its programming. You over-rode the built-in safeties which allowed it to achieve that"—he motioned to the holographic image frozen in the air around them—"combination of cyclic rate and projectile velocity, but you also channeled power from your suit into the weapon through the inductive pads in the gauntlets to supplement its internal power pack. Otherwise, its battery charge would have only lasted maybe five or six shots. Do you remember any of that?"

The room looked at Ben and he just shrugged. "I remember willing my rifle to be a conduit for my anger, but it's not like I purposefully hacked its firmware or anything," he said. "Truth be told, I wasn't really doing much thinking about then." He nodded at the image before him, eyes still fixed on the scene.

"Incredible... Let's continue." The holovid came to life again as his dad restarted the playback.

The rifle stopped firing and Ben's stomach did a little flip when he saw the gruesome result of him hurling it with all his strength at the poor bastard that was just coming through the hatch. The vid paused again.

"We did the math, and that rifle was doing better than three hundred kph when it struck that trooper," his dad said, and Ben's eyebrows shot straight up to his hairline. Three hundred kph? How had he managed that? "The APEX suits are strong, but not that strong. We're still trying to figure out how you managed to put that much force into your throw. Anyway..."

The playback resumed again, and Ben watched himself coil like a viper and charge toward the alien line. The playback slowed mid-charge, and Ben saw enemy plasma bolts that should have hit him diffuse and flow into a harmless aurora around his suit. The air in front of him distorted and shimmered just before raw electricity exploded from his APEX and arced between it and his surroundings. The memory of the searing pain came back to him as he watched, as did the emotion that was driving him: vengeance. The aliens began clutching at their heads and screeching as the electromagnetic energy Ben had willed into existence focused in on them and began broiling their insides. The playback paused again.

"We examined the alien corpses after the battle and found that their brains have been extensively augmented with technology similar to the DNI implants we use." His dad's tone was dispassionate and clinical, the words of a scientist reporting an interesting fact, nothing more. Ben, however, found he wasn't feeling quite so detached. Just the opposite, in fact. His dad continued. "I don't fully understand how you did it, but you channeled a strong electromagnetic field through your APEX and focused it like a weapon—the effect was actually very similar to a maser beam. It disrupted the magnetic fields they use to stabilize their plasma weapons, rendering them nearly harmless, and we found nothing but slagged and burned-out components when we autopsied the bodies—you cooked them from the inside out."

Ben stared at the grisly scene and thoughts tumbled through his mind. What had he done to make that happen? "I don't know how to explain it," he said after nearly a minute of silence. "I just wanted them to feel my pain—to make them suffer as I have suffered. I wanted to wipe their stain from this galaxy, and I wanted them to *burn* while I did it." Tess squeezed his hand again, bringing Ben back to the present for a moment, shocked at the malice that had crept into his voice while he recounted his thoughts during those moments, the emotions still as potent as they had been during the fight. It was almost like his emotions were now somehow tied to the memories themselves. He couldn't just recall an event and remember how he felt; now he recalled an event and *felt* how he had felt, if that made any sense at all.

"I wanted them to die," he snarled. "All of them, for what they had done to Tess, to Jim, to Mom, and to the millions of other people across Terran space." His voice had a dangerous edge to it, and he was sitting up now, laser-focused on the carnage his past self was wreaking on the aliens in the holo. "I wanted them to burn for the suffering they had inflicted and for the tens of thousands of spacers they were slaughtering around this station. I wanted them, in their final, agonized moments, to know that they had awoken a righteous fury like they never could have imagined." Ben's hands were clenched into tight fists as he relived the swell of emotion that had driven him in that moment, blood roaring in his ears as his vision narrowed. He found himself consumed with a desire to kill them all over again, and a part of his mind sought ways to make that happen.

The monitoring station that was keeping tabs on his vitals went berserk with flashing lights and audible alarms, and waves of rippling static cut through the frozen holovid around them as Ben played those last moments over and over in his thoughts. Several nurses rushed into the room, responding to the alarms, and froze when they saw the havoc Ben was apparently wreaking with his mind.

"Ben!"

Ben's focus snapped back to the present as the fury of the past receded into the depths, and he felt his father firmly gripping him by the shoulders. He took a deep breath and focused on controlling his emotions. "I was done being helpless," he said in a quiet, much calmer tone, "as those I loved and cared about were ripped away. I wanted them to see what they had wrought, that I was coming for them, and there was nothing they could do to escape. I channeled all of that into a single thought that drove me on, and I *willed* it to be."

The room was silent as Ben took in the faces of those around him and saw that their expressions ranged from shocked and horrified to thoughtful, but the deep concern etching Tess's face as she involuntarily recoiled from him froze him in his tracks. "What the hell is happening to me?" he said, looking at his hands like they were alien objects. "What have I become? What kind of monster am I, Dad?"

His dad sat down on the edge of his bed and hesitated, finally deciding on resting one hand awkwardly on Ben's leg while the other tucked itself into a pocket. "The damage to your implant from when the Alarians attacked Earth resulted in a malfunction," he began.

"To the dendritic controller module," Ben said. "Yeah, I know. Mabel told me."

"Right," his dad confirmed. "A normal DCM is supposed to limit dendrite production to certain areas of the brain. Under normal circumstances, that would allow an implant to send and receive signals to the various cortices that control sensory and motor functions, the thalamus, etc. Basically just the areas needed to integrate someone with their APEX suit. Your implant is a prototype—it was built to support a link with an AI, and as such, the DNI in your implant was a bit more complex because it needed to create pathways to nearly your entire brain. It still has the same hard-coded limitations that the regular fleet implants have, but when your DCM was damaged, it allowed for unrestricted dendrite creation."

The SEARs were of course already aware of the nature of Ben's implant malfunction, but the medical staff that were present looked utterly horrified as his dad laid out the situation.

"Over the last four years, it has slowly been building electrical pathways that mirror every single nerve in your body—essentially a complete copy of your nervous system composed of filaments specialized for electrical signal conduction. I've been talking to Mabel while you were out, trying to get a handle on things, and everything points to something that we never even considered being a possibility.

"Normal human neurons have action potential speeds between a half to about ten meters per second—think of it as how fast a signal travels from one point to another. But the dendrites your implant created can transmit signals nearly at the speed of light—just a hair under three hundred *million* meters per second—with the only bottleneck being the biochemical processes at the neuronal junction itself.

"Your implant is designed to be adaptive by nature. We were out on the bleeding edge of technological development, and we wanted a system that could change and adapt to unforeseen needs. We think that all of these factors created an environment in which your brain had the potential to learn how to process information at the same speed the processors in your implant or suit computers were able to—or close to it—and the several times you linked with Mabel showed it how."

"That's great," Ben cut in, annoyed at the science lesson he was receiving, "but it doesn't explain how I was able to shoot fucking lightning bolts out of my hands! Just give it to me straight, Dad!"

"Through your linking with Mabel," his dad explained patiently, "your brain didn't just learn how to process information faster—it adapted and learned how to take advantage of the technology linked to it. Even though Mabel wasn't present in your suit at the time, your mind forged a link with your armor. In essence, your suit became an extension of your body, indistinguishable from any of your biological parts. When you focused your emotions into an actionable thought, your suit responded because it was no less a part of you than your hands or feet. Your implant translated the emotion into data that was fed into your suit's processors, and the result was an electromagnetic cascade that you focused toward the enemy in a burst.

"The searing pain you felt during the discharge was not enemy fire hitting you—it was your biological nervous system burning up from current bleed-through from your artificial nervous system while you channeled all that energy into and through your suit."

Ben looked at his hands again, trying to figure out how he had done that. Could he do it again, if given another APEX? Could they find a way to harness this ability without frying his insides every time?

"Ben," his dad said, bringing him back to the conversation, "when you say you *willed* your thought to be, you actually did."

"So what was that a minute ago, when the monitor went nuts

and the holovid went all wonky?" Ben said. "I'm not in my suit right now. How did *that* happen?"

"Your biological nervous system was so badly damaged that some of your autonomic functions were affected, but fortunately, your runaway implant had created a backup system for us to utilize. We had to supplement your DNI with an additional processor to handle the task because the original implant doesn't have the horsepower needed when you aren't linked to a suit or AI. Mabel was actually the one who came up with the new design, and I must say, it's far more elegant than I likely would have come up with—" His dad cut himself off and waved a hand in the air as if to wave away the thought tangent he was on, then continued.

"Basically, the situation is this: without the dendrites your runaway implant created to supplement your biological nervous system, you'd likely be permanently in that bed, hooked up to life support, because your body wouldn't be able to do basic things like control your diaphragm for breathing, and we had to tweak your hardware to allow for it—hardware that is apparently capable of linking with the medical equipment hooked up to your body, judging by that little display."

"How long have I been out?" Ben said, putting two and two together and realizing that it must have been a while if they had designed, built, and installed a specialized implant for him.

"Six weeks."

Six weeks? That wasn't good. Ben's mind raced as he realized this little science lesson had been his dad's way of setting the stage for a bombshell of some sort, and based on the topic and the fact that he'd been in a coma for a month and a half, he had a feeling he knew what was coming.

Ben looked to Tess for an assurance that there was still hope. When she gave him a reassuring nod, he sighed. "Okay then, what's the bottom line, Dad? I'm ready."

"You'll need intensive physical therapy to relearn how to work your body now that your nervous system is essentially a hybrid. It'll be slow going, though, because we're in uncharted territory here and we'll probably have to stop and figure out what is happening and why along the way. Setbacks are to be expected, but with hard work and a little luck, I think you'll eventually be back to your old self again... maybe even better."

His dad hadn't changed, dropping a cryptic teaser at the end for the sole purpose of getting his interest up. He knew from long experience that his dad wasn't going to give him anymore than that, so Ben didn't even try to pry at him. Instead, he looked from his dad to Kravczyk and Valdez, and then Tess. He locked eyes with her, and she gave him a mischievous smile. *Dammit, she's in on it, too.* "When do we start?" he said.

EPILOGUE

THE SHRIEKS OF AGONY SLOWLY FADED TO A WET GURGLE, AND THE violent thrashing that had accompanied them became less and less coordinated and energetic. Fleet Admiral Tarok Na'al watched in stony silence as the smoking corpse of First Admiral Trax was carried out of the chamber to be unceremoniously dumped into the nearest garbage chute. The acrid stench of melted implants and broiled flesh was oppressive in the small room, and it took all of his considerable discipline to not vomit.

"Hubris." The word rumbled slowly through the room. The deep, sinister tone of the Master's voice sent a wave a primal fear coursing through Na'al's body. "First Admiral Trax was a fool. He allowed himself to grow complacent, and nearly an entire battlegroup was lost as a result. His incompetence allowed a fleet of Alarians to escape their destruction, and then his arrogance allowed them to fester, multiply, gain allies, and develop new technologies while our forces were occupied with subduing the rest of their race. His failure to prioritize locating the refugee fleet in a timely manner not only allowed the Alarians to recover and establish a new stronghold—it allowed them to taint the natural development of an uninitiated species.

"These Terrans are a menace. Were it not for one of my agents disrupting their relations with the Alarians, their coalition could have posed a significant threat within the next ten to twenty cycles, had their divergent technological path been allowed to continue unabated. As it is, the remnants of the Terran fleet were still able to defeat an entire Imperium battlegroup. Though the cost was high for the Terrans, we are now in the dangerous position of having two alerted enemies with no significant combat power available to finish dispatching them."

Na'al had recently learned of the utterly disastrous operation being conducted by one of their older battlefleets in Terran space, so it was no surprise to him that the Master would seek to punish those involved. What he didn't understand was why he had been summoned—he'd had no part in planning or executing that operation, and the Master was not known for eliminating his people without good cause. Still, his palms were dripping with nervous sweat and he had to fight the urge to wipe them dry.

"First Admiral Trax allowed his arrogance to cloud his judgment, assuring himself that Battlegroup 21 was more than capable of dispatching the broken remnants of two lesser species. I trust you will not make the same mistakes as your predecessor, *First Admiral* Tarok Na'al."

"No, Master," Na'al said, dropping to one knee and bowing. He was being promoted to first admiral? The Master's pronouncement shocked him—he was being promoted ahead of at least four other fleet admirals, all of whom had decacycles more experience than him. "I shall prep a fleet and depart at once. I intend to oversee the annihilation of the Alarian scourge personally, as well as these upstart Terrans."

"Good," the Master rumbled. "Do not return to this place until it is done."

Tarok stood and quickly turned, striding from the room

with a greater confidence than he felt. Battlegroup 21 had comprised vessels that, while not the most advanced in the Imperial Navy, were still generations ahead of anything the Alarians had had when the refugee fleet had escaped their conquest. The newly minted supreme commander of the Imperial Fleet had seen the reports from Battlegroup 21's initial contact with the humans, as well as the intelligence reports sent by the Master's agent that had infiltrated the Terran datanets. He found it troubling that such a powerful force had been overmatched by a primitive species that had only been capable of interstellar travel for little more than sixty standard cycles. He was missing something, and unfortunately it was going to take a considerable amount of time before he would get any answers.

Earth, the Terrans' home planet, was located nearly five thousand light-cycles from the edge of Imperium space. The journey alone would take nearly a full cycle, and it was going to take a quarter cycle, at the very least, to assemble and outfit a fleet for extended operations away from their home space.

Na'al strode out the anteroom doors and straight down the polished stone floors of the hallway toward a bank of lifts that would take him down to the garage level and his personal ground car. The dark expression on his face—and the stench of death pervading his clothing—had staffers and junior officers diving out of his way as he walked directly into a waiting lift car. After the lift doors slid silently closed in front of him, he allowed his composure to crack, and his hands trembled as he straightened his uniform.

These Terrans are a menace. The Master's words rang in his memory. He had no intention of sharing Trax's fate; the Terrans would be put down like a rabid animal. From what he had seen in the intelligence briefs, Earth was a beautiful planet located in a star system rich in mineral resources. Perhaps the Master would grant it to him as a gift after he brought the upstart species to its knees.

———

BEN'S FEET hammered against the rubberized surface of the running track that ran the circumference of Icarus's central hub. Sweat poured down his face and his breath came in ragged heaves as he pushed himself to the absolute limit of his physical endurance. *Faster! I have to go faster!*

He crossed the white line on the track marking the end of his sprint and collapsed to his hands and knees, chest heaving as his body struggled to supply enough oxygen to his exhausted muscles. A slow, ironic clap began from off to one side where an area was set aside for stretching and observation.

"Not bad, kid," Kravczyk said. "Maybe I should ask your old man about getting me some of those fancy upgrades, too, huh?"

Ben looked up at the large digital readout that listed his split times and overall time for the seven miles he had just run, and he smiled as best as his gasping mouth would allow: he'd run the last mile in just under four minutes, and his average mile time was three minutes and thirty-two seconds. The past months had been grueling, but he'd not only learned how to function normally again; he'd truly mastered his condition.

"You're... going to need... Some upgrades... if you want to keep up with me... old man." Ben's gasping was slowly settling down to rapid, deep breaths as his heart rate fell and his vascular system worked to clear metabolic waste and reoxygenate his muscles.

As the months dragged on and he became more attuned to his unique systems, he started pushing himself. Once he learned how to use it, the lightning-fast response time of the artificial nervous system the runaway implant had created granted him reaction times that were orders of magnitude better than the average human. He was still limited by the speed at which his biological muscles could contract and relax, but he was able to control them so quickly and precisely that his movements now had an efficiency and fluid grace to them that couldn't be matched.

He'd also spent significant time with Mabel during his downtime, spitballing about the possibilities his condition could unlock, and after months of trial and error, the two of them finally figured out how to manipulate his hormone levels in order to boost his potential even further. The end result was a body that handled like a supercar: he had greater agility, could run faster, and could jump higher than any human before him, and he got the absolute maximum possible benefit from workouts and training due to the hormone-regulation techniques.

And if the chatter he was hearing was true, he was going to need every last ounce of improvement he could squeeze out of his body. His dad had broken the news to him that they were going to try to bring the Alarians in on the situation with the Imperium and that there was a chance he and Mabel would be needed in that process. Not to mention the fact that somewhere out there was an advanced alien race that was utterly terrified of the potential danger a weapon like Ben and Mabel represented, regardless of their intent.

But those were thoughts for later. His dad had told him he would have to undergo months of training in order to prepare for what was to come. So for the moment, Ben was making sure he enjoyed the time he had with his dad and his friends to the fullest. He'd learned the hard way that you never knew when you might lose the things otherwise taken for granted.

Kravczyk was still spluttering indignantly next to the track as Ben stood up and turned in his direction. He had discovered that the burly SEAR was sensitive about his age—something Ben had been exploiting to the fullest.

"You're just jealous 'cause he can kick your butt now," Tess said to Kravczyk as she came through the glass doors that separated the running track from the weight room. She had only recently been cleared for duty after having completed a lengthy rehab program of her own, and this was the first time Ben had seen her in workout clothes since that embarrassing train wreck on the *Wraith*... and he still very much liked what he saw.

What she said about Ben's fighting ability was true. His reaction times were so fast compared to the average human that there wasn't a spacer, marine, or special operator who could touch him in hand-to-hand combat—sometimes literally. His mind processed moves and countermoves so fast that more than one of his opponents in recent weeks had complained that he was reading their minds.

Ben still had moments where he felt disoriented or off-balance as he worked to recalibrate his brain to the increased speed at which he now perceived the world around him. It was getting better with time, but there were still moments when he felt like things were moving in slow motion.

"And you're not? Not that long ago we were the baddest SOBs on the block, but now we're pedestrian compared to him," Kravczyk said, jerking a thumb toward Ben.

"Maybe a little," Tess admitted as Ben hopped the low wall on the side of the track and walked up next to her, though the big SEAR noticed his eyes were aimed much too low for conversation.

"He's checking out your ass again," Kravczyk said with an evil grin.

"Yeah, well, she's got a nice ass," Ben said casually, tilting his head slightly to get a better view as Kravczyk's jaw dropped open. "Come on," Ben said as he gave Tess a playful slap on the butt. "We don't have much time to get cleaned up. We've got plans."

"We do?" she said, allowing Ben to drag her toward the locker rooms, leaving Kravczyk standing flabbergasted next to the track.

"Yep. We're having dinner at Pinnacle," he said, referring to the very exclusive and ludicrously expensive restaurant that sat atop Icarus's central hub, where it catered to the most influential people in Terran space. "Then we're going for a little cruise on a runabout I managed to secure, and after that I'm going to show you what my new hardware can do," he said with a wink.

He ran his fingers lightly over Tess's shoulders and she shuddered when a faint electrical current danced over her skin from his touch.

"It's about damn time," she said in a husky voice as she turned him around and kissed him passionately.

———

KRAVCZYK WATCHED the kid walk away with McCollum, and his lips twisted up into a grin as the two smashed their faces together in what had to have been a release of the most pent-up sexual tension he had ever seen two people share. Then they practically sprinted into the locker room.

"Goddamn, kid," he said aloud to the empty space around him. "Maybe you're not so hopeless after all."

AUTHOR'S NOTE

Thank you for reading *The Terran Menace.*
Ben and the crew will return.

If you enjoyed this book, please consider leaving a review on
Amazon. You can also check out my website for news on
upcoming projects at:

http://jrrobertsonauthor.com

Printed in Great Britain
by Amazon